The Year
of Past Things

ALSO BY M. A. HARPER

The Worst Day of My Life, So Far

For the Love of Robert E. Lee

M. A. HARPER

The Year of Past Things

A New Orleans Ghost Story

HARCOURT, INC.

Orlando Austin New York San Diego Toronto London

www.HarcourtBooks.com

This is a work of fiction. All names, characters, places, organizations, and events are
the products of the author's imagination or are used fictitiously for verisimilitude.

Library of Congress Cataloging-in-Publication Data
Harper, M. A., 1949–
The year of past things: a New Orleans ghost story/M. A. Harper.—1st ed.
p.   cm.
ISBN 0-15-101116-8
1. Remarried people—Fiction.   2. New Orleans (La.)—Fiction.
3. Haunted houses—Fiction.   4. Restaurateurs—Fiction.
5. Restaurants—Fiction.   I. Title.
PS3558.A6247937Y43   2004
813'.54—dc22   2004005913

Text set in Requiem Text
Designed by Linda Lockowitz

Printed in the United States of America

First edition
K J I H G F E D C B A

For Tom, and the house

Prologue

November 1, 1996

A FEW RACY ADULT costume parties in the French Quarter's gay community might still be under way at this hour, but all the trick-or-treaters here in this tamer neighborhood have gone to bed.

Orange illumination the color of candlelight filters down from tall light poles through cottony fog. The moon is still up. Early morning traffic squishes by on Prytania Street, two blocks over.

Renovated Victorian houses slumber side by side upon small green urban lots, windows dark behind curtains. Volvos and BMWs sit parked in driveways or out on the street beneath looming live oaks and crepe myrtles, magnolias, and the occasional royal palm. Election day is near and some of these front yards display plastic political signs, most of them for Republicans.

A yellow cat is locked out on the front porch of a smaller sign-less house, kept company by a carved pumpkin several days past its prime. Foul liquid puddles on the green paint beneath the jack-o'-lantern's chin. Its ragged smile is sinking into itself. The fat cat stretches and then paces past it, turns at the front door, meows, and paces past again.

If he had a vocabulary for tonight's smells, it might include *rotten vegetable* and *squirrel nest in tree* and *fenced rottweiler.* Certainly *cigarette smoke with patchouli,* an all-time favorite. He hasn't detected both smoke and scent in combination like this for a very long time, in fact, and it makes him expectant. His tail goes straight up in hope.

But the sleeping people inside, insulated by closed windows and an operating air conditioner, neither hear him nor wake.

Rotating both pointed ears, he goes to the nearest French window to peer in.

Night-lights shine along the route that leads to his food bowl, not that his retinas require that extra illumination. But light means people and his people mean mealtime. Touching the glass with one paw, he leaves a foggy print upon the slick and damp surface.

No good.

Where's the man? Where's that man who doesn't like him, the man who let him out?

He doesn't smell the man. He doesn't see the man. What he smells is patchouli.

But encouraged by it he pats the pane again. Again and again. Its touch is smooth and cold. He has no idea what glass is but does know from experience that it represents an impenetrable barrier of some kind.

And yet…

Those people who live in this house, they'd better wake up.

In every sense of the word.

ONE

New Family

"CASPER CUT UP *ALL NIGHT LONG*," Nicole started complaining the next morning. "That's why I'm too sleepy to eat, Mom."

Michelle pointed at her daughter's uneaten eggs, yellow goo, dammed on one side of the plate by congealing white grits. "What you heard was Hendrix cutting up. He was a very bad kitty. Now hurry up and finish, if we're going."

Nicole scrubbed at her face and made small mewing noises and then searched behind her for the fat cat lying on the bricked floor. "Hendrix can have my eggs. Hendrix loves eggs."

"What Hendrix needs is Weight Watchers," muttered Phil.

"Who wants seconds?" his stepson called from the kitchen where he lounged at the hot griddle, spatula twirling among the fingers of his right hand. Hot oil droplets leaped unnoticed from the spatula, spattering Michelle's folk art terra-cotta candlesticks on the little windowsill over the sink. "Mom?"

Michelle bent from her chair to wave her fingers in a summons and the cat got up to trot over and push his head into the palm of her hand. He purred very loudly, and Phil, who had never known or cared for cats before, tolerated this one only because its presence in the family predated his own. He watched with no interest as his wife and the animal mutually discovered the exact spot underneath the furry fat chin that held ecstasy. Michelle's fingers probed and the cat stretched out his broad neck, leaning hard into her fingertips. The transaction seemed, to Phil, a lot like sex.

"Mom? Seconds?" Cam called again from the kitchen.

Phil turned his head and noticed what the spatula was doing. "Don't twirl it like that, Cam."

Michelle swiveled to look up and back.

"It's okay," Phil told her. "He's okay."

His fifteen-year-old stepson stood silhouetted against the light from the glass pane of the front door, spatula stilled now but held straight up in readiness in an almost military pose. Cam's forearm was still childishly smooth, not yet ridged with any veins, but you could almost see him growing. He was blond like Michelle, tall like her. He shared some of her mannerisms, Phil was discovering, plus that cool reserve that sometimes masked emotion but on other occasions was merely the indifference that it looked like. There was no way yet to tell which was which early enough in any given situation for Phil to automatically formulate a correct response, but he was forgiven when he got it wrong. Just as he always forgave both mother and son for being hard to read.

"I'll have more coffee, I think," Michelle answered Cam, "please."

"What?" The spatula moved.

She turned in her seat. "I dislike shouting in the morning!"

"More coffee!" Nicole shrilled.

Phil stood, hands splayed on the tabletop on both sides of the handwoven Guatemalan cloth place mat he didn't particularly like. "I'll get it. He's got the gas grill on. It makes noise."

"No, you sit." Michelle lay a palm atop the back of his hand. "He's coming."

Cam's athletic shoes thudded down the three varnished wooden steps from the kitchen's level. He sloshed a half-full carafe rapidly past Phil's ear and began to top off Michelle's cup, and Phil leaned to one side to keep from getting his cheek burned when Cam pulled back his arm, careless but not hostile. When Phil looked up and met Cam's eyes, he couldn't recognize anything in the kid's facial expression except inquiry. Cam voiced it: "How'm I doing, Phil?"

"'S'good. Real good. My compliments to the chef."

He wanted more praise. "Mom?"

She pushed back her plate and looked up at him and smiled. That smile was one of Phil's favorite things about her, and he was still discovering good things. Those delicate lines underneath her eyes made her appear very kind whenever she smiled, punctuating the curve of her mouth with generosity. Phil thought and hoped that she was, in truth, a very kind person.

She was also a classic beauty, even at this time of morning, even without the cosmetics that she rarely wore, even at this middle age that he shared with her but wasn't sure he was adjusting to yet. He wasn't sure just how well she was adapting to it, either. When her kids were out of the way, Phil could put Jimmy Buffett or the Temptations on the CD player without suffering from Cam's derision, and he and Michelle would share wine and nostalgia and compare their high school days and college experiences.

What great cheekbones she still had, and a complexion like porcelain, even with the damage inflicted by all of that long-ago Yucatán sun. Underneath the rough Guatemalan cotton of her loose dress hid perfect breasts. Phil began to think about her breasts.

"Breakfast was delightful." She looked up at her son, wrapping one long and thin arm around his upper thighs, and Cam didn't seem at all embarrassed by her embrace. He leaned his body against her face and shoulder. "*Two* chefs in this family." Her grin was for Phil now, and she rubbed his shin under the table with her bare toes. "Double the pleasure."

"So when can I go to work with you, Phil?" Cam bantered. "How much will you pay me?"

"You got the whole rest of your life," he drained his coffee cup, "to go to work."

"You cooked with your dad."

"What makes you think I got paid?"

Cam sat down at the table and reached for all three of the remaining slices of French toast, dumping them onto his own plate. Phil saw Michelle open her mouth to say something but she closed it again. Amazing how much food this kid could wolf down. They pay no attention to what they put in their mouths, these kids, and most of it's junk, he thought. Hypes them up and clogs their arteries, if they don't get any exercise. Cam doesn't get enough exercise. All he does is lie on his bed and play Nintendo.

"Nicole," Michelle spoke to her daughter, "you haven't eaten a thing."

"I'm not hungry."

"But your brother slaved over a hot stove all morning, sweetheart. To make this delicious breakfast. You could show him how much you appreciate it, couldn't you?"

The child's face twisted itself into a grimace. She rubbed at her cheeks with both hands, pushing the powdered sugar from her French toast up into her hairline. "I ate some of it. Look."

"Three bites of French toast won't keep you going all day long," Phil told her. "Nothing but sugar. You need to finish that hen fruit, Nick."

But Michelle contradicted him. "Well, we could always get McDonald's on the way, I guess. I know she'll eat a Happy Meal. All that trick-or-treat candy last night…"

Excuse me, Phil thought, sitting back, careful to keep his mood in neutral, I still don't know all the rules around here. "Well, you did make some big haul last night, for real," he nodded at the small girl in affirmation. "That purple princess costume must've gone over real well with the neighbors."

She glanced at him for a moment, frowned, and then decided to ignore him. "Casper cut up all night, Mom! I'm too tired to go see Mamère!"

"I thought you wanted to go. Skip school. It's me who doesn't want to go."

"I plan on going, Mom," Cam reminded her, an edge to his voice. "Nicole did, too, the little weasel, when we decided. Weeks ago. Isn't that right, Phil?"

"I'm not getting in the middle of this, y'all. I don't know anything about it."

"But you know we're going to Bois Sec, right?"

"Yeah. That much I know."

"Okay, then." Cam sat back, satisfied, and folded his arms across his chest. "Phil's planned on us going. Even Casper would expect us to go."

"Of course he would!" Nicole said. "He's a *ghost*!"

"Mamère hasn't seen you in a long time, though, Nick, remember." Michelle's white hand brushed the dark hair back from the child's forehead. "Maybe she'd like to see how big you are now. You could take your colored pencils. And paper. And draw everybody."

"And we're not going just to see Mamère," Cam added, standing, wiping his mouth and then his buttery fingers on a paper napkin. "Me, I'm going mainly for *Dad*. Because that's what we said we'd do. And because this is the day you're supposed to go and say the prayers. Right?"

"I'm under that impression," said Michelle, "but I'm only nominally Catholic."

"Yeah," said Phil. "This is the day."

"EXPLAIN TO ME AGAIN exactly what all this Casper stuff's for." He sat on the bed and studied Michelle's slim backside as she stood before the mirrored sink in the bright bathroom and blow-dried her short pale hair.

"The Friendly Ghost?"

"Yeah, I know who he is," said Phil. "I remember the comics."

She killed the noise of the hair dryer and then reached for a brush. "All the creaks and pops this house makes. Nicole was scared when we first moved in, mainly at night. Old houses make noises, you know what I mean."

"I just wonder if you might not dwell on it too much now, though."

"But we just make up bedtime stories, honey, that's all we do. She loves the movie; we rented it soon after we moved in here. Casper's become like this imaginary guardian angel."

Phil lay back on the bed, in his faded jeans and pullover golf shirt and bare feet, and put both hands under his head. His hair was becoming more meager these days, right at his crown. The feel of its relative thinness disturbed him. He moved his palms to the thicker and darker gray hair near the back of his neck and watched the ceiling fan turn. "I thought Anne Rice had a lock on all the neighborhood spooks."

Michelle laughed. "Not all."

"So what time you think y'all'll be back here?" He tilted his chin, watching her.

Shoulder blades moved and shrugged. "Exactly what is on tap in a situation like this?"

"You haven't observed All Saints before now, I take it."

"Never could face doing it until now." She gave her hair a final lick with the brush.

"Well, there'll be a Mass at the church, visit to the cemetery. Rosary said for the departed, usually. Some socializing. They might have different customs out there in the country, I don't know."

"I've got a pot of mums in the car for Cam and Nicole to bring, I hope that's appropriate." She padded into the bedroom on panty-hosed feet across the white berber carpet and opened the closet. "It's over an hour and a half just to get there, and another hour and a half to get back. And we'll have to schmooze with Adrien's fam-ily—I can't just take Cam and Nick all the way out there and then not let them spend some time with everybody. So I don't guess there's any way to be back here before you have to be at work."

"'S'okay. Just call me when you get back. So I'll know you got home all right."

She passed close to the bed in a shoe search. "Cell phone'll be in my bag, you can reach me if you need to."

"Be careful, Shell."

Smiling, she stopped and bent to give him a quick kiss. "You know I always am." And then she kissed him again, not so quick. "Love you. *Lots.* Lots and lots. I sound like Gidget."

"Love you, too."

She did this hand thing, caressing his fingers and abandoning them before he could reciprocate, and then spoke in that throaty Texas cowgirl voice she affected when she wanted to be humorous. "You and ol' Casper watch out for each other, darlin'. Cook good. Be safe."

But tension and mild sadness were always present in her leave-takings, Phil noticed, even when she was trying to be jocular.

Well, she's haunted, was his reasoning. Understandably. By more than just Nicole's Casper. And I guess it's none of my business, when you get right down to it.

And I can't do anything about any of it, anyway.

WHAT NICOLE'S IMAGINARY Casper the Friendly Ghost mostly did, Phil reflected, was take some of the heat off Hendrix the family cat, who was actually responsible for the louder household crashes and nocturnal thuds.

Disgusted, Phil frequently got up in the middle of many insomniac nights now to silently urge the animal out of the front door and onto the quiet porch, knowing full well that Michelle worried about feline safety hazards out there like cars and unleashed dogs. But Chestnut Street was always deserted this time of night, reasonably safe for a cat, unless somebody was gunning for him in a drive-by shooting.

So Hendrix would finally amble down the front steps to the area that might've been a tiny front yard had it not been paved over with bricks, tail in the air with alacrity, to sniff the night wind. And that's when Phil Randazzo would lean against a squared porch support and look out into the orange streetlight and wonder just how he had gotten himself into all of this. This second wife. These stepchildren he barely knew.

To be honest, he wasn't at all unhappy. It was actually a relief to be married again, to be looked after and worried about again, to have regular sex. To be out of that depressing divorced-guy utilitarian apartment on Camp Street that smelled of beer and dirty socks and into a real home again, with this pretty woman to curl up with after a killer night on his feet at the restaurant. It wasn't even too bad to have the noises kids could make echoing all around him again. Except that these two kids didn't make much normal noise.

No, what Phil always privately questioned was just how long it could last, this initial period of cordiality in their recently combined lives, when every one of them, even six-year-old Nicole, seemed to be making the efforts of guests at a party to be nice to each other. It was like a group honeymoon. Phil wondered which of the four of them would be the first to become either comfortable or disenchanted enough to let himself go, act rudely, show bad temper. He couldn't say for sure that the first one would not be himself.

Because I'm wooden. He recalled Regan's reason for not staying married to him. I'm never in touch with my own true feelings, he remembered her diagnosis, except in a restaurant kitchen. I'm a stranger to myself. I'm an overgrown adolescent, according to a couple of hundred hairy-legged female authors who write those self-help books I'll never read.

So there's absolutely no telling what I might do here next. Hey, I might be about to relocate to Australia or join the circus or run off with an underage underwear model and not even suspect it about myself, who the hell knows? Not me.

BUT YOU KNOW, there's no telling what Cam might eventually do here, either, he realized one very recent night, folding his arms and staring out into the empty illuminated darkness. Cam's that age, that fractious age, which I'm apparently still emotionally stuck at.

Phil leaned against the porch pillar and thought about his stepson.

Cam had already been in trouble at school a time or two, caught smoking on school property on several occasions right before Phil and Michelle had decided to marry. When the cigarette lighter he was carrying that last time, an old Zippo that had belonged to his father, had been confiscated by a ninth-grade teacher at Newman, the boy had reacted with enough furious tears and pleadings and even nausea to warrant mandatory family counseling.

"I guess what he needs is more security of some kind," Michelle speculated later, lying in her bra and panties on Phil's mattress in his apartment during one of their nooners while Cam and Nicole were at school. She had seemed so literally blue then, listless, all of the pinker tones bleached from her skin. "You'd think he'd be over the worst of it by now, but that's not what this looks like. He doesn't make friends, I'm told. His grades aren't anywhere near what his potential indicates. Nicole still wets the bed. Guess I'm Mother of the Year."

"You think some of his problem might be with me?" he had to ask. "Having to sort of share you with me, like he does now?"

"I was thinking that you were bringing a little fun into their lives for a change, Philip. Arnold Schwarzenegger movies on your night off. You don't have to do stuff like that, but you do."

"You think he suspects that we—ah—are having sex, you and me?"

"Of course he does."

"Maybe he has a problem with that."

She deflated even further. "I don't imagine it's making anything any easier."

"Well…"

Her short hair had been like silk against his naked shoulder. She pushed her face into his neck and her voice came out muffled but very near. "But don't I have a right to have somebody in my life? I've been so miserable. Being with you makes me happy, Philip, and don't I have a right to try to love somebody?"

"Would it help…," he had heard himself suggesting after a long and companionable silence while her slim fingers stroked the hair on his forearm. And he had remembered his own bitter solitude then, and how sick of himself he was sometimes. And he had realized just how much he wasn't ready to give this woman up yet, her occasionally bawdy oil-field twang, her silences, her intelligence and sadness. "Would it help things any, Shelly, if you and I got married?"

Married. Get a marriage license.

Muster up some witnesses, how hard could that be? Find a justice of the peace. Because the church wasn't about to bless a second union for him, not as long as his first wife Regan still lived. Unless he and Regan got an annulment. Which was highly unlikely after having three children together.

But Michelle was irreligious and a born Protestant anyway, so what did it matter?

I don't believe anymore, Phil thought. I don't know where I lost it, but I can't believe in a God who would send me to hell just because I choose to legally bond with this fragile widow in some civil ceremony. That's not adultery, Momma, for cryin' out loud; I think it might even be some sort of charity. He would vaguely address these private realizations to his deceased mother in the days leading up to his second wedding.

It's not like I'm demanding Holy Matrimony here, no sacrament, he'd tell himself. Just some divine understanding that the planet Earth blows and sometimes you just need somebody in your corner.

She won't take my name, since she says she's already been published and is too well-known in her field now to change it. Like I've got a leg to stand on, since she never used her first husband's surname professionally, either.

So maybe this won't constitute a genuine marriage to Michelle Wickham, Momma. I don't expect you to understand that. But maybe it doesn't have to.

SOMEDAY SOON, he thought now on the morning of All Saints Day, watching Nicole waving good-bye to him from the backseat of Michelle's messy Saturn, Cam is going to decide about me.

He's going to stop humoring me or indulging me or being afraid of me, or whatever it is that mannerly kids like him do with their new stepfathers. He's going to be himself around me. I have no idea what that self is. Probably he doesn't, either. He's barely fifteen, those hormones are just beginning to really kick in.

But I can't be his father, and that's exactly what Michelle wants me to be, and he's going to resent the shit out of me.

He dropped his hand when he couldn't see the car anymore and then went back up the brick steps to the porch. And there it registered with him for the second time today just how foul Nicole's Halloween pumpkin was beginning to smell.

The cat was crouched in front of the closed door in an expectant posture when Phil came back that way with black garbage bags and paper towels under one elbow. It darted to squeeze its bulk through the opening when Phil cracked the door now, but Phil's sneaker blocked its exit and shoved it back—gently, all things considered. "Get your fat ass back inside!" he scolded, pushing the animal with his foot and then watching it scurry with flattened ears across the hardwood floor where it slunk behind the sofa. "Don't want to have to scrape your tire-marked blubber off any asphalt right now, you doofus!"

The cat hid and stayed hidden.

Phil stepped out onto the porch and then closed the door with a crash when the pumpkin stink hit him. Wrapping the large mushy orb in black plastic before attempting to move it, he slid the edges of the bag up under the mess as much as possible. His knees popped as he hefted his bundle and he walked it to the corner of the porch to dump it into the metal garbage can hidden in the small alley between the house and the high wooden fence. The thing landed with a loud squishy thud.

What had the pumpkin's ooze done to the paint? He glanced behind himself to the place where the jack-o'-lantern had rested.

Right over there on the welcome mat sat the substantial yellow cat, licking its paws in the sun.

All Saints Day

"AFTERNOON THERE, Chef."

"Good afternoon, Chef."

"How ya doin', Chef?" the staff at Tasso continued to greet him, already busy with what the more formal restaurant Les Plaisirs had termed *mise-en-place* as Phil came into the kitchen at three o'clock on the dot. These luminous stainless steel surfaces—worktables and freezer doors and the satiny finish of the Bonnet range—all reflected brilliant fluorescent light onto bustling white-coated shoulders. His office, where he had spent the last hour catching up on payroll and bookkeeping, was always comparatively dim, the one window curtained, plants suffering. Coming into the kitchen could be like being born.

"Hey, ya'll," he said, becoming vaguely happy. "'S'up?"

"Same old, same old," Frank answered, lifting fresh trout from a bed of ice. "Quarterback controversy. Offensive coordinator who shoulda been fired two seasons ago."

Phil patted Frank's back, and Tyrone's. The two men resumed their melancholy forecasts for the upcoming football weekend, the Saints and LSU and less-cherished Tulane, as Phil did a small balancing dance to first get out of his sneakers without untying them and then stepped into the clean pair of black polyurethane German clogs he had washed in the dishwasher here the night before. They were a new purchase, these nonskidding clogs, comfortable and easy to clean. They did what they were supposed to, supporting his arches during the ten hours or so he spent working on his feet here from two to midnight almost every day. They, too, made him happy.

Thick pierced rubber mats overlay the kitchen's concrete floors for cushioning and traction, but he never thought there was such a thing as being too comfortable or too sure-footed once the floor acquired its daily oil slick. Vanessa had discovered the black clogs in a local store and had been the first to wear them once Phil had given the shoes his approval. Frank, still a boot loyalist, loved to ridicule the boxy clogs on everybody else's feet, calling them "elf shoes" every chance he got. But they were an undoubted godsend to Phil's painful knees, easing the nagging inflammation caused by years of lifting plates and loading dishwashers back in his boyhood. He also hoped they might counterbalance whatever further abuse his lower joints were taking these days from his compulsive morning jogging habit.

"Shut up, Frank," he'd defend his footwear when attacked by his old friend, but then laugh. "You're not a runner, you couldn't drag your fat ass from here to the curb if the place caught fire and your life depended on it."

"Ain't nobody put a gun to your head to make you race streetcars, Chef," Frank would josh, "now, c'mon! You've already met and married that beautiful professor, what's your problem? Gain a few pounds, what's the problem?"

But if I ever stop running I might lose her, Phil would worry during those daily five-mile workouts of his, pounding his knees and ankles and hips across grass and unavoidable concrete, noticing the middle-aged looseness of his belly and back muscles. Michelle didn't marry no big fat-assed moose, she might get grossed out and leave me if I get big and fat. Regan left me, and I was still skinny. I may be wooden, but I sure don't feel wooden when I'm running, and aching, and sensing my body aging and growing soft.

Might be nice if I was made out of wood. Wouldn't have to worry about cartilage and cholesterol and what I wear on my feet.

With my luck I'd get termites.

He appreciated the comfort of his elf shoes now as he carried his sneakers back to his office, whistling something by the Grateful Dead, lightheartedly supposing that the dining public might not exactly welcome the knowledge that Chef Philip Randazzo and three of his employees routinely cleaned their polyurethane clogs in the same dishwasher that handled the restaurant's plates. There was nothing unsanitary about it—extremely hot water was extremely hot water, after all. Still, Phil merrily reflected, stomping his feet in their thick athletic socks down into the clogs' cushioning as he returned to the kitchen, *Gourmet* magazine might not have been so effusive or so forthcoming with that award they'd given him and his restaurant Tasso last year had its representatives been present at cleanup time to see the footwear get loaded in.

The notion made him laugh now, mostly through his nose.

He finished his own setup at the ceramic-topped steel worktable where he could expedite tonight's orders and supervise the plating of each dish, the garnishing, the composing of each laden white porcelain disk like a painting. Phil's onetime classical specialty had been that of saucier and it was primarily from this background that he devised Tasso's recipes. But he had begun his chef's apprenticeship on the line at Commander's Palace and was still more than competent at any station if Tasso got really busy and one of his people needed help. Slow nights might offer him a chance to go home early and leave the cleanup to the staff, but these nights could also depress him.

"—what they been needing," went the continuing conversation at his back, "is a running game, man. You got to establish the run. Take some heat off the quarterback. Third down, they passing into coverage every time, how many conversions they been making on third?"

"They making 'em."

"Where at? You, me, the opposing team, my two-year-old grandbaby knows third-and-long, hell, 's'gonna be a fuckin' *pass*—!"

Phil turned to the speaker. "Frank, you got dogs, right? Not cats."

The full red face nodded an affirmative above the white collar-band of its tunic while the man's pink hands continued to bone trout. "King Charles spaniels. Two of 'em."

"Chef, I got cats," spoke up Vanessa from her station, slicing raw vegetables into tidy mounds.

"How the hell they get out of locked buildings, Vanessa?"

"This a riddle?"

"Nope. Observable reality."

"Windows?" she guessed, working on bell peppers. "Heat vents, maybe?"

"Windows're all closed and locked and all your heat vents are screwed on good," said Phil. "I mean, they crawl up out of chimneys or what? Is that something cats are known for? Like Santa Claus?"

"Snakes come up out the toilet," said Da'Shaun.

Phil laughed with everybody else and lathered up his hands at the sink. "I'm serious! We got this one big ol' fat fucker, big ol' neutered male, and he got out on me this morning, someway. I don't give a shit if he runs off to Bulgaria, you understand, but it'd break my stepkids' hearts. Damn cat is older than Nicole, she's had it all her life. Wife'd kill my ass."

"Maybe he got keys," said Da'Shaun and grinned at Tyrone, the newest cook, a young product of the culinary arts program at Delgado Community College, who nevertheless lived and died with the LSU football program and wore a purple Tiger T-shirt underneath his kitchen tunic every Saturday on game days.

"As a matter of fact," Phil thought out loud, noticing the absence of a faint lavender undertone showing through Tyrone's white attire and correctly concluding that this meant it was still Friday, "I don't know who let him back in before daylight this

morning, either. I threw him out on the porch along about two
A.M., 'cause he runs up and down the stairs and it sounds like somebody bouncing a basketball."

"Your wife's kids, maybe," said Tyrone.

"Probably."

But the clock ran out on the cat question when the hostess and
two of the waitstaff came charging through the swinging doors to
consult about the evening, and Phil immediately turned his attention to getting busy and turning his back on anything that couldn't
be spiced, diced, or iced, sautéed or pureed, blackened or broiled.
He briefed the waitstaff on the qualities of the pecan-encrusted
trout—tonight's special—and his own wine recommendations for
it, and then helped Frank finish the boning. Phil was watching the
clock, ready for trout and sauté pans to come clanging down onto
the hot Bonnet like an opening bell, for the sizzle of popcorn
shrimp appetizers in the deep fryer, for onions reaching fragrant
transparency among green peppers and celery.

He got out the flour for Frank's roux, happy.

Philip, the second son born to Vince and Shirley Randazzo of
Randazzo's Restaurant on Esplanade, grew up in a food service
family. His father had been chief cook and bookkeeper, his mother
serving as both cashier and bartender. Phil and his three brothers
were pressed into service at early ages as busboys, then waiters or
cooks, after school and on weekends. He had learned firsthand, la-
boring from morning to night during the summers and school holidays, just how much hard work running a restaurant involved. His
brothers had all bolted eventually, two of them to sell Chevrolets
in Metairie and the eldest, Dominic, to the priesthood. Phil, too,
had hated Randazzo's, but that hatred was exactly what had im-
pelled him to stay in the business initially. Get some classical training, go Poppa one better. Beat the old man at his own game. But
maybe that had been some early evidence of woodenness in me,
Phil had concluded in later years. A possible indication of a lack of
imagination on my part, or sense of adventure.

He had tried, some few years back, when he and Regan had first begun to acknowledge the seriousness of their marital discord to each other but had had no idea what to do about it, to feel guilty about this shortcoming. He had tried to view his lifelong involvement in the restaurant industry for what it surely must have been: an insufferable routine, the rut of a dull workaholic. The refuge of a second-rate intellect. The unquestioning drudgery of a stunted spirit with no romance in his soul.

But satisfaction just kept getting in his way, and it had been the simple satisfaction that any artist got from the pursuit of excellence in his art. Phil had long been aware that he could taste flavors too subtle for most people to pick up, and he'd read that this was a gift, because males generally had fewer taste buds than most females. He'd also read that taste buds are lost at a drastic rate after age fifty, so he'd felt satisfyingly young and smug and creative as he invented recipes to bring unanticipated levels of delight and discovery to the palate as well as sustenance to the stressed inner beings of those well-dressed people who came in to dine. Who loosened their ties a fraction or smoothed their skirts into comfortable chairs, then relaxed over bread and wine and salad, almost unwillingly, soothed in spite of themselves and their harried lives. Primed for the perfect entrée that arrived just at the right second to transform joylessness into celebration through this most basic but elusive of magics.

This is how Phil thought about what he did, almost in those exact terms, *soothe* and *delight* and *celebration* and *discovery,* never speaking them out loud to Regan, but saying them in his mind. He experienced it as power, this ability of his to attract and enslave the wealthy and important.

Plus, there could be decent money in it, and even fame.

But when you came right down to it, he had just never wanted to do anything else.

During his college years as a business major—he'd kept in mind his father's bookkeeping and how necessary that end of the restaurant game was—at Loyola, where he had met Regan, Phil had found a night job as a line cook at Commander's Palace. When the executive chef there left to start his own wildly successful restaurant, Phil had been invited to interview with him. Within this fortunate association, Phil rose first to saucier and then to sous-chef and was eventually offered the executive chef position at trendy new Les Plaisirs in the Warehouse District—where he immediately won the Best New Chef award from *Food & Wine* and runner-up recognition from the James Beard people. Les Plaisirs was named one of the top ten restaurants in North America by Michelin for three years in a row.

So it had been the most natural of evolutions when Philip Randazzo and his wife opened what would start out as an intimate thirty-seat place called "Tasso" on Magazine Street in 1989 with all of their savings and a hefty bank loan. They took more time deciding on a name for this restaurant than they had spent picking one for any of their kids.

The overhead was kept as low as possible, Regan laundering all the linen herself, taking reservations, and operating the cash register while Phil ran the kitchen and oversaw all else. They served no breakfast or lunch, even after a modest expansion, and limited the menu to ten unique seasonal dinner entrées. Rather than attempting to offer too much, Tasso made its name through nouvelle Louisiana perfection. Tweaking the Cajun/Creole regional idiom, it dished up seafood so fresh it still swam, the tenderest duck, rabbit, veal, and free-range chicken, prepared in handmade sauces and marinades. Tasso baked its own breads and made its own sausages for seasoning. Its wine list was decent, its occasional holiday drinks—Regan's forte—superb. The decor was simple and clean-lined, white on white, relieved by green palms and Jazzfest posters. Phil's reputation had drawn national gourmands who came and dined and praised. He won more awards and was featured on the *Today* show. The restaurant quickly became, in the collective New Orleans epicurean mind, a small but utterly perfect jewel.

Tasso was an unqualified success for the Randazzos, who had worked their butts off to make it happen. Too bad their marriage hadn't been up to the challenge.

All through the whole miserable failure that became their home life, the drawn-out crash and burn of separation and then divorce, Phil was happy and became steadily happier to flee to Tasso and cook there, finding relief in the simple acts of creation, its kitchen camaraderie a sure balm for whatever ailed him. And he looked around himself now at this gleaming stainless domain of his, inhaling the aromas of fresh garlic and French roast coffee, cayenne and celery and lemon juice, shrimp and onion, French bread straight from the oven. I am one lucky bastard, he thought again, happy, as he always thought. Thank you, God. How lucky I am to have all this at forty-five—or still have all this, after Regan's savage divorce lawyer did his satanic best to pry it loose from my fingers.

"...From my cold, dead fingers," he muttered, remembering. Let her have the house, hey, I don't care, the kids need to live in their own house, I can accept that. But I've got to have the restaurant to leave a little something for 'em, for God's sake, Regan! Let me buy you out, if that's what it takes. But where else you think the child support is going to come from?

"Whassat, Chef?" asked Frank.

"Nothin'. Talking about how much I hate lawyers." Phil took up a large Sabatier knife and waved it in small circles.

"Love to carve up a few tax auditors," grumbled Frank.

Vanessa turned her head and laughed. "Hey, you don't want another divorce, Chef, then you better take real good care of your wife's cat."

"ARE YOU GOING TO BE buried with Dad, Mom?" Cam asked Michelle as they drove toward home on Highway 90 behind the red taillights of a muddy pickup. There was little but swampy woodlands visible on both sides of the narrow two lanes on this stretch and they were very dark. The evening had turned balmy and damp, true capricious November weather. Clouds covered the moon and transformed it into white fuzz.

Ridiculous, she thought, to have to run the air conditioner this late in the year. She reached to turn it to a warmer setting but left it on.

"Mom?" Cam prompted.

"Probably not." She spoke the truth and hoped that he would drop the subject, but knew he wouldn't. All Saints Day had drained her. She had gotten through it by keeping all emotions at arm's length, and only wanted everybody else to do the same now.

"That sucks," he commented.

"I'll probably be buried next to Philip, son. On our side of the river."

"That really bites."

The Saturn's white headlights created a traveling island of visibility in the blackness. The twin red eyes of a pickup pulled rapidly away up ahead, exceeding the posted speed limit, and Michelle pressed her lips together in disapproval, knowing that it almost certainly had to be a kid driving like that, a young male, afraid of nothing—not the state police, not darkness, not death, not even unintended injury to the innocent. Young men let their balls do the driving, she thought, blind anatomical features situated a very long way from their brains. "Cameron," she said, "I'm married to Philip now. And we live where we live, son."

He said nothing. He was a dark profile in the seat beside hers, long-nosed and remote.

"Is Nicole asleep?" she asked him.

He turned his head and body after a lengthy and drawn-out moment, as if he had to consider many things before acting. She saw him look at the backseat and then face forward again.

Michelle waited. "Well, is she? Is she buckled up?"

"She's asleep."

"Is she buckled up? It's a safety rule, son!"

"*Dad* was obeying all the safety rules. Lotta good it did him."

"Cam."

"I don't see why you can't be buried in Bois Sec, Mom! So that Nicole and I could visit both of you at the same time."

It was her turn to consider a proper response. "I don't live in Bois Sec, son. I don't go to that church. I'm no longer a member of that family."

"Yes, you are!" His voice grew louder. "You're my mother, and I'm family, I'm a member of that family, I'm Cam Savoie! And Dad is my dad. *Was* my dad. And when you remarried him, you married him *for good,* that's what everybody told me: This is in front of a priest this time, this is in a church, and it's for keeps this time!"

"But what were the words we said, Cam? Sweetheart, you were there, you heard what we said to each other. 'Until death us do part,' son, that's what we promised. And we kept that promise." An unsummoned wedding-day video flitted past on the screen of her mind's eye before she could turn it off and she had to glance down again at her own remembered long ivory-lace dress for a second. But she determinedly avoided looking at the man holding her hand. "Cam, death did part us, sweetheart. And life has to go on."

She was aware as she heard the hoary platitude coming from her mouth of how utterly unsatisfying and even cold it actually sounded. And she wished she had kept it from mindlessly slipping out like this, in this automatic and chilly way, because her son began to make snuffling noises at it and then finally choked up.

"Oh, Cam, sweetheart, I'm sorry, son. I'm sorry."

He didn't respond, and Michelle knew better than to put out her right hand and touch him when he was like this. He would only flinch and twist his shoulder away from her and grow more upset. The darkness pressed in on them from all sides. She riveted her eyes onto the white stripe in the road ahead and sucked in breath. "Cam, when your father died, I thought I'd die, too. I thought my life was over. I wanted to die. Don't you remember?"

No answer. No movement. No sounds except muffled grief.

"Surely you remember, sweetheart. I was a basket case. The only two things that kept me from going off a bridge were you and Nicole, the only two things. I knew I had to live. For you guys."

All Saints Day had certainly been too much for Cam. Wet bright stripes of reflected dashboard light ran down his smooth cheeks, she saw. This trip most definitely had not proved to be the really good idea that the mandated family therapist, six whole months ago, had assured her that it would be.

Why didn't I speak up in therapy? she asked herself, aware of her rising anger. Why wasn't I better able to defend myself and my own instincts, and what I thought my children really needed?

"You never loved Dad," Cam accused her like a sudden shark attack, so unexpectedly now that she jumped.

The raw feelings had been so carefully entombed inside her, shoveled over with layers and layers of glib terms that no longer held any personal meanings for her, that she could offer Cam some of these cheap words now without paying much of a price in pain. She wasn't lying, because the words were the truth. But there were so many of them, and they had been spoken and thought so often that they had become a sort of homeopathy, constant tiny doses of poison that ultimately rendered a patient immune. "Cam, your father was the love of my life, it's just that simple. *The* love. Of my life. I know you don't understand about Philip, son, and there's no way for you to understand, not until you're older. Philip isn't the love of my life, and I kind of suspect that I'm not the love of his, either. But I was lonely and miserable, and Philip was lonely and miserable, and so we've kind of teamed up. To keep from being lonely and miserable. Romance is one thing, son, but needing somebody in your corner to grow old with is another. All kinds of love are valid."

He was quiet for so long, for at least two more miles of white lights behind and red lights in front, that she almost concluded that he'd been offended beyond any kind of immediate repair. The lonely swamps were past, and businesses, fast-food eateries, the ubiquitous political campaign signs that sprouted everywhere like weeds, stores and gas stations, all lined the Saturn's passageway. She considered buying him off with a stop at Burger King or a visit to Blockbuster for yet another video game rental. She thought about waking Nicole, consulting her.

"What happens to us if *you* die, Mom?" Cam's voice came like a quiet flat tire.

"My job," she inhaled, "is to raise both of you so that you'll be able to stand on your own two feet when that time comes. And I'm going to do that."

"How would we live?"

"You're the sole beneficiaries of my will, plus I've got some money already socked away for you, both earned and inherited from my family. And your father's estate'll be receiving royalties for many years to come, all those songs, the recordings. He never spent a penny of that. We lived on what he earned from his day job, and mine, and invested everything else for you kids. So y'all can both afford Harvard if you want to go."

"But where will we live, Mom, if we're not grown up yet? Will we live with *Phil*?"

She glanced at him. "What would suit you best?"

Shrugging, he began to sniffle again.

"You'll definitely have a home with Philip, if you want it," she assured him, her chest tightening a little, hoping that she was telling him the truth. She believed in Philip Randazzo while she was alive but wasn't so sure about what his priorities might turn out to be if she died. "That's one of the things our marriage means, Cam. We have this life together now, Philip and I, and you guys are a nonnegotiable part of it. Plus, he likes the hell out of both of you, you know that. I know you can tell that."

"He already has kids. Three."

"Well, what if he were to adopt—?"

"*No! No way!* I'm Cam Savoie till I'm dead!"

Her head hurt. She didn't need Burger King or Wendy's, she needed aspirin and bourbon. "So would you rather go live with Mamère? In Bois Sec? Or with Grandmom in Houston?"

But he was sobbing freely and loudly now, unable to answer, and Michelle gripped the steering wheel until her knuckles ached. She drove past all the neon and kept the lid bolted onto herself, an act of will that required detachment and deep breathing and the promise of whiskey at the end of her journey.

"*What I want,*" Cam finally shouted, pulling at his hair with both hands, pounding his denim thighs, smacking the dashboard with one fist, kicking out with his big feet among all the Happy Meal toys and crumpled notebook paper on the floor, "*is for Dad to be alive!*"

Her response was soft when it came in his echoes. "I know, pal."

"Where are we, Mom?" Nicole spoke up from the backseat, her high-pitched voice heavy with sleep. "It's real dark out there."

"Yeah, but we're almost home, sweetheart."

"What if there are monsters out there, Mom? In those trees?"

Cam made a razzing sound. "No monsters at Wal-Mart, you little virus, that's a Wal-Mart parking lot out there, you microbe! Jeez!"

"No such things as monsters," Michelle reminded her daughter. "And look. Here's a shopping center. Right over there."

"Could Casper watch over us out here? If he was real, I mean."

She had to think about the proper answer to this, too, briefly questioning the wisdom of her Casper mythology again. But she still saw no harm in it, and maybe it did provide Nicole some reassurance, since Michelle had been unable to give her children a God because she didn't have one. "Yeah, sure."

"Mamère always keeps on about Jesus and the Blessed Mother," yawned Cam, "all the time, since Dad died. Y'all heard her, she went off on all of it again today. Always saying that that's who's really looking out for us, and all. What I want to ask her is, if the Virgin Mary was on the job and looking out for Dad, how come he got killed?"

"Well, different people," observed Michelle, somewhat carefully, "have different ideas. About the way the unseen world works."

"*Is* there an unseen world? A real one?"

"I don't know, son."

"So are, like, Jesus and God and Mary just made up, then? Like Casper? By priests and whoever?" he asked.

"I don't know the answer to that one, either."

"You don't seem to know much," he muttered, but fondly.

"No," she said, "I don't."

"GOOD THING tomorrow's Saturday," she was whispering to Phil nearly six hours later as she pressed the length of her long body against his, with her fingers in his chest hair and her mouth at his. "You get home so damned late, my darling, and I usually have to get up so early, my night owl love. But this is so nice, isn't it?"

He smiled against her soft lips. "You call that *late,* the time I get home? How the hell you ever manage a sex life with a musician?"

Something, maybe a small muscle in her face or her neck, flinched. It was a tiny reaction, minuscule, but he noticed.

"Hey," he apologized, "me and my big mouth."

"Today just sucked," she gave him her own apology.

"I'm sorry."

Her cool palm lay itself against his stubbling cheek and then retracted to rub her nose. "There's just so many Savoies, and they won't shut up about him, and now they've got Cam all whipped up again. He had another one of his scenes in the car coming back."

"Kiss might make things a little better. My momma used to say that."

"He won't let me touch him when he gets like that, Philip."

"I wasn't talking about anybody kissing Cam."

They got in a good ten minutes of uninterrupted intimacy before Hendrix the cat jumped up onto the foot of the bed. Phil felt him there but it wasn't worth it to break the mood to shoo him away. No, I ain't hurtin' her, he saw himself through the animal's curious yellow eyes, pumping away like this, hearing Michelle's sporadic gasps. At least I hope I'm not hurting her. She's supposed to be enjoying this.

I'd be enjoying it more myself if I was sure that she was enjoying it.

Hendrix hunched up at a corner of the mattress and waited, patient eyes like metallic golden coins blinking. He folded his front paws inward against his breast and then lay on them, in it for the long haul.

At the brink, Phil had to stop worrying about his wife or the cat. One last fugitive neuron told him how strange he must look and sound now to some other species, bare ass bouncing, just before he went over the edge.

Maybe even ridiculous.

Hendrix crept up to the pillows for Michelle's tickling fingers and low croonings.

"Boring night outside?" Phil razzed him. "Kitty *Wild Kingdom* in here more interesting?"

But Michelle looked from the animal to the man. "Why would he be outside?"

"He got out on me this morning. Someway."

"How?"

"I don't know how."

"I wish," her tone changed, "that you'd just stop letting him out at night, Philip. It's given him a taste of freedom, and he's going to want to go out all the time now, honey."

"Y'all got Hendrix so spoiled, doll," Phil couldn't resist speaking now to Michelle's shoulder blades, "that he's always going to stay close to home here. For the chow, if nothing else."

"He might get into a fight outside, though."

"So?"

She looked over her shoulder at him. Her tousled hair and kiss-swollen lips were fiercely sexual but the expression her face wore was noncommittal. "Any wound he'd get would be real slow to heal. With his leukemia."

"That ain't no sick cat, look at the size of that mother!" he heard himself bark like a dog.

"Philip," her withering tone implied how stupendously ignorant he was, "it's like AIDS."

He wasn't ignorant and he didn't want to play Doberman. He knew the cat had leukemia. But it wasn't sick yet. It was fat and sleek and apparently content, and arguably even entitled to enjoy the natural outdoor life of a cat now, especially since it was already terminally ill.

And what was so wrong with speaking lightly and not being so goddam morbid all the time?

Of course, Phil did know why: "Cam's father found this cat and brought it home to us. Kitten, actually. Rescued it from a garbage Dumpster behind a club in Mobile. Nicole wasn't even born yet," said Michelle.

"I know that," he was quick to tell her. "Cam's told me that."

She bent from the waist and placed the animal on the carpet and then rose to open the bedroom door. The cat galloped through it toward its food dishes on the brick floor, two steps down. Michelle closed the door and then just stood there for a moment like a slender marble statue, and there were so many other things that Phil wanted to point out to her but did not. Like, people die on kids all the time, that's just the way it is. It's a tough world for a kid. For everybody. But this guy's been dead now for three whole years, and from where I sit, all this walking on eggs for Cam and Nicole is complete bullshit. Get the hell over it, y'all. Get the cat put to sleep, take some time off, and let's go to Disney World.

Michelle stepped slowly back to the bed where Phil held the

sheet out and open for her like a wing. She settled into his welcome with a sigh, her elbows sharp and feet like ice. He reached over and clicked off the lamp on the night table and the large room became dark and still. Only the ceiling fan moved, a shadow in the dim orange light that came from the street. "Crazy," she muttered, "to have to run the ceiling fans this late in the year."

"It'll cool off again," he said. "Always does."

"I know."

His hand tried to find something pleasant to do for her, a caress of a shoulder or the smoothing of her hair. "The kids're going to be all right, baby doll, no matter what happens with the cat. Cam's straightening up. Grades are better. Nicole's just about quit her bed-wetting."

"Oh, Philip," she sighed again. "Oh, Philip. If you only knew."

But Phil knew. And he could guess at the rest of it. He cradled her head in what he hoped was comfort.

Hendrix suddenly began to run up and then down the steep staircase almost directly over their bedroom, sending the drumbeats of his large padded paws right into the marrow of Phil's bones and causing him to tense up the muscles of his jaws so tightly that his teeth hurt.

"He'll wake up the kids," he tried it on Michelle, when the thuds moved elsewhere upstairs but did not stop.

"Cam sleeps with his TV on. I'll go comfort Nick, if I hear her."

"What about me?"

She laughed low in her throat. "Put a pillow over your head. He'll get tired in a while."

"Just trying to suffocate me, I know," he muttered, removing the arm that held her and then turning onto his side, awkwardly folding his pillow around his head. "'S'a conspiracy."

She rolled over into his contours and then repeated that laugh, settling her buttocks comfortably into his groin. Which might've aroused him again had he not been so tired and so forty-five.

The pillow did cut down on some of the noise, but wasn't comfortable. His ears felt mashed and his face too hot. He wondered how long it was going to take leukemia to finish off the obese pest and hoped it would be soon.

"Think how you'll feel," he spoke again to his wife right before dozing off, "to wake up and find me dead."

He didn't mean anything by it.

Entombed

MICHELLE WALKED AGAIN to the grave in Bois Sec that night.

She approached it in her sleep. Alone this time, she carried the pot of yellow mums down the short bricked walkway from the church to the cemetery near the levee that bounded the Intracoastal Waterway, stepping on the short ferns sprouting between the bricks and from the worn crevices of old tombs, passing their incisions displaying the surnames of familial connections, CHERAMIE, DUFRENE, GAUTREAUX, COIGNET, HEBERT—over two centuries' worth of marriage and intermarriage having produced such tangled bloodlines here that her own children had come into this world related to absolutely every individual interred on this relatively dry ground.

A high water table made actual burials in south Louisiana tricky, something that her Texan upbringing still found terribly disturbing. Families here usually buried their dead aboveground, in communal resting places, each new coffin holding its occupant for a mere year and a day. When the corpse was removed from the coffin to make space for the next inevitable death, it was then unsentimentally and very efficiently shoved backward into the tomb's depths among the remains of earlier family members, virtually cremated by summer's blazing heat, so that bodies mingled with bodies and bones with bones.

The week leading up to *La Toussaint* had brought the local housewives out of their kitchens with whitewash, weed whackers, white shrimpers' boots, and gardening gloves to clean and mow and decorate the tombs. Their handiwork gleamed on each side as Michelle passed down the short walkway to one of the more modest plastered-brick edifices near the water. Her mother-in-law's own raw hands had swept the path here, had plucked the weeds. Had arranged pots of chrysanthemums, lit votive candles, and left mementos—a dilapidated teddy bear, an empty valentine-shaped candy box covered in red synthetic satin, framed photographs, and a figurine of Our Lady of the Assumption—having first brushed whitewash over the weathered incised letters, SAVOIE, where, mingled with grandparents, her husband and two of her sons lay.

The elder son was the latest lost, cast atop his father and little brother like a fallen tree limb raked from a yard.

He and I, we should've had one of those pre-need funeral plans they keep advertising on television, Michelle thought, so that I wouldn't have had to put him way out here, separated from me. But I never planned on losing him so soon. Why did God get us back together again, him and me, only to take him away from me forever and so quickly?

There can't be a God. I knew that.

SHE SAW NOBODY LIVING. She saw no dead. They were hidden away in their whitened dwellings, crosses on their low roofs like TV antennae, unspeaking, unhearing, oblivious.

What did these exiled French Canadians think, all those years ago, unable to keep their buried dead from washing up to the surface after floods? she wondered. Better to just bury their dead aboveground to begin with, then, to lessen the possibility of future floating heartbreak and horror. Adapt to the circumstances—something they've proven to be so good at. Adapting to these storm-scoured bayous and marshes, as unlike either France or Canada as a place can get. So that south Louisiana is inconceivable now without them, it's like they were always here, like the Chitamacha or Houma tribes. Always here, surviving. Enduring—another ethnic trait.

The Savoie tomb was open, she suddenly saw.

She almost dropped her mums.

Oh no, she protested, still four paces away, oh no, no way. I'm sorry, folks, but I'm really not ready to look inside, thank you very much. I'm not ready to see anything inside. My field is Central America, Maya culture, so I can sit out any kind of fieldwork here, this is not my dissertation. So fuck this, I'm sorry. But y'all know what? I'm going home.

Yet with the illogic of dreams she found herself, dressed in widow's black, closer to the dark interior where the heavy slab that formed the tomb's door had been slid back. As she became aware now of a surrounding accumulation of the living—her in-laws calling jovially to one another and guffawing, socializing among the raised graves with Styrofoam ice chests and Wal-Mart folding lawn chairs, rosaries dangling from the hands of the women dissecting weddings and births and scandal, young children giggling but obediently trying not to run, cigarette-smoking men in wilted knit shirts arguing about football and politics and layoffs at the shipyard—her own repressed tears finally began to cascade.

Please show me some mercy here, she tried to get the attention of Adrien's family. I am the widow here, people, after all. And I certainly do applaud your stereotypical joie de vivre, but I lack it, remember. I'm a Texan. I'm bereft.

Bereft. What a forsaken word.

...But Michelle could not speak, as she suddenly noticed that the polished lid of an inner wooden coffin had been raised, its year-and-a-day tenure apparently not yet expired. Her heart bumped and jumped.

None of the other people there seemed to notice, with their mouths relating anecdotes and their eyes streaming both with

laughter and fond tears for the deceased. Nobody else seemed concerned at all. Michelle's own hands grew slick with perspiration.
Something lay there.

Unable to look away, she looked.

But the rotting head that rested on the stained satin pillow beneath her bludgeoned stare wasn't Adrien Paul Savoie's.

It was Philip Randazzo's.

FOUR

Belated Birthday

WHAT SHE HAD NOT TOLD ANYBODY, certainly not Philip, was
that she had been having vivid dreams of Adrien lately. In Technicolor, complete with audio and reasonably logical scenarios. They
took place in the surreality of dreamland, resembling little that had
ever actually happened in real life. But Adrien was palpably Adrien
in them, true to the living self he had been. And she was she.

"Shell?" Philip reached across the table for her hand now and
she was slow to react, again, to this abbreviation of her name that
nobody but he ever used. It wasn't that she didn't care for it, it was
just that she couldn't think of herself as *Shell* or *Shelly*. Falling in love
with Philip, she had fallen in love with the idea of becoming someone else, of starting over. But *Shell* always reminded her of the oil
company her father's outfit had been in competition with, so she
was still waiting to feel reborn.

"You want an order of guacamole for the table," he was asking,
"or just the salsa?"

She interlaced fingers with his, enjoying his warm and dry
touch, what large and strong but flexible hands he had. She loved
those capable hands on her body, the way they braced and comforted, bolstering her while she was standing or sitting, exploring
her when she lay down.

"Whatever the kids want," she said.

Cam shrugged, drumming the edges of the table with his thumbs.

"Is guacamole that yucky green stuff?" asked Nicole.

"It's green," said Michelle. "It isn't yucky."

"We'll split an order," Philip told the young waitress, indicating himself and Michelle. "Two Cuervo Gold margaritas, rocks— salt for the lady, please—none for me, thanks. Cokes for the kids."

The corn chips were fresh and crisp. Michelle scooped one into the red salsa and listened to the silence of her husband trying to decide what to have for his entrée. Cam and Nicole never deviated from nachos and coconut ice cream. Michelle always got the chicken chimichangas here.

Philip settled on beef tamales while the waitress was away. He took the menus from the four of them and stacked them on the edge of the table as if it were his job.

Michelle's birthday had actually been last Thursday, but they had waited until now to celebrate it because Tasso was closed on Monday nights, and Philip could be with them. "Thank you so much, honey, this is lovely," she took his hand again and assured him, a little giddy to be out like this with him, with the kids, enjoying something as a family, out of the confines of the Chestnut Street house. He had wanted to fete her at Tasso but she had turned him down because she knew that although Philip might physically be near them on such a night, he would still be working. Serving them himself at a chef's table set up in the kitchen, but busy and distracted and loud and happy and spread thinly among his tribe. She wanted his undivided attention for her family.

He was good about eating other people's cooking with grace and a minimum of criticism as he was good about so much else. He raised his margarita to Michelle now, clinking it against the kids' cola glasses. "To the birthday girl."

She covertly studied him from across their cluttered table and underneath the garish Tex-Mex colors of the room, watching him read the dessert menu to Nicole. Nicole would order ice cream, that was a foregone conclusion, but Philip didn't yet know that. His reading glasses were at half-mast down his curved nose, dark brows lowered in an effort to make out the print half-obscured by the pointing and darting fingers of the small child, but he was giving Nicole as much attention as a grad student gave his faculty advisor.

He had silver hair and a cleft chin and was nearly six foot three—courtesy of a part-Irish grandfather whose genes had supercharged those of an ordinarily short Sicilian build. Philip was a man who didn't know he was handsome and would never believe any woman who told him that he was. It was possible that he had never possessed especially good looks until now, it occurred to his second wife, not until his hair had gone spectacularly gray like this and his bone structure had begun to show in his face with this maturity.

And maybe it's mostly because I love him, she thought, that I find him beautiful. That I do.

"He's so adorable, but he's a dreadful workaholic," had been the confidential warning from the mutual female friend who had first introduced him to her. "He's at that goddam restaurant office most days by noon and then won't leave the kitchen until eleven, that's what really broke up his marriage. And he's inwardly inaccessible, is what Regan says. He doesn't know how to let himself go and really *relate* to a woman. So she just eventually outgrew him, you know what I mean? I mean, she's so *evolved*."

Since I don't think in *italics,* Michelle had reasoned, maybe I'm not all that evolved, either. So Philip and I might have at least one thing in common.

But what can he possibly see in me? I'm a bundle of nerves, I have to get up early, I have two emotionally disturbed kids, he doesn't like my cat, and I'm not young. Is he nuts as well as repressed?

"Mom," Nicole looked up confidentially from the menu, "Phil snuck in a fantastic cake for you and gave it to the lady in the back. They're going to put candles on it and bring it out in a little bit."

"Nick!" spluttered Cam. "Hey, tell *all* the secrets, why don'tcha?"

"What if Mom has to go to the bathroom first? I'm just telling her in case she has to go—!"

"Mom?" Cam appealed, stricken, his body language both apologetic and outraged. "She's ruining everything, little virus, big mouth, tell her to shut up!"

Michelle felt both of her hands reaching to cover her ears, too taken with tequila to be diplomatic, but she was smiling. "Cake with candles? Set this place afire, y'all, I'm so old."

So what the hell is in this for him? she asked herself again, watching Philip preventing Nicole from stabbing Cam's hand with a fork. He didn't stay single long enough after his separation to realize that he's capable of bedding delectable twentysomethings, not just some worn-out old bag like me. He didn't have time enough in the evenings to date around. He caved too early. Gave up too soon. Just settled for the first woman he came across who was willing to forgo all nightlife and screw him at lunch.

"Philip," she spoke up, emboldened by alcohol and the contagious good cheer of raucous diners all around them, the festive bustling of the waiters and waitresses, the turquoise blues and serape reds, "I'm really *old*, honey, you realize that?"

"Like I'm some college kid?" He removed his reading glasses and stowed them away. "See all these gray hairs?"

"I mean," she licked salt from the edge of her glass, "I am really old, no kidding. Older than you, kiddo. Forty-seven is way older than I know how to be."

"Mom's fantastically old," nodded Nicole, eager to agree, having only recently learned the big word *fantastic* and determined now to say it at every opportunity. She used crayons to color the drawing she was making on her place mat of a sky with a moon, stars, and a rainbow.

Nick is the one who takes after Adrien, not Cam, Michelle thought, watching the movement of her daughter's hand. Compact and dark and neatly made. Precociously talented. But not musical at all. Neither of his children has any musical ability that I can detect. So maybe artistic proclivities are passed down in different formats, musical to visual to narrative, or whatever. Or maybe the talent's not passed down in any pattern at all and is just a random accident of the genes. Adrien's huge family currently displays no talent to speak of, unless it's procreation. Although his musical mentor was a deceased uncle on his father's side, yeah. Plus, I mustn't overlook that maternal grandfather of his who was supposed to have played six or seven musical instruments with no training of any kind. The *alcoholic* grandfather, significantly. As my kids get older, I'm starting to really worry about that.

"Mom?" Cam spoke.

"Yes?"

"You having a good time?"

"Absolutely," she said, and she was. Her eyes locked with the brown ones of her son and she recognized his unblinking desire that she be happy. "I love your guts, ol' Cameroony-boony."

He rolled his eyes at the rhyming name, a relic of his toddler-hood. "But Nicole's screwed up the whole surprise now, though. Little big mouth."

"Who says good things have to come as surprises?" she forestalled Nicole before the child could begin to protest. "Sometimes it's better to look forward to something, that's what I think. Like my cake!"

So when the fantastic chocolate cake was ceremonially carried out from the kitchen, ablaze with a few token candles, she was prepared to bask in its flickering light in happy embarrassment, listening to the waiter and two waitresses leading her family in the caroling of "Happy Birthday"—Philip's tenor light but on-key, Nicole and Cam enthusiastic but completely atonal.

A. P. Savoie might be the last man anybody in here would ever guess had sired these two tone-deaf little sweethearts, Michelle thought to herself.

———

LAST NIGHT'S DREAM, the latest in a series of many, suddenly began to replay itself in part as they drove the shortish distance home. Michelle sat in the passenger seat, dulled by margaritas, looking out of the Saturn's window at the bright prismatic lead glass doors of the dark Victorian houses amid their shrubbery on the avenue. And she remembered now that this particular reverie had been erotic.

"Forgot to get gas," Philip told her, pulling the car to the curb. "I'm leaving you with an empty tank for tomorrow, doll, I'm sorry."

Adrien had made her weak. He had done unspeakably sweet things to her.

"Shell?"

"It's okay," she answered slowly, undoing her seat belt, gathering up her purse and the box that held the remains of her cake, coming back to her waking life. "I can fill up on the way to school."

If Hendrix had somehow escaped the house again, none of them knew it yet, because the cat was nowhere to be seen. Cam and Nicole struggled sleepily out of the automobile and up the steps of the front porch while Michelle cheered them on. "Bath time! Y'all run go get your baths, tomorrow's a school day!"

"Yeah," Cam mumbled irritably, flinging long bangs out of his face while Philip unlocked the door, "don't rub it in."

"It's a school day for me, too, pal." She stooped to pet Hendrix, who arched and met them just inside the door, on the short thick fur of his yellow head: "Good ol' Hendrix, nice kitty, there you are, sweet ol' booger boy! Mean ol' Philip got all your escape hatches sealed up?"

"Haven't sealed up a thing," her husband admitted, turning off the porch light and switching on the overhead reflector bulbs in the front room. "Never found out where he was getting out from."

The kids scrambled past her and began to toil up the staircase with heavy feet. "Well, he seems to've quit getting out, anyway, whatever," she said, watching their backs. "Maybe we'd just left a window open or something and just didn't notice. Maybe it's closed now."

Philip's face wore that I-checked-for-open-windows-baby-doll expression again but he didn't speak.

She stepped close to him and he reached behind her to cup a buttock in one of those marvelous hands. "Nice ass for an old lady," he teased.

But she was compelled to sniff at his neck suddenly, just under his earlobe, knowing that men didn't dab cologne underneath their ears like her own mother did but not knowing where else to sniff. "You aren't wearing patchouli, are you, honey? Philip?"

His smile was tolerant. "Whatever you gave me for my own birthday. Calvin Klein."

"What the hell am I smelling in here, then?" She lost the scent and then found it and then lost it again. "This is so odd."

"Cat piss." He gobbled at her earlobe until the tickling of his emerging beard stubble made her laugh.

"Not cat piss!" she insisted, pushing him away and then immediately pulling his head back against her collarbone. "You're the one with the great sense of taste and smell, Chef, what *is* that?"

"All I smell is beautiful woman and cat piss."

Her thin arms were like whips when they wrapped around him in glee. "Oh Lord, I feel so wanton all of a sudden! This must be menopause!"

"Sorry," he kissed her three times on the lips, lightly, quickly, "I do not do Chinese soup."

"Philip!" She swatted him gently for his bad pun.

The lights went out.

BY THE TIME the offending circuit breaker had been located and reset, and both kids calmed and bedded down, and Nick's school clothes selected and laid out for her, and the cat fed; and by the time Michelle had had a brief opportunity to sit down for just a moment and glance over tomorrow's lecture notes and wash her face and then go up to turn off Cam's television, Philip was already asleep.

With a pillow held in place over his ear by one forearm, in mute protest over the noisy and chaotic household his wife and her children inhabited, he had checked out on her.

She stood in the doorway of their bedroom and looked down at him in the darkness, her arms entwined beneath her breasts and around the rib cage of her special black lace nightgown, leaning her shoulder against the doorjamb, watching the sheet rise and fall with his unconscious breathing. She felt loving and indulgent and vaguely pissed off.

He doesn't even have to get up as early as I do, she thought, weary.

Setting her alarm clock, she climbed into bed and tucked herself around him and held him for a while, her bosoms to his shoulder blades. But when he neither waked nor responded, she finally rolled over into what was for her a more comfortable position and turned her back.

FIVE

Thanksgiving

PHIL ROSE VERY EARLY—for him—that next Thursday morning before the televised Macy's parade had even come on and drove the thirty-two miles across the Causeway to Mandeville to pick up his kids for the holiday. He was in the Acura, his own car, where he exhumed his oldies collection from the glove compartment and played some of them as he crossed the lake—the Beach Boys and Otis Redding and Marvin Gaye, cranking them up really loud. Lowering both front windows and opening the sunroof, he sang along to his favorites, strands of his hair twisting and the wind making his face pink.

He was pursuing happiness, trying to yank himself into a noisy and expansive good mood, but failing. The tall tidy pines of the north shore depressed him because they sheltered the large beige-bricked and azalea-flanked ranch house where Regan lived with her husband, Lyle.

Phil always dreaded dealing with Regan. It wasn't that she was not pleasant and cordial, because she always was. But just the sight of her in her present situation, with his own past failings always implicit in every encounter, had the power to make his scrotum contract. The childless Lyle Gaspard was a cardiac surgeon and he made obscene amounts of money and Regan hadn't had to lift a finger to help him make a dime of it.

So here now were Phil's own three kids, growing up with a swimming pool in their backyard and a Honduran housemaid running the vacuum cleaner several days a week, *buy me, bring me, get me* an everyday part of their adolescent vocabularies over here among these lush lawns. Where all the neighbors were both monied and Caucasian on the nearby streets. The housemaid went elsewhere when she went home.

Do you begrudge your kids this? Then what would you rather have for 'em? Phil asked himself as he watched the manicured lawns slide past and the houses get bigger. Half of a stinky shotgun-double next door to a restaurant like what you had? Bus traffic and high crime? No, but that new house in Lakeview wasn't half bad, Regan and I had a real nice house in Lakeview, kids were happy there. Yeah, maybe I brought home more disposable income when I was still at Les Plaisirs, they paid me a shitload at Les Plaisirs. But Tasso was *ours,* and it took money to get it off the ground.

And I thought Regan was happy. In Lakeview.

With me.

It was still early Thanksgiving morning and Phil quieted his music and closed his sunroof to keep from disturbing the innocent, and felt the resulting loss of sunlight as actual darkness.

Lyle Gaspard's social transactions with him always boiled down to one long and ongoing lecture about needed changes to Tasso's menu to make it more heart-healthy. "I'll supply my name and professional endorsement to any selection of lighter entrées you'd like to offer, Phil, and then my office'll handle the press releases. You can even have sort of a second grand opening. Guaranteed great coverage in the *Times-Picayune,* with our photos," Lyle would offer as if he were some celebrity. "And maybe we should have a companion cookbook ready, to get it out to the bookstores at the peak of the publicity. What would be involved? How much time would it take you?"

Yeah, Phil sighed now as he turned the corner onto the Gaspards' street, let me get this straight: I do all the work, Doc, and you suck up half the profits for officially assuring people that my food won't kill 'em.

He pulled into the driveway behind twin Lexuses, wondering if the plural should properly be *Lexi*. Well, let the fun begin. The kids were certain to bitch and complain about everything in the entire universe on the way back. They weren't enthusiastic over leaving their own home today, and Michelle and Cam and Nicole certainly hadn't seemed all that thrilled about having them over. But it was Phil's turn to get them for Thanksgiving this year, with Regan keeping them for Christmas. And he knew that if he ever passed on one of these visits, he'd probably wind up never getting to see them at all. That's how these things went.

He loved them as much as he knew how—Brendan, sixteen; Kerri, fourteen; and Hunter, barely thirteen—but might've already traumatized them forever, according to Regan, by making her so desperate that her only reasonable salvation had been divorce. Making her work so hard at Tasso that she'd actually risked her health. Emotionally freezing her out so thoroughly that she'd been driven to seek solace in the arms of patron Dr. Lyle Gaspard from right over there at Touro Infirmary, all of which was Phil's own fault. According to her.

Fuckin' breaks my heart, he thought, stalking up the immaculate walkway in his sneakers, leaning into the doorbell, hoping that he was waking somebody up.

But no, both Regan and Lyle were having coffee and the three kids were ready to go with overnight bags all packed, videotaped movies and CDs in shopping bags, and even several sandwiches in a Ziploc bag.

"Goddam, Regan," Phil said, "we got food."

"But Kerri seems to be developing that allergy to peanuts, remember, you know how serious that can get. And I'm not sure she's as cautious yet as she should be, either."

"Michelle's been warned about it, it's not like it's some secret, she can read a label. And she's just doing a turkey, not Chinese."

"It's so easy to be careless, is all I'm saying."

He was mystified. "Not if you're a chef."

"So why aren't *you* doing the turkey, Dad?" asked Brendan, once the Acura was back out on the Causeway. "You're a better cook than Michelle could ever be."

"She wants to give me a little holiday, son. From work. And I think that's real nice of her."

"What'll we *do* there?" worried Kerri. "We don't know anybody."

"You know Cam, sort of. He's a good kid. And Nicole."

She flopped back into the seat cushions behind Phil and he heard her deep sigh. "What if somebody expects me to *babysit* for Nicole? I'm not coming all this way to *babysit*."

"Kerri, nobody wants you to babysit. If Michelle and I have to go someplace while you kids stay behind, then Cam looks after Nicole, sweetheart. That's his job."

Hunter remained silent beside Phil in the passenger seat, looking out of the window onto the shining steely water, and Phil was grateful that his youngest had made no complaints so far. Hunter clutched a translucent plastic grocery bag that held a Super Nintendo console and several games. He rubbed his cheek while Phil watched, and he yawned in the morning sun that came slanting in.

"Dad?" Hunter turned his head, finally. "Why can't just the four of us, you and me and Brendan and Kerri, just go someplace, like a hotel, and just hang out by ourselves? Just the four of us. The Four Musketeers. With no outsider to bother us. Just us."

Here it was. Phil had known that it was coming. "So. I should just check out on my wife and her kids and just run off with you guys for Thanksgiving," he said. "Is that it?"

"Basically." Brendan's snicker was deep, and Phil couldn't see him but he could imagine him shrugging, all sharp shoulders and elbows and nodding brown hair. "*Yeah,* as a matter of fact."

The other two amplified the laughter with their braced teeth and high voices. Phil finished with the Causeway and headed toward uptown, frowning.

"I brought my own Super Nintendo, Dad," Hunter held it up, "in case Cam won't let me play. Can I play it in your bedroom on your TV?"

"Why wouldn't Cam let you play?"

Hunter shrugged.

"Cam's stuck-up," Kerri explained.

"Cam's such a little fag," said Brendan.

Phil felt his face getting too warm and he gave up and turned on the air conditioner. "Cam's not a fag and he's not stuck-up, y'all, and I expect all of you to be just as nice to him as his mother is going to bend over backwards to be nice to you guys. Is that clear?"

They chorused, "Yes, sir," but Phil detected insincerity in it and heard muffled wheezed snorts coming from the backseat. And it made him angry, their response; not so much because he favored Cam Savoie over them—he did not—but because they were so anarchic about it. They took their noncompliance to his order so lightly. Their disrespect of him was so deep and pervasive that they weren't even aware of it. It was like their breathing, unintentional and effortless and daily. They held no malice for him they unquestionably did love him—but Phil was irked at their dismissal of him and his wishes.

He got off the expressway at the St. Charles exit. "Guys," he took a deep breath and went for solemnity if he couldn't get to them through a direct order, "Cam lost his dad just about three years ago to the day through some kind of traffic accident that wasn't anybody's fault. But he blames himself for it. So ease up here."

Brendan eventually spluttered in predictable young-guy giggles and Phil glanced into his rearview mirror and saw him hugging himself in the backseat, face creased with the unreasoning and uncaused mirth of adolescence. But when Kerri spoke again it was in a new tone and Phil realized that he had gotten through to her. He met her green eyes in the rearview reflection, her curiosity if not her concern.

"How old was Cam's dad?" she asked. "When he died, I mean."

"A couple of years younger than I am right now, I believe. I don't know for sure."

She thought about that. "Was it Cam's fault?"

"No."

"Mom says he was sort of famous," she said, "Cam's dad."

"Well, around this region, yeah, definitely. He was a recording artist—rhythm and blues. Sang and played guitar. Couple of his records got national attention, nominated for a Grammy, even. He opened for Bonnie Raitt on her national tour the summer before he got killed, I think it was that same summer."

"Had you ever heard of him?" Brendan, calmer, spoke up.

"Your mother and I," Phil answered, driving up St. Charles behind a white airport limousine, "went to see him at the House of Blues in the spring of '93, as a matter of fact. And we always tried to see him at Jazzfest. First time we saw him was at Tipitina's in about 1990 or '91, right after he'd been written up in *People* magazine. We'd have gone out a lot more back then, heard more music, if we could've found babysitters for you guys and if Tasso could've run itself. We used to bring you guys with us to Tasso, those times when Nana couldn't watch you—y'all remember that?"

"Vividly," said Brendan. "Watching *Batman* in your office while Mom would come in and yell at us to be quiet."

"Did you know Michelle then?" This was Kerri.

"No." He turned onto Seventh Street. "Seeing A. P. Savoie perform, didn't even cross my mind that there could be a Michelle."

"Did he look like Cam?" She sounded fascinated.

Phil tried to recall. "Well, maybe more like Nicole, on the whole, real dark-headed. Kind of an interesting face, probably would've been real handsome if he'd been more clean-cut. And he wasn't near as tall as Cam's going to be. What he did, he wrote all of his

own stuff. Slapped a lot of idioms together—blues, zydeco, Alge-
rian *rai,* even. Between numbers, he just came across as this ordinary little guy from out in the country, didn't take himself too
seriously, no pretense or spandex or big hair, always laughing and
easygoing. But when he got cranked up, he could bring the house
down for real."

"So why didn't he become really *big* famous?" asked Hunter.

"Got discovered too late in life, I guess." Phil shrugged and
yawned, not knowing for sure. "Plus he was sorta handicapped."

Kerri's eyes met his again in the mirror. "Like how? Like in a
wheelchair?"

"It wasn't that obvious, except when you noticed that he never
moved around onstage much, just sat on a barstool with his guitar
on his knees. But we saw him out front at Tip's one time, talking to
some people, and he was leaning on this walking cane with a silver
handgrip. He could get around reasonably okay, but with a bad
limp, like more than one thing was wrong with more than one leg."
Phil braked at the Prytania Street stop sign. "Plus, he was missing
a couple of his fingers."

"But he's *so* sexy," had been Regan's assessment of A. P. Savoie's
appeal that last night in '93 at the House of Blues, the fourth or
fifth time Phil had gone with her to see him. "I know you don't get
it, honey, but that's what's bringing in all these women here, not
just the music. You, when you look at the stage, here's just this little
gimpy guy, big deal. But silly women see a tragic boy inside who's
absolutely begging to be taken home and looked after. He's so talented and so easy on the eyes, and then there's that whiskey voice.
I'm sorry, Phil, but you did ask me why on earth any girl would
throw her bra at the stage like that fat brunette did awhile ago, and
all I'm doing is telling you."

Phil hadn't much wanted to go back to another such perfor-
mance with Regan after that. Nine months later, the object of
her interest was dead and gone. But Regan and Phil had already
stopped making the effort of going out together by then, anyway.

"So he was good, huh, Dad?" Kerri was still pursuing the subject of Cam's father for unfathomable reasons, daughter of her mother, as they turned onto Chestnut Street.

Phil parked the Acura at the curb in front of the house he shared with A. P. Savoie's widow and children, and sighed. "He was the real deal."

THEY FOUND MICHELLE in the kitchen when they came inside, and the aroma of the roasting turkey did smell good, Phil decided. Maybe some of what I've been teaching Cam is rubbing off on her, he thought, giving her a quick kiss on the lips. If you just soak the bird in a bucket of salt water in the fridge overnight, nothing special, you're already on your way.

"Traffic bad?" she asked him, her face all pink from the heat and her hair in little wet spikes at her temples, as his kids thundered up the staircase in search of Cam.

"Naahhh. Not all that many people out yet." He put Kerri's sandwiches in the refrigerator.

She watched him close the door upon the Ziploc bag. "What's that?"

"Regan being an idiot."

Nicole, who had been in the dining room drawing a picture of the fruit basket centerpiece, trotted into the kitchen now to display her work to Phil. "Look!" she said, not altogether modestly, holding up artwork done with colored felt-tip pens.

It was spooky, he thought, how good this kid was. It was, like, impossible that a six-year-old girl could render images this accurately when most children her age didn't have the hand-eye coordination to even color inside the lines of a coloring book. Nicole had produced a likeness of oranges and apples and grapes in a large brown basket, and each fruit was an appropriate hue. Okay, so the coloring was too bright and unsubtle, felt-tip marker—jeez—and her round shapes had wobbly places. But, Jesus Christ, the kid could *draw*. You could tell what it was all supposed to be without being coached. Her purple grapes were, correctly, much smaller than her apples or oranges. She had even attempted the woven pattern of the basket, with some success.

"Nick," he took it from her, "that's real good, sweetheart. Wow."

"Is Kerri upstairs?" Her large eyes were fixed upon him and he noticed again what long and thick lashes she had. She wasn't a conventionally pretty child—her narrow nose was too long and her jawline too harsh, her chin too square for moppet prettiness, coffee-black eyes certainly big enough but somewhat downturned and mournful at their outside corners. She looked Parisian French, Philip sometimes thought, like a kid who could be nicknamed Zizi or Gigi or Fifi, when most Cajuns seemed like anything but. The delicacy of her flexible hands and wrists was uncanny and something in her posture and countenance promised compelling future beauty.

"Nicole," Michelle warned, "remember what we said about not bugging Kerri while she's here?"

"Okay."

"She's upstairs, sweetheart, and she's playing Nintendo with the guys. You may go up and watch them if you want to, but please give her a chance to just relax and chill out for a while, okay?"

"Okay, Mom."

Phil felt the child's disappointment, and he held her drawing up high now and made a big deal over it yet again, finally affixing it to the black surface of the refrigerator door with two discreet magnets. It was the only thing he had allowed up there so far since the new appliance had been delivered, besides a small family message slate, and he felt magnanimous for having broken his own no-magnetized-crap rule. He straightened the picture so that it would hang level.

But Nicole had disappeared, escaping up the same staircase to the computer loft and kids' bedrooms that the Randazzo children had escaped up earlier. Phil stood there empty-handed and considered taking the drawing down again.

"She worships Kerri," said Michelle, noticing. "Kerri's a Big Girl. Therein lie many mysteries."

"Kerri's a pretty good kid," he left Nicole's picture where it was, "in spite of the fact that Regan and Lyle are spoiling her and the boys rotten."

"Isn't there some kind of football game on today?" she asked him, beginning to dice apples for the salad.

He saw. "Shell, let me do that."

"No! It's your day off from cooking! Go enjoy your day off! I want you to!"

He would never have left her now if he didn't believe her, but he did believe her. He was able, lately, to recognize a certain little edge to her voice when she really meant something. He watched her laboriously chop at an apple half for a moment or two until she said, "Honey, I'm going to cut my finger right *off* with you watching over my shoulder this way! Makes me nervous! Go sit down somewhere, for God's sake."

He kissed the corner of her white smile and bounded down the three varnished wooden steps onto the enclosed patio. The master bedroom suite opened onto the patio from underneath the staircase and the biggest television set in the house was hooked up in there, on top of Michelle's father's antique chest of drawers. Adjoining the bedroom and merging into it was a second room filled with free weights and Phil's golf clubs and a stationary bicycle that nobody ever used. But three steps down from the weight room was a very large and extremely private Jacuzzi-type spa, four feet deep and nearly eight feet square, set right into the bricked floor of its own enclosed room and hidden away from and unsuspected by all adult guests except the most ill-mannered and intrusive—which so far included only Michelle's mother. The yellow cat slumbered insensible on its deck in a pool of sunlight.

Phil sank down onto the king-sized mattress in the master bedroom, clicking on the TV, and wondered how many minutes of blessed tranquillity he would have before all of those kids upstairs rediscovered the Jacuzzi and put on their swimsuits.

None of the teams playing football today were favorites of his, he discovered, and he leaned back into the pillows in gratitude. He would not have to stay awake for games he cared nothing about.

Michelle appeared at the door of the bedroom now with a cold long-necked Corona and a slice of lime. *"Pour toi,"* she held out the libation to him, *"mon amour"*—said facetiously, since she had hardly a drop of French blood in her Texan body and he himself had little more. Her cheeks were hollow but rosy and her smile was very self-satisfied.

"Whoa, you sperlin' me rotten, dawlin'!" He exaggerated his native midcity accent. "I ain't gon be woith a damn afta today, thank you ma'am, queen of wives!"

She grinned and waved and disappeared. Phil sprawled against the multiple pillows at the head of his own king-sized bed with the bottom of a cold beer resting on his sternum, football on TV, kids out of the way, bills all paid, and a beautiful, sexy blond preparing a bountiful dinner in the kitchen.

I have, he decided in utter contentment, become my own beer commercial.

He was sunk in some sort of football reverie, paddling in the warm and comfortable shallows between deep sleep and awareness, when waves of loud music began to wash over him.

Not completely conscious, he heard his wife scream, "Turn it down! Turn that down, y'all!"

Her entreaties became incorporated into his dream, becoming the cheers of fans, while he visualized a dancing woman dragging her brassiere out from underneath her blouse to toss it high over the end zone. Soul-searing rhythmic blues blared from the stadium speakers: A. P. Savoie live at Tipitina's, a gumbo of percussion and slide guitar and backup band culminating in the broken vocal plea, "Baby, baby, baby...let me kiss you where you bleed..."

"What?" hollered his own son Brendan from somewhere above.

"Turn it down! Turn it off!" came Michelle's surly orders again. "Cam? You hear me?"

The music abruptly stopped. Phil was left with fuzzy football commentary as the sole sound track to his hypnopompic imagery. Kind of a shame, he thought, woozy. Can't dance to football.

"Philip?" Michelle called, footsteps drumming down the three small steps from the kitchen's level.

He opened his eyes.

"Philip, dinner's ready." She stuck her head into the bedroom and her voice was no longer a beer-commercialish purr. "Wake up."

"Hah?"

"Get washed up, please. Dinner's ready."

He sat up, passing a hand over his forehead and nose, but she had disappeared again. He looked at the television screen until it again made sense to him.

He didn't know how long he sat there like that, but it was long enough to irritate her, and she came stomping up the wooden steps onto the bedroom's carpeted floor now, oven mitts clutched in one hand.

"What?" he said.

"Thanksgiving dinner," she huffed, "if you want any."

He slid across the mattress. "Yeah, sorry. I fell asleep."

But he said it to her spine because she had already turned away and was scurrying back to the kitchen's steps, her shoulder blades prominent and stiff. "Would you go call the kids, please, honey? I don't think they heard me," she said without turning.

"Did you tell 'em it's time to eat?"

She spun slowly and looked at him and her eyes were unreadable.

"Okay," he told her, standing. "Will do."

Moving beyond the doorway of the bedroom across an expanse of bricked patio, scratching his ribs through his blue golf shirt, Phil trudged sleepily up the three steps to the floor level of the kitchen.

He yawned so widely that something clicked in his jaws, and then he turned to consider the painfully steep stairs. The large landing at the top, where a burdened computer desk sat unconsulted, was brightly lit by a high row of uncurtained windows. The brilliant sunlight made him blink and he sucked in a deep breath, intent upon shouting the kids out of their lairs so that he wouldn't have to climb the stairs with his sore joints. But when he looked up, there was already one kid in view, seated on the steps near the top with his back to the computer, elbows on knees.

"Hey!" Phil called up to the boy in the sunshine, a vaguely familiar-looking kid probably from a family down the block whom Phil was supposed to know by name, but didn't. "Hey!"

The kid didn't budge, he just looked off toward the windows. He wore a wilted black football jersey with gold numbers on it, cleated and muddy athletic shoes.

Phil instantly hated the shoes and pointed at them. "Son, if you plan to eat with us, then please take off your cleats and just come to the table in your sock feet so we won't get our hardwood floors down here all scarred up. Okay?"

When the kid looked down at him from his high perch, he did not quite make eye contact.

"Go tell the others to get washed up," Phil waved. "Dinner's ready."

The boy turned his head toward the open doorway of Cam's bedroom where several high voices echoed. His profile was a dark silhouette, long-nosed and alert.

Phil about-faced and hobbled toward the kitchen, still stiff from his nap. Michelle, wearing oven mitts, crossed the floor in front of him carrying a casserole dish of oyster dressing. He followed her into the dining room where she had set the table beautifully with linen napkins, lace tablecloth, her antique sterling flatware and inherited china, two unlit white tapers in silver candlesticks bracketing the fruit basket centerpiece, and name cards at each place setting. Phil, astounded and delighted, must have shown both of those things in his facial expression because she smiled at him now in the reflection of the mirrored back wall.

"You can carve." She indicated the turkey, golden and lacquered, steaming beneath the chandelier. "As a matter of fact, maybe you'd better."

"Wow!" he said, and meant it.

"I'll light the candles and serve Nicole's plate, if you'll take care of the carving."

The gelatinous cylinder of cranberry sauce on the table was of the canned variety, but Michelle's children probably wouldn't eat any other version. Phil suspected that his own wouldn't, either. "Jesus, baby doll! I've married Martha Stewart!"

She hesitated with the matches. "Where're the kids? Didn't I hear you calling them?"

"I told that neighbor kid to get 'em." He jerked his head in the direction of the stairs. "They're coming."

"What neighbor kid?"

"Boy in the Saints jersey, friend of Cam's." He flapped a dismissive hand.

"Well, dammit," she said, "I didn't invite any friends of Cam's and I don't have enough food for anybody else if they eat like our own little barbarians do. It's not Gavin Whatsisname, the one who keeps 'borrowing' Cam's video games and never brings them back?"

"No, not him, another one," Phil answered, and then remembered the cleated shoes. "But I'm sending him home if you didn't invite him. He's all muddy."

She held a match but didn't strike it. "Well, see what's keeping them, because the food is getting cold."

Phil moved across the hardwood floor of the dining room and went back through the kitchen archway to the bottom of the staircase. The boy in the Saints jersey was nowhere to be seen, but at least he hadn't despoiled the varnish on the flooring here at the side door. Very little mud and a few dried brown leaves showed on the welcome mat. Loud laughter and video game sound effects echoed from above.

"Guys!" he cupped his hands, shouting up the stairs. "Hey, guys!"

But they were making too much noise to hear him, hollering over that game stuff. And Cam was playing that rap music of his now, thug music, Phil thought: incitement to criminal behavior. He took deep and frustrated breaths at their distant hooting and derision of each other, the electronic beeps and tinny sound track music of the contest, Nicole's excited high shrieks.

For the love of Christ! he thought, putting his hand on the railing and angrily climbing the unusually steep steps, feeling his knees complain.

Five white faces turned to his red one when he poked his head into Cam's yellow-painted bedroom. "I *said*," keeping his voice even, "turn off all the stuff."

Cam didn't move but Brendan did, and he flicked out a hand to stifle the CD player. The rap noise stopped in mid-rant. "Sorry, Dad."

Cam was still absorbed in his game, something called *The Legend of Zelda*, with formatted castles and islands and brightly colored forests on the television screen.

"Cam?" Phil prompted.

The boy's brown eyes lifted. His long fingers moved a toggle, and shut off the light and color.

"Time for dinner, y'all," said Phil, letting out big breaths. "And it's time for your company to go home. You guys get washed up and come on downstairs."

Kerri's blue-jeaned legs started to unfurl where she sat cross-kneed on the carpet. Hunter stood.

"I told him to tell y'all." Phil looked around himself. "He left without telling y'all?"

Brendan twisted the waistband of his jeans back into place. "Who?"

"That kid in the Saints jersey."

All five of them looked at Phil now like he was wearing a fake mustache and a Groucho nose.

"The *kid,*" he began again, already starting to recognize a futility in his own insistence, "who was up here awhile ago. In a Saints jersey. Right out there. On the stairs."

The five blank faces looked at each other and then back at Phil.

He began to backpedal, covering for himself, unwilling to look like an idiot in front of all these children he was supposed to be raising. "Never mind," he muttered, "just some neighborhood kid, maybe he didn't even come up here to see y'all. Come on downstairs."

"Who was it?" asked Nicole, her face smeared with color from her green marker.

"A kid from down the block," he repeated, "no big deal. Sweetheart, you've got ink all over your right cheek, go look in the mirror and get all of that washed off before you come downstairs. Okay?"

"Was it Gavin?" Cam asked. "Did he bring back my new *Mortal Kombat?*"

"No, it wasn't Gavin," Phil shook his head. "And stop loaning anything to Gavin, son, because he never brings stuff back, you know that. Whatever, just forget it, he's gone home now, let's go eat. Smells real good down there, the turkey and all. Don't want it to get cold. Y'all smell that?"

They began to emerge from their ablutions, jocular again, getting louder. And the anarchy was back as the three boys pounded down the stairs in high-dollar sneakers, jousting with words and elbows, throwing each other off balance and snorting. The two girls stepped carefully in their wake, thinking about the placement of each foot but separated and oblivious to one another.

Phil glanced back over his shoulder at the sunny top of the stairs as he descended, seeing nothing but daylight and the bare carpet, the computer desk against the far wall, all quiet and empty and normal.

Have I just seen *Casper*? The silly notion flitted through his mind like a drunken bat, ludicrous, come and then gone, too farcical to fly.

On his way to the kitchen he grasped the brass doorknob of the side door and tried to turn it, but it wouldn't turn. The door was as securely locked, with its key hanging from a nearby hook near the burglar alarm panel, as if it had been nailed shut.

Sleepless Night

"WHATCHALL KNOW ABOUT GHOSTS?" Phil asked his staff at Tasso that next afternoon as soon as he was done with his paperwork and had left the restaurant office to come into the kitchen.

"Know I don't want to meet one," answered Da'Shaun.

Frank looked up. "Thought what you had was cat trouble."

Phil raked off his sneakers and stuck his feet into his clean black clogs. "Cats, ghosts, kids, divorce. Just your basic American Dream," he said, and then tried to fake the same sort of condescension his father had once used in references to his mother. "My wife thinks she saw a genuine wraith yesterday, y'all believe that?" he lied. "On Thanksgiving? In broad daylight?"

"Before or after aperitifs?" spoke up Tyrone, the new guy who rarely said anything unrelated to LSU football, probably because he was still new.

"Now, y'all know my wife, she's a pretty levelheaded person, no flaky stuff," Phil went on, relating the vision of the kid at the top of the stairs, how utterly ordinary it had seemed. But he told it as if it had been Michelle's sighting, not his own. He wasn't about to become the kind of boss who saw ghosts or believed in alien abductions or knew anything about New Age matters. It was important always to him that he instigate the laughter in Tasso's kitchen, not become its whispered-about and ridiculed subject.

"Strangest damned thing," he finished up, shaking his head. "Normalest thing you ever saw, according to her. Nothing scary, nothing transparent or floaty. Just a kid whom none of us knew, and who didn't leave by the only door he could've gone through unobserved. Maybe he went out a window. But I don't know why a kid would climb out through a window unless he was stealing something."

"Y'all missing anything?" This was Frank.

"Not yet," said Phil, "and I checked."

"Sound like you got a secret entrance, Chef," said Da'Shaun, "like in the movies. Cats, kids, they know the password. In and out." The young cook went softly *hee-hee-hee* at his own words after a moment, over there near the fryer, and Phil was dismayed by the gold-toothed mirth, the promise of cool and easy derision for anyone older and whiter and more peculiar.

"'In and out.' Guess I'm screwed," Phil observed, speaking up quickly before anybody else could exploit him. He smirked at his own deftness.

"Chef," Vanessa was at her station among her salad vegetables, "your wife, she's, like—what? An anthropologist? I mean, she's had to've heard and read about weird stuff from all over the world."

"Well, Central America and the Yucatán is where she did her fieldwork. She's even the author of a couple or three books, heavy-duty ivory-tower subjects like matrilineal descent among the Mayans." He raised his head, realizing how ambivalent he was about Michelle's professional authority. "Smartest damn real blond God ever made. So if she says she's seen this ghost…"

"Well, there you go," said Vanessa. "She's had to absorb a whole other view of things, instead of just your usual cornflake America. So she's probably more open to interpreting some things as actual visions. Because she's been trained not to view the folklore of other

cultures as benighted. Not to pass judgment. Y'all ever read any of
those Carlos Castaneda Don Juan shaman books?"

Phil vaguely remembered the Don Juan material from the sixties drug scene but could call up no specifics now. He did marvel
at how overqualified for her job this woman Vanessa was. "But
could she have seen a *real* ghost is I guess what I'm asking. An actual American ghost, under the influence of nothing stronger than
one little twelve-ounce Corona?"

"Nobody's sure if there are real ghosts, Chef. At least, not in
our culture."

"Yeah they are," Frank's red and meaty face nodded disagree-
ment, and Phil couldn't say how much of Frank Favrot's permanent
flush was due to his gifted way with cayenne and curries and
jalapeños and how much was uncontrolled high blood pressure and
an incipient drinking problem. "Seen it on *Unsolved Mysteries*. Real
people, normal people like us, not your kooks or your nutcases.
Having ghosts in their houses. Aboard ships. Seeing 'em on the
street, even."

"No such thing," scoffed Da'Shaun. "Bible don't talk about no
ghosts."

"No?" Vanessa turned. "What about that witch of Endor who
called up Samuel's ghost?"

"Some researchers believe," Tyrone spoke up again after a moment while Vanessa and Da'Shaun argued biblical history, "that
ghosts are actually some sort of recording, not conscious or alive
in any way. Just something that's gotten recorded someway, and
gets played back. Like a mirage, just some kind of image. On, like,
damp air or something. Something about electrical fields, I don't
remember."

Phil visualized his own Casper, the kid in the football uniform,
the way the eyes had failed to make contact with his own. "Yeah.
Okay. Interesting."

"Chef, you wanna hear something real mind-blowing?" Vanessa
straightened and put both hands to her arching back. Tiny yellow

flakes of raw squash stuck to brown forearms where the white sleeves of her tunic had been rolled up above her elbows. "I've read somewhere that these ancient pottery pieces, Greek or whatever— that if you could put 'em back on a potter's wheel and exactly duplicate the speed the potter spun them at when they were orig- inally being created, and if you could devise a laser gizmo like a CD player to read their surfaces while they were being spun around, then you could actually play back and actually hear the sounds of whatever was going on in the pottery studio the day they were made. *Hear* the ancient Greek being spoken, or whatever. Voices, or whatever. Isn't that wild?"

"Vanessa, you read too much," Frank shook his head. "Ain't healthy."

"Then I know *you'll* certainly live forever," she said.

"I mean," Phil threw up his hands, "look: normally, somebody you love says this kind of thing, 'I've seen a ghost,' and you just go, 'Okay,' and then laugh about it with 'em, and so on. And explain to them what you think it was, and so forth. And it all becomes just one more wacky family story, eventually. But I've got my own three biological kids in the house for this weekend, and then there's my two stepkids. And so when somebody says, like, they've seen some- thing or somebody who doesn't belong there, who's got no business being there…"

"I hear ya," said Frank.

"Coulda been an intruder, Chef," Tyrone weighed in, "yeah."

"Kids messin' wit yo head," Da'Shaun suggested.

"Kids just messin' couldn't keep a secret this long, is what both- ers me." Phil looked right at Da'Shaun and stopped waving his hands in the air and put them down. "Somebody would've yelled, 'Gotcha!' long before now, seems to me, right? Kids today got no patience, right?"

Da'Shaun didn't laugh or smile. "I don't know."

Phil kept looking directly at him because Da'Shaun was the youngest person in the room, the closest to the mind of a kid.

"You'll figure it out, Chef," said Vanessa, "just like y'all figured out how your cat's been—"

Oh *please* don't mention the fucking cat again, Phil thought. As if I could forget the fucking cat.

"—escaping," she finished. "You really kinda smart for an old white man."

"And you got a big mouth for somebody who don't write out the checks," he genially shot back to general laughter. The clock on the wall said that time was going by very fast. Phil realized how anxious he was to abandon the subject of ghosts and get back onto a more substantial footing before the evening rush hit. His brain felt unaccountably attenuated and tired, as if he had just taken a college placement exam. He wiped a forearm across his forehead and thought about those color publicity shots of notable chefs, himself included, relaxing at restaurant tables in spotless tunics with glasses of merlot raised companionably to the cameras. As if they had nothing more pressing to do than enjoy their own cooking over red wine. "So hey— Whatchall think about that game yesterday? That lame-ass call on pass interference?"

And the topic of Tasso's ongoing kitchen conversation, just that easily, changed to football.

"BUT GHOSTS DON'T wear football uniforms, honey," Michelle objected in amusement much later that same night while the two of them were sharing her Spanish recipe for sangria in their large private Jacuzzi.

The five kids were still awake. Phil could hear all of their young-teen noise, even above the roilings of the spa. What he and Michelle had in here was probably more properly termed a hot tub, but it wasn't tub shaped—it was square, lined in blue-and-white Mexican tile—and it wasn't always kept hot. Yet it did bubble and produce great gouts of water from its subsurface jets. And it was a terrific place to relax, even if it couldn't drown out the loud rap music from upstairs, and the stompings and the laughter, the beeping music of a video game.

"Philip," Michelle insisted, smile lines appearing underneath her eyes now, "you saw a *kid*. This house is infested with kids. Listen to them up there!"

He let the spa do its magic, buffeting his lower back with warmth. The hot water dissolved the restaurant ache from his feet and his knees. "Christ, but this is great, this little brick refuge from the world, how private it is. Exactly what stroke of genius came over you to buy this particular house anyway, doll?"

She shrugged and sipped at her sangria. "First house the Realtor showed me."

Phil regarded the framed prints high above his head, hanging from hooks in the beige wall just under the tallest green reaching fronds of large potted philodendrons: bright Mexican colors, skeletons riding bicycles, the Day of the Dead depicted in rollicking humor that he didn't get. "Good spaces for all your stuff, yeah."

"That wasn't it," she said. "Hell, I was ready to take anything, frankly, I told Joe the Realtor—house trailer, *anything*. Condo next door to a biker bar, Formosan termites, *anything*. In the middle of a parking lot, I didn't much care. We just needed to get out of where we were."

He reached for the sangria pitcher and poured himself another. "I hear ya."

She genially rubbed the top of his foot with the bottom of her own. "You think I bought a haunted house! Poor dumb Michelle, she let somebody sell her a haunted house!"

"I didn't say that."

"Philip, you'd been asleep!" She was laughing, her bare face pale and clean, her short hair soggy at the back of her neck. "You'd fallen asleep watching football, honey! Is it so hard to believe that you could still have been half asleep when you looked up those stairs and just imagined Cam or Brendan or Hunter silhouetted up there against that glare, in a football jersey?"

"I certainly would've recognized a son of mine, doll, thank you very much. And it definitely wasn't Cam up there, either. But you know what? It doesn't matter. This is a wonderful weekend, we're having a great time. My kids're having a great time here."

She turned her pleased face up and he kissed her lips. "It absolutely does not matter," he repeated.

The water surged around them in calming turbulence and Phil found himself no longer much caring about strange kids in his house or the noisy bunch upstairs or whatever was going on in the world outside. He draped his arm around his wife's shoulders, content, feeling the warmth of the red Spanish wine inside him like an inner hearth. He had no bewilderment or even lust in him now.

"But it's easier for you to think 'ghost' than to think that you had a normal sort of thing like a waking dream or something." She crowded up against him like a wet seal.

He leaned back against the surge. "Aw hey, I don't give a rat's ass what I saw or what I thought I saw, it doesn't matter. Maybe you're right. I know that the mind can play funny tricks on people." The sense of relaxation was almost supernatural, all worries and preoccupations leached from his muscles and tissues so that he could feel trouble being literally drained out of him. "People can play funny tricks on minds."

They stood side by side against the Jacuzzi wall, chortling at nothing, laughing out loud. Phil realized that he was actually supremely happy.

"Precious, infallible baby doll," he hugged her with one arm, "you're so right, you're absolutely right about everything. Maybe the kid I saw up there was really Nicole, I dunno."

"Nicole." She shook her head at this, smiling.

"Yeah." Phil put his chilled glass to his forehead. "Certainly looked more like Nicole than any of the four others, actually. Eyes. Nose."

The sangria pitcher sat on the bricked deck behind Phil's head and shoulders and she reached up for it, its floating citrus slices beginning to pinwheel among the ice cubes at her touch.

"Here, Shell." He took her glass from her. "Let me."

He poured her another cold ruby serving but when he handed it back to her, she held it in her fingers for a long moment and then carefully set it down upon the red bricks. "I don't know," she was muttering as he watched, "maybe I shouldn't have any more. Maybe I've had enough."

So did that mean she expected him, too, to stop with the party? he wondered, the clear glass pitcher suspended by its handle over his own glass in midpour. Dismayed, he was even irritated at her unanticipated prudence, her sudden readiness to let all the helium out of their fizzy ballooning mood. "Shell, I'm—" He relinquished the sangria and reached for a towel. "Doll, maybe I've had a little too much here myself, I'm sorry…"

"No, you go on, you're fine."

"You okay?" he asked her.

"Yep. I just believe I've already had a little too much, now that I think about it," she repeated herself, "but you're fine."

"We can both sleep late tomorrow," he reminded her, "like the dead."

"Most dead people don't have a houseful of kids to entertain."

"They're total video zombies, since when did they let us entertain 'em?"

"Well," she said. "Yeah."

"Us two, we can sleep till—oh, about nine, before they come downstairs for a sugar fix. Spend all day watching football, before I have to go to work. Eating turkey leftovers. Drinking whatever we haven't already drunk."

She moved closer and became herself again. Or at least became the self that Phil knew, as she began to laugh softly and bump him with her hip. "I don't know about all this drinking. Bad example for the kids."

"What about this?" He slid an underwater hand up her belly and then inside her bikini top to cup one breast, kissing her neck as she stepped into the embrace. He licked water from the top of her shoulder where its narrow fabric strap fell down. "Bad example?"

Her breath came warm and invasive into his ear, pelvis floating into his groin, away and then back again. "Won't leave a hangover. They'll never have to know."

But he wasn't hard yet and wondered now if maybe he'd started something he wouldn't be able to finish. She pushed his swimsuit down past his hips and then took him in hand, seeming neither impatient nor patient. The humidity clumped the light brown lashes of her eyes in spikes. Blue veins beneath the skin of her temples carried cool blood to an expressionless face that was neither excited nor unexcited. Now I know what *existential* means, Phil thought unwillingly. And with that academic reflection, any possibility of an erection vanished.

"Too much sangria," he apologized, embarrassed. "You were right."

THEIR BEDROOM WAS dark and quiet and the whole house was silent except for rain on the roof and the faint chatter of television. The kids had finally fallen asleep upstairs wherever they had dropped in their antic tracks. Michelle listened to their distant TV but could make out no intelligible speech. Still, she listened, not wanting to but unable to help herself, lying too alert and sandbagged against a snoring Philip by the weight of Hendrix purring at her ribs. She'd never be able to fall asleep if she kept trying to make sense out of an overheard talk show.

Philip never even twitched when she irritably gave up and tiptoed upstairs at about two A.M., she guessed, not wearing her watch, to turn off the offending television in Nicole's room and then all the video game rigamarole in Cam's. Exhausted young bodies lay on the carpets or sprawled across the bedspreads, five children, fully clothed, dreaming in the colored light of electronic screens, arrested in their determined amusements by sleep.

She put out a hand and almost touched Cam's unaware face, blue in the glow of his video game, and knew how little of anything Cam trusted when awake. Then thank God for sleep, she thought, recognizing the phrase as just a figure of speech. There was no God. She had suspected his possible nonexistence for most of her life since adolescence but hadn't really known for sure until December of 1993.

But I'll let my children decide for themselves, was how she always handled it. I won't preach atheism to them but I won't allow them to be raised with any more lies from me, either. If they want to believe in God, Santa Claus, aliens, Zeus, or the Tooth Fairy, fine by me. That's their business. But I'll never tell them what to think.

So maybe it's time I stopped the Casper mythology, she reflected, shutting off the video screens and then returning to her own bedroom in the rainy street light that came from shrouded windows. Nicole's pretty mature for her age but I'm not sure that she can always tell the difference between imagination and reality yet. I keep stressing to her that we're just making this up, like a story, but who knows? I'm not doing her any favors if she starts to believe in Casper as an actual entity. I'll just be setting her up for more disillusionment. And loss. It's time I call it quits, if this is getting out of hand.

Hell, even Philip's beginning to believe in Casper, bless his heart.

Michelle lay herself down again next to her sleeping husband, expecting him to wake at her approach, but he didn't. It was the cat who awoke and then assumed his own accustomed position near her elbow, first kneading the coverlet with his front paws and then circling in that spot in a nesting motion before curling up against her side.

She expected to fall asleep in this fresh silence. But didn't. She pushed Hendrix away from her a little so that she could have the freedom to turn over.

Because I'm trying *so* hard, she said silently to the big cat as she scratched him under his chin and he purred like a lawn mower. Philip's the best thing to happen to us in years, you know that? He's so much finer than what's mostly out there, all those multiply divorced neurotic navel gazers. So much better than what I deserve. How on earth did we ever stumble across such a man, Hendrix, so unassuming and intelligent and affable? And what must we do to keep him happy, to always make him glad that he married us?

I don't want to be in love with him any more than I already am, because you and I both know I can't survive another love. But he is lovable and I'm scared.

Because what will become of us, of me and Nicole and especially of my poor little Cam, if I somehow louse this all up and lose him?

The cat purred so loudly in response that Michelle was afraid that the noise would disturb Philip. She stopped stroking the fuzzy head but Hendrix just rolled over onto his back and invited her to consider his expanse of rounded belly now, regarding her from upside down in the dim street light with his ears mashed flat against the mattress and his inverted eyes comical. Her stifled laugh came out as quiet sniffs. She kicked off some of her own covers—could this be her first hot flashes starting up?—and fluffed her pillow. It felt like a trap when she lay her head back into it again, hard against her ear. She couldn't find comfortable placement for her arms. She became aware of her own breathing.

Hell! she said to herself, suspecting what this was really all about, this sleeplessness. She had been warily circling the issue all night, waiting for it to evaporate and just disappear like rain so that she could occupy the center of her own consciousness once again. By not thinking about it, maybe it would go away. Just fade.

By going to sleep without thinking about it, maybe she could wake up to find her mental TV channel magically changed. To a program less troubling. To something sane and safe and ordinary.

But no. Sleep was not coming.

Okay, she instructed herself, let it in. Let's be crazy and entertain looniness and just get it all over with, if that's what it's going to take to fall asleep eventually. But let's also make it entirely clear here that we're not to go on thinking this way, this is just a onetime shot at serious lunacy. We're just getting it out of our system so that we can go right back to reality, okay?

Okay. Here goes:

He looked like Nicole.

And the football jerseys of the New Orleans Saints aren't the only ones colored black and gold. Hell, the high school I graduated from had black jerseys with gold numbers. Bois Sec High School, the Bois Sec Stingrays—where I became a cheerleader after Daddy moved us from Houston, hell, Bois Sec's uniforms were black and gold.

He looked like Nicole.

Hell, Adrien Savoie was forty-four when he died, he'd never be up there on my staircase in his old high school uniform, looking like a kid, mistaken for age fifteen. Not even in the imagination of Stephen King. Not even in dim light.

Okay, that's it. Time to fall asleep. I'm sure glad I don't know what time it is, I'd be so bummed out if I knew. Move your cat self over, Hendrix, and give me some room, she thought.

She turned over and faced the window. She began to weep.

Nightmare

WITH A LATE-NIGHT SNACK of leftover turkey joining all the sangria in his digestive system, and with his wife awake and silently crying at his side, Phil lay on his back in bed and began to dream of driving up St. Charles Avenue in the rain.

His dream-self knew very well where it was going, but didn't think to tell him. That was the trouble with these kinds of dreams. You could never pin them down afterward, Phil would later reflect upon awakening with his heart racing and the metallic tang of terror still in his mouth.

He drove an anonymous stretch of the avenue on some urgent errand, noticing the reflected glimmer of streetlights in the long parallel puddles of the streetcar tracks, feeling distinctly upset. It was raining in the dream, very hard, and his windshield wipers broke the images of oncoming headlights into fragments like sparks.

I'll feel better with the radio on, he thought, reaching out to turn on some music. The familiar sound of the oldies station comforted him as he approached a wide intersection where the traffic light up ahead was still red. It had been red for a while. Impatient, he anticipated its change at midblock, slowing so that he would not have to stop altogether.

The rain pounded on the roof of the sedan like a car wash. Lightning struck nearby, across the river, and Phil's retinas were branded by lashing black limbs of live oaks outlined against the pink afterimage.

A streetcar, large and olive, its interior brightly lit, was chugging along parallel to his left like a moving barricade. He overtook it and heard its circuit breaker pop when it responded to the same new green light that he did. He pulled even with it for a second as he accelerated, glimpsing seated tourists behind its rain-streaked rectangles of lighted windows.

Phil's car was far faster and he was in a much bigger hurry. He nosed past.

…Too late to respond to suddenly revealed and blinding headlights, no longer obscured by the streetcar, barreling toward him from his left.

Dickhead's running a red light, he had time to notice in that curious slow motion and dispassion that accompanies disaster. In dawning certitude, he also had time to realize: *Dickhead's gonna kill me.*

Dickhead's coming right at my door.

The impact, and his simultaneous non-word, which was going to be *"Shit!"* but never got the chance, came in an explosion of glass and steel and fury that blew out his eardrums with its violence.

One high oncoming headlight passed directly in front of him, left to right. The other went dark as it came through the side panels of his door and tore his aorta and splintered his face and snapped his spinal cord. He was still able to see and understand for only seconds afterward, but he saw the rain and the uncontrolled dark red of his own flooding blood and understood that he was dying. He saw Michelle's face.

It took him much longer to understand that he was lying in his own bed now, his shaking hands clutching clumps of sheet, while she wept next to him in the night.

EIGHT

Michelle, Ma Belle

AFTER AN UNEASY WORKOUT that next morning, jogging down the middle of those same St. Charles streetcar tracks all the way to Napoleon Avenue and back, Phil came back inside the Chestnut Street house and found nobody home. He already knew it—the Saturn was missing from the curb out front—and he stood at the kitchen counter and toweled his face and neck and read Michelle's note: "Gone mall cruising to Lakeside, McDonald's for lunch. Love you."

He knew how much she wouldn't have liked cramming those five kids into one car, leaving one of them unbelted. They had to've been driving her stir-crazy, he said to himself as he trudged into the large master bath and pulled his T-shirt over his head. We got no back or front yard, and they got all that energy. Yeah, let 'em whoop it up out at Lakeside, all that Christmas stuff out there by now, decorations and music. Walk 'em to death.

He imagined the way Michelle would've handled the seating, worrier that she was. The Randazzo children, her guests, would have had pride of place, all three of them buckled up. And then she'd drive the way she always did, very deliberately and defensively as if she were chauffeuring the president of the United States.

Well, thought Phil, I can't blame her, not after what she's been through. After a few more damn wreck dreams like that sumbitch last night, I might be ready to turn in my own license.

After showering and shaving, he dressed in soft old jeans and a yellow golf shirt, telling himself that he might actually take up golf again one of these days. But the house now was what needed attention. He padded barefoot into the kitchen to rinse off the breakfast dishes that had been piled on the counter. And then loaded the dishwasher, careful to keep any resentment at one remove. It was nobody's fault that he had to do kitchen scut work here today, that's just the way things could turn out in a houseful of lazy and bored kids whose mamas never expected them to even lift a sponge.

He climbed the stairs afterward, prepared for the worst. And it was nasty up there. The kids had slept sprawled on top of the bedspreads in street clothes, snacking on apples or granola bars or fruit roll-ups, drinking root beer. And now there were dried apple cores among the twisted coverlets, and candy wrappers, dirty socks.

The carpets in both bedrooms lay littered with downloaded cheat sheets for video games, Nicole's Barbie and hairbrush, soft drink cans, CDs, videotapes of movies, and Cam's outgrown macho action figures that had been dragged out from the toy box in the closet to either date Barbie or assassinate her.

Phil stood in the doorway of Cam's room, hands pinching his hips, trying not to think about all of the powerful disapproval he wanted to express to Michelle. But if I had just once left a room in this condition back when I was a kid, he realized, I wouldn't've been able to sit down on my poor blistered little ass for an entire—

Something caught his attention, right over there on the carpet by the bed. He stopped thinking about the mess. When he stepped over to the object and looked down at it, he was no longer thinking at all.

He stooped. Grasped its rectangular crystal surface and then lifted it up.

It was a copy of A. P. Savoie's last CD. This was what Cam had been playing so loudly on Thanksgiving afternoon, probably in response to Kerri's curiosity, right before Michelle had started yelling for the kids to turn it off. Phil knew what it was, all right.

What had stopped him in his tracks now was the photograph on its cover.

Jesus Christ, he breathed, his thumb covering only the smallest corner of the picture.

He had seen photos of this man before. He had encountered the recording artist in person on several memorable occasions. But this was the first time that he was looking at a photo of Savoie right after having seen that kid on the stairs.

Phil felt for the edge of the bed and sat down on it and held the hard plastic rectangle in both of his hands, and understood suddenly that the universe was a much stranger place than he had ever been taught by the Jesuits.

Because under the dark beard stubble in the photograph, even allowing for crow's-feet and gravity and the gray-threaded hair of middle age, Phil was able to identify these features. The droop of lids over black irises that did not quite make eye contact with the camera. The angle of the nose.

"Son of a bitch!" he yelped like he'd been stung.

But A. P. Savoie had been handicapped by a limp that would've ruled out football. And a couple of fingers had been missing from one of his hands. Exactly when had he lost those two—?

Phil threw down the CD and galloped downstairs to the master bedroom, trying to picture the kid's hands in his racing mind. Had both hands been visible? Yes. Had they been whole?

Yes.

"Beat it!" he shouted at the cat who was dozing in the middle of the mattress. Hendrix had no chance to move before Phil dropped to his knees alongside the dust ruffle to fling the draping hem of the bedspread up onto the animal and then pull several flat cardboard boxes out from under the box spring. Hendrix sat like a

lump for a moment, covered by the spread, and then found the situation intolerable. He jumped off the bed and was retreating down
the steps to the brick patio when Phil tore into the first box. And
then into the second.

Which hand was it, you bastard? he tried to recall, sweat seep-
ing out of his scalp and into his eyes as he rifled through packed-
away legal papers, baby books, birth certificates. Just what happened
to your goddam hand, when did it happen, were your hands intact
in high school?

Because Casper's hands are okay. And if *your* hands are okay…

Shell was sixteen the year her family moved here from Houston. How many fingers did you have when she met you?

Were you playing football?

He struck sudden pay dirt almost before he was ready: her high
school yearbook from 1966. His hands vibrated as he dragged it out
from underneath dusty manila envelopes and felt its black, grained
leatherette binding. He flipped like a madman to the football team
pages, scanning each of the young Stingrays, one by one, who
scowled up into the sunshine of a long-ago day.

In these black-and-white photos their jerseys were very black,
the numbers on their chests light gray, yes. Could be black and gold,
most definitely.

Where the hell are you, you bastard?

But Casper was nowhere among them. There were no Savoies
at all on the printed roster.

Phil turned to sit on the floor and leaned his tense back against
the bed, trying to figure out if this fact made him feel better or
worse. He laid the yearbook on his knees and turned the slick pages
to the juniors and accidentally unearthed cheerleader Michelle
Stafford Wickham, Miss Junior Class, shining hair and the face of
a fashion model, not having been prepared for her. Aw jeez, he responded to her extreme youth and vulnerability as he touched a
fingertip to her gray cheek. She wore a strapless formal gown for
the beauty queen photograph, displaying a hint of tender cleavage

beneath the baby-fat softness of her collarbone. Her lashes were striped at their collective base with a thick slash of dark eyeliner.

Flipping the junior class pages to the S's, he suspected the presence of but did not find an Adrien or A. P. Savoie. The two Savoie kids pictured were both girls, maybe A. P.'s sisters, although both of the girls were fair-haired.

Aw shit, Phil thought, leaning back and pinching the bridge of his nose, how crazy does this make me look, sitting here on the floor with all of this stuff dragged out from under the bed like this? I don't know for sure that he was ever in her class. Maybe he was some older, maybe a year younger. And I'm just assuming that they went to the same high school.

He leafed through the remaining photographs to the end of the junior class, headed for the seniors, but then stumbled over it, right after the surname Zeringue, in small type: "Not pictured: Marianne Adams; A. P. Savoie; Bobby Theriot."

His chest gave a jittery heave of satisfaction although the yearbook could furnish him now with no other documentation. It was as if A. P. Savoie had attended only his classes and had done absolutely nothing else on school property at all. Phil shut the yearbook and closed his eyes and tried to recall what else he'd read about the man in *People* magazine or the local weekly *Gambit*.

Well, he thought, I remember he was the eldest of a zillion kids—and I see younger Savoies here—so he probably had an after-school job to help out at home, not just that weekend bar band thing.

What if he'd had to give up the one and only extracurricular a kid like him would've ever been allowed in the first place—football? Lafourche Parish has always had its football powerhouses, Bois Sec was state champ. All of those boys down there probably catch the football bug at least once in their lives. What if he'd already quit the team before Michelle met him?

Phil sat there and tried to put his mind back into the head of a teenager and was successful enough, after a few minutes, to recall

something very important to look for. And he found it easily, turning to the blank white endpapers in the front and back. Students
had scrawled all over every available space, in the corners, down the
margins, all with notes for Michelle. Closing with "See ya!" and
"Luv," the *i*'s of the girls' signatures dotted with little circles or
hearts, the names of the boys frequently illegible.

But where does your boyfriend write? he asked rhetorically,
feeling like a cultural anthropologist himself, remembering. Why,
he writes in the very best place, because he is the very first person
you ask to sign your yearbook, luv. He writes where you want him
to, and that's right smack in the middle of the very first blank page,
isn't it?

And there it was, a legible missive done with a black ballpoint,
in large and vigorous printing, all capitals, beginning with the quote
from the Beatles' song of the day: "Michelle, ma belle"—all of the
words spelled correctly throughout, punctuation perfect.

> MICHELLE, MA BELLE, SOMEBODY WISE ONCE
> SAID THAT WE SHOULD ALWAYS BE CAREFUL WHAT
> WE WISH FOR, BECAUSE WE JUST MIGHT GET IT. BUT
> I DON'T KNOW IF I'M THAT CAREFUL.
> SO DON'T GIVE ME JUST THAT COY LOOK WHEN
> YOU READ THIS. YOU'RE NOT A REAL CAREFUL
> PERSON EITHER.
> ALL MY LOVE WHEN YOU'RE READY FOR IT,
> A. P.

Goddam, thought Phil, careful to keep his damp fingers from
smudging the ink, the little fucker goes right for the bra hooks.
Straight for the panty hose, unless I'm reading something into it
that isn't really there.

A bullshitty kind of style, not to mention sexual confidence,
seemed to be just jumping right off the page here. Phil laid the
yearbook opened and flat onto the carpet and took his hands away

from it, trying to recall what inferior and juvenile sentiments he himself had inscribed in his own girlfriend's annual all those years ago: "Roses are red, violets are blue…"

Wiping both dripping palms on his thighs, he finally put the book back where he had found it. That's when he noticed the wide furred face of the cat peering at him now from the second step of the doorway. He became very still and listened for any sounds that might indicate that Michelle and the kids had returned home, but heard none.

Good, he nodded. Marriage is dicey enough without her discovering she married a nutcase.

But it occurred to him as he started to push all of the boxes back under the bed that although Michelle could have had no earlier yearbooks from Louisiana, she would certainly have had a later one, for sure. From her senior year.

Oh yeah, thought Phil, an old hand at this by now, digging around in the lower strata of the third box. This is going to be The Book, you know that. Crushed orchids between its pages, graduation announcements, you remember how girls did this stuff…

He found it almost immediately.

And this time, A. P. Savoie's photo was included among those of his class.

Oh Christ, Phil thought, taking his reading glasses from the night table to examine it better as the implications of his discovery and the perspiration of his body chilled him. Look at this face.

Great teeth for a poor kid, Nicole's eyes, thick straight brows, all the features I saw on Casper, definitely. Just several years older, in sharper focus, more cleanly planed.

Real tanned coastal France, that long straight nose—high dimples like dents in the tops of his cheeks. Son of a shipyard welder, glancing at the camera without posing, thinking about something funny that catches him in a shit-eating grin as the shutter snaps…

Here's the guy who always knows exactly what to say to girls to make them laugh. Who never gets tongue-tied or turns into a pathetic goofball, I remember guys like this. Able to touch a girl just about anywhere, partly because he's good-looking but also because he's not scared of her. Lots of sisters—he lives with girls, he teases them, he eats breakfast with them, he smells them.

And since he's a musician and he's in a band, he can get all the girls he wants. He gets phone numbers without asking for them.

Warming to his task now, dismay building, Phil began to thumb randomly through the pages and accidentally encountered the edge of one protruding slightly from the uniform edges of the others. The irregularity caused the book to fall open at yet another significant photograph, taken at the 1967 senior prom.

The first interesting thing about the page was that it had been carefully cut from the book, as close to the inner binding as possible, only to be reinserted in its original place at some later time without benefit of glue or tape to hold it there.

The second interesting thing was that the photo showed Michelle and A. P. on the dance floor of some crepe-papered auditorium, in formal dress. They had been captured in profile, forehead to forehead, in a slow-dance embrace. Her lips were parted, as if she were confiding something to him in whispers.

Phil could have laughed, because old photos like this were always comic, that archetypal consuming teen romance. But he stopped laughing when his own throes of adolescent passion flashed back, anything but funny at the time, those after-the-movie struggles in the backseat of his Ford Galaxie, the *no* from his well-raised girl that he'd kept hoping would somehow magically transform itself into acquiescence but never did. Well-raised girls had been expected to save themselves for marriage. To guard their reputations.

But here in this picture Michelle Wickham didn't seem to be on guard against anything. The caption under the snapshot read: "One More Dance for Old Time's Sake?"

I've always thought, Phil reflected, troubled, I've always just assumed that she was some taller than him. As if that mattered. But it's the impression I've always had, I guess from the way he leaned on that cane and couldn't straighten up to his full height, that he always had to look up at her. She's about five-nine. They're exactly eye to eye here. She can't look down on him unless she wears spike heels.

Check this out: Both of those groping hands of his are visible, one where it grips into her dress material and cups her ass cheek, the other wrapped around her waist from the opposite side. And both of them are entirely intact.

Casper, you son of a bitch, I've got your license plate for sure.

Phil slammed shut the yearbook, blowing short whuffing breaths like a swimmer.

Okay, he thought, Phil Randazzo aces the ghost hunt. End of mystery. End of story. Bingo.

But the question of Casper's identity was no longer at issue, he knew, nor had it been for some minutes. At issue instead was the irrational jealousy he was beginning to feel for his wife's past.

And that's just so fucking silly it's pitiful, he acknowledged, embarrassed again, rolling onto his knees and beginning to stack everything back into its proper carton. He shoved the three shallow boxes beneath the dust ruffle and under the bed. The 1967 yearbook was all he kept out.

His whole worldview, on this most ordinary of mornings, had gotten itself flipped right over like a flagstone with unsuspected creepy-crawlies scuttling out from underneath— At my own instigation, he nodded to himself, accepting the blame.

But he wanted very much to just flip the world back over now and return to yesterday and let Shelly laugh at him again and tell him that he'd just been sleepy or mistaken about the kid on the stairs, and then let it go at that.

I'll listen to her this time, he vowed. I'll tell her she's absolutely right, you'd better believe. We'll tell each other that I had a little football hallucination and that what I saw was Cam, and we'll let it go at that. And then get on with everything else.

Because I just want to be normal. I don't need to be right anymore. I want to see only normal things and have only normal things happen in my house. Anything that ain't normal, I don't want to pay attention to. It might not go away, if I pay attention to it.

It might grow.

Phil stood and tidied up, pulling the bedspread back down over the dust ruffle like a curtain. Trying to focus on noises from outside, songbirds and traffic and faraway barking dogs. Goddam, he thought, I've got to get the house some straightened up before Shelly gets back, haunted or no, that's a fact, unless we want to start right in on *Jeopardy,* and the category is *Phil.*

Let's see if she and I can approach this subject later tonight, off the cuff—like, by the way, here's your old yearbook, honey, and you'll never guess what—in as normal a way as it can ever be addressed by two first world adults. Then just see what happens.

Jesus, just let her laugh her head right off at me.

MICHELLE SHUFFLED into their bedroom in her house slippers toweling her hair much later that night, after Philip had returned from his stint at Tasso and after the kids were all upstairs and settled down. She was tired out and frazzled by the addition of the Randazzo children to her household this weekend and way too wired, she feared, for easy sleep.

She hadn't been expecting anything in particular. It was just an ordinary night two days after Thanksgiving.

So she certainly was not expecting to see her old high school yearbook spread out on the sheets like this, with Philip Randazzo pointing at the senior class photo of Adrien Savoie, the tip of his index finger resting upon the photographed chin.

"Look, Shelly," he said, his tone light but ultimately unreadable, "*Casper,* I swear to God. I'm not kidding."

All she could think of to say was, "I know."

NINE

Pillow Talk

"NOT A WORD OF THIS to the kids," she warned him immediately. "I mean it, Philip. I mean, I really, really mean it."

He stood there with his fingers still inside her yearbook, surprised at how unsurprised she seemed. "You actually think I'd say anything to the kids?"

"All I'm saying is, it would be a really terrible idea." There was a tigress tone to her words now, a wary mama watching out for her cubs.

He slapped the book closed. "I'm not a total idiot, baby doll."

"Nobody said you were, honey."

But neither the *baby doll* nor the *honey* could lessen much of this sudden tension between them. Phil watched her kick off her slippers and lift the coverlets to crawl into her side of the bed. The cat came out of nowhere and hopped onto the bed's vacant side, tunneling under the covers, but Michelle scooped him out and deposited him onto her knees.

Phil tossed the yearbook onto the large television set. "What the hell kind of moron do you take me for?"

Now she looked at him. Both her facial expression and tone were mild. "Honey, I'm very tired. I'm sorry."

He waited for something more abject but it wasn't forthcoming. "You're too tired to appreciate how strange all this is? What I'm saying?"

"Philip, I know what you're saying." She held the coverlets open for him. "But come on to bed. I'm just too tired to be real weirded out right now. Maybe I can get more weirded out in a minute. Gimme a sec."

None of this was what he had expected of her. She held the sheets and bedspreads high, motionless, like she would never move or relax again, keeping the cat from taking his place. Phil finally took off his pajama top, clicked off the bedside lamp, and got into bed beside her. She let the coverlets fall. He felt what a warm and soft presence she was and he turned over to throw an arm across her and half embrace her, so totally baffled by her and her weary impenetrability that he had nothing more to say.

Her breath came hot against his chin. The heavy cat walked up the length of their bodies and Phil heard its purring grow louder as Michelle reached out a hand to scratch its ears. It was awhile before she spoke. "I know I'm coming off a little bizarrely here, Philip."

"No, I think I could understand it more, if you acted more bizarre."

She sighed. "Honey, I'm an anthropologist. I've heard of things you could not begin to imagine, told as true by people who absolutely believe them to be the literal truth. I was confronted with all kinds of things in our village those years in Yucatán: spirits, gods, ghosts, babies who weakened and died of dysentery because of the evil eye. And I can't say objectively what was reality and what wasn't, Philip. Reality itself is subjective."

Don't lecture me, he thought but did not say. You would've never lectured *him*.

"I've even had some prophetic dreams, myself," she went on in a monotone. "Most people have. Haven't you? Ever?"

He thought back, unwillingly. "Yeah, I guess so. I dreamed that my father was going to die. The next day, he did."

"Well, there you are."

"Yeah, but he had lung cancer, so it's not like he was going to get well or anything. It wasn't a question of whether or not he was going to die. Just when."

"All I'm saying," she shifted position and put her arms up over her head and spoke softly to the ceiling, "is that no one else can ever know the actual objective nature of what you saw, Philip. Because it's unknowable, that's all I'm saying. I don't know what you saw. I can't know what you saw."

"It was *him*." Phil couldn't say Savoie's name. He felt an arcane sort of fear, suddenly, of speaking the name. Of giving voice to something, as if he would accordingly be giving power to it.

"Yes, honey, I accept that. I do accept that your mind might've projected an image of him somehow. I know that. I'm not arguing that."

"Shelly, call me crazy, call me nuts if you want to, but you know what kind of guy I am, baby doll. I am not an imaginative guy. The only time I'm halfway imaginative is in a kitchen, you know that."

"Philip…"

"So how could this've been any kind of projection?" He blinked at the empty air. "How in hell would I be able to visualize him as a young boy in a football uniform, even if somebody put a gun to my head and ordered me to do it? Shell, I never knew the man. Never even laid eyes on him until he was in his late thirties. So if what I saw up there on the stairs was some kind of projected memory, out of somebody's mind, it sure wasn't mine."

She was silent for a moment. "Well, it couldn't be Cam's. For sort of the same reason. Or Nick's."

"So who does that leave?"

"But it couldn't be mine, either, Philip. I hadn't even met him yet, back when he was still playing." She paused. "Aren't American ghosts the images of how people looked when they died? Not how they looked in, like, sophomore class or something…"

But that second sentence of hers was what he had picked up on. "Playing what? Football?"

"Yes."

Phil released a breath he didn't know he had been holding. "So he did play. Once upon a time."

"Oh yeah." She moved and stiffened. "Running back. Just fifteen, not the biggest guy on the team, people told us, but a great broken-field runner, hit a hole and just run like hell. And hold on to the ball no matter what, that's what impressed people—he never fumbled. Not even when some giant opposing player once stood him right on his head, so I understand… Gave Adrien a concussion so severe he thought George Washington was still president. Shame his daddy made him quit the team."

"Then his daddy is the one who needs to be haunted."

"Honey, Philip, my darling, my ghost buster…" She sounded too depleted to be thoroughly coherent. "I just can't think straight until I've had a little nap. Kids ran my legs off at Lakeside. Gimme about fifteen minutes."

"You're kidding. You could actually sleep now?"

She raised two weak fingers in the dim light and then lay them across his lips to shush him. "Philip, honey, even if you're right. Even if what you dreamed up was an actual ghost. I don't believe that, but let's say it was. Am I supposed to be frightened? Of *Adrien?*"

"But it's a more normal reaction to be shook up by ghosts, right? Even the ghosts of people you love, or people you're related to. You're the cultural anthropologist, you tell me."

"I've never claimed to be normal."

"You're normal enough to've been a cheerleader."

"All I know is," she mumbled with force into her pillow, "Adrien Savoie would never harm me or his children, dead or alive.

And he'd never allow us to be harmed by anything, either, not if he could help it. Dead or alive."

"What about me, though? Maybe he wants me to get hit by a damn bus."

"Oh, honey, what would people think if they could hear us right now? I've read about waking dreams but I'm just too pooped to remember what the experts say can cause 'em. Let's just take a break and get some sleep."

"I don't think people who've just seen a ghost usually drop right off. Without having a drink or taking a pill or something."

"Philip," she sounded exasperated, "whatever it was that you saw, you saw it *two days* ago."

"Well," he said, "yeah." He felt a soft weight plop onto his left ankle—Hendrix the cat settling into the spread at the foot of the bed, purring. The purring sang of sleep.

And no self-respecting ghost of a jealous husband would ever appear, to his replacement, as a fifteen-year-old kid in shoulder pads.

"Good night then, honey. Sweet dreams."

"You too, doll." He found a comfortable position for his head and was just beginning to let go of his resentment and have it replaced by random and pleasant hypnagogic images like sautéed onions, Fats Domino singing "Blueberry Hill," a Saints wide receiver catching a pass in the end zone...Regan Dwyer in a thin yellow cotton dress at Audubon Park, long red hair like a flame and pale freckled arms outspread, dancing to her own inner music, spinning, spinning, spinning...

He felt Michelle moving as she began to slip out of bed. Cold air hit him as she drew back the covers.

"'S'up?" he asked her.

"Don't want to leave that yearbook out like that," she said. "One of the kids might find it."

"'S'not pornography, Shell."

She ignored him. He heard her tugging one of the cardboard

cartons out from under the bed on her side. There were rustlings and then came the sliding of the box back across the white berber carpet to its proper hidden place. He sensed her straightening again, standing.

She stood there like that for a long time, in the dark. Not moving.

"What's up?" he asked again.

"Shhh!"

He started to sit up, suddenly worried about the kids upstairs. "Wha—?"

"I hear Hendrix meowing," she muttered, stooping and fumbling at the dust ruffle for her house slippers, "from out there, on the porch."

"Hendrix?" Phil sat up all the way and began to feel around at the foot of the bed, slapping gently among the covers for the cat. "No, he's right here. Right down here on my feet. Somewhere."

"Philip, I hear him out there on the *fucking porch*. There's a fucking cat out there meowing its guts out on the fucking porch, how many other neighborhood cats would do that?" She clicked on the bedside lamp with a crisp snap and headed for the bedroom door.

The sudden light lasered into his retinas with pain. "He was just here a minute ago."

"Then somebody's let him out again. I'm getting sick of this."

"But we've had our door here closed. To this room." Phil wasn't sure what he was trying to say. "All this time."

Michelle didn't answer, she just yanked on the doorknob and jerked the door open. Phil could suddenly hear, clearly and unmistakably, the yowlings coming from the front French windows.

"Four-legged Houdini," were all the words that he could think of, his mind racing. "Son of a bitch."

T E N

Dreamsicle

AS DREAMS GO, it wasn't a very lurid one that he was having now. Compared to the car wreck dream of Friday night, rating that nightmare as a ten, this one wouldn't register anything higher than a four. It wasn't even a nightmare, in fact, and Phil would remember little of it that next morning.

He was a small boy again, out in the backyard of his boyhood home next door to the restaurant on Esplanade, holding an emptied Red Ryder air rifle—its ammunition spent on fly-buzzed cardboard cartons in the Dumpster—in one hand and an orange-and-vanilla Dreamsicle in the other.

The Dreamsicle was melting too fast for him to catch all the drips with his tongue and the cold liquid plopped onto his bare toes.

"Phil?" his oldest brother Dominic called out through the screen door again. "Telephone!"

He couldn't take the messy ice-cream bar inside like this, Momma would kill him. "Who is it?"

"How should I know?"

There was nowhere to lay his ice cream. Neither Joey nor Martin was around to hold it for him. He licked at the melting goo until the rest of it avalanched into the unmowed clover at his feet. The bared wooden stick felt rough to his tongue. "Coming," he called out.

"Hurry up, lardass! It's long-distance!"

He took the air rifle into the kitchen with him and crossed the linoleum with sticky bare feet, and then raised the heavy black telephone receiver from where it lay on the countertop near Momma's flour and rice and sugar canisters. Painted yellow daisies decorated their sides. Their bottoms displayed rust spots. "Hello?"

Nobody responded.

"This is Phil," he prompted in his uncertain, treble voice.

The line hummed.

He replaced the receiver in its cradle and then turned to look at Dominic, who was wrapping containers of snap beans and chicken parmigiana from the restaurant in aluminum foil and then placing them into the wheezing refrigerator. "Nobody there."

"Not my fault, don't look at me. I'm not the lardass who didn't answer it in time."

"You're a jerk, Nonnie, you big shitweasel! Stop calling me names."

"Come inside and do a little work around here for a change, you can answer your own damn calls."

"Was it a kid or a grown-up?"

"Operator's voice. Lotta interference."

The telephone jangled again, alarmingly loud in its belling, sudden enough and close enough to make Phil jump. He reached out with short fingers and took it up. *"Hello?"*

"Long-distance call," said the metallic voice, "person-to-person, for Philip Anthony Randazzo?"

"Yes, ma'am. That's me."

"Please hold."

He held, and held, but heard only the electronic hum of silence.

"I'm sorry," said the operator, "but we're unable to establish a clear line right now. This is an extremely difficult connection to make. Would you like to try to place the call again later?"

"Well, I wouldn't know how, exactly," he told the lady. "I'm not trying to call anybody, ma'am. And I don't have any idea who it is that's trying to call me."

"Of course you do! And it's a matter of life and death!" she said with asperity, and hung up.

Phil looked at the back of his brother's neck where the brown crew cut bristles turned inward between the twin tendons at the base of the boy's skull. "That was kind of strange, Nonnie."

"You're gonna be sorry you missed it," Dominic spoke without turning around. "You should've hurried."

"I lost my Dreamsicle for this," muttered Phil, and went back outside.

Dominic called out through the screen, "Yeah, well, if you think *that's* so terrible, Filbert, just wait'll you get a load of what happens now."

ELEVEN

Old Addictions

"SO ABOUT HOW LONG have y'all had Casper problems," Philip was asking her, "would you say?"

Michelle let her eyes sweep the sky and the tree-shaded slate roofs of pastel Victorian houses as she matched him step for step, Philip in his sneakers and sweats. She saw doves and crows flying.

The weather had turned colder again but the sun was blinding in an almost audible way like the clanging of a church bell, as alarming, as intense. His shadow fell upon her for a moment and chilled her.

There was only one subject of conversation between them this morning, now that Regan and Lyle had shown up early to treat all of everybody's kids to pancakes and the breakfast bar at Shoney's. Michelle and Philip were free now to speak about anything at all, but they spoke of one thing only, over and over, turning it this way and that in their minds, looking for fresh perspectives.

"I honestly don't know."

"But this is why you had to move out of your former house, right?"

"No. Not because of anything like this."

He stopped at the curb at Washington Avenue and waited for the light to change with his hands on his hips and his head lowered.

She saw the sheen of perspiration in front of his near ear, the way his squinted lids darkened his eyes. "I thought you had Casper stuff on Dufossat Street. That's what you said. Awhile ago."

"What I meant was about memories haunting us."

"That's not what you said."

"There were too many memories there, honey, not literal apparitions. Just— Everywhere we looked, every room we went into, reminded us. Reminded me."

Philip reached for her hand as the light changed and she registered the warmth of his touch, the reassurance. He broke into a trot and urged her along the last seven feet to safety as the changing traffic light sent cars and trucks and slanted black shadows charging over the asphalt their bodies had just cleared. "You don't make a very good pedestrian," he told her.

She stepped up onto the concrete of the beveled curb. Her pace slowed. Her mind slowed. "Adrien started staying home more. Cam and Nicole were growing up so fast, and I guess it had finally begun to dawn on him that he was missing it, being on the road so much. That was something I had always nagged him about. So he was playing mostly local club dates. And composing like crazy when he was home with us, which was a lot."

"So this was, roughly—when? About the same time where he wrote that song for the movie?"

"Yes." Her breath was fast and gappy with the rapid walking and this telling. She smelled woodsmoke and dog feces. "Somewhere right along in there."

"Y'all go to the Oscars?"

She looked up at him. "The movie didn't even come out until about five days after he died."

"Oh."

Tourists wandered along the uneven herringbone-bricked sidewalks of the Garden District, maps deployed and their cameras and fanny packs strapped on. Some of them were Asian. Michelle found it strange that people should want to come all the way from

Japan to visit her neighborhood and eat at, like, Philip's restaurant. The idea made her feel like an inadequate hostess now and she wished that Philip would find another site for their garbage can instead of leaving it in the alley near the front porch where stray tourists might smell it.

"He never even knew the song was nominated," she shook her head. "It's just something that happened. Allen Toussaint had put some guys at Miramax in touch with him, they just wanted something evocative and Louisianian over the credits for this hurricane movie, and one thing led to another."

"So who would've picked up the Oscar? If he'd won?"

"My mother. She went."

"You and Cam should've been the ones to get to go."

"I was still on tranquilizers. They make you a little indifferent. To stuff. Like Oscar night. And our problem wasn't Casper on Dufossat Street, we hadn't even dreamt of Casper on Dufossat Street. Our problem was that we couldn't go on there. In that house."

"Well, yeah…"

"Even before we moved," she tried to explain her actions of two years ago to her husband of six months, "I'd already had to take Cam out of Country Day and get him into Newman. You can imagine how much he associated Country Day with his father's death, and began to hate school and became such a problem there. This is what I'm talking about."

"But Shelly, people do die every day on kids, excuse me," here it came, the rest of his unfinished observation. "If changing schools did y'all any good, then that's fine. But as far as the housing thing goes, most of the time, isn't it sort of better to let grieving survivors remain where they are? Where their memories can comfort 'em?"

Michelle rubbed aching sinuses under each eye with the fingertips of both hands. "I think that the operational term here is *comforting* memories, honey. Ours don't comfort us. What we remember is a catastrophe, that I sort of caused. That's a very hard memory to live with."

"Now you've lost me. I thought it was Cam who blamed himself."

"Yes, we both blame ourselves. And when Nicole's old enough to understand how it happened, she'll probably blame the two of us, too." She sucked a breath. Keeping up with Philip was work. "Look, honey, I don't know how much you know. But I assume, since it was public knowledge, that you know that Adrien was a recovering alcoholic."

He nodded.

She was unsure of how much she should defend Adrien because she didn't know how much of his behavior had been defensible. "The same week we conceived Nicole—Cam was about eight years old—that was when he finally quit drinking. And this was someone who enjoyed the hell out of alcohol, not only because he was addicted to it. That was part of the paradox. How can I explain this?"

"I never said that you had to explain anything, Shell."

"Adrien," she spoke the name slowly, hanging on to Philip's sweatshirt-sleeved biceps and trying to slow him down, "was a very animated sort of person, at home or among friends."

Philip's pace slackened with her holding him back this way, but she felt his own vitality or stubbornness urging him on.

"He loved to play on the floor with the kids," she said, "some really noisy French game that went *Plume ou piquant?* He sang everywhere, under his breath, fingering imaginary guitar strings sometimes while the rest of us would be watching television. And Motown? He'd crank up his favorites loud enough to make your teeth hurt. Yell at televised Saints games, cussing bad officiating or whatever, then get on the phone with one of his brothers to commiserate. But laughing, ultimately. Glad to be mad, you know what I'm saying?"

Philip prompted: "The paradox—?"

"For somebody who enjoyed life so much, he could be self-destructive as all get-out. Well, until there at the last, I mean. The last three years he was alive. But before that, he was unquestionably killing himself. I mean, we all recognized that, even Cam."

A teal Taurus passed them with a bound Christmas tree tied to its top, the driver honking his horn in what might've been recognition, but Philip failed to notice. "His disability...? Like, I know that he had some kind of problem, he had to walk with a cane..."

"It wasn't just that. I mean, it was that, yes." Her words were a slow sighing. "He didn't know how to be. Anymore. He didn't know how to *be*. In the world. As he was, now. We knew that, me and Cam. We understood that. Cam had never known him any other way."

His bright head nodded.

"All of those legal pain meds doctors had been prescribing for him for years and years, on top of the alcohol... When he was depressed he'd try to solace himself with Jack Daniel's and pills and marijuana and whatever else he could get his hands on. Just as maintenance, mostly, but it could turn into some real scary binges on occasion. Me, I'd cry and nag, and all I might end up with was him pissed off enough to stay out a night or two, or three, just to get back at me. Screwing some little groupie and making sure I knew about it, reaffirming his own manhood, whatever...

"Anyway," she softly clapped her palms together, "what the rest of us lived in fear of, me and Cam and even Adrien's own mother, was that his body would one day just give out from all the damage, even those last three years after he'd quit with the booze and wasn't using anything but legal pain meds. What we foresaw, I guess, was something on the order of a drug interaction, or cirrhosis of the liver, or heart disease and lung cancer from cigarettes. Or even HIV belatedly showing up, my private concern.

"So we were all psychologically prepared for that, if you can ever be prepared. Maybe we were preparing ourselves on some level to blame him for his own eventual death, I don't know. All I know is that none of us was prepared for some drunk driver in a Jeep Cherokee just smashing him to pieces."

Philip squinted up at the cold sun.

"As far as I know," she went on, "he never took another drink or touched another groupie once we'd conceived Nicole. He'd even cut down on the pain medication, talking about giving acupuncture a try. Now, none of that was my doing, because I'd given up. Given absolutely up on him. He just straightened himself out, for reasons of his own. It's like he reached way down into his own soul and hauled the best of himself back out into daylight, finally."

She waited for something judgmental but Philip remained silent.

"Life with an alcoholic…," she began but didn't finish, perspiration chilling her scalp over her forehead and temples. "Well. Ups and downs. It ended on an up. I can't say it would've never come down again. But I loved this person dearly. I did, Philip. I loved him dearly."

"Sounds to me," he shifted his weight from one foot to the other at the curb while they waited for another light to change, "like you and Cam both might've been better off *without* this guy, Shell. I'm sorry if that sounds harsh."

"Well, sometimes, you know, that's pretty much what I thought, myself. I knew he loved me, I was never in any doubt about that. But so much of our past was always poisoning our future."

"You're probably going to take this the wrong way, but you know who sounds like the real addict here."

She shook her head. "I left him a whole bunch of times. For good in '84, when Cam was almost four. With no intention of ever coming back, not ever. Hey, remember what I said awhile ago about giving up? Here's where I gave up."

"Hmm."

"We bottomed out. Both of us." She walked faster. "It's like, sometimes, you dive into water too shallow and you hit the bottom of the swimming pool, and you either drown or you float back up. Drown or float, it's a toss-up. Maybe it depends upon whether

you've broken your neck or not, and how much air you've got in
your lungs...

"Anyway, we miraculously seemed to be floating, by the time he
died. When we remarried in May of '90, with Nicole already on
the way, he was actually able to stay sober and keep every single
marital vow he made to me. And we were *so* happy those last three
years of his life there on Dufossat Street. All four of us, him and
me and the kids, just like some stupid TV commercial, so well-
adjusted and functional and loving that you'd just want to smack us.
Happy at last. Shit."

"How do you mean, 'bottomed out'?"

"He was—"

"Not him. You."

"There are some real bad boyfriends out there. Use your imagination," she said, but imagination wouldn't even begin to cover it.

"You want to stop for coffee or something? Go to PJ's?"

"Regan and Lyle'll be back with the kids..."

"Shell," he said, "do we ever get to do anything? Just the two of
us, no distractions."

"We're walking."

Distractions. Adrien's damaged body asleep beside her. The la-
boriousness of his limp, the effort it cost him, the discomfort. Her
dresser mirror's occasional covert reflections of him reaching up to
catch hold of the framing over the bathroom door with both hands,
hanging from it by his few fingertips for as long as he could,
straightening out a spine at war with gravity.

There had been such tender history to those hands, fingertip
stirring at her entrance as the two of them lay mouth to mouth in
the middle of cool nights, her leg thrown over his scars to receive
him, love passed back and forth between them like whispers.

I caused it, she remembered whenever she became conscious
of what those ridges interrupting the smooth terrain of his skin sig-
nified. Even when she knew for sure that he didn't blame her.

And attached to that nasty old guilt now was this newer guilt, just three years old but showing every sign of comparable longevity: *I killed him.*

"Shelly, you okay?"

"Just too damn dumb to live," she said.

THEY HIKED BACK to the house in fake good humor, Phil thinking about the things she had told him and what she might have left out. God alone knew what Michelle was thinking, striding along beside him in flapping folkloric drawstring pants and Mexican striped hooded pullover and Danish clogs, bare face polished by the crisp weather.

There were ghosts in her, vestiges of grief, the remains of the unspoken. And maybe she couldn't begin to speak of them yet without ceding them power over her. Maybe he was wrong to pry.

He reached for her hand.

She interlaced fingers with his and pressed his thumb.

That one phrase about a Jeep Cherokee driven by a drunk suddenly worked its way back into his awareness just as the two of them turned onto Chestnut Street—a vivid image, much more disturbing now to him for some reason than it had been when she'd first spoken of it awhile ago.

And then his recent nightmare just exploded like a bomb into his conscious memory, Jesus. That very real dream of rain and darkness, the horrific violence of the crash, the blood, the certainty of death. *And those high-off-the-ground headlights,* higher than those of his own sedan, heading right for his door.

Phil's scalp began to pour sweat. His pace slowed. He dropped Michelle's hand and then wrapped his fingers around her upper arm in a disconnected movement, feeling like he was underwater or had taken too many antihistamines. "Shell, exactly *how* did A. P.'s accident—?"

"They're back," she nudged him, pointing to the Lexus parked at the curb up ahead.

His chest felt constricted, crushed. "I need to talk to you."

But she pulled away and raced ahead to make that cooing voice to Regan that women made when they didn't know each other well enough to skip it, and Lyle got out of the car to shake Phil's hand. Five kids jumped up and down, women hugged, and Phil thought he was going out of his mind.

"You look terrible," Lyle told him, one brow raised. "You feel okay?"

He nodded and gulped air. "Exercising."

"You ever take a medical stress test? Before you took up an exercise program?"

"Nope."

"Big mistake, man your age."

"Mom! Mom! Mom!" Nicole was screeching, bounding around Michelle like a rubber ball, tugging at her striped pullover. "Mom!"

"It's rude to interrupt," Michelle turned and looked down at her daughter, "when I'm trying to talk to Miss Regan."

"But Brendan and Kerri and Hunter want me and Cam to come spend some time with them over Christmas!" Nicole's smile split her face.

"I'm just getting to that." Regan beamed cordiality at both Michelle and Phil. "We'd love for Nicole and Cam to spend a few days with us in Mandeville."

Phil leaned over to brace both of his hands onto his knees. He took big breaths.

Michelle noticed. "Honey? You okay?"

He nodded. Perspiration poured down both of his temples. "Just winded."

"From a *walk?*" She had begun to work herself up into one of those big Michelle morbid worries and he certainly wanted to short-circuit something like that before it could get going.

He forced himself to become calm, to breathe evenly. "I'm fine."

"Mom, can we?" Cam spoke up from the front porch. "Can we go to Mandeville? Over the holidays?"

Regan put her freckled hand into Michelle's and Phil remembered what Regan's hand once felt like, encrusted with rings. "Because we really, really want them to come spend a few days with us. My three have had such a good time here this weekend, and they've all hit it off so well."

"Um," Michelle was looking helplessly around herself for some reason, "well, I don't know. We'll have to see."

Phil was slow to take it all in. He was winded by his insight, his mind was blown by the implications of his car wreck nightmare, and Regan's presence was disturbing him. So he was slow to see what Michelle had certainly already noticed now. Hunter and Brendan had climbed into the backseat of the Lexus with a Game Boy and were oblivious to everything else. Nicole was still jumping around. But Cam stood close to Kerri on the green front porch, Phil finally registered, and he was holding her hand.

Phil's Monday

HE WAS USED TO TROUBLE and he was used to being troubled during his daily jogs along the streetcar tracks before work. There was never any end to it—sharp increases in the percentage of health insurance premiums he paid in order to offer an affordable group policy to Tasso's employees; inspections ranging from the state fire marshal's office to the board of health; child support due Regan; auto insurance rates going up; profits at the restaurant leveling off or going down.

But the Cam-and-Kerri thing had brought about his first real fight with Michelle, late last night, with Phil second-guessing the wisdom of having left all of those kids upstairs and unsupervised for two entire nights, and Michelle insisting upon the innocence of it.

"Honey, Cam is just barely fifteen! And this is the first indication I've had in years that he might somehow just manage to turn out normal, and I welcome it! It's not like we can't supervise them!"

"All I know is, nobody's going to Mandeville for any overnights, that's all I know."

"Philip, you're just being silly."

"She's my daughter and she's Cam's stepsister, and there's something about encouraging them that just makes my skin crawl."

"Nobody said anything about encouraging them! Hell, if you get onto this big Daddy-forbids-it high horse, I guarantee they'll become more attractive to each other. They're so young, this is just puppy love, good Lord."

"How old were you when Savoie got into your pants?"

She had given him a look of pure outrage at that. "I see what this is really about. I see where this is going."

And he couldn't say for sure right now, as he turned around at Felicity Street to begin his run home, that Michelle had been wrong. The morning was foggy and cloudy and Phil felt the ambiguity of the fog—not quite rain, not quite not—going down into his lungs with every breath.

And Christ, I hate ambiguity, he shook his head, pounding back up the avenue in his hard trot, loose fists held close to his rib cage. Cars and service trucks swished past him on the dank black asphalt. The headlight of an approaching streetcar shone through distant shrubbery. It wasn't coming very fast, but Phil went ahead and switched tracks, leaving it a clear route. The conductor still clanged her warning bell even though he was well out of the way now, and Phil nodded and held up a hand in acknowledgment as he heard the motor uptake. The streetcar rumbled past him in a blur of olive green siding and rusty metal wheels, and he jogged back onto his original track, head down.

The streetcar only reinforced the immediacy of his recent nightmare. Plus his growing dread of all the things he didn't know. Phil embarrassed himself with this dread. *Dread* had once meant nothing to him beyond an upcoming date for divorce court or a dental appointment, or suspecting the presence of Formosan termites in his Lakeview garage. This was different. A skinny boy in outsized shoulder pads perpetually turned his head in Phil's memory and did not quite make eye contact; did not quite make eye contact; did not quite—

Maybe there is such a thing as male menopause, he told himself now, tasting the fog as metallic when it rushed into his open mouth. Maybe dreaming about a dead guy's death and having his cat jump out some closed windows on you are just typical symptoms of it, I don't know.

But today was a Monday, and Phil was almost abjectly thankful to have a day off like this where he could be alone with himself now. Michelle had quickly forgiven him for the fight and they had made up like college sweethearts, but he was still glad that she had to be at Tulane today. Cam and Nicole would be at school until three. He raised his head and looked into the distance at dark overarching oak trees, white fog, and vehicle headlights.

I'll take a long shower, he promised himself, and then make a fresh pot of coffee and read the paper. Maybe take a nap, if the caffeine'll let me. Maybe I'm making mountains out of molehills, overreacting to some little trivial phenomena that human beings experience pretty often on the whole, I'm finding out. And worrying about Kerri, maybe that's silly, she's just a little girl. Cam's not a bad kid, he's not his father, it's unfair to him if I start to look at him like he is.

And I won't pay any attention to the damn cat this afternoon. Wherever the cat is, it's cool with me.

Phil sprinted across the downtown-traffic side of St. Charles and onto the sidewalk at First Street and jogged into the Garden District. Tourists stood in clots at the corner of First and Prytania, looking at street maps. He dodged them without breaking stride, hoping that they'd notice the Tasso ad on the maps' borders.

Raising one end of the towel draped around his neck to wipe fog and perspiration from his forehead, he saw the black limousine parked up ahead.

He knew that house, knew the black iron gate. Knew whose spacious lot it was, where an enigmatic statue of a very large dog, rumored to conceal video surveillance equipment, sat high up on a second-floor balcony. And he saw the lady herself now, coming through the gate in a white lace dress, with a man, possibly her husband, two paces behind her. Phil increased his speed, suddenly

needing to intercept her before she could get into the waiting limo,
acting on impulse, surprising himself when he pounded up to her
like this from out of nowhere like some crazed fan. He supposed
that the novelist was somewhat used to crazed fans, but that her
chauffeur and her husband would take measures to protect her if
somebody seemed just too crazed.

Christ, they might shoot me, he thought, wiping his right hand
on his sweatpants and then holding it out. "Ma'am? Excuse me, I'm
Philip Randazzo, of Tasso restaurant. Got a stepson at Newman, a
couple of years younger than your son. I think they sort of know
one another…"

She took his hand without hesitation and met his intrusion with
a nice face for a horror writer, a pretty face, brows raised in inquiry
beneath long straight bangs. "Mr. Randazzo. Of course. A pleasure."

Phil was diffident in the presence of celebrity, no matter how
ridiculous he thought the whole fame game was, no matter how
many celebrities he routinely met and fed at Tasso. He understood
that he was something of a celebrity himself but wasn't sure if that
status allowed him to waylay a world-famous author like this. "I see
y'all are on your way somewhere, I'm sorry, I won't keep you. I've
just got to ask you one quick question, ma'am, since you're the only
authority anywhere around here on this particular—"

"What grade is your stepson in, did you say?"

"Well, this is not about him. I mean, it concerns him, yes, but
it's not anything about school." He never looked at the faces of the
two men nearby and couldn't spare a thought for whatever they
might be thinking. "What it is, ma'am, is my house is haunted.
What do I do?"

"Move!" she laughed, approaching the open door of the limo.

"But the ghost isn't in the house. I mean, it didn't come with
the house. It came with the people who moved in. My wife and her
two kids."

Her facial expression never changed. If she thought he was
crazed, she didn't let on. "You know anything about poltergeists?"

He puffed out his cheeks and blew. "Only that movie."

"There often seems to be a relationship between disturbed adolescents and poltergeist activity…" She made eye contact with one of the men who had been looking at his watch. "Ahh… You might do well to read up on poltergeists, that's about all I can tell you."

"Okay. Thanks. Thank you." Phil bobbed his head, signaling that he was ready to take his leave. "Will do."

"Oh, and are you familiar at all with psychometry?"

"Doesn't ring a bell…"

"It's more complex than I can go into right now, but let's simplify it all into the theory that some individuals are able to read the past from an inanimate object," she explained, "as if objects are capable of recording their surroundings."

"You know, I've just recently heard something about that," he remembered out loud, nodding. "Somebody was telling me a few things about something kind of like that, just a few days ago."

"Okay. Good. So if your house itself isn't that object, then some other object might be generating your ghost for you. Does that help?"

"Potentially."

She smiled. "You might also want to speak to a priest."

"My brother's a priest, I'll do that." He extended his hand to her again. "Thank you kindly, ma'am. Sorry for keeping you. Y'all have a nice day."

"Good luck," she said, and Phil sensed how much of a hurry she was in.

But he couldn't just let it go at that. "Look, y'all come to Tasso anytime, you and your family and however many people you want to bring, it's on me. Just tell the waitstaff. Anytime."

"How kind of you."

He stood on the sidewalk and waved as she got into the limo and then understood that he'd thoroughly outlasted his welcome. The two men were stirring and Phil turned away without looking either of them in the eye and began a slow jog home.

Nice lady, he mused, knowing what a disheveled and sweaty figure he himself had cut. For all she knew, I was a psycho. She could have called the cops.

He kept thinking like this for a while as he ran up Chestnut from First Street to Second and then to Third, and on toward Seventh Street and home. Because it kept him from thinking about what she had told him. About what he knew he had to embark upon this morning and early afternoon, before Michelle and the kids could get home. His new project.

His search.

I've got enough time to get it under way, he thought, leaping up his own steps and onto the porch, key already in hand. More than enough time, if I skip the newspaper.

And he'd certainly postpone his shower, because climbing into the attic and searching up there for an unknown ghost-generating object was going to be sweaty work.

THE ATTIC WAS FULL OF STUFF like the box of Christmas decorations that would soon have to be taken out of storage, plus cartons upon cartons of her mementos from Yucatán—enough Mexican objets d'art to open a goddam gallery, Phil thought, standing on the ladder with his head and shoulders inside the airless space. He pushed around boxes and bent back their flaps to look inside but saw nothing that suggested her first husband in more than just a general way. Nothing musical, no item of clothing. Just a couple of old shoeboxes full of letters and photographs. And although he was tempted to snoop among these private archives, especially when he recognized the printed handwriting on some of them as Savoie's, he knew his limited time could be better spent if he concentrated upon his primary task.

I have no idea what I'm looking for, he realized, churning through yet more yuletide tinsel. But it can't be a photo or a letter, can it? Whoever heard of a haunted Polaroid?

Maybe she wouldn't keep anything real precious up here anyway, like a guitar. Gets too hot up here in the summer. Shit, I don't see anything up here.

He gave up on the attic, noticing what disorder he was leaving it in, belatedly beginning to grab at Christmas boxes and take some of them down. They'll be my cover story in case anybody gets home early and catches me like this, he thought. It's December, this is what people do in December.

Michelle's own closet was in their bedroom and Phil opened the louvered doors and looked down at neat pairings of boots and shoes. Embroidered ethnic clothing and handwoven ponchos swung from hangers as he pushed them over the high and low bars, but there were normal American garments in there, too, like that navy blue outfit she'd worn to Bois Sec on All Saints Day. Her academic gown and hood were way in the back, protected by a dry cleaners' bag. Unsuspected festive things hung with them, sequined short dresses and long velvet coats with rhinestone buttons that glittered.

Several hatboxes were stacked upon the high shelf above his head and he stuck a hand up there to explore amid and under them, beginning to see himself as slightly ridiculous. But if he was going to do a thing, he'd do it right.

A kitchen step stool boosted him up and let him look down upon an orderly shelf of his wife's stuff. No guitars were up there, nothing masculine. The hatboxes held only two hats. But a chunky gray strongbox way in the back caught his eye, and he pulled it toward him. When he lifted it, the box was heavy. Phil knew that these fire-retardant strongboxes were heavy even when empty, so he couldn't guess what was inside it. But there had to be something important in there, he concluded as he tried its catch, because the box was locked.

He simultaneously realized he might even know where the key was.

When borrowing Michelle's dental floss, he had several times glimpsed a small silver key in her personal drawer, there among feminine hygiene stuff and cosmetics, but had never once given a thought to what it might be for or what it might open.

He went into the bathroom now and pulled open the drawer, violating her privacy very gently, pushing tiny eye shadow compacts out of his way with his large hands, feeling furtive and dirty. But there it was, way in the back. He brought it into the light, ran back to the strongbox, and inserted it into the lock.

Yes.

Having had no idea what he would find inside, he was nevertheless disappointed to discover only a single videotape cassette, as ordinary looking as anything Cam or Nicole routinely rented at Blockbuster. Phil held it up, identifying Michelle's own handwriting on the label, several words: *Twelfth St. apt. / us.*

That *us* had been underlined three times, and Michelle wasn't the sort of woman who underlined everything she wrote.

Phil didn't think twice. He just popped the cassette into the VCR slot in the large television on the chest of drawers and sat down upon the bed.

THE TAPE HAD NOT BEEN fully rewound after its last viewing, so he was unprepared for the abruptness of the noises. He leaned forward for a moment, unable at first to understand what he was seeing.

The images were too close to the camera to have heads or faces. They consisted exclusively of skin, navels, buttocks, genitalia.

But Phil's own face understood the imagery and flushed deep red in the millisecond before his mind got a handle on everything.

No, he thought, nope, can't be them. These are just some actors, some strangers—even as he registered the hand with its missing fingers and Michelle's voice.

A matchstick thigh labored to propel a scarred pelvis. The videotape went blank in a flurry of reaching hands.

It immediately flashed on again, the camera lens set at a broader angle this time. Establishing a bed with white sheets, matches and a hash pipe in a saucer on the nightstand. Savoie's facial features were redundant and expected, the long nose, a small gold earring in an earlobe.

Phil couldn't make himself look away.

They're taping themselves, he realized, and they're playing to the camera. To their own private audience of two, stoned out of their minds, for themselves and by themselves.

It was a younger Michelle here, light hair very long and entwined around her bouncing breasts. Her body strained atop her partner's, her posture a study in rapture as her hips worked him.

Savoie pulled her down to kiss her mouth. Blond hair became entangled with black. He looked directly into the camera.

Intelligence leaped from his eyes, his grasp of these ludicrous circumstances—this overacting, the camera's potential of offering up this taped intimacy to anybody who eventually stumbled across it, the unphotogenic quality of deformity. Implied, too, was his awareness that his own youth, recorded at this moment, would decay and pass and was already passing.

Michelle came to herself after a few seconds and followed his glance into the camera lens. But then she slowly collapsed, overcome, onto his chest in a spasm of giggles, his incomplete fingers combing through her hair—a hippie nymph no longer, just a tickled young woman from an X-rated blooper reel.

One of her thrashing hands reached for the camera to shut it off but failed to connect with it. She nailed it on her fourth try, drunken with mirth.

The screen went blank.

Phil just sat there in front of it, devoid of emotion. The tape's content and the very fact that Michelle had preserved it had been burned permanently into his brain beyond any ability of his now to somehow erase or forget it.

He sat there in silence, long after the television screen had become nothing but empty roaring snow.

THIRTEEN

Michelle's Monday

THIS WAS A BITCH of a morning for her, too, with Tulane's exam week rapidly approaching and both faculty and students trying to tie up loose ends in haste.

She had not yet finished composing the final for the single undergraduate class she taught—something she felt compelled to do more or less from scratch instead of just handing out identical versions year after year to students who saw nothing wrong in file sharing.

Most of them don't give a shit whether or not they actually learn anything from me, she thought, closing her eyes and rubbing fingertips over both brows, leaning back in an office chair that was too wiggly and loose in its swivel. I wonder how long I can continue giving a shit.

Kids constantly dropped by her office now to quiz her about material that might be on the final. Others came in to complain that they'd been unable to obtain last-minute access to certain books in the Latin American Studies section of the university library. As if I cared, she thought, pretending as much sympathy for them as she could. Little assholes should've been reading these books weeks ago.

Several students, girls wearing thumb rings or boys in sweat-shirts and baggy jeans, showed up only to stand hopelessly in her doorway, mute in their woe.

Maybe next year, Michelle promised herself, I'll stop with this. I've always favored, in principle, the idea of full professors teaching a class of undergrads, but I've done my time.

"Yes?" She glanced up at the next unwelcome face at her open door, one of her grad students who was still having trouble choosing a topic for his master's thesis, a young man whom she suspected of having a crush on her, damn. She let her reading glasses slide unappealingly down her nose and wished him faraway down in Mérida with no telephone.

"Dr. Wickham?" she heard from the hallways all day, from the doorways, everybody making their claims upon her while her attention flew to Cam and his own looming exams. She prayed that he'd be able to pull up that D in English and felt guilty for being relatively well-off, knowing how poorer kids on scholarship at a private school who came up with Ds wouldn't be welcome to stick around for very long. "Dr. Wickham? Dr. Wickham?"

"Yes?" Yes and yes.

She was late leaving campus, late picking up Cam and Nicole from Newman, late in grabbing cat food and a few groceries from Ferro's nearby.

And then she had to deal with this huge mess that Philip had inexplicably made of the weight room at home, where cartons of holiday tinsel and Christmas decorations spilled their freight onto the carpet.

"You had to take all of this stuff down from the attic *today*?" she greeted him, mystified and dismayed, with a quick kiss.

It took him a moment to answer. His hair was still shower wet. "Well, I just thought I'd better inventory how much in the way of decorations we've already got. In case we need to buy more."

A few strands of crushed tinsel lay underfoot.

Cam and Nicole raced upstairs for their refuges. Twin televisions immediately sounded overhead, tuned to two different but loud channels.

Michelle let go of her tote bag full of papers and books, dropping it onto the carpet by the bed in the master bedroom. She sat down on the coverlet and then collapsed backward onto the padded mattress, feet dangling, kicking off her Danish clogs and freeing her toes.

She lay there and Philip stood mute in the doorway like one of her students, and she had the urge to prompt him with a professorial yes.

"So when you want to think about getting a tree?" he finally spoke.

"A tree? Christmas tree?"

"Yeah."

She closed her eyes. "Honey, it's only December second, we have plenty of time."

"But y'all do put up a tree, right? I mean, usually?"

"Yes." She raised her head to better look at him. "But not until after. The anniversary. You know."

"So if I understand all this correctly, none of us dares make merry until after December fifteenth." There was a new opacity in his face.

She lifted herself up onto both elbows. "What's with you?"

"Not a thing. Ho ho ho."

She sat all the way up and took him in. "Philip, honey, have I said something wrong?"

He pinched at the bridge of his nose, massaging the inner corners of his eyes with a finger and thumb. "It's too goddam humid outside for a good run, maybe that's all it is. And I'm just getting a little tired of living like this, I guess."

"Living like how?"

He stood completely still for a moment. And then spread apart his empty hands at his sides, swiveling from the hips, taking in the entire environment, his mouth eloquently, speechlessly, open.

"Philip?" She was alarmed.

"'S'okay." He closed his fists loosely and let them fall. "It's okay, let's just forget it. I don't want to say anything stupid."

But she stood. "Honey…?"

He let her approach him. He allowed her to put her arms around him but he was slow to return her embrace. He looked down at her through brown eyes slightly reddened at their rims with what might be perplexity and even veiled ire. "Shelly, don't you ever get just a little bit tired of living in the shadow of a dead man? Because me, I'm starting to get really pretty goddam tired of it myself, if you want to know the truth."

She could only explore his face, searching for something to say.

"You know, if he is here, haunting this place," Philip went on, but relenting enough now to place his arms more fully around her, "it has to be because none of the three of y'all will let him go. Ever think of that?"

"Honey, I can't deal with this right now."

"Just let the poor bastard go, Shell. Just let him go on to purgatory or heaven or hell or whatever floats your boat. And let the rest of us just get on with it, for Chrissake."

"I'm doing that," she said.

"No, you're not."

"Philip, that's exactly what moving out of our home on Dufossat Street was all about, honey. That's why I bought this house. That's what falling in love with you was all about, honey."

"Wow," he said. "And all this time here I've been thinking it's because I just swept you right off your feet with my studly charm."

"It *was*. It *is*."

"Shell," he took his arms from her and left her feeling chilly, "I have no earthly idea of how you really feel about me. You know? And I'm not always a hundred percent sure about how I feel about you, when you come right down to it."

"Philip—"

"No, doll, let me finish. I love you, yeah. And we have this marriage, yeah. But there are definitely more than just two people in it now and it's getting kind of crowded."

She opened her mouth, unsure of what she could bring out of it except the vague anger that her defensiveness was starting to give birth to.

…But was short-circuited by the sudden hammering of feet on the stairs overhead—Cam's big sneakers—and then the slap of their rubber soles as they came jogging over the bricked floor of the indoor patio. With two bounding steps up, he leaned through their open bedroom door now, hair in his face, eyebrows raised.

"Mom?" He looked from Michelle to Philip.

"What is it?" she asked.

"Um…Sorry, Phil," Cam said. He touched his nose and then his chin with the fingers of one hand. "Um…Hendrix's sick."

Michelle turned fully to him now. *"Sick?"*

"Yeah. He's all scrunched up under Nick's bed."

Michelle looked at Philip.

"Don't ask me how long, because I don't know," he said. "I haven't seen him all day."

She stepped down to the bricked floor. "Maybe it's just a hair ball."

"Well, his eyes are sort of real glassy," Cam followed behind her, "and he's kind of panting."

Dammit to hell! Michelle thought, mounting the stairs. Not now. I can't deal with this, Hendrix, don't get sick on us now, of all goddam times.

Nicole stood waiting at the top of the stairs, staring down at her with Adrien's eyes. "Mom, Hendrix's sick."

"I know, I'm coming." She quickened her pace, pulling herself up with her right hand on the banister. "It's prob'ly just another hair ball, Nickyboo, sweetheart, you know we've talked about how often cats puke…"

But Nicole did not giggle at all at the word *puke,* something she would certainly have done under less anxious circumstances. Michelle felt her stomach lurch.

Please, Adrien, she thought, if you're really somewhere and if you can read my mind and if you're not pissed at me for causing you to get killed, please don't let your fucking cat die on your children, not now.

She reached the landing and took Nicole's small sticky hand and then belatedly realized that she had left Philip standing in the doorway of the downstairs bedroom without even an *Excuse me* or a *Come with us.* "Philip?" she called, turning, looking back down the steep and empty flight of varnished wooden stairs to the vacant bricks below. She wouldn't be able to see him from this angle, anyway, if he'd remained where he was, but still. "Philip? Honey?"

Nicole tugged at her hand. "Come *on,* Mom!"

"Philip?"

He didn't answer.

FOURTEEN

Hendrix

IN ONE WEEK'S TIME, it became apparent that the cat Hendrix just wasn't capable of recovery. Michelle found that she could no longer bear the strain of balancing her duties in the Anthro Department with the needs of her children, plus Philip's increasing irritability, only to make these daily futile and sad visits to the veterinary hospital where the animal lay in his clean cage and watched her with transparent eyes.

In spite of all the modern medical care she was able to buy for him, he was losing ground and a great deal of weight, and it crushed her to see him so thin and dejected. He didn't seem to be in any pain and his appetite was ferocious, but he panted constantly. There was no longer any pink color to his gums and nose and ears, and Michelle saw that he could get no rest at all, panting like this day and night, craving iron as his body tried to oxygenate itself.

Oh, Hendrix, she thought on Friday, scratching his wilted ears, seeing that he took little pleasure in her touch. How exhausted you seem. You're ready to go, aren't you, pal? They hint to me here that keeping you around like this isn't a kindness to you. Maybe they're right.

But if you're a genuine Houdini, if you can walk through walls and jump through the sides of a closed cage, isn't this the time to do it, dear little friend?

She accepted the idea of uncanny animal abilities that no human might be privy to. So she silently urged him to heal himself or lay himself down to a final gentle sleep, because she didn't want to be the one to have to decree that.

But he was still alive on Saturday morning when she called to check on him, still trapped in both the cage and his failing body. She decided right then and there to take the veterinarian's hint this very day, when she would have no classes or office appointments to cancel.

"But wait until I get there, because I want to be there for him," she told her vet over the telephone at ten. "He's just a cat, I know. But he's always been there for all of us, and I know it sounds sentimental, Rocky, but I do want to be there for him." *I don't want him to die alone* were the words she couldn't say and they were like swallowed glass fragments, because her husband had died alone.

"Well, he's a member of your family," Dr. Buchanan assured her, "and you have every right to be sentimental. What's the point of even having a pet if you don't emotionally bond with him?"

"I just never thought it would hurt this much." She wiped her eyes in bitter amazement as her nose began to clog up. "But he's been through so much with us. Lord, where does the time go?"

"Yeah, seems like only yesterday when A. P. and Cam first brought him in, Hendrix just this little skinny, sick kitten. What was that, six or seven years ago?"

"You've kept him alive for a long time, against all odds, and I certainly appreciate the humane way you're handling *me* right now."

"Well, here's what you do," he instructed. "You come by here today at around one, after all my appointments, and my office manager'll bring you right on into the back, and I'll be ready. Okay?"

"Thank you, Rocky," she told him. "I'll be there. Thanks so much. Bye."

The line clicked. She put down the phone and rubbed her face and looked at nothing.

"So you're going to go through with it?" Philip watched her from the bathroom doorway now, toothpaste tube in hand.

Her hair was in disordered spikes and felt greasy. She raked both hands through its oiliness. "What time you have to be at Tasso?"

"Frank and Vanessa can always start without me. Anything I can do for you?"

The neutrality of his tone encouraged her because neutral wasn't what he had been this past week. Irritable and almost hostile, rather, were what Philip had actually been. Neutral would be a gigantic improvement here.

She turned her head to look up into his face. It encouraged her further. "Well, could you maybe get the kids out of the house for a little while? Take 'em out to Lakeside or somewhere?"

"Poor little guys, I'm sorry." He squeezed toothpaste onto his brush. "I didn't care for the cat much, no secret about that. But you know I'm sorry for Nicole and Cam, yeah."

"So can you?"

"But if it's all wall-to-wall jingling shopping-center Christmas out there, that's okay?"

She didn't understand for a moment.

"…So close to the anniversary," he faced around to run water into the sink, "of you-know-what…"

"My Lord." She had to stand up suddenly and go hug him, getting toothpaste on her sleeve. "You're too good for me, Philip Randazzo, and I love you so much, and I'm so sorry for whatever crap I'm always putting you through."

She experienced his small laugh as a vibration in his chest. Then: "So when d'you want to tell them?"

"The kids? Afterwards, I guess. I can reach you by cell phone."

"You want me to tell 'em? While we're out at Lakeside?"

She considered the wisdom of this, knowing that Nicole, especially, would have a fit, regardless of whether she heard the news at a mall or at home. "I don't know. Do whatever you think is best, I don't know, honey. Just don't say anything about euthanasia. Just say that Hendrix died, and let it go at that. I can't have them thinking that I made the choice, because I don't think that these particular two kids are ready to understand that choice."

"I agree," he nodded. "So maybe if I just wait for the right time, somewhere in the day, to let it slip that Hendrix died this morning, and that what you intend is for the rest of us to try to have a little fun while you go off to be sad by yourself for a while...? How does that sound?"

"Like pretty much the exact truth," she admitted, and tried to laugh.

"But I also think maybe we should stop trying to compartmentalize everything so much, Shell. Trying to keep all the happy things walled off from the bad things. You're wearing yourself out trying to do it. Plus it's useless, ultimately, because that's not the way things're going to be for Cam and Nicole during the rest of their lives, you know what I'm saying?"

How on earth did I ever stumble across this lovely man? she wondered, struck by his wisdom. "Maybe you're right."

"So let's get ourselves a knockout Christmas tree. Today."

She didn't know whether that was a bad or good idea. She couldn't decide. All she could do, right now, was just hold on to Philip and try to trust him. When it came to her children, she didn't know if his instincts were trustworthy or not but she saw no alternative now except another surrender to her own knee-jerk reaction to say no. She thought about the staleness of it, her own predictable sour sadness. "I don't know, honey. I don't know if that's wise."

"Shelly, look: They're gonna need a decent Christmas tree in this house *tonight,* doll, you know that. We'll invest in some special ornaments out there, like at a Hallmark store, I'll let the kids pick 'em out—new ones, Randazzo ornaments, not just all of that old shit from the attic—and they can decorate the thing tonight instead of just sitting around grieving for the cat. Or while they grieve. Or whatever."

Adrien would've agreed with him a hundred percent here, Michelle realized. That's how he lived his own life, although much of what he found joyous was actually toxic.

But I can almost hear him saying now, *Christ, Mick, let him buy da kids a Christmas tree, whass your problem? He's just tryin' to make 'em happy, babe, and dass what we want, right?*—unable or unwilling to pronounce those English tee-aitches unless you hold a gun on him, looking at me as if I have just grown two heads.

She sniffed an involuntary voiceless laugh at the memory and felt a load fall from her shoulders, or perhaps it was just Philip's arms lifting from her body. But she did feel suddenly better, realizing that for the very first time she was about to allow Philip Randazzo to parent her children. She took a deep breath through her mouth and the air tasted wholesome, like vitamins.

DR. ROCKY BUCHANAN was waiting for her in his clean jeans and lab coat, and he hugged her briefly and then began to show her what to do.

She shook, her heart battering at her rib cage like something trying to escape, when he deposited Hendrix's frail and sick yellow tabby hulk into her arms. Tears began to drip despite all the pep talks she'd given herself on the drive over, and she hugged the little emaciated armful and then fervently kissed the cat on top of his skull. Escape, she told him mentally, that's what this is all about, pal. We're going to help you escape this misery, Hendrix. Jump through that window for good.

"You okay, Mickey?" came the vet's soothing voice near her ear as he helped her position Hendrix on a cold stainless table where she supported him in her arms, elbows on the steel. She wished the table were warmer and soft, even though she knew it couldn't matter now. "You don't have to do this—"

"No, I want to. To comfort him."

He wrapped something around the cat's front paw and then took up a syringe as Michelle stopped watching. She put her head down very close to Hendrix's and willed herself to be serene, wanting so much to communicate something to this animal besides dread. She looked directly into his glassy eyes and mentally told him what a great cat he had been. She tried with all the ESP she could muster to thank him for just being there all this time, distracting her children during their darkest moments with his purring solicitations and high-spirited antics, so thoroughly on rodent patrol in their Dufossat Street house that they never needed to hire an exterminator like other homeowners in the city. She thanked him for curling up to sleep against Adrien's injured side all those times, fuzzy belly upturned and paws kneading the air in bliss, so that her husband's amused concern at such moments became more about making Hendrix comfortable and less about the shape of his own thigh.

And she tried to communicate her own personal gratitude on that unthinkable night of nights, that unreal blackest night of all black nights, when she had finally collapsed onto the sofa in stupefied new widowhood after getting her exhausted and cried-out children into bed—solitary, soul-chilled, unable to lie down in her bedroom in that empty bed alone now, too blasted to weep—until this cat could come wheedling onto her lap and then stretch up with sheathed claws at her collarbone to gently butt his own little bristling forehead into hers. As if he had known something or could guess something, or was thinking animal thoughts in an animal mind that nevertheless resonated with her emotions. He had slept on her knees the whole of that night, sharing her vigil right there with her, while neighbors and friends and family came and went.

But now you may go, she told him with flooding eyes as she cradled him on the chilly table. Go on. I know you're tired of suffering.

You're free now. Go free.

Here comes Hendrix, Adrien, she thought, feeling the cat's tense muscles suddenly relax. Catch him, baby.

Dr. Buchanan patted her back. "You okay?"

She couldn't speak, she just nodded.

The cat's eyes had subtly changed. The veterinarian put a stethoscope to the animal's ribs for a moment. He straightened.

"Well," he said.

Michelle nodded again and then reached for the tissue he held out to her. She smiled through the water that glazed her face. "Lord, I'm sorry, he was just a cat…"

"Don't start with that in here, remember who you're talking to."

Her smile came easier. She blotted her lids and cheeks with one hand and then blew her nose.

"So, Mick," lines of concern deepened around his eyes, "you want us to…um…handle—?"

"I have no backyard at all now, no place to bury him." She relinquished the small cooling body and never looked back at it. "So yes, Rocky, if you could do whatever it is you do."

He walked her to the front of the clinic building, to the door that led to the small lobby. "You're one tough lady, Mickey Wickham."

"Gotta be."

"How long ago was it? Three years, about?"

She nodded. "Three years exactly, the fifteenth of this month."

"He was a great guy, Mick. I'm proud y'all chose me. I'm just glad I got to know him a little."

Michelle saw her own hand reach up and out to touch a pale blue wall. "Yeah."

"You need me to call you a cab or something?"

"Nope, I'm fine, I can drive."

"How the kids doin'?"

"All right, I guess. Cam's just turned fifteen, can you believe?" She stirred among the crumpled receipts and Rolaids and ballpoint pens littering the bottom of her bag, seeking the jingle of car keys. "But Nicole's sure going to take this hard."

———

AND NICOLE WAS taking it very hard, even though a stupendous blue spruce was standing naked and fragrant in the front room when Michelle got home to Chestnut Street. The two kids and Philip, who was already half-dressed for work in houndstooth check chef pants, were unboxing ornaments and Christmas lights in companionable but somber quiet when she let herself through the door. "Well, hey," she unslung her bag and dropped it onto the sofa, unable to contribute any verbal content of her own.

Cam glanced up from beneath his long bangs. "Hey, Mom."

Nicole stood in the middle of the Oriental carpet that covered the hardwood floor, untangling last year's plastic icicles for yet another debut, both of her eyes streaming two small rivers. Her breath came evenly, not in catches, and she made no sound as she watched her own small hands performing her task amid the silvery Mylar, but those eyes never stopped flowing.

That's the way Adrien wept, Michelle remembered, stricken. Utterly silent, with only his eyes.

She crouched to take his daughter into her embrace. Nicole felt hot and solid in her arms and under the palms of her hands, but yielding. "Hendrix is better off now, sweetheart. He felt really terrible, there at the last. He was so tired."

"I know, Mom."

"We bought some presents," Cam offered from where he sat on the edge of the sofa unpacking colored lights. When he lifted his head and slung the hair out of his face, he, too, looked like Adrien, especially the shaping of his brows and eyes, the angle of his nose. "But I'm not going to tell you *what* we bought, Mom, since some of the presents are for you."

"Is that right, Nickyboo?" Michelle still knelt, smoothing the hair back from the child's forehead, watching those magical little hands of hers undo the knots in the icicles. "Are some of them really for me?"

"Yes."

"Spill the beans, Nick. Give me some hints, if Cam won't tell me."

"It's a secret," said Nicole, trading slow glances with Cam and then Philip, glances that would have appeared more conspiratorial if her eyes had been dry. "You'll have to wait until Christmas."

"You should've seen me and Phil, Mom, trying to get this monster tree tied on top of the Acura," Cam said while Philip disappeared into the kitchen. "You would've laughed."

Philip returned almost immediately with a punch cup of something creamy, holding it out to her. "You look like a lady who could use some festive eggnog."

"My Lord, you are psychic," she marveled, taking the cup from his warm hand. She inhaled its aroma of nutmeg and whiskey and rum, and closed her eyes in surprised gratitude for a moment before taking the first sip.

He waited. "How is it?"

"The nectar of the gods."

He held her elbow. "I've gotta be at Tasso in a little while, but Cam's tall and strong enough to get the stepladder out of the weight room and get that angel up there on top."

Cam held out the multicolored light string with arms spread wide. "Mom, Phil wouldn't buy any of those little all-white Italian lights like everybody else in the world has, and he *is* Italian."

"Christmas should be just as gaudy as it needs to be," Philip countered, pulling on a leather bomber jacket over his tee shirt at the front door, car keys in one hand, knife case in the other. "Like Mardi Gras."

Michelle crossed the floor to kiss him good-bye. She rubbed the thick hair at the back of his head. He was the cleanest of men, smelling of soap and aftershave and Calvin Klein, and she wanted to pull his face down and just smell him.

"Be careful, honey," she said, suddenly a little frightened, or maybe it was the eggnog. It was still daylight outside and the sun was low but evident. And yet there would be drunks out there even now, driving around too fast, young men with immortality complexes, all tanked up.

"I will," he promised. "Y'all just get that tree decorated."

"Watch out for bad drivers." She couldn't drop the subject. "Really."

He lowered his voice to a whisper, right at her ear. "Sorry about the lights, but I could tell that Nicole didn't like the all-white kind, she wanted multicolored. 'Z'at okay?"

"Good work."

"Nicole's job today was to select most of the ornaments we bought," he turned and raised his voice in significance, aiming it at the small girl who stood on the blue Oriental carpet, "since she's the artist in the family. She really worked her butt off for us, too, I mean she really put in some effort. Isn't that right, Nick?"

The child raised her head and just nodded. Two stripes of clear water still flowed down both of her cheeks.

BUT NICOLE WAS her old self the next morning at breakfast, blithely taking her Sunday place at the dinette table on the indoor patio for the meal that her brother Cam was dishing up. She bounced to the table in her flannel nightgown, a coloring book in one hand and a box of well-kept crayons in the other.

Phil watched her pull out her seat and plop her art supplies onto the table and was gratified to see her smiling at something Michelle pointed to through the clear glass of the window, a blue jay on the high wooden fence outside. The grief of the child yesterday had brought back some of his own childhood losses, a beloved pet mutt run over and killed on Esplanade right in front of Randazzo's, the sudden death of his raucous and good-humored grandfather from a stroke.

It's sure a tough world for everybody, he had reflected out at the mall right after breaking the bad news to the kids, trying to dry Nicole's leaky eyes in front of the mobbed Dillard's department store entrance with a brown paper towel from the men's room. It's

a tough place especially for kids, poor little guys, maybe it's time I
cut these two some slack. They're not spoiled, exactly—I used to
think they were spoiled but it's actually something else, I don't
know what to call it—and they've been through a lot, when you
think about it. Maybe all we're haunted by is just ordinary grief, not
some ghost.

"You sleep okay?" he asked Nicole now from over the top of his
Sunday *Times-Picayune,* seeing her open her coloring book and reach
for a crayon.

She nodded a bright affirmative. "Is Cam making pancakes?"

"French toast, for you." Michelle rested both elbows on the
place mat in front of her. "How's that?"

"That's fine, we're French, me and Cam."

Michelle smiled and raked a hand through her uncombed hair.
Her eyelids were puffy, wrinkles at their corners stressed. Phil
knew that she couldn't have gotten much sleep herself last night
because neither had he, and he secretly seized her knee now under
the tabletop and squeezed it in gratitude and friskiness.

She slipped her own hand over the back of his while he put
last night's lovemaking on his mental VCR. She had been awake
and receptive when he got home from Tasso, and he had become
suddenly inspired for some reason by stubborn images from that
homemade porn tape to indulge his own imagination a little, beyond what Regan had customarily expected and exacted in his
first marriage. And Michelle had been very responsive—if a mite
surprised.

So what he was feeling this Sunday morning was sleepy but
great.

And the welcome sight of little Nicole contentedly coloring
away to the sound of her own atonal humming was lagniappe, icing
on the cake.

Cam deposited a plate of eggs with bacon and grits in front of
him now, exactly the way Phil liked his eggs done, their whites
cooked just enough to solidify, both yolks unbroken but still liquid.

"Cam, my man," he looked up, "this is dead solid perfection! When you want to come to work for me, boy?"

"Cam's going to go to college," Michelle spoke with just a suspicion of that old edge.

"Guess what, Mom?" Nicole didn't look up, she just went on coloring.

"What?"

"I dreamed about Hendrix last night," she said, and Phil noticed the deftness of her small hand as it sketched in more subjects upon the page than the coloring book artist had originally put there. Her fingers had taken up a black crayon and were drawing a bird with a big worm in its beak.

Michelle yawned. "You did?"

"Yeah." She put down her black crayon and took up bright colors, red and yellow and blue, to make a rainbow. "Look, Phil." She saw that he was watching her. "Red and yellow make orange, and yellow and blue make green. Did you know that?"

"I do now."

"Hendrix was alive in my dream." She worked on her rainbow. "He was big and fat just like he used to be, and he wasn't sick anymore."

"No?" said Michelle.

"Nope. And you want to know what else?"

"What else?"

Her oval face tilted up and her big new front teeth shone in her smile. "Dad was there, and he was holding Hendrix in his arms. And you know what else?"

Phil saw his wife's facial expression change imperceptibly and he could barely hear her response this time because it came so softly: "What else, sweetheart?"

"You were in the dream, too, but I couldn't see you, Mom. You just said something like, I don't remember, something to Dad like, 'Catch him, Adrien,' and Hendrix fell from out of the sky, and Dad caught him."

Michelle blinked four or five times and then sipped at her coffee.

Nicole glanced up at Phil now, frowning, her eyes narrowed, as if she suddenly doubted something. "Dad's name was Adrien, right, Phil?"

"Yes," he said. "His first name."

"But we don't say it the way he did."

"No," Phil answered, because Michelle did not. "I imagine that both he and his family gave it a French pronunciation, which the rest of us aren't used to. You know, like the way some tourists might call y'all *Suh-voy* if they don't know it's *Sav-wah.*"

"He went by his initials," said Cam from the steps, bringing coffee. "Mom is the only one who's ever called him Adrien."

Nicole seemed relieved. "Well, okay then, that was my dream. But one other thing."

A vertical line appeared between Michelle's brows like a slash. Phil reached under the table for her knee and squeezed again but got no response this time. "What other thing, Nick?" he finally asked the little girl because somebody had to.

She wiped her hands on her napkin and studied her picture with satisfaction. "Hendrix was purring, and Dad had him in his arms and held him out to me and told me that he'd take good care of Hendrix from now on, and that I could come and visit Hendrix anytime I wanted, because Hendrix would always be right there, and all I had to do was to go to sleep and dream. That's all I had to do. And Hendrix wasn't sick anymore. He was his big, fat, lazy old self. And you know what else, Phil?"

"You can't remember Dad, you little microbe," Cam scoffed. "You didn't even know what his name was."

"Yes I do!" she insisted. "He sang songs to me and he had a hurt leg."

Phil was intrigued now, remembering that terrifying dream of his own, not about resurrected cats but about wreck and death. "Go on with your dream, Nicole. What else?"

"Dad wasn't hurt anymore, either, in my dream," she smirked with the ridged edges of her new teeth overlapping her lower lip, glad of Phil's attention. "And he didn't need to walk with a cane anymore. He just put Hendrix down, on this, like, little grassy hill, and he showed me: Dad could *run*."

"Y'all please excuse me." Michelle pushed her chair back with a scrape, and she hurried up the few steps into the master bedroom and then the bath, and closed the door.

FIFTEEN

Truths

SHE MADE IT THROUGH the rest of that Sunday because she had
no choice.

But if there hadn't been these two kids to tend to, she realized,
and no Philip, her own preference would have been an immediate
return to bed.

To the comfort of slept-on pillowcases and coverlets where she
could curl up to privately ponder Nicole's dream, regarding it from
all mental angles, turning it over, examining it like an artifact. Until
her mind might wear itself down enough to be overcome by pro-
tective sleep like the screen saver eclipsing an image on her computer monitor whenever one threatened to burn it out.

She got on nevertheless with her Sunday routine, dressing herself, doing laundry so that she and Philip and the kids would have
clean clothes for Monday. Working at the computer to give shape
to an abstract for the academic paper she'd like to submit for next
year's meeting of the American Anthropological Association on the
reinterpreted role of paternal grandmothers among the Zinacantec,
Yucatec, Tzotzil, Tzeltal, and Quiché peoples.

Philip left for Tasso at four, trusting his staff to begin the
kitchen's routine without him. He had managed to watch some

football before leaving and Michelle had joined him there in their bedroom in front of their big TV with her notes, her reading glasses suspended from their chain around her neck. Away from the computer so that she could be with her husband for a while.

But the Saints were playing poorly under their interim head coach, and so what was the point? It doesn't matter who gets into the play-offs, Philip had pointed out, we won't be there. Same old Saints. He seemed testy. He seemed distant.

"Be careful," she told him at the door.

His kiss good-bye was quick and obligatory. "Catch you later."

What goes on inside that head? she wondered as he went down the front steps and out to the Acura at the curb. What piece of emotional landscape gets shifted in there, imperceptible to me, that makes him affectionate one moment and then distant the next? Did Nicole set him off, Nicole and her dream, and is Philip entitled at all to be jealous over my first marriage if I am not expected or encouraged to be jealous in regard to his?

THE DARKNESS CAME DOWN very fast now in December, and Sunday night was a school night. And by the time both Cam and Nicole were done with their supper and homework, and had watched the *X-Files* on television with her, Michelle was glad of the approaching solitude and silence.

"Y'all get upstairs and get your baths and get on into bed," she urged them, anxious to get back to the Maya. And then watched them trudge up the stairs and away from her without a word.

"I love you guys," she called after them.

Cam turned his head at the top of the stairs so that he appeared in profile to her and she wondered, What did Philip see up there? Did he see only what I'm seeing, a boy with this profile, something ordinary, just this son of his father?

"G'night, Mom," he said, his voice beginning to change. "I love you, too."

"Night, Mom." Nicole didn't even bother to turn her head.

Michelle knew that she should shelve her outline and work instead on that final, but the fatigue she had been fighting all day came over her now with such power that she could only pad into the kitchen in her sock feet and pour herself some bourbon. She put five ice cubes into the glass and not much water but it still looked way too pale to do her any good. So she added another dollop of whiskey.

Hell, she said to herself, checking the front door to make sure that it was locked, setting the electronic burglar alarm, and then turning off all the lights, how can you get this tired on a Sunday? How will you make it through tomorrow if you don't settle down now and relax and get some rest?

Stop obsessing about the goddam anthro paper, it's not due for nearly a year yet. We know what this is about, it's about being too lazy and uninspired to go finish that stupid final, that's what this is actually about.

The drink was strong but did not make her feel better. What she really craved now was chocolate, but there was nothing sweet in the house except syrup and sugar and Nicole's breakfast cereals.

Bourbon and Cocoa Puffs, she thought. A new low.

Damn perimenopause. I'm nothing but a sagging bag of hormones, right on the verge of becoming a blithering emotional wreck, worse than any of my pregnancies. I think if I were God, I could've come up with a better female reproductive system.

She sat down on the sofa in the darkened front room near the silhouetted cone of the Christmas tree, and gulped at her drink in the stillness. When her glass was empty she poured herself another. And came again into the darkness, sitting in an armchair now, facing the windows and the orange street light that bled through their sheers, missing and mourning her warm yellow cat.

Cam's television was still yakking away upstairs by the time she had finished her bourbon and was finally willing to call it a night. She considered just leaving it on but realized that it might disturb

Nicole. And it would certainly disturb Philip, once he was home and in bed beneath it.

Her brain was too tired to even generate a cussword as she dragged herself up the steep staircase to shut off the TV. Cam lay asleep in its blue light, half under the covers and half on top of them, and his room reeked of sneaked cigarettes. One of his windows was open a couple of inches, probably to let the smoke out, and Michelle closed it with a quiet snap and then stood in the doorway for a moment with her arms folded across her body.

What if that's really all that's been going on here, she wondered, Hendrix just opportunistic enough to find the windows left open by a kid sneaking a smoke? Cats can climb down trees and there are a lot of trees around this house. Hell, it's just a drab and ugly world, and I don't know why I keep expecting it to be anything else, this magical place of light and shadow, a mythic Maya universe, when what it really is is Taco Bell and beer cans.

She noticed the Zippo lighter on the top of the dresser, amid the clutter of Cam's wallet and house keys and coins, and heaved her chest up and then down with the effort of breathing. What'll I do if he gets expelled from Newman? she wondered, considering confiscation of the lighter, thinking better of it. I can't risk a blowup with him now, not over the lighter again, not this close to December fifteenth, *shit*.

But I can certainly confiscate the little asshole's cigarettes if I can locate them in the dark.

She found a mashed soft pack of three in the front zippered section of his backpack and she shredded them into his wastepaper can, leaving their remains highly visible there on top of the crumpled papers beneath.

I'm going to bed. It's certainly screen saver time for me, before I burn out some mental circuitry.

But she had to pass close to the kitchen again to get to the first-floor master bedroom, and there was more bourbon in the kitchen.

So finally, when she had at last achieved the privacy of the bedroom and it was already ten o'clock and she knew that Philip wouldn't be home for at least another hour, and she saw how wired and unsleepy she was becoming, it seemed reasonable to her to bypass the alarm system on the rear French windows and then just throw off all her clothes and give up and walk nude through the weight room to the Jacuzzi. A click of a wall switch caused the hot, still water to begin to roil and bubble. She went to the tall windows, opening both of them to the winter night, and took deep breaths of the crystal air, hidden from any neighboring eyes by the high wooden fence.

I'm drunk, she realized in a pleasant fog, seeing how the cold darkness made gooseflesh of her upper arms. And this is glorious. I can even see stars up there, holding their own against all this man-made light.

Wisps of steam rose from the Jacuzzi's surface.

She stepped down its steps into the deep warmth, sighing with almost childish satisfaction at the delight of hot water on chilled skin. She watched her own breasts bobbing in the turbulence. Wavelets licked at the nape of her neck. She leaned backward into them, buoyed in their rocking embrace.

What a wonderful place this little pool is, she thought, for stressed muscles and whatever else ails you. Wouldn't Adrien have loved this thing? With its heat and massaging hydrotherapy almost tailor-made for him?

Yeah, but you know if we two were living here, he and me, there'd be a lock on the door to keep the kids out. He'd have music speakers in here and I'd have candles. And after both kids got tucked in upstairs, we would have thick, warm towels in here. But no clothes. And no clocks.

There'd be some nostalgic oldie coming over the music system like "Layla," and there would be this lulling lapping.

In this hot water he could wear me like a garment, my arms around his shoulders. Steadying my floating weight with his hands, he could wear me like a sheath, so deep inside me that I would feel him in my heart.

Wow, am I drunk out of my gourd! I need to get out of here and dry off and go to bed, that's what I really need to do. Shit, I'm drunk, I'm going to wake up with one hell of a hangover, how idiotic is that? What this is is chlorine in here, but I'm even drunk enough to imagine that it smells like patchouli.

Weirdly inspired, she suddenly wondered what would happen if she were able to angle her pelvis at the water jet pounding at her buttocks. It might be fun. It couldn't hurt her unless she drowned. What the hell, Esther Williams in a porn flick.

The spouting water prodded her like a living thing.

Moving in as close as she could to it, breathing out lungfuls of vapor, she held on to the deck with her hands and half floated— twisting her body in an attempt to accept the hot surge inside her, slightly frightened of its force, but driven. She wasn't sure that she could even achieve a position that would admit it.

But she could.

She did.

The pleasure was amazing.

SIXTEEN

Friday, December 13, 1996

"PHIL, I'M NOT SURE that any of this sounds genuinely demonic to me," the Reverend Dominic F. Randazzo, SJ, contradicted his younger brother over breakfast at the Pontchartrain Hotel coffee shop five days later, "sorry to disappoint."

"I'm not married to 'demonic,' Nonnie, when did I say that? But what I need to do is make sure you understand how unhealthy this all is," Phil said, pushing away an omelette and taking up his fourth cup of coffee, "for all of us. In my household."

"But I don't know that it sounds all that unhealthy, either."

"But Michelle knows a lot more than she's telling me, I saw by the way she reacted to Nicole's dream."

Dominic shrugged with only his bristling brows.

"Nonnie, there's only two points of view that she can hold about these happenings," Phil tried again, "think about it: Either she secretly believes that he's actually come back and just doesn't want to give me the satisfaction of hearing her admit it—"

"Please pass me the salt."

"—or," Phil complied, "or, she refuses to believe it because she's afraid to get her hopes up. Either way, I come in second."

"But you might be better off consulting your own parish priest here, Phil, I'm a high school principal," Dominic grunted, shifting his weight on the booth cushion and adjusting the white napkin that lay upon his fleshy lap. "Not used to counseling adults."

"Bones McCoy on *Star Trek:* 'I'm a doctor, Jim, not a marriage counselor.' Did I say that I needed marriage counseling?" Phil paused. "Look, I was told to talk to a priest. I'm just trying to talk to a priest."

"About your marriage."

"About a haunting."

There went the eyebrow thing again.

"Hey," Phil pursued it, spreading wide his open palms, "I don't want to believe in ghosts, Nonnie. The church didn't teach us to believe in no ghosts. Poppa didn't raise us to believe in no ghosts. I need you to talk me out of believing in this ghost."

"Well."

"As my brother. As my big brother, then, if not as a priest. If you don't want to approach it as a priest."

"Phil, I approach *everything* through my vocation," Dominic spoke in the sententious tones of a man who valued his own opinion and did not care to be misunderstood.

"Okay, that's fine." Phil waited.

"Why don't you start over about this anniversary business, then."

"Today's Friday the thirteenth—not that that means anything in particular, except weirding me out just a fraction more than I was already. But Sunday'll be the third anniversary of Savoie's death."

"And?"

"You tell me."

Dominic was half a head shorter yet heavier than Phil, and only eighteen months older. But his black suit and Roman collar imparted gravitas that even a sibling might find difficult to ignore. Phil could easily recall the big brother that showed no mercy during boyhood fistfights, pounding him into the greasy dirt of Esplanade Avenue one time until Momma made him stop by spanking him with the flyswatter—Nonnie taunting him one minute, ignoring him and Joey and Martin and God and everybody else the next.

But that moody and enigmatic Nonnie finally had forever morphed, nearly twenty-five years ago, into Father Dominic, dedicated educator, exemplar of the vows of poverty, chastity, and obedience that he had taken upon his ordination, a wholly different person and a publicly substantial one. Phil still could not see what had drawn him to the priesthood unless the call had initially been suggested by the piety of their mother. He understood now that he would never understand Dominic.

Beefy red hands slowly folded themselves and then came to rest on the edges of the white tablecloth. "From what you tell me, and from what I'm getting from what you tell me, Phil, this is not a phenomenon that warrants any kind of attention from the archdiocese."

"But the church still does do it, right? Exorcism?"

Dominic reached up under his glasses to rub his eyes at their corners. He resembled their late mother, Phil noticed now; and the thought of Momma, dead only two years, reminded him anew of the implacability of time and loss. "We saw way too much sci-fi, you and me, didn't we? Yeah, sure, it's still done upon occasion. But they are exceedingly rare occasions, Phil—like practically never. Incontrovertible evidence would have to be presented to the archbishop to even get permission to proceed. And then it gets turned over to a priest with some experience at it—a designated exorcist, if you will."

Phil put his fingertips together and then lightly rested his forehead on them. He felt a headache coming, one of those dishonest allergy-induced ones beginning in the sinuses behind his eyes.

"No priest of my acquaintance has ever performed one," his brother noticed after a moment and offered further explanation as if it were an aspirin. "We're psychologically sophisticated enough now to reject demonic possession whenever Freud will suffice. Plus, there's the fact that nobody in this case is possessed, so we have nobody to exorcise. Looks like you're pretty much S.O.L. here."

"Nonnie, there are just some things—" Phil thought about sin.

"There are just some things that seem to summon Savoie up. That I associate with the dark side."

"I hear what you've been telling me, don't think I don't. And I realize what a strain these past seven or eight months've been for you, what with Regan's remarriage and your own. All the legal bills of the divorce, two new stepchildren," Dominic nodded, "coupled with long work hours. But I do think that what you really need to hear from me now is just how normal a situation you're in, not how ungodly."

"Bullshit. I know you think we're all ungodly. Divorcing and remarrying."

The tone was unctuous: "What do you know about the practice of modern grief counseling?"

"Not a lot." Phil carefully took up his coffee, repressing his mild but burgeoning rage at his brother's condescension. Nearby diners might take it the wrong way if they overheard him calling a priest a dickhead.

"Well, then, you might benefit from a visit to the Internet. The church is finding it quite routine these days to hear of all sorts of postmortem visitations. There was a time—"

"Nonnie—"

"—there was a time, Filbert, some years ago, when we most un-charitably insisted to grieving survivors that what they were seeing and hearing and dreaming about were mere hallucinations, I'm sorry to say." He reached for the check over Phil's protests, still an-noyingly the responsible eldest brother. "But what with the recent work done by researchers like Father Andrew Greeley and Dr. Louis LaGrand, and so forth, some counselors are beginning to view these phenomena as a natural and perhaps even necessary part of the grieving process."

"Phenomena." The last of the coffee was cold. "Plural."

"Yes. Like dreams of the deceased, very vivid and real dreams, that both instruct and comfort."

"Aha."

"Or floral aromas that have no source. Or the disembodied voices of loved ones, or actual apparitions. All fairly normal happenings, apparently, for perhaps one-third to one-half of the widowed survivors surveyed. And we aren't speaking about lunatics or publicity seekers here, either, Phil. We're talking about just plain, normal people," Dominic's gaze became level, "who are very afraid, after having already suffered the loss of a loved one, that they are also about to lose their minds. What they have to relate to researchers about these phenomena, they relate unwillingly."

"What about cats jumping out of closed windows? Where do cats come in?"

He received a frigid stare through eyeglasses topped by brows growing gray and wild with age. "I'm here, Philip, only because you asked me to come. If you don't want my input, there's no need to get cute about it."

"Okay. You're right. I'm sorry. I apologize."

The waitress returned with Dominic's credit card and topped off their coffee cups again.

"Phil, you know, several influential Catholic grief counselors are posing the interesting question these days of whether these contacts might not be heaven-sent. Literally."

"You gotta be kidding."

"As an act of divine grace, to assuage grief. So that the survivor can feel that his or her loved one also survives and is in a better place, and can get on with the business of living."

"So our ghost comes from God? *Whoa,* I ain't buying that."

"Well, how can we know? These counselors can no longer just automatically assume that either it's a hallucination or its origins lie in something darker."

"But I'm hardly one of Savoie's loved ones. Why the hell should I experience anything?"

"Louis LaGrand addresses third-party contact, which is the most rare. But it's also the most affecting, because the survivor can't just dismiss it as mere wishful thinking, conjured up by her own grieving mind, if it comes from someone else's. Like yours, for instance."

"Nonnie, what bothers me is you're dodging the question of objective reality here. Are these researchers of yours claiming that these contacts are literally *real,* actual contact with disembodied personalities who are as *real* and as conscious as I am? Or are we talking about just some nonliving images, plus assorted smells and dreams and tricks like a cosmic magic show performed in order to make somebody feel better about losing somebody?"

The priest raised both black shoulders and spread apart his fat palms. "I can't see where it makes any difference, as long as the effect is positive."

"Well, shit, Nonnie!" Phil suppressed the even stronger language he might've used on a layman. "It makes a real big difference to third parties like me!"

"Phil, hey, what can I say?"

"—and just where do 'normal' grief phenomena end, and your standard nasty Stephen King–type, *Amityville Horror,* really badass hauntings begin?"

"What can I tell you? 'By their fruits ye shall know them,'" Dominic quoted scripture. "Have any of these experiences that your household has had, you or your wife or Nicole, have any of them led to anything harmful?"

"Not yet."

"Have there been any suggestions, like…oh…that any of you should commit a harmful act? Like suicide?"

"No."

"Murder?"

"Nonnie, stop trying to fit us into a pattern and please just *listen* for a minute, okay?"

"Okay." He smoothed his black garments over his bulging midsection. "I'm listening."

"See," Phil began, "none of this stuff was going on three years

ago, right after Savoie died, when Michelle might've been comforted by it, know what I'm saying? If she experienced anything
strange then, she won't tell me. But I don't think she did. And she
shows no signs of having been comforted."

"Better late than never."

Phil leaned onto his elbows again, rubbing his aching forehead
with one hand. "Here's the thing. Because of the creakings that old
houses make, like ours, what with tree limbs against 'em in the wind
or whatever, she can't say exactly when those normal noises ended
and the other kind replaced them. Hey, maybe the ghost was somehow able to take advantage of natural noises and make his initial
breakthrough on the noise channel, damn, I'm starting to sound
like a nutcase here…"

"It's okay," Dominic modulated his voice into relative anonymity,
the nonjudgmental tones of the confessional. "Please continue."

Phil accordingly lowered his eyes so that all they could register
would be the darkness of the clothing and not its wearer's familiarity. Maybe he could make it seem more like confiding in a usual
priest whom he wasn't related to and whom he hadn't seen naked.
"What I'm afraid of— Look, it all started out as just creakings,
apparently…"

"Okay."

"But then along about All Saints Day, it starts becoming about
the cat getting in and out of the closed-up house, through closed
doors or windows or whatever. Cat couldn't do it all the time, but
it definitely did it some of the time. No explanation, we kept
checking. Even Michelle was spooked."

"Okay. Go on."

"Okay," Phil echoed. "Then I see the kid on the stairs, as if all
the creakings and cat stuff had just been warm-ups like a battery
being charged. The cat goes out the windows some more. And then
right after that is when I get this vivid Technicolor nightmare
about how Savoie got whacked. I mean, it's *real*. It's like I'm living
it, Nonnie. Like it's happening to me."

The priest nodded in Phil's peripheral vision.

"And now here he is, coming through to Nicole, too. That's two of us so far, that I know of. Cam might want dreams of him but isn't getting them yet. I don't know about Michelle. If she's dreaming him, she won't say. Won't admit it."

"So what you're afraid of—?"

"What I think is, he's getting stronger. Like, every time he succeeds in getting through to one of us, it opens new channel bands for him. Like a radio station. It boosts his signal, every time one of us tunes him in."

"Hmm."

"Nonnie, I don't know if it's because he was in the recording industry or what—if it's just because I hear his records over WWOZ—but I . . . ," he struggled for words, "I conceptualize all of this like a broadcast. Like he's someway able to fine-tune his signal every time he detects that he's gotten through to somebody. And he gets stronger."

The silence in the coffee shop was unnatural. Phil came to himself, noticing that he and his brother were the last of the breakfasters. The few people coming in now were ordering lunch. He glanced at his watch.

Soft light reflected off the lenses of Dominic's glasses, rendering them opaque.

"So when do I check myself into DePaul's rubber room?"

"You say that the presence is getting stronger. To what end?"

"I don't know. This is where the priest comes in."

The priest was silent for another interminable pause, lacing his sausage fingers together, staring across the room at the Victorian wallpaper.

"Look," said Phil, "let's say I was this guy. Savoie. This disembodied spirit, or God's little consolation prize, or badass ghost, or whatever. Okay: I've been dead now for three whole years, my wife and kids are surviving without me, for better or worse. But they *are* getting along, bottom line. Okay. So *why* do I suddenly go to all this trouble now to make myself known, to manifest myself to her new husband, to make myself stronger, unless it's the very fact of her re-marriage that gripes me?"

"I see your point."

"So what would it hurt, Nonnie, if you were to go to my house right now and just sprinkle around a little holy water, like?" Phil tried a laugh. "Look, I know how nuts I sound. Savoie was raised Catholic, he might not be any more lapsed than me. Maybe he's even sent by God, what do I know? All I'm saying is, a few prayers for his soul in purgatory might do all of us some good, him in-cluded. Could we do that?"

"Is it possible that he's trying to warn y'all of something, not threaten you?"

"Nonnie, what is the exact meaning of the word *haunt*?" Phil sensed suddenly that he was right about everything. He had not known it for sure before, but he knew it now. He saw his rightness reflected in his brother's facial expression and increasingly uncom-fortable posture. "As in, my wife is haunted by this man? As in, even now, she's so haunted that she won't let his kids play his music and she can't stand to see photos of him? There are no pictures of him on display anywhere at all in our house, not even in his kids' rooms, believe it or not. You'd better believe she's kept them all, oh yeah. But stashed away in boxes, like in the attic or under the bed, or under lock and key in her closet. And I can make her break down and cry if we dwell too long on the subject whenever I push her to really talk about him, I'm learning. I haven't exactly meant to, up until now, and she can't help it. But does this honestly sound like the successful outcome of modern grief counseling to you?"

Dominic sat still.

"Shit, Nonnie. We need a *priest*." Phil rested his case and rested his forehead one last time upon his fisted hands.

Maybe a full minute passed. Maybe longer.

Phil's brother finally cleared his throat after that very long silence.

And then he began to slide six inches across his booth's bench toward its open side, but tentatively. "Well, Filbert, you know I've got to get to my school, I'm afraid…Monsignor's dropping in for a scheduled visit this afternoon…" He glanced at his watch. "Would Michelle be at home now?"

"No, she's at Tulane."

"Nobody's at home at your house right now, I take it."

"Not a living soul, and I say that with all my heart." Phil took his head off his fists and put them down.

"Then I guess there's no harm in dropping by for just a minute."

"Sure," was Phil's one-word response. His relief was so paralyzing that he couldn't find a way to feel it. He watched his brother first pull down the hem of his black suit coat in back and then smooth both lapels.

"I'm just going to bless your house, Phil, that's all I'm going to do, you understand." Dominic began to walk to the door. "Nothing major."

"You're the boss." He fell into step.

"So you're free to tell Michelle about it. Say anything you please."

"Shit, I'm not going to tell her, make her defensive about the whole situation." He stripped cellophane from a mint and then took out his car keys. "I don't want to put her through anything else."

"Fine," said Dominic.

"No," Phil sucked on the candy. He pushed at the glass door and held it open. "I ain't saying a word."

SEVENTEEN

Anniversary

WHATEVER PHIL HAD BEEN expecting to happen on December 15, whether demonic or nothing—now that the house had been blessed—this wasn't it.

It was a Sunday of long telephone calls and all of them were for Michelle. They started early that morning, the first one coming before Cam had even begun preparing the weekend breakfast.

Phil made it to the phone first and it had been the voice of an older woman, Michelle's mother, making brief and distracted pleasantries to him in her Texan drawl and then demanding her daughter's ear with no further ado.

"That was Mom," said Michelle unnecessarily, returning to the dinette table after Cam and Nicole had both taken over the call from Grandma on their respective extensions. "Calling just to tell me that she's thinking about us."

"Uh-huh," he acknowledged over the sports section of the *Times-Picayune*, understanding that he was not included.

She ran both hands through her short hair while Cam and Nicole continued their long-distance chatting. "She's called us every year on this date. Well, she does call us on other days, too, like birthdays. But I guess it's actually pretty thoughtful of her to remember me this way on every anniversary of the accident, since she openly hated Adrien's guts."

He turned a page of the paper, hearing Cam bounding down the stairs and back to the kitchen. "Why?"

"Because he existed, to begin with."

"She might not find a greasy cook any more lovable. She hardly talks to me."

"You just make her tongue-tied, Philip: You've been on the *Today* show and written up in *Food & Wine*. Every time you win another award, her old bitch friends all call her for a victory rally."

"What happens when I stop winning?"

The cordless phone shrilled again from the middle of the table before she could address that. Phil thumbed its button and put it to his ear, said his hello, and heard the raspy honk of a Cajun lady, nearly unintelligible. He held the phone out to Michelle: "Has to be for you."

She took it from him and began what promised to be a very lengthy conversation, punctuated by her own "I'm fine," and "They're fine," and other disjointed musings, until Phil rose from his seat and went into the bathroom to shave.

She was still at it when he came out. Pacing up and down the length of the front room in her espadrilles, phone to her ear, listening and nodding and intent.

Cam had deserted his post at the stove, probably on grandmother duty again upstairs, and Phil took over without a word, flipping hash browns in their pan with one hand while breaking the eggs for western omelets with the other. Having diced onions in a flurry, he took up the wire whisk and then belatedly felt dismay at how dull the knife here had become. And he wondered, similarly dully, why nobody in this whole house besides him ever thought to sharpen anything.

Breakfast was pretty much a done deal when Cam reappeared, and he looked crestfallen to see Phil finishing up. "Oh, I'm sorry,"

Phil apologized, having had no idea that the boy's feelings would be hurt by this usurpation. "I figured it might be hard on you, reminiscing or whatever with your maw-maw. I just thought you could use the morning off if it's going to be this way all day."

Cam merely stood there, useless and silent.

"We do need a fresh pot of coffee," Phil groped for a suggestion, and was pleased when the boy seemed glad to have something to hop to.

The phone kept going, both during breakfast and after, and he very much wished that his wife and her kids would just allow the answering machine to pick up and record. One deep African-American voice, inflected with Ninth Ward pronunciations, began like so many of the others by asking to speak to "Mickey"; but when Michelle got to the phone and addressed the caller as "Bee-Bee," Phil realized he had been speaking to Walter "Bee-Bee" Legendre, A. P. Savoie's former manager and a big honcho with the House of Blues and the Jazz and Heritage Foundation. He was retroactively impressed, both as a music fan and as an ordinary guy susceptible to celebrity. He would've liked to converse further with Bee-Bee Legendre if he had had anything at all to say to the man.

Can't even fall back on *How 'bout dem Saints?* Phil realized glumly. 'Cause they suck.

"Your dad sure knew a lot of people," he grunted to Cam as they scraped dishes and loaded the dishwasher while Michelle fielded telephone calls and Nicole withdrew to her own room.

"Well, no, not really," Cam answered after a long moment's thought. "A lot of these calls are from his family."

"Oh."

"It's more like a lot of people knew *him,* if you know what I mean." Cam's hair was in his eyes. "Dad could be a shy person, on the whole, if he didn't know you very well."

"Interesting. I never got that impression."

Water splashed into the sink. "Well, he used to say that he'd been performing for so long, since he was a little kid, that it was just like paying bills, for him. No stage fright, nothing like that."

"Hah."

"But offstage is where he got nervous, interviews, stuff like that. Mom says his accent kind of bothered him whenever he thought about it. People used to make fun of real country French talk back when Dad was a kid. Call it ignorant, call it 'coonass,' stuff like that, not like things are now. *Cajun* was even sort of a bad word then, you believe that?"

"Have to reprint a whole lot of restaurant menus, I know that much."

"My mamère, Dad's mom, she still won't use it, she just says, 'French.'" Cam sponged at another plate and then rinsed it off. "All Mom's friends from the Anthro Department, they used to beg Dad to talk for them. Like they wanted to study him or something."

"Jerks. Let 'em pay a cover charge."

"Yeah! Dad would've liked you, Phil."

"Well, he came across onstage as a genuine and sort of humble guy." Phil watched the boy from his eyes' corners. "That's what a lot of his audience really liked about him."

"That was the real him," Cam nodded. "We'd go out to eat or something, and he'd always be surprised when people wanted his autograph. He'd never say no, not even one time when Nick was cutting up so bad nobody could hear anybody else talk, and it was real embarrassing."

"I guess nobody had to actually go out to clubs and hear him play to know who he was." Savoie's left hand and his cane had been markers to even casual observers, Phil knew.

Cam's voice was noncommittal when he spoke. His face and gaze watched his own fingers scrape with a plastic spatula at congealed egg yolk. "Both of the cops who were first on the scene that night when he was killed, both of them recognized him right off."

"Yeah. Wow."

Cam slung the hair out of his eyes with a toss of his head.

"Why do you think you caused it?" Phil heard himself suddenly seize the opportunity, not having planned it, feeling something wake and shake itself like a grizzly. He deposited three coffee mugs into the open dishwasher.

"Who says I think I caused it?"

"Your mom. And she worries a hell of a lot about it, Cam. You have no idea how much she loves you and worries about you."

"Well," his face adopted that deadpan, shutdown look that teenage boys affected, a neutrality so thorough that it could appear hostile, "I know I didn't *cause* it, not really. I mean, I know that."

The telephone rang again. Michelle answered it, speaking to someone in somber tones as she mounted the stairs toward the laughter of Nicole's televised cartoons.

"You want to talk about it?" Phil ventured, but not exclusively out of empathy. The shape that rose up against his inner skies now was his own nightmare of wreck and death. "I was out of town when it happened, at this restaurant thing up in Chicago. Regan mentioned it the next day or so when she phoned. I just couldn't believe it."

"Neither could we."

"I'm sorry, son, for what it's worth."

"Well," Cam's tone was flat, "Dad was on his way to this really stupid Christmas concert at my school."

"Country Day, huh?"

"Yeah." A smooth forearm flexed with the lifting of a grease-encrusted pan. "It was this really lame concert like they do every year, all of us kids having to sing stupid Christmas and Hanukkah songs that nobody ever heard of, and even a few for Kwanzaa."

Phil remembered his own dutiful paternal attendance at similar events. He wondered now if his own kids were participating again this year in concerts on the north shore to which he had not been invited. "Yeah. I know the drill."

"Well," Cam said, "the kids in my class who could play the

piano, they played. A couple of the girls sang solo parts. But since I can't sing, some retard thought it'd be cool if I recited this dumb poem."

"What, like 'The Night Before Christmas'?"

"No. Just something I wrote."

"You wrote it yourself? A poem?"

"Well, this embarrassing one that really sucked, yeah. I mean," said Cam, "it wasn't worth making some special effort to come hear it. It certainly wasn't worth anybody getting killed for."

Only the sound of water trickling into the sink broke the silence that followed. The humdrum horror of it was what first struck Phil—what a really sitcom way to die. Getting whacked in an auto accident on your way to your kid's Christmas pageant. He tacked on this new preamble to his nightmare.

"But you know what else really bites?" Cam measured out the correct amount of detergent for the dishwasher, closing its door with a bang. He pushed its on lever into position without delicacy.

"What bites?"

"Just how pissed off both me and Mom were when Dad never showed." Pale hair curtained his cheeks. "She'd been nagging him about it all week, like, to take off early—his day job was at this recording studio on Clematis Street, it wasn't as if he'd have to drive all the way in from Slidell or somewhere. He kept saying he'd see what he could do. But he was producing this CD for somebody, I don't remember who, and they'd been having all kinds of trouble with it.

"So anyway, when he didn't show, and we were all out front after it was all over, out there with the other kids and their parents and the teachers, and Mom holding Nicole in her arms— She kept going, like, under her breath to me and really pissed off, 'The *asshole,* I can't believe it! The *asshole!*'"

Cam leaned against the dishwasher, head down. "And you know what, Phil? I was like, 'He keeps telling me how important school is and all, what a laugh. I know I'm not that talented, but he could've at least gone through the motions!' This is all while Dad is lying dead in the hospital, you understand, and cops are already parked at our house on Dufossat, trying to find us."

Phil shifted his weight. "Well, but you had a right to your anger, son. It was honest. You had nothing else to go on."

"Yeah, but even before I got up to recite, Dad had already died. He didn't live more than ten minutes after he got hit. I get up to say that *stupid, shitty* poem, and I'm, like, looking for him, trying to see if he's way in the back." His face crumpled.

Phil ran out of words.

Cam's right arm suddenly launched a fastball of dishwashing detergent into four juice glasses and a jar of orange marmalade. The whole mess splatted into a wall and then came crashing onto the floor, broken. His tall and slight body shook with sobs as if a sci-fi movie alien had come alive inside him and was trying to break out through his chest.

Phil grappled with him to comfort him, to restrain him, but Cam became a human tornado, kicking cabinet doors in the narrow space, smashing his fists on the stove, the rims of the sink, the black refrigerator, until he was cut somewhere by something and bleeding.

Phil got both arms around him, finally, in a chokehold that became a bear hug. "Here," he was saying, "here. Just come here. Just come here."

"*Oh God,* Phil!" Cam wheezed out.

"It's okay. It's okay."

"Oh *God,* I loved him so much! I loved him so much!" in thin wails. "I miss him *so much,* Phil! Oh, Phil! Oh, *God!*"

"I know, son," his own voice came out gruff because if he let it come out the way it wanted to, it wouldn't help. "I still miss my own dad, and he could be a real son of a bitch."

He noticed, over Cam's shoulder, Michelle standing aghast in the doorway that led to the indoor patio, the cordless phone gripped in one white and tight fist, held like a weapon.

"It's okay," he told her. "Everything's okay."

"Philip?" She was on the verge of some implosion.

"Just a little flashback, it's all over now." He patted his stepson on the back but continued to restrain him. "Just some male bonding going on here, nothing earthshaking."

Her lips were still parted. Her face was the color of milk.

"We'll just beat our drums in here for a little while longer, doll," he gestured with his head, "just give us some time," but his arms did not relax.

"PHONE'S FOR YOU," he told her several hours later after Cam's fingers had been bandaged, the broken glassware swept up, the relative normalcy of televised Sunday NFL games established. "It's another 'Mickey' call."

But Michelle had been very shaken by Cam's upset, and Phil could see that she was still shook, even now, long after Cam himself was again evened out and back at his Nintendo console upstairs with muted rap music on his CD player. Nicole was up there, too, playing with a Barbie in her own room, brushing out its platinum Dynel hair and talking to herself.

Michelle sat in the front room on the sofa, arms folded across her stomach. "Who is it?"

Phil shrugged. "Cajun accent."

She looked up at him, the whites of her eyes inflamed. "How can you stand this, Philip, people treating you like you're my servant or bodyguard, not my husband?"

"I don't take it personally. They don't know me."

Her smile came, a thin one, and she reached out a hand to him. "Come in here and sit with me when you've gotten rid of 'em, and we can be quiet and together for a while."

He nodded. And then informed the caller, a woman who gave her name as something that sounded like "Bay-bay," that "Mickey" wasn't feeling well, and could he take a message?

"Sister-in-law," Michelle said when he'd hung up.

"She told me to take care of you. And she let me know she knew who I was, but in a nice way. Nice person."

"Very nice, and funny." She looked at her thighs. "I'm sorta surprised she didn't tell you a knock-knock joke."

So maybe Michelle and I ought to take the kids out there sometime this spring and just let them spend some time with that family, Phil thought now. I guess I really ought to start making a stab at getting to know these people since my stepkids are related to them and they're not going to just go away.

And the old lady just might have some killer family recipes tucked away in a kitchen drawer somewhere, you never know.

Goddam, Cam and Nicole are just so *isolated*. Cam's fucked up, and it can't be healthy for little Nick, either, to spend all of her time in the house like this, playing all alone, so quiet. Maybe what they've been needing all along is a thousand rowdy cousins, weekends in the country, shrimp boats and alligators and whatever.

Would it be disloyal to my own sons if I brought Cam to Tasso with me sometime, just let him mess around the kitchen if he's really that interested? Take him and Nicole to the Saint Joseph's Day parade next time, tell them how the Italian people still do the Saint Joseph's Day altars like my momma did and see if my aunt Rita and her sisters still do one. They could get to know everybody, old Uncle Sal—take home a lucky fava bean from the altar. Damn, I haven't seen my aunt or uncle in over eight months, myself. Where does the time go?

When he sank down into the sofa cushions beside her now, his wife took his hand. She rubbed the tips of her fingers over his knuckles. He waited for her to say something.

But her chin was turning red and her lips had begun to melt, and he saw that she wasn't going to be able to talk for a while.

"Cam is a fine young man," he said, finally. "Fucked-up because he's insightful."

She nodded and just rubbed, mute.

"None of y'all, you didn't do anything wrong that night, baby doll. You didn't cause this thing."

The dam of her lower eyelids gave way. She held Phil's hand to her face.

He started to say something else, to tell her that after having thought it over some more, he was deciding to relent and allow Cam and Nick to go spend some days out across the lake with Kerri and Brendan and Hunter. That's what he was opening his mouth to say. But the mirrored wall in the dining room didn't let him get to it.

No, the mirrored wall one room away showed Phil to himself, seated next to Michelle, but it also reflected the image of someone positioned just behind them.

His short hair was cowlicked in some places, matted to his skull in others, and he looked very normal. Except that Phil could see the windows through the edges of the kid's elbows, and that was a very big *except.*

Sleeves were rolled above slick tanned biceps. Phil could smell the rank dampness of unwashed clothing. A steel bead chain shone against the browned neck. Military insignia were stitched in black to each shoulder. An automatic weapon dangled at the end of one arm.

Phil heard Michelle make a noise and he knew that she, too, was seeing something.

The kid fumbled with his free hand among the sweaty pockets over his chest for a pack of cigarettes, shaking it up and then pulling out a smoke with his lips, stowing the pack away again in its place. A lighter audibly clicked and Phil recognized the gleam of Cam's familiar Zippo as its flame caught.

He wasn't prepared when those wary and weary eyes made deliberate contact with his own, squinted against the spiral of smoke. The barrel of the automatic rifle swung toward the back of Phil's head now, just above his right ear.

Every hair follicle on his body contracted. He smelled smoke.

Michelle shook her hand from his and gasped something unintelligible. His peripheral vision registered the motion as she fell right off the edge of the sofa and onto her knees.

When it finally occurred to him to turn around and look behind him, he saw no one.

EIGHTEEN

The Psychic

NEVER BEFORE IN HIS LIFE, not even once, had Philip Randazzo foreseen that someday he might be willing to visit a psychic.

What he associated with psychics were those cheesy ads on daytime television for telephone readings. That, plus the faded fame of Jeane Dixon, who had correctly predicted the 1963 assassination of John F. Kennedy and then had gone on to get everything else wrong for like the next twenty years. The so-called genuine psychics he had sometimes glimpsed on talk shows had been only slightly more impressive: big-haired, overweight women wearing lots of silver jewelry and going by a single name, like Rain or Maya or Dawn, semifamous for having worked with police departments in Colorado or San Diego, finding missing children, solving crimes.

But even Phil was willing to admit now that there might be no other reasonable recourse left to him and Michelle, not after that shared vision. So send in the psychics, he had thought, up to his eyeballs in Christmas at Tasso: special seasonal menus and many large office parties in the decorated dining room; bonuses for the staff and huge energy bills; testy diners with frayed nerves; waitstaff with the flu—all coming on top of his own frantic attempts to shop for presents. No psychic can be any less effective than the priest was, he reasoned.

What was odder was his ability to just go on about his work these jam-packed days as if it were the most natural thing in the world to have had an armed ghost show up in your living room. But he had a theory—and had said as much to Michelle—that the two of them now had at least one clue as to the *how* of the mystery: the Zippo lighter.

When Cam left it in the house like he was supposed to, Phil pointed out, like he'd probably done when he and his mother and sister had traveled to Bois Sec for All Saints Day, the cat had jumped through windows. And those rare times when Cam risked discovery and carried it with him, secretly, to school or elsewhere, were likely the same occasions that phenomena ceased in the house altogether.

These phenomena don't require Cam's presence, Phil put it all together in his mind while making out paychecks at Tasso that Sunday evening. But they do require that lighter, is my hypothesis. And if I can ever separate him from it for long enough, I can test it.

"IT WAS IN ADRIEN'S POCKET when he died," Michelle confirmed, as Phil drove them both to Texas Avenue in Kenner on the following Monday afternoon for their appointment. "When the hospital people handed over all of Adrien's personal effects to me that night, and Cam noticed the lighter on my dresser a week or so later and asked me for it as a keepsake, well, how could I say no? Adrien had been so careful with it around the kids, rarely letting them even touch it—he had a thing about kids and flammable stuff. I wasn't sure if he would've wanted Cam to have it now.

"So I'd have much preferred Cam to choose the watch or religious medal. But he saw that old lighter in use every single day of his life with his dad, and the memories must go very deep."

"But don't you see, doll," said Phil, "that this is exactly what I'm talking about? Some object so deeply associated with a death that it's been imprinted somehow, and can sort of generate the images or act as a channel." He braked at a traffic light, glad that today was Monday and that there would be no Tasso tonight. He had no idea

how he'd be feeling later. "If we get rid of it, Shell, it's a pretty safe
bet that we'll also be rid of this haunting, or whatever it is."

"A haunted Zippo," she muttered and sighed. "Zowie."

"Well, I've never heard of ghosts appearing in mirrors, either.
I didn't think they could make any kind of reflection, from what
I've always heard."

"That's vampires, honey. I've yet to marry a vampire."

They rode in silence for a while, tires humming on the asphalt,
and he considered Cam and Nicole out there across the lake now
with his own sons and daughter. He suddenly wondered if Cam had
taken the lighter to the Gaspard residence, secreted in his pocket.
Could it generate the apparitions way over there in Mandeville,
away from Michelle's proximity or Phil's own? After all, the phenomena did not require the late cat, that much was evident now.

The idea began to gnaw at him.

Michelle spoke. "Philip, I'm not about to make my son give up
that lighter. Not yet. I'm not ready to fight that fight."

"I didn't say you should."

"We don't even know for sure that it's the true culprit, anyway.
What about Adrien's wallet or keys? And his watch? Or that medal
that was around his neck, nearer his heart when it stopped beating
than anything else?" She began to sound troubled.

"I doubt any saint's medal ever becomes haunted, Shelly.
They're all blessed, I think," said Phil. But was remembering simultaneously: so was our house. "Whose medal was it?"

"Adrien's. Some of his bandmates gave it to him."

"I mean, which saint?"

"Oh. Saint Jude—hopeless cases, lost causes. Nothing to do
with the paranormal, probably more about rehab." She was silent
for a few minutes. "They bought it from that shrine over on Ram-
part Street right before we remarried, sort of as an affectionate
joke, I guess. But he wore it. I thought about letting it be buried
with him, but decided to keep it for the kids. Maybe Nick'll remember it. She used to reach up and finger it while he held her on

his lap and sang to her, when she was real little and just learning to talk. *Zhewd,* she'd pronounce it, for 'Jude,' just like him. Daddy's little girl."

"You left his wedding ring on him, I take it?"

"Well, he couldn't wear one, his ring finger was gone. So what I did was, the first time we married, I bought a man's wedding ring but had it reworked into a gold loop earring. That's what that earring was for. He looked like a pirate but it suited him."

Phil remembered.

"So yes," she answered his question, "I left it on him. He never once removed it, no matter how badly he was behaving or how many times I left him."

HE FINALLY LOCATED the psychic's house, an unpretentious redbrick and single-story affair set back from the street on a wintry tan lawn. He pulled into the driveway as he had been instructed to do behind a very nonmystical Toyota Camry. "Okay, Shell—before we go in. There are like five personal objects that could be generating the apparitions: the lighter, watch, wallet, keys, or medal. Do we subdivide the wallet into its contents?"

"Credit card, driver's license, he didn't have much in there. I doubt it."

"Well, think about this: He didn't show us any watch or medal when he came to us last week. What he showed us, and what we even heard, was that goddam army lighter."

"Well," she said, getting out of the Acura, "you know, if I were him and if I really needed that Zippo to materialize, I sure as hell wouldn't have shown it to somebody like you. Who is interested in preventing me from coming back."

He pocketed his keys and then both hands. "Shit."

"Maybe we're about to find some perspective here," she blew out white vapor and then faced the walkway. "Learn a few things."

Phil registered the neatness and normalcy of the house and shrubbery, a lawn mower visible inside the raised garage door. This was certainly not the abode of anybody named Rain or Maya. Kenner wasn't the usual place you'd expect to find a wizard, either, and he didn't know if that observation made him feel better or worse.

Warren Pailet looked nothing like a wizard. Phil had expected someone a little more on the hippie side or at least sort of bohemian-looking. But the person who answered the doorbell was an inoffensive-looking young man in a long-sleeved and buttoned-down shirt, wearing eyeglasses with thin tortoiseshell frames. Michelle knew little about him, since her contacts in the Tulane University Psychology Department knew only of his casual but extremely impressive sherry-party readings for some of the professors and a grad student he had been dating at the time. None of them were professionally suicidal enough to follow through with an on-the-record departmental study of Pailet's abilities. Yet his name and phone number remained discreetly tacked to a couple of select bulletin boards in the psych offices.

He took no money for his readings and would read only for those who approached him through his psychology contacts, careful not to jeopardize his own occupational standing in the personnel department of the *Times-Picayune*. But if you're checking out job applicants, Phil silently reasoned as Michelle joined him on the sofa, clairvoyance might even be a plus.

"Y'all want some Coke or tea or something?" Pailet asked them.

Michelle shook her head and Phil could feel her anxiety. She was coiled and tense beside him now, legs wrapped around each other, both of her arms crossed over her body. The room was cozy and well heated but she still wore her sheepskin coat. "No," she said, "but thank you."

Pailet inclined his head. "You, sir?"

"Yeah, I'll have some Coke, please. Thanks." Phil noticed a menorah near the front window and it made him feel better. Most Jewish acquaintances had never struck him as flaky. And nothing at all like a crystal ball was in sight. A folded copy of the *Wall Street*

Journal lay on the coffee table with a ballpoint pen and a box of Kleenex.

Pailet returned with a tumbler full of cola and held it out to Phil. "Thank you," Phil told his host. "Look, I've been instructed not to introduce myself, so I won't, but I feel a little unmannerly here. What do we call you?"

The young man was settling himself into an armchair beneath a floor lamp, across the coffee table from the couple. He clicked on the lamp and flooded himself with brightness, spotlighting his curly dark hair, neat spectacles, crisp collar. He made a long reach for the ball-point pen. "Just call me Warren, if you're comfortable with that."

"Fine."

Warren took up the pen and the yellow legal pad he held in his lap, looked up, and smiled slightly. He glanced at his watch. "Okay, let's cover a few of the ground rules here. I don't know who y'all are, except that you've come to me through acceptable channels, and that's all I want to know. If you volunteer any information to me, it could influence the reading and bring in some element of doubt, okay?"

"Okay," said Michelle.

"I don't know what you're expecting. But the way I work, I don't go into trance and channel some entity like Ormolu from At-lantis, or anything like that. So if that's what you're looking for, you'll have to go to somebody else."

Phil found himself liking Warren, if not actually trusting him. "Fine with us."

"Okay." Warren's thin fingers twirled the pen. "For me, the messages come through in visual or aural dream symbology, mostly, while my eyes are open and I'm talking to you. And what I do is try to interpret it. Like, if I see a Barbie doll and hear hoofbeats, I might speak to you of a little girl who loves horses, but I could be interpreting things incorrectly. Like, the impressions might really mean a fashion model who owns a racing stable, y'all follow me?"

Michelle laughed and Phil could feel her relax.

"So," Warren went on, "what I need for you two to do is, I need you to give me negative feedback if I'm going down a wrong path. If you're not willing to do that, then this is all just a waste of time and you might as well go home. Okay?"

Phil nodded.

"Because there's nothing in this for me, no motive to trick you or anything like that. I don't get paid for this. I'm not here to do a Vegas act."

"Fine," said Phil.

"So I want you two to work *with* me, since my readings are a collaboration among my mind and yours, plus the mind of anybody else who shows up here disembodied. So if I get something right," he looked at Michelle now, "please let me know. A yes will do. Okay?"

"Okay," said Michelle, and took Phil's hand into her damp one.

"Okay," Warren echoed, crossing one knee over the other, getting comfortable, putting his pen to the legal pad. "Here we go: Do you know a letter C, first initial, man's name?"

But C was not what they'd been expecting and neither of them could answer for a moment.

Warren looked up and made eye contact with Michelle. "Older man, he's passed over?"

"My father, I guess," she said after a slight pause. "Cameron."

"—because I'm getting a father vibration." Warren pushed up his glasses and wrote something. "He passed in regret?"

Michelle seemed puzzled. "I don't—"

"There was an issue, confrontation, between the two of you."

"Yes," she said.

"Because he loved you very much, but he never apologized."

"*Yes.*"

"He says, 'I've seen the baby.'"

Tears glazed her eyes and her next breath came in catches. Phil, alarmed, took his hand from hers so that he could put that arm around her shoulders.

"He's saying, like, its spirit is very loving and is going on to an-other rebirth, okay?"

She could only nod her head with two emphatic movements and pull several tissues from the box on the coffee table.

"He says he's sorry. He's saying he loves you."

"I love you, too, Daddy," she blotted her lower lids and told the empty air as if she were actually believing in all of this. Unease began to fester in Phil's gut as she focused on Warren and then spoke louder, her voice unsteady. "What was it?"

"What was what?"

"Boy or girl?"

He stared at the legal pad for a moment. "A boy."

She put her face into her hands. Phil embraced her shoulders and then turned his head. "Hey, Warren? You want to give this par-ticular line of questioning a rest before—?"

"No!" Michelle said through her fingers, turning to stone. "I'm okay."

"You're sure?" Warren asked her. "Because maybe the gentle-man is right, maybe—"

"No." She raised her head and dropped her two fists and their wet tissues into her lap. "Go on, I'm fine. This just isn't what I'd expected, is all. I wasn't ready for *Daddy,* that's a whole other can of worms. But I'm fine, really. Please go on."

Phil could not have said which was the stronger now, anxiety or his mystification.

"Okay with you, sir?" Warren pushed up his glasses.

"Yeah. I guess."

"Do y'all know a name—woman's name—begins with like a *B* or a *P*?" Warren's pen tapped the yellow paper.

Michelle looked blank, lips parted. Phil had no ideas either, al-though a roll call of deceased female relatives did unwillingly begin to scroll down in his brain, but none of them with the initials *B* or *P*.

"'Betsy,' maybe?" Warren prompted with just a suspicion of impatience.

"No," Michelle shook her head. "I—"

"Okay. Who's 'Cam'?"

Her voice, when it came out, was weak. "My son."

"—because I keep getting that this isn't your father Cameron, this is someone younger. Named for him."

"Yes."

"Not passed. Still among us."

"That's correct."

"Cam is in serious psychological danger, says his grandfather. Your daughter is also in psychological danger of some kind."

"Okay," said Phil, thinking: This isn't exactly news.

"Ma'am, do you know a letter *P*? Or sounds like an *F,* maybe. Man's name, not passed over."

Michelle looked at Phil now and he looked back at her, into her clear eyes like aquamarines. "Yes," she said, "I think so."

"—because he's very important to you."

"Yes, he is." Her eyes didn't leave his.

"This man," said Warren, "is in physical danger."

Nobody really believes that their hair can stand right straight up on the backs of their necks, Phil thought now, until it happens to them. The eyes of his wife were deep pools.

"That's *you,* sir," said Warren, "because I see this older man right above you, all around you, and his name begins with a *V...*"

"'Vince.' My father." He closed his eyes.

"...Vince is saying, 'This is Philip, my know-it-all son Philip. He'd better watch his step.'"

"Yeah, that's me."

"Vince isn't sorry for anything he did to you, he's saying. Because he disciplined you out of love, and you've turned out pretty good."

This is all an act, Phil reminded himself, this is just a load of slick bullshit. Maybe this guy isn't consciously faking, I'll give him the benefit of that doubt. But he's just guessing, that's all he's doing, and maybe sort of reading our minds, picking up on my own unease here.

And we keep giving him clues, I mean, *goddam.* Just like he's asked us to do.

So he wants me to get emotional now. I refuse to play along.

"He keeps showing me knives," Warren said, frowning. "But not because you're in real danger from knives or sharp instruments, I don't think."

"Nope."

"I think he's saying that he taught you to always keep a clean edge on your blades, and always keep a clear head, too. He says to keep a sharp lookout, is how I interpret this."

"Warren?" Michelle spoke up, her voice very soft, as if she were afraid to disturb the mood or break a spell. "Can we go back to that business about Philip being in danger?"

Warren tapped the pen against the paper. "Do you know the letters *A* and *P*? Passed?"

Phil felt her sharp intake of breath. "Yes."

"Some repeated phrase here: *'savoir faire'*?"

"Oh Lord. Yes."

"— that phrase..."

"A pun on his name. Please go on."

"Philip's danger originates with him. He's the source of it."

Michelle gripped Phil's hand. "Because he's angry at us? At me? Because—?"

"Oooohh, wow—this is coming through very strong," Warren interrupted, his brows lifting in surprise. "Excuse me, ma'am, but he's *singing* to you!"

She blinked rapidly.

"This is something about, I don't know—something that goes, 'My treasure, my pleasure, my love, my desire...'?"

Michelle doubled over and buried her face in both fuzzy sheepskin sleeves.

Phil's hand hesitantly went to her exposed back and began to rub it in circles.

"I'm sorry, honey," she suddenly straightened and turned so that the two of them could make eye contact, but Phil was unable to even begin to hack through the jungle of emotions that he saw there. "He wrote that for me, that song, a long time ago, way back in high school after my folks broke us up. Never recorded—too juvenile an effort, according to him. I don't know what to say. I'm babbling. I'm speechless."

"That's okay, I understand," he lied. Himself speechless.

"*Two* things," said Warren, all business, holding up two fingers on his hand now. "One, he comes to you in the only forms he can take, for out of the body— I have no idea what that means…"

"Go on." He never took his eyes off his wife's face, just wanting to get it all over with now, get all of the cards out onto the table, go home and try to start all over.

"Two," said Warren, "he comes to you in images of his strength, initially, to show you how strong he is—"

"He's showed me," said Phil.

"—because he needs you to add to his substance. You have to see him as strong."

"Why?" It was Michelle who asked the question.

"To add to his substance, he keeps saying. I have no idea what that means."

"Which one of us, both of us?" She swiveled her head. "Philip? Me?"

Warren glanced up briefly at each of them. "Well, a lot of this might be garbled, because he speaks very rapidly and in a rather… uh…"

"Yes."

"English is not his birth language."

"No."

"—because his thoughts aren't always in English and I'm not sure if I'm getting this right."

"You're doing fine," she encouraged him. "Please go on."

"Well, he's saying, like, 'I'm not going to let her be hurt again'—he's pointing at you, ma'am. He's saying, 'I'm not going to let my children be hurt again.'"

Phil looked at Michelle and she stared back at him.

"What I'm getting," Warren pushed up his glasses and doodled on the legal pad, "is, he's showing me, like, he has a very hard head. He's saying how hardheaded he is—"

"Yes," Michelle nodded.

"—because he keeps going like this," Warren slammed his own forehead with the heel of one hand, "and I don't know how that's supposed to be important, but it is."

"Okay," she said.

"—and then he points at Philip here, and says how he's not going to let Philip hurt you again. You and the children. His little girl. All the children, he stresses. *Touts les enfants.* French."

"Yes."

"He's still pointing at Philip."

"And he speaks of the children?" She leaned forward. "Both children?"

But Phil raised a flat palm and said, "Wait just a second here!" as his objections began to roil, out and up, past all mystification levels. "*'Hurt'* this lady here? *'Hurt'* the children? Somebody's reading me as a wife beater or a child abuser?"

"I'm probably getting this wrong, I'm sorry." Warren ducked his head. "I never made real great grades in French…"

"Hurt them *'again'*?" The sound of his own voice made Phil angrier. "What's this 'again' stuff? Damn, I've yet to hurt 'em even once, and you'd better believe I never intend to!"

"Philip—" Michelle lay her thin hand gently over his.

"I'm very sorry, sir," the psychic shook his head, "but you know, it's like I told you, I can't always interpret these things correctly, I never said I was infallible. Do you know a letter *E*?"

"No." His irritation was like a wall.

"Not passed, male, about thirty-five."

"*No.*"

Warren looked at Michelle. "Ma'am?"

She shook her head, finally. "No, I'm sorry."

"Wow, I see a—um—dead body, a corpse laid out on a steel table," said Warren, "and a red Ford pickup, with, like, some kind of bumper sticker. Somebody is being autopsied or maybe just embalmed. Female."

Michelle's hands curled listlessly in her lap. "I don't know."

"Sir?"

"No. No idea."

"—because I'm getting very negative vibrations here, y'all. *Very* strong."

"Somebody else's spook, not ours," Phil finally muttered. "Can't relate to any of that, I'm sorry, no red truck, no autopsy. Unless the lady here—?"

"No." She looked at their host and then shook her head again. "I haven't a clue who that could be, I'm sorry, Warren. My concentration is slipping, I guess. But I can't think who this is."

"No, it's me who's slipping." He put the pen down onto his pad and then straightened and rubbed his eyes under their lenses for a moment. "I've just lost it, I do that. Lost your signal. I apologize. I pushed it too far and I'm getting all the wires crossed. Maybe your cousin or something, red pickup truck. Maybe not, maybe just the type of crap I see whenever I start to run on empty. Well," he stood, and appeared unaccountably tired to Phil in this instant of defeat. His shirt collar was wilted, his sleeves wrung out. The curly hair at his temples was damp.

Michelle hurried around the coffee table to take his hand, and then she hugged him. "Thank you so much, Warren. That was really incredible, *my Lord.*"

"Does it help y'all any?"

"Oh my Lord, you'd better believe. You've given us such real food for thought, you cannot imagine."

He was whuffing like he'd just finished stacking sandbags.

"Well, I lose it whenever I read for any one person too much, that's a problem. It's like I bond with them or something, begin to lose my objectivity or something, I don't know. But it just starts to come out all crappy."

"Most of this was nowhere near crap, Warren."

Phil certainly wasn't going to hug him but he did take his hand in a handshake, and the guy had a firm grip. Warren's eyes, when Phil's own contacted them behind their thick lenses, appeared guileless. "So when're you going to turn pro?"

"Oh, I'd never take money for this, sir. No way."

"Why not? You're pretty good."

"Because then I'd be tempted to tell people only what they wanted to hear," he said, smile fading, "and I'd lose whatever shot I have at satisfying myself, eventually.... In my own little private investigations, what I'm trying to do. What I'm trying to find out."

Phil nodded and pulled out his wallet and took out one of his business cards. "Well, at least let somebody feed you. Who knows how. You come in any time, you and a guest, give the waiter this card, and it's all on me. Including the wine list."

Warren read the card without surprise and Phil tried to decide if that made him seem more genuine or more phony. "Why, thank you, Chef. I'll take you up on that, one of these days. Many thanks."

Phil shoved the wallet back into his hip pocket. "So just what is it that you're trying to find out in these little investigations of yours?"

"The most important thing in the world," Warren answered without irony, pushing up his glasses. "What really happens to us. When we die."

AT THE FIRST RED TRAFFIC LIGHT they came to, while Phil waited for it to change, he took Michelle in: the way she was sitting, buckled into her seat, with her folded and defensive arms across her body, her weary slump. Her silence.

"Honey," he reached over and patted her thigh, unable to call her *baby doll* because it no longer fit. "Shell, you've got to fill me in on some particulars here."

"I know."

He got on the expressway. He waited. "Like everything."

She looked down at her hands.

"I don't know about the accuracy of what we've just heard, maybe it's all bullshit, I don't know, Shelly. But if you're in any psychological danger, you and the kids, and if I'm responsible for it, then we immediately need to figure out how. Red alert. First order of business."

"You're the one in physical danger, he said."

"Yeah, the ghost is planning to whack me because I'm messing with all your heads—still first order of business. You sorry you married me, Shelly?"

Pink blotches instantly bloomed on her cheeks. "How can you even think that?"

"Because I would cut my arm off for you and all our kids, yours as well as mine. And that's the God's honest truth. I hope you know that."

Her lips were white. "Let's not talk right now about you *cutting* yourself, sweetheart, not even as a figure of speech. I know what you're trying to say. But don't joke about causing harm to yourself."

"I ain't laughin'."

"I just want to get home, Philip, I feel really creeped out right now." She hunched herself up into a curl and then unhunched, forced by her seat belt to straighten. "The traffic is crazy out here, Christmas shopping, everybody and his brother on the expressway, look at all these lunatics driving eighty miles an hour..."

"Shelly," his gaze swept there and back, "if you've made any connection between what Warren said—about you getting hurt again—and the possibility that I'm cheating on you or anything like that, I just want you to immediately unmake it. That's just not my style. Guess I work too hard to get into trouble. But you can ask Regan about me." He navigated the multilaned waltz of tractor trailers, vans, SUVs, sedans, not quite fearlessly. Her fears were contagious. "Maybe I have a hard time opening up, but that's all it is. I don't mean to be distant."

"He said you were in physical danger, Philip. *You*. Your actual self."

He kept his eyes on the traffic. "Well, yeah."

"Do you connect that with the apparition?"

"Warren did."

Her voice came thicker. "I'm more upset by that than I am about anything else he said."

"Well. I'm in somewhat of a generalized upset mode myself, yeah…"

Neither of them spoke for some moments. Faster traffic screamed by on their left.

"I guess," she said, "you must have a lot of questions about some of the rest of what you just heard."

"I guess I do."

She was quiet for another mile. He kept sneaking glances at her and finally saw her lick her lips. But then she closed them.

He prompted her. "You are going to fill me in eventually, right?"

"I'm not the person you think I am, Philip." The tendons in her very white jaw and neck were pulled tight. "I'm selfish and I'm ignorant."

"So am I."

She smoothed back her hair, pressing it with both hands against her temples as if it might fly off. "You don't understand. If Adrien's come back now to haunt somebody and cause somebody some harm, it has to be me, honey, not you. You're not the one who ruined his life."

"You didn't ruin his life, come on. You were a saint."

"You know next to nothing about us, Philip, about him and me," the reminder came with a sour little laugh. *"Nothing."*

"You told me, that day we went walking."

"Tip of the iceberg."

"Maybe he needs us to add to his substance just so he can hit the Jack Daniel's for one last pub crawl. Maybe he's met some cute little groupie demonettes there, in the Great Beyond…"

Michelle didn't even smile. "Don't try to laugh this off, Philip, listen to me. This is a big, gigantic, fucking iceberg."

NINETEEN

Past Things

HE DROVE HER straight to the Trolley Stop Café on lower St. Charles as soon as he got off the expressway, having been made suddenly reluctant by the tone of her voice to examine her past in that haunted house of theirs on Chestnut Street.

The Zippo might be in Cam's room in that house, upstairs.

Plus, Phil reflected, holding the door for her, if you need to feel safe anywhere, this just might be the place. Unless you've just committed a felony.

Four uniformed cops sat at a table near the back of the café in tight blue shirts, drinking coffee and talking LSU basketball, their staticky radio squawking, when Phil and Michelle took seats several tables away.

"You want anything to eat?" he asked her, glancing at the menu. "Belgian waffles, whatever?"

She shook her head no. "I don't think so. Just coffee."

"Two coffees, black," he looked up at the waitress and ordered for both of them, "please."

The girl, a burgundy redhead with a pierced eyebrow, scurried away in black sneakers. Michelle pulled at a wisp of her baby-fine hair, glancing around herself at the framed prints of streetcars on the wall, the Christmas decorations, the cabdrivers in the smoking section.

"Well," Phil asked her, "how much of what Warren just told us is true?"

She shrugged. "I don't know. Maybe all of it, I don't know."

The waitress returned with their coffee. It was cop coffee, cabbie coffee, opaque and black, steaming like boiled tar. Phil was glad for the solidity of the chunky stoneware cups, basic and classic, protecting his fingers from the heat. He watched his wife dump artificial sweetener into hers and then take a cautious sip.

"Okay?" He reached across the small table and took her free hand and held it in his own. "Ready to tell me some things?"

She returned his squeeze but didn't meet his eyes. "Ready as I'm ever going to be, I guess."

"So start wherever you want. But don't leave anything out."

"I had an abortion when I was seventeen."

"I've sort of figured that out already." He didn't let go of her hand. "Tell me more."

"I'd barely lost my virginity, Adrien had been so careful with me," she said without emotion. "And we'd already been accepted to different colleges—me at Newcomb, him at Nicholls State in a work-study program. I found out I was pregnant about three weeks before graduation."

"So he freaked out."

"Well, not really." She pulled at that strand of hair again. "I mean, you're talking about a boy who'd been born to teenagers himself. We weren't supposed to be seeing each other anymore— my folks had broken us up—but we were."

"Go on."

"Well, so when he kept saying a baby wouldn't be the end of the world, we could be together openly now, we'd just get married and raise it and be happy— Well, I believed it. And remember what things were like back then, Philip. I didn't have a whole lot of choices, not like girls today."

"So your parents—?"

"When I finally got up enough nerve to tell 'em, he was right there with me, holding my hand. They both seemed to take it pretty well, on the whole. I mean, nobody screamed or passed out. My mom cried some. Daddy could've yelled at us but didn't—he wasn't someone to waste time in recriminations or how I'd violated their trust. All spilt milk, now. It was like, 'Where do we go from here?'"

Phil shook his head. Rubbed the back of his neck. "I guess we do need to discuss your dad."

"Adrien spoke up and just told him and Mom that he loved me and that he was going to marry me. As if that were something they'd be real thrilled to hear..." She summoned the waitress to top off her cup. "Okay, Daddy was this George Bush Texan, a Yalie with a trust fund, come down to the oil fields after the war to grow his pile. He started his own company, sold it to Chevron, and got a top-floor corner office in the merger and a huge chunk of shares. Married a Houston socialite with pretensions and a pedigree. But I was all the two of them ever produced in the way of progeny. So they did have certain aspirations for me."

"None of which included A. P. Savoie, I take it."

She raised a brow. "Well, Louisiana was supposed to be just this temporary inconvenience on the way to more money. Technology for drilling in much deeper waters was a coming thing and Chevron already knew Bayou Lafourche would be a natural staging point for deepwater exploration, what with its shipyards and access to, like, the Intracoastal Waterway. My father loved challenges like this one but my mother sure didn't. He had to bribe her with an old nationally registered historic sugar plantation house to get her to move."

"I'm still thinking major culture shock for all of y'all..."

"Well, yeah, we'd known there wouldn't be any country clubs, no private schools—except for Catholic ones—but Daddy always believed in being close to the wellhead, you know? He didn't figure it'd take him much more than a year to get everything up and running, so we still kept our house in River Oaks, back in Houston. We visited Houston every chance we got, for Mom to golf and gossip and mostly complain. Which is where I was supposed to have been for my senior year, graduating from Lamar. Except I wasn't."

Phil couldn't think of a safe comment.

"This is awful." Michelle tossed her head and her light hair became a nimbus. "They sound like shallow, materialistic creeps, my parents. I'm making them sound awful. Maybe they were."

He walked his fingers across the table to take her hand again. Its bones were like a bird's, fragile and restless. "So what happened?"

"Daddy'd already scheduled us a big European vacation for that summer, I already had my passport. What I think he was worried about was the possibility that Adrien and I might just jump the gun and elope. So he was taking pains to appear just as reasonable now as anybody in his position could ever be."

Thinking of his own daughter Kerri, Phil wondered how that particular position might feel. He twisted the wedding ring on his wife's slender finger. "I'm trying to imagine reasonableness."

"Well, what you do in that position is, you've got to say something like, 'All I ask is that you two kids just wait until we get back from Europe, A. P., that's all I ask. My wife and my daughter've been looking forward to this trip for a long time, son. It's Michelle's graduation present.'"

"Reasonable."

"Oh absolutely, except that all I wanted to do now was marry my boyfriend and live happily ever after on love." She pulled at her hair as if she would yank it out. "And this brings us to the second issue Daddy raised that night, which also seemed eminently reasonable at the time. Like, he wanted to know exactly how Adrien was planning to support me and a child."

Phil blew an unwilling laugh through his nose.

"We had anticipated this. Adrien had already applied to the shipyard as a tack welder and still had all those regular club dates with his uncle's band at night. And he was working weekends— days—at a marina. So college might have to be postponed indefinitely, but we thought we'd be okay." She tasted her coffee, and it had to be cold now. "I know what you're thinking, Philip. My father could've sent him to school and supported both of us on what he spent on lunch."

"Maybe it's not a father's place to do that."

"What would you have done if you had been in my dad's place and this was Kerri?"

"Yank the kid up by his shirtfront and bang his head against the wall."

"What if the kid *wants* to marry her? What if that's not the problem?"

He rubbed his face and the back of his neck again where stiffness was beginning to set in. "Shit, I don't know. Buy him off. Smuggle her away to a home for unwed mothers."

"Well, I'm not sure Adrien could be bought off, since he didn't know how much anything cost in the big world, including himself," she shook her head. "There was this salvaged little houseboat set up on blocks in his parents' backyard, that's where he was living—real tiny, nothing in there but an army-surplus cot, books, his guitar and prized matchbook collection—a real strong wind could lift the whole thing up and down. But what he focused on was having his own room, and he was thrilled."

Phil played with his spoon. "He was above envy?"

"Philip, this is going to sound naive of me, but I honestly don't think he thought in those terms." She shook her head again. "Adrien *loved* his life. He'd been performing with his uncle's band on weekends since he was barely nine, in lounges and dance halls all over Lafourche and Terrebonne Parishes. Places so rough, some of the bandstands were protected with chicken wire to ward off the bottles thrown during fights. Regular gigs, late Friday nights after the games before he quit football, late Saturdays, Sunday afternoons—he absolutely loved it."

Phil tried to imagine Michelle Wickham behind chicken wire. "That would've been a hell of a life for you."

"Oh, but I could've handled it, I loved sneaking off to watch him play at some of the nicer places. We wouldn't've starved—his dad had taught him to do a perfect weld, like, even inside an oil barge, Adrien was able to squeeze into tight places where many of the older men couldn't easily fit, he knew he could be hired on. So if he wasn't going to get to go to college now, well then, this is how we would live and raise our own children. No big deal, no great tragedy. Adrien Savoie was the happiest person I've ever known in my whole life."

I sort of like this guy, Phil realized, and I don't want to like him. It scares me to like him. I have to think about him now and I don't want to think about him. I want him to stay dead. "Yeah, okay, but let's be realistic here, Shelly. Living in some little rented house, stuck on the bayou with two or three kids by the time you're twenty-one—no luxuries, no travel, no career, no academia, no intellectual conversation... *You'd* have been the alcoholic, honey."

"Don't make me out to be some spoiled princess! I lived in Yucatán for almost two years, don't forget. No running water. Dirt floors. I didn't even have Adrien in Yucatán."

He waved the air in front of his face, dismissing Yucatán, her fieldwork, plumbing. He didn't want to sidetrack himself into an argument. "So your father—"

"My father," she expelled a deep breath, "advised us that we were going to need more income, young marrieds just starting out with a baby on the way. So he offered Adrien, right there on the spot, one of those high-paying jobs offshore with Brown & Root, welding and laying pipeline. Making six times more than he could at the shipyard. 'I'm not going to let you starve my daughter, A. P.,' he said. 'So I'll just have to pull a few strings here, son.' Daddy had to lie about Adrien's age and lie about his qualifications, but got him the job. Adrien vowed he could do the work, and he did it well, as it turned out. Daddy was very proud. Lucky us."

"Lucky you." Phil thought he saw where Cameron Wickham had been going with this. "You wouldn't get to see a whole lot of an offshore worker, would you? Two weeks on and two weeks off, or something like that?"

"That's once the rig is built. Hell, they'll keep somebody out there a month or even three months at a time when they're building something. He was laying pipeline from one rig to another. Only guy who never got seasick, including his foreman. And after day three, it was all overtime."

"How much music playing was he getting to do?"

"Well, okay then, we were pretty stupid," she nodded. "Young and stupid. But it seemed like we had everybody on our side now. Everybody who needed to know, that is, since my condition was so hush-hush.

"So!" She steepled her long fingers, gold wedding ring glinting. "Mom and Daddy and I flew off to Europe, and Adrien was offshore, and I sent him love letters from France. On our way home, we just happened to make a swing by Sweden to see whatever sights people normally see in Sweden. And where abortion was legal and safe."

"Goddam."

"They had to've had it all rehearsed. I'm pro-choice, but they didn't let me choose. Once we got checked into our hotel suite in Stockholm, they began to double-team me right off. It was like... I don't know... I guess like these deprogramming sessions that parents of religious cult members do now, kidnapping their own kids and then brainwashing them day and night." Her free hand groped for napkins. "I'm sorry, Philip. I promised myself I wouldn't bawl like this in a public place..."

"Here." He unfolded a napkin for her. "It's okay."

"I didn't know much about abortion, honey. It wasn't legal in the U.S. and I didn't know anybody who had ever had one. So when my own mother and father kept harping on it and *hammering* on me this way, telling me how it would all be for the best... how I could still go on to college in the fall and pledge Kappa Kappa Gamma, how Adrien himself would be able to pursue his own education... Mom screaming that if this were really and truly *true love* that the two of us would still be interested in each other after our college graduations and then would be able to start married life off on the right foot…

"And then Daddy changed tactics, about how I was still only seventeen, not of legal age yet. How he could have Adrien arrested for statutory rape or something—"

"Christ."

"I caved," she said. "I just caved."

"What happened when you got home? When you told A. P.?"

"Oh, he wasn't there when we got back," her voice took on an edge, "since he was still stuck out there in the Gulf welding fucking pipeline, remember. I had to tell him by letter."

"Oboy."

"Yeah, so maybe that wasn't the best way, but there was some real urgency involved here, Philip. He did need to know as soon as possible so that he could unmake some plans. I put a really great spin on everything, like how it was all for the best, blah blah blah, we could both go on to college now and I could pledge Kappa. All the upbeat shit my parents had force-fed me."

A cluster of brown coffee grounds remained at the bottom of Phil's cup. "He didn't take the news all that well, I imagine."

"*Oh Lord.* Completely inexplicable to him, like I'd had a sex change."

"You should've lied. Just told him you'd miscarried."

"That's sort of what I implied, I'm not an idiot," she said. "But he was too intelligent, Philip, too good at putting two and two together. He could tell something was really, really wrong."

"So y'all went on to college."

"Well, *I* did." She leaned back in her straight chair and put her hands in her lap. "It was too late for him to reclaim that work-study arrangement he'd had with Nicholls State."

"What about the you-and-him thing? Was that over, too?"

"In his eyes, yes." She looked down. "In his eyes he'd been totally repudiated, rejected on about every level you can reject a man. It took me a while to realize that—I was just so naive. So when I never heard from him, after my first letter, I wrote him again: 'Baby, I still love you. Baby, let's talk this over.' And again. And again. He sent all my letters back unopened," her voice lost strength, "from then on."

The waitress freshened their cups in passing, a vapor trail of steam following her back to the coffee machine at the bar.

"Well," Phil began, looking out through the slats of the window blinds at the gray sky. He was unable to add to this beginning.

"But wait, it gets worse," she said.

He waited.

"Since he had no student deferment now, and since he was already eighteen, and since he wasn't anybody's father and breadwinner, he got drafted."

IS THIS HOW WE LOOK TO GOD, if there is one? Phil wondered after a long silence that he didn't know how to fill. Our lives all of a piece, lucky or unlucky, woven around some pattern that we can't detect, with a dominant theme, a dominant texture?

"It happened so fast, and I know that Daddy never meant for it to happen." Her long fingers tore paper napkins into strips. "He was only trying to separate the two of us. People like my father, Vietnam just wasn't a priority of theirs, except to make damn sure it got fought. College, political connections, the old-boy network—the draft just didn't exist for their sons. But Adrien—my Lord, he was so bright, so aware, he had to have seen it coming, Philip. He must've been terrified."

She took up her coffee again. The cup reached her lower lip and paused there. "While I was JYA in Spain my junior year, I got this letter from Delphine Savoie, Adrien's mother, totally out of the blue. She made it newsy, this and that, real offhand. I was pretty surprised to hear from her, after several years of no contact at all between our families.

"But okay, I read it through a couple of times and it was obvious that her real motive was to get me to contact Adrien, who was back in the States now but not doing real well, apparently. I mean, she didn't come right out and say that, she just alluded to a few unspecified wounds sustained during his tour of duty, plus some sort of recent bereavement of her own that he probably shared. And since we'd both recently been living overseas, he and I, she thought we two might have various insights to exchange now. Take his mind off the bad stuff. That, of course, was not the way she worded it.

"So here I am in Madrid, in the middle of a torrid flirtation with an anti-Franco communist painter named Juan who's preaching how Americans are fascist pigs. So the last thing I need is a politically incorrect blast from the past."

Phil raised his brows and then lowered them.

She put down her drained cup. "I also didn't care to receive any more returned and unopened letters from Adrien Savoie, so I answered his mother and told her that. But she writes me again, literally begging me to just drop him a friendly line."

"Hmm."

"I finally decided to send him this short, impersonal note—mainly to get Delphine off my back—and mailed it in downtown Madrid one afternoon. But when I recognized his handwriting on a blue airmail envelope in my mailbox about three weeks later, well, I just busted out crying."

Phil signaled the waitress for the check.

"I wish we had a tape recording of everything Warren told us awhile ago," Michelle said, standing. "I'm already fuzzy on some particulars."

He put a hand to her back and then around her shoulders as they went down the two steps and out through glass doors into the gray day. "Your father never explicitly apologized?"

Her breath was a white plume. "He died unexpectedly. Of a heart attack. My senior year."

Phil looked up St. Charles Avenue and then down it, and the air above the sidewalk was cold and hostile. He needed to be active now, to process all of this new knowledge with exercise. The warmth inside the café had made him relaxed, even with caffeine, and he couldn't afford to relax yet. He didn't understand Warren Pailet's warnings of danger yet.

He touched Michelle's forearm. "You want to just walk around for a little bit, honey? We can leave the car right here, nobody's going to tow it."

"Don't you want to go home?"

"Oh, I sorta want to get stuff straightened out in my head first," he said. "Because we never know what we're going to find at home these days."

"True." She took his arm. "Okay. Then let's take a stroll."

"You know...," he squinted into the gray distance, "I used to wonder what the matter with him was. His handicaps, watching him perform. But nobody ever said."

"He wouldn't talk about it in interviews. He knew he'd be politicized, by one side or the other."

The wind combed through Phil's hair, finding the thin places, chilling his scalp.

"Let's walk faster," she gripped his biceps and urged. "I'm freezing my butt off."

Phil complied. "Okay, fast-forward past the rest of Spain. Stop at the point where you actually see him again."

"He met my plane when I flew back to New Orleans for my senior year at Tulane." She stared off toward Lee Circle in the distance. "Looking pretty much the way he always had, a few years older, but still himself...

"But he was on crutches, those tubular metal ones that kind of clamp to your forearms. His hips weren't level and one of his knees seemed hyperextended, and his steps were just lurches. His left hand was mangled. I was so shocked I was babbling, small talk, nonsense, but he acted like it was no big deal, trying to help me with my luggage and everything, when you could clearly see what a hard time he was having just walking.

"—and how nervous he was. We were both nervous wrecks.

Totally unsure now of what to say to each other, how to behave around one another."

Phil slipped his arm out of her grasp and then draped it over her shoulders. He felt the tension in her body like a tremor, like her teeth were chattering.

She took a deep breath. "Long story short: We take a cab to my hotel and head straight for the bar, he's buying. He gets loosened up enough to explain how he can still play guitar by turning it upside down now and playing left-handed with a pick. But is he getting any gigs? Well, no. I finally get loosened up enough after a pitcher of sangria—I'm buying—to ask him up to my room. Where I make him take off his clothes and show me the damage.

"Oh Lord, his poor body. He was barely twenty-one years old, Philip. When I knelt to kiss his scars, he cried, standing there on the Roosevelt Hotel carpet with his head bowed, naked on his crutches.

"He'd been in the Veterans Hospital here for seven or eight months," she went on, "for I don't know how many operations. They had him scheduled for physical therapy several times a week, but it was hard for him to get there and back, climbing in and out of taxis, even if he could've afforded the taxi fare. He had no car, and buses were impossible. So he didn't always go."

Phil had managed to sit out the Vietnam War in Loyola University's Business Department until the lottery system had kicked in, giving him a providentially high draft number. He experienced the stale survivor guilt of the male boomer who had not served. "Goddam, I don't even know what questions to ask. Had it been a booby trap, or a mine, or—?"

"Oh. A big Vietcong offensive, February 22, 1969. Artillery, specifically."

Lowering his jaws into the collar of his jacket, a sudden victim of the wind, Phil recognized his own fortunate noncombatant history as an additional reason for A. P. Savoie to resent him. The idea chilled him, the idea and the weather, and he remembered the black stare of that kid soldier now, the sizing-up stance. Were those dead eyes somehow still watching him right at this very minute, even out here?

"I cannot begin to imagine…," he said, trying not to imagine what artillery could do to a human body. "I can't imagine living through anything like that."

"Well, he was made of some tough stuff, I can tell you. He'd even tried for college again, the first time he got out of the hospital, while I was still in Spain. Got as far as a few months in the Loyola Music Department, here on the G.I. Bill." Michelle stopped cold as if she, too, felt creepy. "Adhesions from abdominal surgery soon put a big stop to that. And I don't imagine he exactly fit in with your typical university freshmen by then, anyway…"

"No." Phil stood still, unprepared for the mention of his own alma mater. And found himself suddenly compelled to scan through memories of Loyola's green lawns and handsome bricked Gothic archways for an unsuspected outsider on crutches. Had he noticed such a person all those years ago while chatting with Regan Dwyer outside the *Maroon* office or over coffee at the Danna Center?

"He knew next to nobody in New Orleans and had made no real friends here," Michelle continued. "His family would've certainly taken him in, but were in no position to shuttle him to and from New Orleans several times a week for physical therapy. He'd rented this cruddy little apartment on Freret Street to be near Loyola and was still stuck there after he'd had to drop out. Scheduled for yet more surgery. Just waiting. With his guitar, many books, a bed, a chair, and four changes of clothes."

"And he was drinking," Phil realized out loud.

"Well, there was another thing…" She let her voice drift. She looked off toward the city skyline, the tops of its buildings like broken teeth against the sky. "Seems his family found a buyer for that old houseboat he'd been living in, so they cleaned out his stuff while he was in the army. And one of his favorite things, something he'd been real proud of, was his matchbook collection—he'd saved all these matchbooks printed with the names of bars and dance halls he'd played at during all those years, you know how a kid'll do. But his baby brother, five years old, got his hands on it during all the confusion of the cleanup and snuck off and managed to burn himself to death."

"Holy God!"

She coughed. "I guess it would've killed Delphine if she hadn't had all the rest of those children to look after, and her grief-stricken husband, and Adrien as well."

"Shelly, I think what you're trying to tell me is that he had a lot of reasons for drinking, and maybe he did," Phil spoke to her profile. "But what we're looking for here, though, is reasons for haunting: big difference."

"Well..."

"And I'm not sure I buy that reason-to-drink excuse, anyway. I mean, all people have choices. He had choices. He made some good ones, he made some bad ones."

The side of her face was as unreadable as marble. To touch her cheek now would be to touch the coolness of sculpture. "Okay, Philip, you win," she said. "He chose to collect a bunch of matches."

"SEE," SHE FINALLY WENT ON, turning around, pulling him with her, beginning a slow walk back to the car, "this is why an apparition of him as a soldier couldn't be coming from my subconscious mind. This wouldn't be an image of his strength to me, the way Warren specified. To me, it would only suggest impending weakness. I never saw him in uniform, besides that pitiful photo they make for the parents, just the head and shoulders of the kid posed in front of the flag."

He let her tow him along to the parked car. Regretting that he had not borrowed somebody's tape recorder to take along to Warren's house, or at least had jotted down some kind of notes during the session.

He unlocked the car doors and they scrambled inside, chased

by the penetrating wind. "I think it's getting colder," she observed while he started the engine and got the heat going.

"Feels like it…" But he was sure of the Loyola thing now, sure of the memory. Of being haunted there at college before he was ever actually haunted, seen from the edges of his youth by a boy newly trapped in a damaged body and alien surroundings. Encountered by a ghost in the making.

"Sure hope the kids're warm enough at Regan's." Michelle fastened her seat belt. "Cam's always running out the door without his jacket…"

"He gets cold enough, he'll come back and put it on."

"I hope Nicole hasn't wet the bed."

Phil looked past his hands on the steering wheel, over it and out onto the avenue, and everything seemed illusory. Insubstantial. "Regan can deal with a little pee." Three pedestrians crossed the asphalt of St. Andrew Street, young Goth girls in white makeup and heavy British workman's boots and billowing black clothing, live kids trying to look like corpses.

"I keep trying to understand that other phrase of Warren's, Philip, the one where he said he didn't know what it meant, either. About Adrien being able to come to us only out-of-body, or something."

"That's pretty much the way everybody is when they're dead," he muttered, pulling into traffic. "I'm still stuck on that business about me hurting y'all. After everything you've just told me, I still don't see any pattern to it, how I could be hurting anybody. Am I just dense?"

"No denser than I am. Oh Lord, let's just go home, get in the Jacuzzi, and get warm." She rubbed her own upper arms through her sleeves. "Turn on some, like, Christmas carols, I don't know. Drink some bourbon."

"Sounds like a plan." He turned left onto Seventh Street.

"Call the kids. See how they're doing."

"They're doing fine, Shell, you know that. Let's just see if we can give the ol' worry reflex a rest here."

"But we're still missing something...," she mused as they came to Chestnut. "We're overlooking something significant, Philip, I just know it... Misinterpreting something Warren said..."

"For God's sake, can't we drop it for five minutes?" He suddenly felt very tired as he pulled up at the curb in front of the house. Twilight was beginning to eat away the gray day, the massive limbs of the live oaks turning blacker. Shadows ruled. "Look, if A. P. wants to bump me off tonight, nothing's stopping him. If not, then great. But I'm just too drained to give a shit right now."

"No!" she wouldn't let it go, she was smacking herself in the forehead with the heel of her right hand the way Warren had earlier demonstrated. "*This* means something, and it doesn't mean that Adrien was hardheaded. I mean, he actually was, he was as stubborn as a mule. But I already knew that, he wouldn't need a psychic to tell us that."

"Bourbon!" said Phil irritably, stomping up the steps to the green front porch. "Jacuzzi! Heat!"

"'Out-of-body images, the only forms he can take...,'" she quoted as they came inside to the hardwood floors and the Christmas tree and the welcome envelope of warm air that nevertheless could stand to be warmer.

Phil flipped the light switch and headed for the thermostat.

"*Oh. My. Lord.*" Michelle froze to the floor and hit herself in the head one more time, but this time as if she meant it.

"I don't want to hear it."

"He's coming back, Philip."

"He's already back, goddammit, that's where we came in at."

"No, I'm talking about more appearances."

"The only appearance I'm going to concern myself with right now," he went past the breakfast bar into the kitchen to take down a tumbler, "is bourbon in this glass."

She trailed him into the small kitchen area, unintentionally standing in his way. "Honey, listen. He'll appear two more times, if I'm right. It's based on head injuries, this ability to come to us. He can only do it twice more, if I'm right about this. So they'll really have to count. He won't waste them."

He nudged her aside to get at the liquor cabinet. "So I'll get to live until the final one?"

"He'd never harm you, Philip, not deliberately. You don't know him, you don't know what he was like. He wasn't like that. He was a good man, honey. A kind man."

"He was a combat veteran, I imagine he tried to harm his share..."

"You know, Philip, I really hate it when you act like you want me to think you're stupid!"

"Aw Shelly, enough *X-Files* for one evening, let's just have a drink and chill out."

"Not if you're in danger," she pushed past him to the sink, "you moron."

"Nobody said *mortal* danger, just physical danger," he watched her. "Could be just a fractured pinkie."

She made no response. Her eyelids looked raw.

"You know," he took out ice from the freezer, "I can take this danger shit pretty well, I'm finding out, as long as the warning comes from a *Times-Picayune* personnel manager who believes that spirits think in foreign languages and speak with accents when they open their spirit mouths."

"I don't know if you ought to be making jokes about this."

"I'm just making the point that I do see some wiggle room here. Margin of error."

"But Warren was right about so many things, Philip." She began to move, pouring bourbon into the two glasses in front of her.

"But only if that's how we choose to interpret what he said, yes."

The bottle settled back onto the counter with a soft clunk. "So many."

"Was he right about you still being in love with A. P. Savoie?"

"Oh, Philip." She laughed. "Good Lord."

"Are you?"

"Warren didn't say that."

TWENTY

Michelle Dreams

THE TELEPHONE RANG in her sleeping mind that night. And since she thought that she was awake, she did what she always did whenever the phone intruded while she was working. She yelled for Cam: "Catch the phone, Cam, will you please?"

But when she didn't hear the pounding of sneakers anywhere, she remembered that he and Nick were at Regan's in Mandeville, that's right, until Christmas Eve.

Dammit, she huffed, having to seek out the cordless phone by its ringing, why isn't the answering machine on? I'd just let it ring, but it might be the kids.

She pushed its button and put it to her ear. "Hello?"

"Hey, Mick," said Adrien.

And she was not astonished to hear his voice because he had always been alive in this dream she was having.

I've been dreaming that he was dead, she realized now, but how ridiculous. Wake up, Michelle.

"Well, it's about time you called me, pal!" She sat down on the sofa, warm with the pleasure of his soft speech, and kicked off her clogs. "Because I really need to talk to you, lemme tell ya!"

"You okay?"

"Not if Philip's in danger, no. *Is* he in danger?"

"Yes."

"Mortal danger?" Her pleasant glow dissipated. "Danger of death?"

"Yes."

"From you?"

"Through me. But not because I want it, Mickey."

Her alarm skyrocketed. "Then why, for God's sake?"

"Because I fathered Cam. Because you and I could make children."

"Cam is the cause?" This was worse. "You're going to kill Philip just because we had Cam?"

"Every action has a consequence. Every act, every life, is so interwoven with all others that existence is like a fabric."

"Stop sounding like some glassy-eyed guru! This isn't *you*, pal!"

"I'm not what I was," his tone was apologetic. "I'm sorry."

"You're not going to make me do a *Sophie's Choice* thing, are you?" She was scared. She trusted the man he had once been but did not know what he was now. "Like, choose between Philip and Cam, one lives and one dies?"

"No. Nothing like that." But he still sounded forbiddingly formal. "The choice is not yours to make."

He was himself, and yet not. He was more than himself.

"So where does your own free will appear in all of this?" she asked him.

Static crackled on the line for a long moment. "I don't know. That's what I'm trying to find out."

Whatever he was, she realized how deeply she missed him. An empty place opened up in her chest. "Where are you?"

"I can't explain."

"Can you be yourself again for me?" Her nails were white where her fingertips pressed into the plastic of the telephone. "Just for a few minutes? Because we never—"

"Yeah, I know. Never got to say good-bye, or nothin'..."

"Yes. That's just how I feel."

"But I kept trying like hell to get through to you that night, Christ, babe!" She heard him draw breath. "Shit, I tried every-thing—audio, video, smell-o-grams…I guess I was just too much of a beginner at this, and you were in such a negative state of mind, you and Cam both, and little Nick so young…"

"That's putting it mildly," she sniffled and then laughed in both sorrow and gratitude, recognizing him: just him now. Just plain him.

"See, it isn't like your AT&T, you hardly ever get any kind of clear line out of here," he spoke very fast like someone with too much to tell and not enough time to tell it. "Nick—she can some-times pick me up, mainly because she doesn't know she isn't sup-posed to. And you, you're happy now that you've got Phil, so you're not so negative anymore. You got a few open channels of your own now. But Cam's still locked up, real defensive and all. *Man,* he won't open himself, talk about negative."

What had been said earlier about Cam, what was that again? Cam and Philip? I must be getting old, thought Michelle, my mind is going. "But I know how much Cam would dearly love to hear from you, pal. He's envious of Nicole's cat dream, I think."

"Yeah, but see—she isn't all guilt-ridden like you and Cam are. She hasn't convicted herself of anything. She's too young to be afraid that her perceptions of me are just wishful thinking on her part. So she lets me come through. But Cam—no way he's gonna let me, babe. He thinks he's wide-open, but he isn't."

"He's hurting, Adrien. He's a mess. He needs you."

The conversation paused for a moment. Michelle felt almost as if she had just typed in new information to her computer and had hit Save, sensing the response of its processing hard drive. Then: "Well, get him to turn on all that video game stuff sometime, just leave it on but don't play it, and maybe I can come in on that line, I don't know. Give me something new to try, at least. Can't hurt."

"How's Hendrix?" she asked. "Was Nick's dream really true?"

"Oh, he's fine. Fat."

"So he's really there?"

"I don't know of any way to explain this, Mickey, so you'd understand— Lemme think a sec." He paused. "Listen, why don't we just say that he's here and let it go at that? 'Cause you'll see for yourself one day soon enough, for real."

"And will you be there? To meet me?"

His tone warmed further. "Babe, I'll already have you by the hand."

"I wish I could see you," she stifled emotion. "The *real* you, not just some apparition you show to us like some old vacation snapshot."

"Then put down the phone," he said after a moment, "and come outside."

An electric thrill shot right through her. "Are you kidding?"

"Ain't my style."

"Where are you?"

"On your front porch." He sounded a little out of breath now, as if he had just completed a very fast walk.

"Will I recognize you?" She was apprehensive, suddenly, beginning to realize that there was something kind of odd about this whole exchange.

"Yeah, I'm—let's see—I appear to be about thirty years old. Got all my fingers and toes."

That did it for her. "I need to see this."

"Then come on."

"Don't scare me or anything," she pleaded, her heart bumping, "because I don't want to see a ghost or anything uncanny, pal, I'm not ready for more of that."

"Hell, babe, I'm only me. Come on."

"Okay." She thumbed the phone's off button and stood.

SHE SAW THROUGH the curtained glass panel in the door that somebody ordinary was on the porch, standing with thumbs hooked in pockets, looking off across Chestnut Street and waiting.

She undid the lock and then opened the door with a jerk.

He turned around, a breeze kicking up his dark hair, looking like he'd just gotten out of bed after a late-night gig and was dressed for hanging out at home—jeans, gray T-shirt—unshaven, sleepy-lidded. "Hey," he said, wiping his old sneakers on the welcome mat. "Real nice neighborhood, by the way."

This is only a dream, warned her subconscious, even as she seized him in profound relief and registered the density of his body. There was nothing supernatural in his scent—just tobacco and patchouli—or in the way his neck felt to her lips. He tasted salty. "You're real," she said, "oh my Lord!"

"Yep." There was such tenderness for her in his face. He stepped back from her a little way and held up his left hand for her inspection. "And look: all healed."

She examined the palm, felt down the length of each intact digit, and then touched the knuckles on the back, rubbing her fingertips over uncoiling veins.

"Don't even have scar tissue now." He laced his fingers through hers as if he were asking her to dance, flexing his knees, dimples beginning to dent the tops of his cheeks. "Smooth all over as a baby's butt, I swear to God. Want to see?"

"No," she said, flustered. "I can't now. I'm married to Philip now, pal."

"Hell, I'm thirty years old, babe. When I'm thirty, you don't even know Phil exists yet."

"But *I'm* not thirty, Adrien."

"Come here." He took her by the hand and pulled her inside the house and it became their old apartment in New York. "Look, Mick. Here we are."

He steadied her in front of the big blotched mirror over the sofa covered by the Indian-print bedspread, centering her in the oval reflection with hands on her shoulders. She saw herself in the silvered glass, her own long and light hair, familiar face, unwrinkled flesh around the eyes. He stood beside her, no taller, fitting her perfectly. "Here we are, Mick: thirty. Cam isn't born yet, let alone Nicole. Phil Randazzo is way down in New Orleans happily married to Regan Dwyer, and he's never even heard of you."

She put a hand to her cheek and felt disoriented but she knew where she was: home.

"Here's the way we should've been," he said. "Got my shit together. Sober. Don't even smoke dope."

"Healed, is what you are," she corrected. "Or never injured in the first place... Oh my Lord, so would your baby brother be still alive?"

"For real. In high school now, I believe."

Her complexion felt like rose petals. "I'm so young, look at this!"

"Well," his reflection shrugged and smiled, "how else should heaven be?"

"Is our first child living in this life?" she asked him. "Our lost baby? Are we raising our lost baby here?"

The black eyes went into a thousand-yard stare. "I don't know."

"So you don't know everything."

"I'm not God, babe."

"Nobody said you had to be, Adrien. Honestly, that wasn't meant as a criticism."

"But here's something I do know," he spoke again after a pause, both intact hands moving down her shoulders to her elbows and then back up again. "You're probably going to laugh. But I still want you, Mick, how crazy is that? I want to make love to you."

She kissed the hand on her shoulder.

They were in their own bed again with Derek and the Dominos on the radio in the front room—"Layla"—and wet gummy snow falling in chunks outside their window there on East Twelfth Street. Her hair cocooned them both in a tangled shawl.

"Oh, my darling," she heard herself say, "oh, my love. Oh, my dearest love..." It was like giving birth in reverse, a drawing in rather than the forcing out.

He liked to take his time, always the artist. "Promise me, Adrien," she kissed and kissed and kissed him, "promise me that we won't ever get too old to love each other like this."

"I promise."

"Whew," she said when she could again speak. "Good Lord."

"So was this the real me, you think?"

"Yeah, pal. That was definitely you, all right."

"So will you believe me when I tell you that you've got to start watching out for Nicole and not just Cam?" he sounded sleepy. "Because, Mickey, that little girl can get into a real dark place real fast where you won't see her, I'm telling you, and I won't be able to do a damn thing to help her."

"HEY, I JUST HAD the weirdest dream, pal," Michelle jostled him, coming out of her own doze ten minutes later, blinking into dim light.

He stirred atop her and said something she didn't catch, his face in her breasts.

"Oh, love—sorry, I didn't mean to wake you." She hugged him and rubbed her palms into the drying sweat of his back. "I'm sorry, baby, I didn't know anybody was asleep but me."

"No, 's okay..." He reached over her to grope for cigarettes. "What'd you dream?"

"It was the future. And I was married to this chef."

"Yeah?" He lit a smoke. Gave her a smile with the free side of his mouth. "Ate good, huh?"

"Well, no, he didn't cook that much at home, as a matter of fact."

"You didn't get enough supper last night?" He rubbed her belly affectionately. "You go to bed on an empty stomach?"

"And you and me, we'd already had two kids together..."

"Oooo-yee-yi."

"...but—" She couldn't say *but you had died on me, pal,* and so she didn't tell him that. She only said, "—you were sick, baby. You'd been injured."

"Damn, and me already low on quality body parts..." Smoke went to the ceiling. So did his soft laughter. He took the cigarette from his mouth with a three-fingered hand.

Michelle woke up on Chestnut Street.

The telephone was ringing.

TWENTY-ONE

Fog

PHIL WAS ALREADY AWAKE, Michelle's thrashings having yanked him out of a light sleep before the phone could weigh in. He put it to his ear: "Hello?"

The line buzzed. He heard no voice. *"Hello?"*

"Is it the kids?" she mumbled finally from her pillow, sounding drugged.

"They've hung up, whoever it was. Dickhead. Least they could do was apologize." He returned the phone to the night table and looked at the clock, at the criminally early hour. "That's sure some dream you were having, you okay?"

"What if it's the kids? In some kind of trouble?"

"They'll call right back if it's the kids, Regan'd keep trying until she reached us. Lyle's a doctor anyway, if anybody needed one. *You* having nightmares now?"

But Michelle couldn't remember a nightmare. And nobody called back.

The drive across the Causeway to fetch Cam and Nicole later that day was uneventful and she was grateful for that.

She had not slept well at all. She felt dizzy and disoriented and wondered if she could be coming down with a sinus infection. Taking a decongestant might make her even spacier, she knew, but she took one anyway that afternoon while Philip loaded up the Acura with all their wrapped presents for Brendan and Kerri and Hunter.

"Not much traffic for a Christmas Eve," he observed halfway across Lake Pontchartrain, obeying the posted speed limit because that's what Michelle demanded he do.

She looked at the sky. "It's clouding up."

"Getting warmer, that's what it's doing." It was warm enough for him to open the sunroof as long as the heat was on. He looked to see if she had any problem with the wind coming in like this, disturbing her hair, but she smiled back at him and indicated that her short cut was no problem. "I like it," she tossed her head. "Feels like freedom."

"'Born to be wild,'" he quoted, one eyebrow up, dim daylight burnishing his cheek and jaw.

A car was stalled in the pull-off lane eighty yards ahead of them and he slowed when he saw it. Michelle felt him begin to brake.

"What're you doing?"

"Not but one head visible, it's a woman," he said. "Give me the cell phone. Bad place for her to have car trouble."

So it was. The pull-off lane was narrow, bounded on the outside by a concrete railing and the vast expanse of lake, no land at all in sight. Traffic roared by when Philip eased into position right behind the car and parked, the turbulence created in the wake of each passing vehicle buffeting the car. As he cracked his door, a semitrailer stampeded by like a mad thing and rocked the Acura on its tires.

"Philip!" she snagged the knitted wool of his sweater, digging her fingers into it at his shoulder. Her fingertips went through the yarn in two places like the claws of a cat, stretching the weave.

His face was both perplexed and irritated. "What?"

"Don't just pop open the door like that and get out without looking, honey!"

"You think I'm not looking?"

"People'll run over you, honey! They're driving like maniacs!"

He stared at her for a moment and then smoothed the bunched

yarn at his shoulder with one large hand. "Shelly, I'm not a total idiot."

"I know you're not."

"So let me go see if I can help this lady up here. Make a call for her, if she needs it."

She watched as he looked at the oncoming traffic behind them, timing the opening of his door. He climbed out during a relative lull. The door slammed shut. Michelle watched him walk the short distance to the other car and she tried to keep from jumping out of her skin, even when he crossed over to the passenger side to tap on its glass in relative safety. The window glided down. But he was still so vulnerable, his heels right up against the concrete railing, bent from the waist to communicate with an unknown driver, just flesh and muscle and bone, while tons of potentially rear-ending powered steel bore down on the two parked vehicles and passed within mere feet of them almost every second.

What did I dream last night? she tried to remember, feeling her fear suddenly spike. Her palms and temples emitted a flood of perspiration. Philip in danger, Philip a fatality somehow?

She undid her seat belt and jerked at the lock, trying to see if the concrete rail left her enough room to open the door and get out, unable to sit here anymore and just watch.

But he was nodding and waving good-bye to the driver now, so Michelle stayed where she was. He straightened, pulling down his sweater in the back, and then ambled back to the Acura with de-liberately slow steps like he was trying to make a point to her. He even chose the exact moment another eighteen-wheeler was due to thunder by to open his door and climb behind the wheel, and she closed her eyes.

"I called the Causeway police." He turned the key in the igni-tion. "They're on their way."

"What's the problem?"

"Generator light lit up a long time ago, engine won't start now after she's pulled over to check the manual about it."

"She should've just kept on going," said Michelle, "if it's her generator, good Lord. Until she got to a service station."

"Yep. But sometimes you don't know what the right thing to do is until after you've already gone and done the wrong thing."

"You frightened me," she told him after a long silent moment. "I'm glad you could help her but I was frightened for you. All this traffic."

He rubbed the cleft in his chin.

She looked back as a patrol car with an overhead light bar approached and began to slow. "Here they come. I guess we can go."

He started the engine and shoved a cassette into the tape player, the Mamas and the Papas, Cass Elliott's satin contralto: "If you love her, then you must send her somewhere where she's never been before…"

"Philip—"

"Just let it go, I don't want to hear it. Let's just try to be normal for at least *one* goddam afternoon, can we do that?"

"I'm sorry," she detected the edge in her voice but didn't smooth it out, "to be such a morbid worrywart."

"Let's just get the kids and go home and try to have a good, bland, normal Christmas like everybody else in the world," he said. "Can we? Can we at least do that?"

"Okay."

"I don't get many days off from Tasso, you know."

He was driving too fast. She glanced at the speedometer and it read sixty, but sixty had to be much too fast for this scary bridge, two narrow one-way lanes stretching a full thirty-two miles across a leaden lake, opposing traffic traveling back to the city on a twin two-lane structure running parallel to this. Vehicles doing way more than sixty miles an hour barreled past the Acura on the left. Philip swung out behind them into the fast lane to pass an old pickup pulling a bass boat on a trailer.

The cell phone suddenly trilled from the console like a demented starling, scaring her witless.

It rang twice more before she could react and summon enough
brainpower to reach for it. Neither she nor Philip ever gave out this
number. Only the kids would have this number, the kids and Regan
Gaspard. Michelle's heart knocked at her sternum and her lungs
were almost paralyzed when she answered. "Hello?"

Nothing but static replied.

REGAN ENTREATED THEM to come in for just a little while—to
please stay for just a cup of coffee—when they pulled up at the big
house in the pines thirty minutes later. She had not been trying to
call them, she said, but come on in, anyway, please! The private look
Michelle gave Phil said she'd rather eat dirt, but he knew it'd be
rude to just sit in the car and wait for Cam and Nicole to finish
packing.

A bright fire crackled in the fireplace in the front room. The
house smelled of cinnamon cookies and evergreen and was decorated as upscale Christmasy as it smelled. All of the crisp bows on
the wreaths and swags and the tree itself were identical, ivory satin
and metallic gold, and the hundreds of tiny lights showing amid all
of that genuine florist greenery were white.

"Look, Mom!" Nicole crawled up into the sofa next to Michelle,
displaying a new box of sixty-four crayons, a gift from her hosts.
"This is every color that there is!"

"That's fine, but finish getting all your stuff together," Phil
urged her when she came to show him, too.

Regan emerged from the distant kitchen with a steaming tray.
A vapor trail hung in the air behind her as she moved carefully toward her guests. "Michelle?"

"Oh my goodness, how nice." She accepted a mug and packets
of artificial sweetener. "Thanks, Regan."

"Phil?" Regan carefully turned.

He sat back amid white cabbage roses printed on chintz upholstery and tried to enjoy his coffee. The big log in the fireplace
whistled. A fire was better than television for watching, almost hyp-

notic, and he supposed that this might be an atavistic reaction in human beings, bred to appreciate the camaraderie and safety and comfort of communal fires since their caveman days. He wished he had his own fireplace.

"Lyle'll be sorry he missed y'all," Regan said at length, offering them iced cookies shaped like bells and then taking a seat near the fire. "He's been in surgery all day…"

"Well," said Michelle, "please be sure and give him our best."

The fire was nice but there was nothing to talk about. Phil had a second cup of coffee and listened to the two women exchange comments on crowded malls. He stood, finally. "I'll go see what's keeping the kids."

Regan pointed to one end of the unfamiliar house and Phil followed the sound of laughter. His boys were watching a video on the kitchen VCR with Cam and Kerri. "Cam!" Phil clapped his hands together. "It's getting late. We've got to hit the road. You got all your stuff packed?"

He nodded, indicating a large duffel bag at his feet.

"Just a few more minutes, Dad," said Brendan, remote in hand. "I want him to see the good part."

"This next part is awesome!" Hunter sneezed and then coughed.

"Guys, it's getting dark outside. Cam can rent whatever you're watching the next time we go to Blockbuster, sorry."

Brendan looked up and met Phil's eyes. "But Dad, just a few more minutes, we promise! Just watch this next part! Watch what Eddie Murphy does when he sees that guy there come out of the door!"

Phil nodded at Cam, who got to his feet and bent to grab the strap of his bag.

"Nooooo!" Hunter protested. "It's not fair! You never let us do anything!"

"Please sit down and just watch this next part with us, Dad," Kerri spoke up from her seat at the table. "It's really funny. Please?"

"You never do anything with us," complained Brendan. "You never spend any time with us."

Well, Phil didn't want to be the bad guy, not in Lyle Gaspard's house. He reluctantly pulled out a chair for just a moment and sat on the edge of it and watched Eddie Murphy pull a gun on cinematic bad guys. His kids' braying laughter was out of all proportion to the comedy. And in the confined kitchen space it was jarring, but he found himself enjoying it more than he did the movie. He even nodded off a time or two, bolt upright, coming awake to join in the guffaws and then falling back into drifting comfort.

"Causeway's closed," Regan told him as she came through the doorway with the empty tray. "Lyle just called."

"What?" He sat up. *"Closed?"*

"We're watching Channel Six out front. Look out the window."

The four kids stayed in place, uncaring and lost in mirth, but Phil jumped up, passing Regan to get to the sink. Above it, the rectangle of window showed both nightfall and streetlights that were smudges. The fog was thicker than Hollywood could have made it. Phil couldn't even see trees. "Holy God! Anybody saying for how long?"

"Until it lifts, I guess. Maybe they'll convoy people over if it doesn't look like it's going to get any better before morning. But nobody's mentioning convoys yet."

"Goddam 747s land in Atlanta in goddam fog all night long, how come the state of Louisiana can't invent a way to get people across one goddam low-tech lake?"

She looked at him. "Y'all can spend the night with us..."

"Can't do that. Tomorrow's Christmas."

"Lyle says the highway to Slidell is unbelievable. Traffic over the Twin Spans is backed up all the way to Pearl River."

He stepped closer to her. "Oh God, Michelle will have a fit."

"She's not having a fit, she's in the front room and asked me to ask you. About staying."

Phil knew as soon as he saw her that Michelle was terrified of the fog. He could see it in her posture, the strained way she held up her head, Nicole asleep on the sofa beside her. "So whatcha think?" he stood in front of her and waited.

"We ought to stay put. If Regan is good enough to have us."

He went to the front window and tried to see something. The house had become an island. This was a twenty-car-pileup night, for sure. His own fear surprised him.

"Okay," he nodded to his wife.

REGAN SERVED THE ADULTS decaffeinated Irish coffees after a light supper of hot dogs, which a drowsy Nicole couldn't finish.

Regan showed Phil to Kerri's room where the two girls had been bunking, and he lay Nicole down onto the soft lavender coverlet amid its printed white daisies. Her eyelids fluttered but she didn't awaken. Her straight brows were like two tiny black feathers.

"What are we going to do about the Santa Claus thing?" he muttered softly to his ex-wife, straightening. "In the morning? For Nick?"

"Oh, it's okay. She doesn't believe in Santa."

"She has to, c'mon. She's just six."

"I overheard them talking, Phil, Nicole included, and she has no illusions whatsoever about reindeer or the North Pole or any of the rest of it. And I do think that a little girl her age should have a few illusions, call me old-fashioned..."

"Ours all did," he remembered. "Brendan writing all those Santa letters..."

Her profile appeared just off his right shoulder. "She's really such an odd little thing, isn't she? So matter-of-fact and undemanding, sometimes I don't even notice she's around when she's been right under my feet the whole time, drawing pictures for hours."

"She sure can draw, though. She's a prodigy. Her father was a prodigy."

Regan's tone became unsure. "Well, Lyle sort of thinks it looks dissociative sometimes, what she does. Not completely mentally healthy, in his opinion."

"Just what the hell business does a cardiac surgeon have, diagnosing stuff like mental illness?"

"Oh, Phil," Regan sighed. "Here you go."

"I don't even know my own kids anymore, they've been so Lyle-ized."

"Don't ruin everybody's evening. *Please.* I don't deserve one of your lectures."

He remembered himself. Remembered her generosity. "I'm sorry. Hey."

"Please." Her long painted nails touched him. "We need to get back out front."

Kerri, matchbook in hand, was trying to get at least one of a trio of ivory candles lit atop an end table near the sofa. She was on her fourth crumpled and ruined cardboard match. Her last.

"Dad?" she turned when she saw him. "You got any matches?"

"What?"

"Matches?"

"No, smoking's never been a real great career move for chefs, sweetheart. Ruins your sense of smell."

"Michelle?" His daughter's head swiveled.

"Kerri, the candles are real pretty, just like they are," he said when Michelle shook her head no and shrugged her shoulders in apology.

"But Mom said I could light them." Her pink face pleaded. "They're scented, all-natural vanilla—they smell really, *really* good. But mainly if they're burning."

"Cam!" Phil called over to his stepson who was examining a Game Boy that Brendan had just unwrapped. "You got that lighter on you, by any chance?"

The boy's straight brows lifted and disappeared beneath his long bangs. "Sir?"

And Phil realized that he deeply wanted to know the answer to this particular question. He gulped at his Irish coffee and then licked cream from his lips. "That Zippo of your dad's. You bring it with you?"

Cam shook his head no, after a longish pause. "Mom says to leave it at home. So I won't get into trouble anywhere."

"Well, that's good. She's right."

Cam still gave Phil an odd look, as if he had been asked some trick question designed to entrap him.

Phil ended his misery. "Cam, that's fine, you've done the right thing here, don't worry. Kerri just wants to light some candles."

"Mom?" Kerri headed for the kitchen in her quest, long straight brown hair swinging from side to side over her shoulder blades.

The sounds of Kerri and Regan conversing in the kitchen floated out to him now in remote non sequiturs. Faraway cabinets opened and closed without haste, and Phil glimpsed cottony white through the large front window. He felt sudden deep gratitude for being indoors like this tonight and out of the Acura and off the roads.

It was that gratitude, coupled with this big cheery fire and several Irish coffees, but also it was the knowledge that the Zippo was home on faraway Chestnut Street that made him come suddenly unwound. His spine and arms and legs went comfortably limp, like one of those huge Macy's Thanksgiving Day Parade balloons with its helium unstoppered. He stretched both arms high over his head and leaned back among the sofa cushions, unflexing his tender knees.

Michelle rubbed his thigh. "Looks like you're enjoying yourself," she said.

He took up her hand and kissed its fingertips. "Just relaxing."

"You need to do that more, honey."

"Don't always have the time and place," he said, and let it go at that.

Kerri finally got the candles lit and they did smell good, and so did that evergreen tree, radiating bracing outdoorsiness from somewhere north of south Louisiana. The three boys disappeared into Brendan's and Hunter's wing of the house where they could make

noise and play video games, but Kerri and her mother got comfortable around the fire, Kerri with hot chocolate, Regan with something stronger. Soft carols played from hidden sound speakers in
traditional music arrangements, none of that *boom-chucka-boom* up-
dated holiday sound.

He must have been smiling at Michelle with his mouth open
because he saw her lips part now in a pleasant question. "I'm sorry,
honey, you were saying—?"

He shrugged. "Wasn't saying anything."

"How many coffees have you had?"

"Too many, I know. I'm sorry."

"Y'all want to watch TV?" Regan pointed at the large blank
gray-green screen midway up the tall bookcases. "*A Christmas Carol*
is on, I think...Tiny Tim on his little crutch and the Ghost of
Christmas Past—"

"No," both Phil and Michelle said in unison.

"Or we could play cards..."

Phil put down his glass, stood, and stretched. "Ladies, I'm
about ready to turn in and just call it a night."

"Me, too." Michelle crossed the floor to give Kerri and then
Regan one of those quick hugs. "Regan, it's been such a pleasure,
hon, thanks so much for letting us crash here."

"Oh, you're welcome. You're very welcome," she said, and Phil
could tell that she meant it. "Let me show y'all to the guest room
and get you some clean towels—"

"Night, Dad," Kerri came over to give him a little bear hug. "I
hope you'll sleep real good."

"I know I will, sweetheart," he said, because he knew that he
would. He was comfortable and wanted happy oblivion and it
seemed like a pretty attainable goal right now.

And oblivion was what he got, until Cam crept into the guest
room at about three o'clock in the morning to wake him with
clammy hands.

TWENTY-TWO

Angels

"WHAT IS IT?" Phil mumbled, not yet fully awake, slow to understand where he was.

Cam's hand on his shoulder felt damp and very cold. "Phil, I really need to show you something," he whispered. "I really need for you to see something, I'm sorry to disturb you like this."

"Right *now*?" He looked at his watch, aiming his wrist where light could catch it. The guest bedroom was black except for the tall rectangle of dim glow that was the opened door. He blinked up into the dark and registered a headache and recognized the dull vertigo of too much slept-off whiskey.

"I need you, Phil." Cam's whisper was as brittle as ice. "Please."

Cam's tone and his manner got through. Phil sat up and swung both feet out of bed. "Should we wake up your mom?"

"No! I can't worry her with this, that's why I'm coming to you!"

Phil rubbed both hands over beard stubble. "Let me get my pants on first."

Cam stood in the diffuse light of the open doorway, bent over from the waist with his hands on both knees, head down like a marathoner just past the tape. He breathed like one, fast and noisy, while Phil jerked on his khakis and zipped up.

Behind him, Michelle pulled his abandoned pillow over her head but did not fully wake.

Phil put a hand to his stepson's bent back. "Okay. Come on."

They padded out on bare feet and Cam waited on the hallway carpet while Phil softly closed the door behind them. The boy looked sleepy and wired and very upset, all at once, and Phil didn't care for that combination. He modulated his whisper into quiet speech. "You sick? Anybody sick?"

Shaking his head no, Cam took Phil's elbow but didn't seem able to speak now as he led him rapidly down the hall. The kid was still in his street clothes, baggy jeans and a hooded sweatshirt. He was breathing fast and avoiding eye contact.

"We need the cops? Fire department?" Phil felt a steady rise in blood pressure pounding his already punished skull as the two of them arrived at the end of the hallway and then emerged into the vacant living room where the fire was an ashy memory. Chilled sweat stuck his T-shirt to his back and chest.

Cam came to a full stop in front of the cooled hearth and Phil was prepared for the same sort of wiseass response he might've gotten from Brendan. But it was as if his stepson hadn't even heard the questions. Cam licked his upper lip. "Have you ever played a video game, Phil?"

The unexpected question snagged on Phil's hangover. "Video game?"

"This is real important." Cam's round brown eyes said that it was.

"No. Well, I've watched Brendan play, and Hunter. And you, a time or two. That's about it."

"But you do know what's involved, sort of?"

"Yeah, in theory. I know you've got some kind of little gizmo that lets you respond to whatever's going on on the screen..."

"Well, Brendan and me've been playing all night, Hunter

wussed out a long time ago and went to sleep on us. Sorry, I don't mean to diss Hunt, he's a great guy—"

Phil waved both hands in front of Cam's face in impatience.

"—okay. Well." Cam's chest rose and fell. He licked both lips. "Brendan crashed about an hour ago but I was still at it, *The Legend of Zelda,* that's probably my all-time favorite. It's about trying to rescue this princess in, like, medieval days or whatever—"

"Cam."

"Okay, I'm getting to the point, *really* I am. But I've got to set it up for you."

Phil leaned a weary elbow on the mantel and rubbed his forehead.

Cam's gaze went all over the dim room. He tried to communicate intangibles with his agitated hands. "It's got, like, this plot that you follow when you're playing it, this basic plot, which is sort of a story line. You meet these characters and they give you choices of things to buy or use—weapons, spells, whatever—and every choice you make sort of changes the story. So it's like you're sort of making up the story as you go along."

"Gotcha…"

"Well, you move your guy all over the place—it's like you're above him, overhead, like you're looking down on him from the sky." His breath grew fast again. Shallow. "You can see whenever he meets up with another character or a dungeon or a boss or whatever. And when he meets up with somebody, they maybe fight or introduce themselves and ask him stuff. The way you know what they're all saying is by these word boxes that appear on the screen, like lines from a play. There are lines for the other guys, and then for you, and then for them, and so on."

Phil reached around to put a hand to Cam's skinny shoulder blades, gently urging him toward the hallway at the other wing of the house where all the family bedrooms were. They could spend all night out here like this, Cam holding forth on Nintendo.

But he stiffened. "Phil, wait. Look. Those words that appear on the screen, there's *no* way to change them. The game's not like that. You don't even have a keyboard, it's not like a computer, okay?"

"Yeah, I know. No keyboard."

"The words come with the game when you buy it, built-in," Cam resumed his quiet walking. "That's mainly what I need for you to grasp here, okay?"

"Yep."

The door into Brendan's bedroom was ajar and Phil could see an achingly bright multicolored television screen from the hallway. Cam reached for the doorknob and pushed the door open another two feet. The narrow bed against the darkened wall held Hunter's short body flung diagonally across its mattress with Brendan himself lying senseless on the carpet, partially covered by a Chicago Bulls starter jacket. Cam's own unzipped sleeping bag lay bunched up and wadded nearby, not far from the game console, along with dirty white socks and empty fruit-juice cartons. Yogurt-covered raisins littered the bedspread by Hunter's thigh like hailstones. He coughed four or five times from the bed but didn't wake.

Cam crept in and beckoned for Phil to follow.

Cam put his mouth very close to Phil's ear and dropped his whisper down to mere breath. "I was getting too sleepy to really follow the game, I guess. I was here on the floor, trying to decide if I wanted to use a spell or a weapon, and I guess I must've been too tired or too spacy to notice exactly when it appeared. So I don't know exactly what happened. But look."

Phil looked at the screen. What seemed to be the green coastline of a cartooned land, seen from above, was bordered by a flat blue sea and there were two squashy-looking little figures near a bridge and a building. A white box of typescript appeared below the images.

Cam pointed at the dialogue box. "*Look,* Phil."

There were verses in the white space. Phil bent to read:

CHRISTMAS ANGELS
by Cameron Savoie

What did those shepherds see?
They must have found it frightening
To hear that awesome song
From people made of lightning.

They came from outer space,
Or inner spaces, maybe,
To celebrate the birth
Of Mary's little baby.

Phil read it through twice, not really comprehending, feeling his hungover brain like some gummed-up engine failing to start properly, when Cam touched him on the shoulder and put his mouth near his ear again: "You remember me telling you about a poem? That I recited for a school thing, the night Dad died?"

The nickel dropped. Machinery whirred and clicked. "So how's it fit into the game?"

Even the quietest whisper could hold exasperation. "That's what I'm asking *you*, Phil! Because *I* didn't type it there, I don't have a keyboard!"

Phil kept rereading the words as if enlightenment could somehow come from them. And then he'd be able to go, "Oh yeah, I get it now," and take his stepson back out into the living room to explain the whole setup to him. Except he couldn't get that to happen.

"Who else has a copy of the poem?" he asked, like it would make a difference. "Your mom?"

Cam shrugged. "I never wrote it out for Mom, so I don't know. I guess it's possible some teacher at Country Day still has a copy. But I can't imagine what for."

And did the creators of video games routinely plagiarize the poems of twelve-year-olds? Still: "Who else did you show it to?"

"I don't remember showing it to anybody at all, except the teachers. It was a class project, like, we had to write these stupid holiday poems and all and hand them in. I got an A+, and then some geek decided I should recite it for the concert."

"So your mom and Nicole were hearing it for the first time? That night?"

"Yeah."

"And your dad—"

"—never heard it at all!"

Phil straightened and wondered if Cam had lied to him earlier about the Zippo. Because it was blindingly obvious, this suspicion that they were both dancing around the edges of now, neither of them able to voice yet. But it had to be addressed because Phil could tell from the way the boy had begun to shake and sniffle that Cam was thinking it and pondering it, feeling once-solid earth melting from beneath his bare feet like tidal sand, freaking out. "Son—"

"It can't be! It can't be! He was dead by the time I got up to recite it!"

"Son, but if it's all true—what religions try to tell us—Cam, if it's all true, then your dad still exists somewhere. In some form that we can't even begin to imagine."

"But you see it, too, Phil, right?" The slow tears were coming. "So I'm not nuts. I'm not just imagining it. You see it, Phil? You can read it?"

"Cam, I've seen a whole lot of stuff that I can't explain," Phil omitted the word *lately*. "Now, I'm not a scientist and I'm not a clergyman. But it seems to me, like, if a man did die alone and separated from the people he most cared about—and if religion is correct about this eternal-life thing—then maybe the very first thing that man might try to do is go be with his young son who's counting on him to be there. Even if the kid's onstage in a school auditorium."

"I couldn't write it down now if I *tried*!" Cam was crying freely but fighting it, mashing his hands into his face, muffling his whispers. "I'd never be able to remember it now, much less punctuate it correctly, Phil! This is not a thing I've ever wanted to remember, ever, ever!"

Phil put an arm around the boy's shoulders and stood there with him in the garish colored glare of the video screen and was at a complete loss for words. He couldn't even formulate a linear thought to himself. Exhaustion pulled down at him. He was aware of gravity.

"So what do we tell Mom?" Cam asked when he was able.

"I don't know. I have no idea. That's up to you." Phil tightened his draping arm, bracing Cam's outside shoulder, wishing that he was free to frisk the boy and locate the lighter and reassure himself. Of its necessity. Of its familiarity. All known things were so much more appealing now than all these unknowns, even that known and hated Zippo.

It's a straw I can grasp at, he realized. Because I'm running out of straws.

"I don't know if I should tell Mom." Cam wiped his eyes and nose on the hood of his sweatshirt. "I don't know exactly what to tell her. I guess I could just show her the game, like I've showed you, if nobody messes with it and loses it before she gets to see it, or if it doesn't disappear on its own. Just let her draw her own conclusions about it…"

"That might work."

"I've just got a whole lot to think about now, Phil, y'know?"

"That makes two of us."

He waited until his stepson was stretched out between the layers of an unzipped sleeping bag. The boy's light hair reflected the bright blues and greens from the television. "You gon be okay, Cam?"

"Yeah."

"Sleep good."

"Okay. Thanks." Cam turned onto his side and bunched up a pillow beneath his multicolored hair and got what looked like comfortable.

Phil's bare feet made two final benedictory steps up to the TV set where his fingers absentmindedly groped for an off switch to render the darkness complete, seeking only to cast blackness over all three boys like a calming blanket, unthinking.

"Phil!" But Cam's eyes showed sudden white, alarmed, and stopped him.

TWENTY-THREE

Christmas Day, 1996

MICHELLE TRIED NOT TO make too much over it when Cam took her into the bedroom where he had spent the night and then showed her the video game screen, because she didn't want to tax his equilibrium.

When her own was so sorely taxed.

And she apologized to the Randazzo children at breakfast for the "tampering" with their game, making out a check to Regan Gaspard for the purchase of a new copy of *The Legend of Zelda,* as if Cam had done to it something inventive but ordinary. God knew what Regan and Lyle thought.

But maybe they aren't thinking anything at all about it, she realized, capping her roller-ball pen. The kids might find it intriguing for a time and might try to download the nonexistent cheat sheet, until they give up and finally lose interest. Because kids always do lose interest, sooner or later, bless 'em.

So I think we're okay on that end. No perceived supernatural weirdnesses.

As for Cam, I'll let him come to whatever conclusions he wants, hell, he seems thrilled so far. Thrilled is a whole lot better than alienated, you bet. When he took me into that room and showed me that poem awhile ago, all the two of us could do was to hang on to each other and be goose-bumpy thrilled.

I'm downplaying it now because I have to. But I still feel it. My heart thuds in my ears while I sip coffee and make inane small talk with these nice and ordinary people here. A modest miracle has occurred and my son's troubled spirit has been soothed, at least for a time. But one person who doesn't seem very thrilled with anything going on in this house today, I notice now, is my husband.

The fog had been last night's problem. Today was clear and much colder, the sky like the inside of a hard blue bowl, as Philip drove all four of them back across the Causeway to Orleans Parish and home.

He said very little as he drove and Michelle had to keep glancing over at him to make sure that he hadn't fallen asleep.

It was still early when they pulled up outside the house on Chestnut Street where their own Christmas awaited them. Michelle darted inside to turn up the heat and then hastened back out front to bring all of Nicole's and Cam's presents from their longtime hiding places.

Philip spun the radio dial in a lackluster manner until he hit Christmas music and then silently went to the kitchen and began to prepare brunch. She could hear him opening drawers and cabinets. Cam passed her to go help.

"Y'all okay in there?" she called out after a while in determined jollity, listening to the clatter of cookware, overhearing and noting Cam's manic conversation. The rather sudden role reversal struck her, Cam the high-spirited one for a change and Philip much more subdued.

"Yeah!" Cam called back.

"Need any help?"

"Not from amateurs!" was the answer, followed by a small crash, an "Uh-oh," and then another whoop of merriment. When was the last time I heard my son really laugh like this? she marveled, piling presents underneath the tree.

Nicole lay on the sofa with a plastic gadget that Kerri Randazzo had given her for Christmas, some kind of little Japanese computer-chip virtual pet that presented itself as a live chick needing nourishment and attention and love in the form of digital reassurance or its tiny screen would go blank and "die." She never looked up, not even when Michelle began to shake presents. Nicole was in a parallel universe.

Can it be, Michelle suddenly wrapped herself in her own arms and worried, that I've been fixated on Cam and his problems for so long that I'm starting to take this good little girl for granted? Her teachers never complain about her, they just award her straight A's and comment on how quiet she is. She demands so little of my time now. She doesn't seem to need anything at all from anybody these days except meals and art supplies.

When was the last time she woke up frightened? When was the last time she wanted or needed a Casper story?

We're really leaving her to her own devices lately, all of us. She's just like her father, smart, creative, capable of existing alone with nothing but a few books and her art, she doesn't need any pampering. Just toss her a crayon and she'll keep herself amused. If she wets the bed, hell, she'll grow out of it, no big deal.

Good Lord, where have I been?

Michelle stopped with the presents and went to the sofa. "May I sit, sweetheart?"

Nicole obediently raised her feet. Michelle sat down and then reached for her daughter's short legs, stretching them out and laying them across her own lap. "Nick—"

"Plug it in, Mom," Nicole made eye contact, her voice low in her chest as her chin bent into her collarbone.

"Hm?"

She pointed. "The tree."

"Oh Lord, what am I thinking, *of course* a Christmas tree should be lit up on Christmas Day!"

Nicole smiled, dimpled.

Michelle stooped to push the brown extension cord plug into the outlet at the side of the sofa. The tree leaped to glory in a sudden blaze of Mylar icicles and multicolored light. Its unexpected beauty caught at her breath now, even though she had seen it lit like this on many evenings. "Better, yes?"

"Fantastic," Nicole confirmed.

She sat down again and rested her hands on her daughter's knees and wondered, Am I affected as a mother because she's beginning to resemble her father so much? Does she remind me of my loss so much that I never give a serious thought to the possibility that she suffers from that same loss, too?

But Nick was so young, barely three, it doesn't seem possible that she can remember him well enough to need to grieve. Yet there's the bed-wetting—although her pediatrician can't say exactly what causes it—and those scary Casper noises that used to keep her awake with dark imaginings. Plus her love for that Casper movie in the first place, what does that tell you? Face it.

"Mom?"

Michelle came back to herself with a jump. "Sorry. You were saying—?"

But Nick wasn't saying, she was just regarding her mother with a puzzled frown between her downy brows.

"What if we got you a kitten this spring?" Michelle patted her feet and changed the subject, since she no longer knew what the subject was.

The small chest rose and then fell in a long sigh. "No, kittens *die*. I think I need some more Tamagotchis like this one, though. They don't really die because they're never really alive in the first place."

"But you were able to love and cherish Hendrix for a long, long time before he died, Nickyboo, didn't you? And he had that bad disease. You'd probably be in college by the time the life span of a healthy new cat ran out."

"The prettiest, most handsome cat in the whole wide world

couldn't replace Hendrix." The Tamagotchi beeped. "I guess because he was Dad's cat. But you know that."

"You still dream about Hendrix any?"

Nicole kept her eyes on her toy. "Yes."

"And is he still fat and happy?"

"Yes."

Michelle had to ask it: "And is Dad still with him?"

"Well, yes…" Nick jiggled the pink gadget on its silver keychain. "He sings me to sleep sometimes, whenever I wake up in the middle of the night and I'm scared. So that's why I don't need Casper anymore. I've got Dad."

You just had to know that, didn't you? Michelle chided herself as unnameable emotion swamped her like a tsunami, a troubling stew of fright and grief and love. She drew two deep breaths to normalize her tone. "Do you see him, Nick? Or just hear him?"

"Oh, *Mom*!" Nicole sounded exasperated. "I can't *see* him, he's not a *ghost*! I can hear him inside my head sometimes, right before I go back to sleep, and he sings, real soft. But I don't get to *see* him unless I'm having a dream."

"Oh."

"People get the wrongest ideas about everything!"

MICHELLE DOZED on the sofa with her daughter's legs across her lap and visualized the military apparition that she and Philip had seen in the mirror. And she knew that somebody in this house would probably soon see another one. And then one more after that.

She acknowledged the small kernel of dread she felt at the very notion of apparitions, at their unnatural mystery. But she also admitted to herself that she was perversely excited at the prospect.

So I'm crazy, she thought, stroking Nicole's delicate socked ankles with her fingertips. But if you can only show yourself two more times, Adrien, then please show yourself to me.

Because I'm not Nick, I can't believe so easily. I crave more assurance that you still live, all the assurance you can give me. Because

I kissed your broken mouth there in the hospital that night and felt your fingers as wax candles when I touched your hand. You know how I am, you know how I always was, needing to hear you tell me over and over how much you loved me, always seeking that reassurance. Driving you crazy, I guess, although you had too much class to ever complain about it.

Okay, so I'm still insecure. So sue me.

But I do know what you were trying to tell us through the psychic, me and Philip. Why you kept hitting your forehead, what you meant by "coming to you in the only way I can, out of the body," or whatever the actual phrase was. Because I do understand a little bit about all of this.

I understand, for instance, that you suffered a head injury playing high school football. A bad concussion. You got upended by a great big defensive tackle and landed on your head, so people in Bois Sec told me and Daddy a year later.

So you were sort of out of your body for that little while, weren't you, concussed and confused? Was the image that Philip saw on the stairs the inner image that you had of yourself at age fifteen the night of that game, benched on the sidelines with your helmet removed, trying to figure out just where in the hell you were?

I think it was.

Just as I also think that you had another out-of-body experience that day you were wounded in Vietnam, only it was a classic near-death experience this time, because you were so critically injured. So again Philip and I see your own idea of yourself, rifle unslung, lost and wandering, roaming out of your body and out of time while you are physically somewhere else. Some*time* else.

And there was that third time, my love, right after we had conceived Nicole but didn't know I was pregnant yet, when we bottomed out as a couple and my then-boyfriend beat you up, not our finest hour, certainly. But what you say you saw then, it changed your life. It saved us. It healed us. You were what—forty? So this will have to be the next way we see you, at age forty, won't it? Coming off your final big drunken binge, blows to the head, beaten to a pulp, both of us at an all-time behavioral low. Philip won't find you so scary then, or so strong.

Oh my Lord, is it really somehow true: Whenever you were like this, those three times, whatever your actual age, whatever the year, were you transported to the future, to me and Philip, and you can't recognize him because you've never really met him? Is that why he's in danger, because you don't know who he is and what he means to us?

Who does this to you? Does God do this? Does God exist? Is this done as a mercy to you, or to me? Or is it a punishment?

And of course, if I'm correct—and I am—there will be that fourth and final time:

The night of Cam's Christmas concert.

I don't know if I can survive it, my love, seeing you like that. I can't interpret that as any kind of mercy and I'm scared to death.

TWENTY-FOUR

New Year's Eve

PHIL TOOK UP A new secret project that week between Christmas and New Year's while Cam and Nicole and Michelle were still on holiday from their classes, the three of them hanging around the house too much to allow him the privacy to pursue his studies over the Internet on the computer at home.

He soon realized that the Internet wasn't the ideal place to research the afterlife, anyway. Too many nutballs all jockeying for attention, making their cases for UFO abduction and alien-human hybrids and spirit surgery in the Philippines.

So he resorted to the public library where he would take a seat at a small oaken desk and get out his reading glasses to consult, day after day, various authors on parapsychology, past-lives therapy, postdeath communications, and ghost lore. New books with rigid spines and old crumbling volumes losing their yellowing pages.

Most of the authors agreed that living people had nothing to fear from the dead, contrary to folklore. Spirits could not, for example, push somebody down a staircase or stab him with a knife or physically harm him in the strictest sense of the word.

But they were capable of possessing the living.

Phil would rub a hand over his jaw and try to determine if an emotionally disturbed widow might be able to fend off possession by a dead husband.

Or invite it, in an extreme case.

You need us to add to your substance now, huh, Savoie? he remembered. According to Warren Pailet, you do. Whatever for, I don't know—but none of the possibilities I'm coming across here in my reading are real big favorites of mine.

Add to your substance . . .

What can that mean, exactly? I can't find much written about a spirit's substance, since you're not supposed to have any. Unless some medium conjures you up and makes you solidify out of, like, ectoplasm.

Does this mean that you're intent on becoming, literally, *substantial*? You making it happen—your own self—without the initiative of a medium?

And where will the energy to do that come from? From me and Shelly?

Substantial. I don't much like the implications of that word.

Substantial enough for what?

BUT THE WEEK ENDED without incident and Phil lost the time to stay worried about any ghost draining his energy, what with Tasso and the approaching new year threatening to do exactly that.

I'll get some more research in right after the Super Bowl, he promised himself. But what I really need to do now is make late-dinner reservations at the Palace for New Year's Eve for me and Shelly, or she'll kill me herself.

Cutting out of Tasso early enough on December 31 to speed home for a shower and a shave was not as difficult as he thought it would be because the restaurant wasn't as crowded after eight as it should have been. Frank and Vanessa and the rest of the staff could easily handle the remainder of the evening with no trouble.

Time for more advertising, he decided, straightening his black

bow tie and getting into his tuxedo jacket. If people aren't thinking about Tasso on New Year's Eve, then that's something that
Tasso should be thinking about.

Super Bowl's coming up in three more weeks, goddam. And
these aren't just your everyday tourists, either, these are people
with incomes big enough to blow on Super Bowl tickets.

Christ, looks like I'm still okay, I ought to get my sorry ass in
gear.

Maybe this'll be the year to add a lunch seating, hire a few more
staff, and open for lunch. New businesses moving in all around us
on Magazine now, people got to eat somewhere and not just at the
coffeehouses. All these out-of-town ladies shopping the antiques
district, not scared to take the bus anymore. Advertise in their
guidebooks. Clear an indecent chunk of money on bar tabs, Bloody
Marys, screwdrivers, mimosas…

Invent a Tasso Sazerac or a special Tasso Cajun martini or
whatever. Get them happy on Sazeracs and make them forget all
about their diets…

Phil forgot all about Tasso when Michelle appeared at the
bathroom doorway now in a short slinky black dress with spaghetti
straps, wow.

She was even wearing makeup, foundation and lipstick and eye
stuff, like one of those well-to-do Uptown ladies who went to the
opera and the symphony, only hipper and sexier. Her short pale
hair was Hollywood-tousled, long, shapely legs in sheer black ny-
lons going on forever.

"Jesus!" he mumbled, startled.

She went from self-assured to suddenly abashed. "Is it too
much?"

"Shell, you're so gorgeous I can't even remember how to
whistle," he told her the truth. Because he had never seen her this
way, not even on their wedding day, this glamorous, in something
low-cut that showed off so much skin and made so much of her
blond looks. The points of her nipples jiggled against the silken

fabric. She wore no jewelry except for her wedding ring and two large white gems in her ears that were probably real diamonds.

It was taking her a while to believe him. "I'm probably too old to wear this now, I guess. Maybe I'd better change. I probably look pretty ridiculous."

"Yeah, ridiculous like a movie star. I have no idea why you'd want to be seen in public tonight with a big clumsy doofus like me."

She lightened up. "Oh, come off it, you jerk! You know you look wonderful!"

Yes, he did know that he cleaned up well. He knew what great hair he still had, even if it required Rogaine near its crown lately. His shoulders filled out the padded seams of this black tux he'd bought at Rubenstein's two years ago for a cooking awards presentation. Glancing down now at a gold cuff link, he smoothed his flat white shirtfront, proud of the flab that wasn't there.

But I'm still going to lose hair and teeth if you let me live long enough, he thought at A. P. Savoie. With knees so arthritic I won't even be able to climb out of a damn bathtub.

But not you, man, oh no. You get to stay forever young in Shelly's memory, cut down in your prime. Enshrined. Preserved in amber.

Or on secret videotape, shit.

"Philip," she said, taking him in, "you look good enough to eat, honey."

"So why are we going out?"

"I plan to have you for dessert," she smiled and lifted a black velvet coat from the bed.

He draped it around her shoulders and checked his pockets for wallet and reading glasses and keys while she patted her hair one more time and took up a black silk purse. Her high heels clattered over the bricks as they stepped down from the bedroom and headed for the front of the house. Her perfume blew back to him.

Cam and Nicole were downstairs in the kitchen baking brownies. There were televised bowl games on tonight, Phil remembered, and wondered if Cam would ever discover an interest in anything as normal as football. The kid was mixing nuts into brown dough now, enjoying the audience his little sister provided, giving her a running commentary like a TV chef.

Cam was certainly a changed person since the night of the poem, spending less time in solitary pursuits like video gaming, frequently going to his friend Gavin's house on Eighth Street during these holidays.

Okay, Phil told Savoie mentally as he saw Cam notice him with Michelle. Okay, you did one commendable thing, man, the poem was a class act. So quit while you're ahead.

Nick's eyes were like big black marbles. "Mom! You look like a princess! You and Phil look like the king and the queen!"

Michelle smiled and stooped to place her long hand across the damp brow of the child. "You still feel a little feverish, sweetheart, you going to be okay here with Cam if we go out for a little bit?"

Nick's hair was glued to her temples in sweaty small curls and her eyes were hot and bright, but she seemed hale and alert enough in her flannel nightgown, thought Phil. "I'm fine."

"Throat still hurting you?"

"Everything hurts my throat," she nodded, "except *brownies.*"

"Cam," Phil attracted the boy's attention, "keep the phone handy and we'll keep checking in with you, okay?"

"Sure."

Michelle called a taxi while Phil watched his stepson pour dough into a rectangular glass dish. "Looks good. Smells great. Whose recipe?"

"Mine." There was a tinge of pride in the boy's changing voice.

"No kidding?"

"Well, I got one off the Internet," Cam smoothed the top of the batter with a spatula, "but I'm substituting pecans for walnuts. And adding some chocolate chips, that real dark semisweet chocolate. I've put in a teaspoonful of instant coffee to give it a little…

um…*bite?* And then I'm going to ice 'em. With fudge frosting. You think that's okay?"

"Way to go, holy God!" Phil was impressed by the improvisation. "That's how it's done, buddy. Save me some."

The straight white teeth of A. P. Savoie shone in the smile of his son, and Phil saw how Cam was beginning to grow into his looks. The boy's pleasure came easy now, unstrained, in the manner of someone who had finally awakened from a bad dream. "Probably keep Nick and me up all night long, all this caffeine, but that's the idea on New Year's, I guess."

"Philip?" Michelle called from the front door where a black-and-white cab showed through the sheer white curtains of the windows and honked its horn at the curb. "Taxi's here."

"Well, Happy New Year, all!" he beamed with sudden inexplicable joy at his two stepchildren, glad to see their faces beaming back at him. He crossed the shining expanse of wood floor with a smacking of polished Italian shoes to hold out an arm for his wife. "Don't wait up for us wild and crazy kids."

"Next year," Cam shouted after him, "y'all two are going to have to hire yourselves a babysitter for the little microbe here because I'll be out on the town with a driver's license and my own date! Get used to it!"

"Cam," said Michelle, when Nicole glowered like an outraged duchess and then began to cough.

"I HATE LEAVING HER when she's sick," Michelle said from the backseat of the taxi as it headed downtown on Prytania Street.

"Probably just that virus Hunter's got." Phil took her hand. "Kids shake off viruses like water off a duck's back. It's old people like us who really get laid low."

"Don't start that…" Her hand squeezed his fingers.

"Start what?"

"That 'old people' crap, honey, or I'll lose my nerve again about wearing this dress." But she was smiling. Her lipstick was dark red and her teeth white.

Their dinner at the Palace Café was enjoyable and they topped off their meal with its famous white chocolate bread pudding. A cashier must've recognized Phil's name on the credit card he submitted for payment, because their waiter returned all effusive with a second dessert, this time complimentary. And then professional courtesy demanded that Phil and Michelle be escorted back to the gleaming and noisy kitchen to pay their compliments to the chef.

—Who is alarmingly young, Phil discovered with some disquietude, exchanging pleasantries with the slim man in white. But then so is Jamie Shannon at Commander's, damn, was I ever this young at Les Plaisirs?

Did I leave Les Plaisirs too early, and open Tasso too early, and miss out on the reputation and stardom that a big famous operation can bestow? I'm rarely asked to do national TV anymore, not like when I was on the *Today* show with Bryant Gumbel in the Les Plaisirs days, several times, and just took all of that national exposure for granted.

I'm no longer up-and-coming. I've arrived, shit.

Shelly was hanging back now, just off the kitchen, checking in with Cam and Nick via cell phone. Phil leaned against a wall and looked at nothing. It was like all the tensions of the past few months had picked this moment to congeal in him. He felt his stomach begin to churn out acid. That second dessert hadn't helped.

Maybe my substance is getting sucked out here and now and leaving me nothing but heartburn, he reflected.

What if it doesn't take a ghost? What if my life has no meaning in the first place? Like my own day in the sun has already passed, and I had my nose so close to the goddam grindstone that I never noticed or appreciated anything or anybody in it.

"You seem blue," Michelle remarked as they headed for the front where Phil could see the neon of Canal Street through the white lace curtains, the crush of underdressed tourists from places like Toronto and Chicago finding this Louisiana winter comparatively warm, the swoosh of buses coming and going on the neutral ground. "You okay?"

He helped her through the revolving door and out onto the cold and windy street. It wasn't until they were seated inside a taxi that he answered her. "Just got a little heartburn."

"Where to?" the cabbie asked them.

"Bombay Club, on Conti," answered Phil and leaned back in the sudden acceleration as the cab pulled away from the curb and nosed into traffic.

"Here're some Tums." She offered half of a fuzzy foiled roll taken from her evening purse. "I thought you never got heartburn."

He popped two mints into his mouth and chewed. "Never been this old before."

"What time is it?"

He held his watch up to the light and was dismayed that he almost needed his reading glasses to make it out. "Eleven thirteen. Another year all set to go down the toilet."

"Please don't get into one of those."

"One of those what?"

"Moods where neither of us can have a good time." The taxi turned off Canal and Phil saw the unnatural lights play over her features as their position shifted.

He knew she was right. "I wish we could just, like, blow off Bombay and just head on over to the Mermaid Lounge and listen to Marcia Ball or something. Go to the Funky Butt and catch Steve Masakowski."

"Then why don't we?"

"Aren't we a little…ah…overdressed for the Funky Butt?"

"But now that you've brought it up…" Her voice trailed off. "I'm just not sure I'm feeling soignée enough tonight for the Bombay Club."

"I'm not sure that I even know what *soignée* means."

She laughed as the cab pulled up to the entrance. "There might be people at the Mermaid, though, who'll know me as 'Mickey.' So this is okay, right here. This is fine."

He thought about the implications of that. "Like Marcia Ball? You know her?"

"I used to."

"Just a minute," he leaned forward to tell the driver, "because we might be going somewhere else."

"Maybe nobody would remember me," said Michelle, but Phil noticed how very memorable she was looking tonight. And he suddenly had a vision of a big theatrical sort of entrance for A. P. Savoie's widow. With people he wouldn't know, total strangers, all threateningly hip, multiracial or artistic, fawning over her.

Yet the Bombay Cub threatened with its own special kiss of death tonight, too, young professional couples power-sipping martinis like the Rat Packers they had never been, bragging about their stock portfolios and Porsches and beach condos in Destin—interspersed with the occasional tourist group having no clear idea why it was there at all, if martinis weren't as "authentically" New Orleanian as Sazeracs.

Phil decided to let Michelle make the call, Mickey or no Mickey. "So what you want to do?" he prompted as she sat watching all of the comers and goers laughing and smoking on the sidewalk outside the club. "Here or the Mermaid?"

"Well, I know I don't want to run into anybody from the old days," she said softly. "I don't want to have to introduce you and explain how we met and talk about Cam and Nick and reminisce..."

"I hear ya."

"So where? Back home to turn on Jay Leno and watch the Times Square ball fall?"

"We have more imagination than that, Jesus!" He pressed her fingers. "Look, you know they've got to have something going on for New Year's Eve at the Rock'N'Bowl, how 'bout it? Vince Vance or somebody like that, oldies night, Frankie Ford hits or whatever?"

"Go *bowling*?" Her eyes goggled. "Dressed like *this*?"

"We don't have to bowl, hey, we can just sit back and drink beer and listen to the band."

"Oh *no*," she grinned, "I'm renting shoes and I'm *bowling*, buddy, you can do what you want!"

Phil laughed and leaned forward and directed the driver to the Mid-City Lanes out on South Carrollton. Then he laughed again—guffawed—at his own dumb and spontaneous idea.

"What?" She playfully jerked at his arm.

"Us."

"Yeah! This is our first *us* thing, isn't it?"

"So maybe this could be a brand-new original Randazzo family tradition, what we're doing, going to the Rock'N'Bowl on New Year's Eve."

"You bet. Unless we absolutely hate it."

The cab pulled into the parking lot where many vehicles were parked, but not so many that there would be too many people inside to make a good time possible. Michelle called the kids again while Phil paid and tipped the driver.

"All is well?" he asked her, stashing away his wallet as the taxi drove off and Michelle thumbed her cell phone.

She nodded. "They're pigging out on brownies and watching MTV, and Nick's determined to stay awake and see it through. She says she feels okay."

"Cool," said Phil, offering her his arm. "So shall we, my baby doll?"

"Cool!" She took it. "We absolutely shall!"

THEY BOWLED for nearly an hour past midnight, Philip in shirt-sleeves and suspenders with his French cuffs unlinked and rolled up, black tie untied. Michelle was beerily amused at how he'd finally forgotten himself in the happy din, becoming thoroughly mussed, hair sticking up in back. She saw how the silk of her own dress adhered to her perspiry skin and could well imagine how goofy she looked in these big tan flat bowling shoes.

But he could really bowl, Philip could. He had unexpectedly fluid form, urban grace, an almost balletic line of energy flowing from his white back on down his outstretched right arm and through sensitive releasing fingertips. Michelle postulated the inheritability of Sicilian bocce ball prowess, swigging her third beer and enjoying just watching him, seeing how he could be overtaken by the moment and finally relax amid mindless hubbub—the resounding crashes of falling pins, the twanging electric guitars of the band, all the bright lights and loud jubilant voices.

"You're *killing me!*" she exulted after losing yet another frame to him, rising on tiptoe to throw both arms around his damp shoulders. "You're *murdering* me, you asshole!"

"Den stop lettin' me win, dawlin'!" One of his hands pressed into the small of her back like a comfortable lumbar support without forethought or possessiveness or apology, there against her body just because it was there.

His face was too close to focus on, but happy and warmer than the red insides of her own closing eyelids. She pressed herself quickly against the slick wet cheek, inhaling cologne, seeing an afterimage of his bodily grace, the proud head on its strong neck, the timing in his fingertips. Her lids opened onto his eyes, amber like sunlight through a bottle of cold beer on a hot afternoon.

That's exactly what Philip *is,* she realized, reaching up to frame this amazing face with both of her hands. He's my lifesaving beer at the end of a long trek across the desert.

"Don't ever go," she kissed the cleft in his chin and then his lips. "You amaze me, Philip. You thrill me. I'm yours."

TWENTY-FIVE

Super Bowl Week, January 1997

HE NEEDN'T HAVE worried about business.

During the entire week leading up to the big game, Tasso was jammed with diners sporting team starter jackets and festooned with the colored metallic Mardi Gras–style plastic beads that every souvenir shop in the city seemed to be selling. Taxis pulled up like clockwork outside on Magazine Street, disgorging Green Bay fans in green or Patriot people in blue. Phil didn't fret about reservation no-shows since there were none.

"Any of 'em fighting it out in the dining room yet?" he asked Frank Favrot on Thursday night when he came into the kitchen from his office, rowdy laughter and uproar from out front echoing through the building.

"They too glad to be warm. Too full to fight," said Frank, red-faced and sweating. "Cold up there, Chef, where these folks are all from."

"Too drunk," Tyrone amended.

Phil's throat had begun to get a little sore by that Thursday, with the virus that Nicole had caught from Hunter beginning to make its presence known in his own system. But he was too busy now and too pumped with the excited crush of diners to feel ill.

Faces he knew only from television stuffed their mouths with his creations and downed his wines. A few of them requested his presence out front so that they could meet him, including one former NFL coach turned prominent sportscaster, and Phil was caught unprepared. It felt unprofessional having to go greet this celebrity bareheaded like this, but he never wore a toque at Tasso. Toques and even bandana sweatbands gave him headaches. His tunic was splotched with a brown pecan glaze for the trout. He knew his hair was stuck to his temples.

The sportscaster, large and gracious, put out his hand and spoke in a softer voice than Phil had expected. He had to strain to hear the man over the euphoric shrieks of the big-haired women at a nearby table. But several of the people in the sportscaster's party asked intelligent questions about Louisiana food and made informed comments about the garlic shrimp, boudin, and tasso gravy.

I only wish Michelle and my kids could see me now, Phil thought. Hear me explaining the one-pot philosophy to this celebrity and his party, and why most traditional dishes begin with a roux.

Why is it people come down here anyway, Savoie? Nothing much to see here except the Quarter and the river, lots of ugly chemical plants next to a few old plantation houses. Rusty petroleum industry shit corroding out in the swamps. Is the food so inedible back wherever it is that tourists come from? Have they been so musically deprived, don't they have any titty bars or sell alcohol anywhere back home?

Well, whatever, I just wish that Michelle was here tonight to see me in my own proper element, man. I know she got to see you in yours.

Here is where I really shine, and I sure wish somebody knew that.

TRUE, MICHELLE WASN'T THERE watching him cook. But he was definitely on her mind. She'd already spent a huge chunk of that week worrying about him because she knew he was coming down with Nicole's virus.

Cam had caught a light case of it and was just getting over it, having missed several days of school. Wonder of wonders, he had phoned Gavin for homework assignments without being urged to do it more than twice.

Nick had bounced back immediately, invited to Saturday birthday parties two weeks in a row now, good Lord—all of these classmates conceived in the lusty month of May. And I guess this means she'll expect her own lavish party in September, Michelle thought, shoehorning in some hasty gift purchases at the Magic Box, juggling her schedule to get Nicole to and from her sudden socializing.

But Nick had wanted to go, and that was novel.

Her mother sat sipping coffee with the other parents at Discovery Zone and could hear Nicole's wild and shrill laughter even when she couldn't see her romping through the ball pit with the other kids.

She was older than these other mothers or fathers of six-year-olds and she knew none of them well. They were all polite, a bit diffident, addressing her as *Doctor* Wickham, as if she was their professor and not their companion.

She had to smile at herself, noticing that she was the quiet outsider now, not Nicole. Nicole was a manic sprite, flushed and rosy, noisy, having a terrific time.

So is it my turn to come out of my own shell? Michelle wondered, not having realized that she had much of a shell to come out of until now. Do I need to begin spending more time with my anthro pals, going out for a beer with them the way I used to? Show up at a few of those parties I'm still invited to? Hardly anyone in the department knows Philip. Like I'll be able to get him away from Tasso to meet anybody...

Oh Lord, I've got so much to do: lectures, my paper, students e-mailing me. Laundry, a checkbook to balance, groceries to buy. But here I sit on my fanny at a birthday party, like a doting young mom on a play date, as charmed by my daughter's spontaneous joy now as if she's just started to walk.

But isn't that the way it should be? What could possibly be more important? Do I need to lose someone else in order to learn about priorities?

Oh, Philip, you diligent sweetheart, we're not going to end up in the poorhouse if you hire whomever is necessary to give you a life outside of Tasso! You deserve it, honey, we both deserve it. Life is short. Who knows how much time we have left together?

As old as we are, we'll never be this young again.

I am so deathly tired of being sad.

TWENTY-SIX

Waking Dream

WHILE THE CAPTAINS for the New England Patriots and the Green Bay Packers stood in the middle of the Superdome field and awaited the Super Bowl coin toss, Phil Randazzo and his staff were already anticipating the postgame rush at Tasso where victors would soon demand celebratory feasts and champagne. Losers would need the solace of comfort food and hard liquor.

It's a win-win thing, Phil thought with deep satisfaction, viewing the evening's capacity-crowd reservations list. Even the earliest reservation slots were taken, a mild surprise since the game would not yet be over by that time. Maybe a lot of them are women, he reflected, football widows, wanting to get away from the game and out of the house, good for them. Terrific for us.

Frank had brought in his tiny black-and-white television set, battery-operated, what he referred to as his Hurricane Special. Both the kitchen and waitstaff had a pool going and Phil had anted up a modest amount. He was pulling for Green Bay since quarterback Brett Favre had grown up in nearby Kiln, Mississippi, just over the state line.

High on decongestant and cough syrup, Phil huddled with the cooks around the small TV screen for the kickoff, shoulder to shoulder with them in white. Everybody was jazzed, impressed by the immensity of this famous event taking place a mere few miles away in the domed stadium their tax dollars had built.

"Green Bay gon whup they ass," said Da'Shaun, "my man Reggie gon take 'em *down*."

"Don't count out the Pats. This is the AFC's year, y'all." Vanessa's voice dropped as the ball was teed up.

And Phil wondered, just for a moment, if the family ghost could see the future and knew which team was going to win.

If you really exist as a separate intelligence, he addressed A. P. Savoie in his mind, and if you're still hanging around, I got three kids to put through college, man. You could make yourself real useful by giving me some point spreads.

BUT THAT WASN'T the sort of information he received much later that night, after he was home in bed and Green Bay's cheesehead fans were still uproariously celebrating down on Bourbon Street.

No. What Phil dreamed of was a mortuary.

It began with him watching the local news on television, just as humdrum as in waking life, with him even drinking a Corona while an anchorman was speaking of a horrific wreck on the I-10 High Rise. An eighteen-wheeler had caused a minivan to become airborne. Taped footage was running on the screen, the white van's remains, upside down, so crumpled and destroyed that Phil couldn't tell if he was seeing its front or its rear. Three people had died in this wreckage, two of them young children. The news camera predictably lingered on a plush stuffed rabbit toy on its side amid broken glass and tortured metal.

The names that the newscaster gave of the dead woman and her daughters meant nothing to Phil but they might to Michelle, since their address was on Calhoun Street, not too far from campus.

He shouted "Shelly?" up at the computer loft above him.

At the mention of the dead woman's name, a photograph taken of her in happier circumstances appeared on-screen—pleasant-looking and in tennis clothes, hugging two small girls to her brown bobbed hairdo.

"Hey, Shell? Where you at?"

But that image was replaced with another before Phil could even finish getting his words out—showing the dead woman's present postwreck condition as of right now in real time: nude, a flap of her scalp peeled away and hanging loose from her skull, one dilated eye open and the other almost closed.

"Jesus!" Phil jumped and spilled his beer, not ready for this.

Overhead fluorescent lights were shining onto the bald spot of someone wearing scrubs who came into the frame of the TV shot and then bent over the body, his chubby hands in latex gloves. He rested one elbow on the steel table, but jerkily, looking at the dead face with no particular interest. What he seemed more interested in was a clock on the far wall.

The woman looked like lard. No blood appeared anywhere to humanize her. Even the scalp wound was bloodless, the loose skin with its attached hair like the edge of a bad wig. Her breasts were dough, nipples purple. Muscles in her face had fallen into bewilderment.

Phil found himself leaning forward, beer forgotten, a memory beginning to itch him like a mosquito bite. Somebody had been mentioning something some time ago—hadn't they?—about some woman on a table in a funeral home. Yeah. Who had that been, Warren the psychic?

Warren Pailet's face came back to him now, plus his voice, but Phil couldn't make the voice say any exact words that might apply here. Only one single word floated back up to the surface of his memory and kept rising and floating, insistently, maddeningly, and that was the word *important*.

"Just got your message, Everett," the television suddenly spoke and broke in on his frustration. "Sorry I couldn't get here any sooner..."

The young mortician straightened with relief as the back of someone else's head came into view. "Probably no hurry. It's our first, I guess you know how that goes. Her contractions are still pretty far apart—"

"But you've gotta be there for the Lamaze thing, she'll kill you. Just run on, I'll do this one here."

"Lady here had two little girls, you know that? Both killed with her. Damn shame. Really makes you think."

"Yeah," the other man's voice was tired and older. The top of his head was balder. "Life's like a bus station: some pulling out, others pulling in. Raining like a motherfucker outside. Be careful."

Everett peeled off his latex gloves, taking up a wristwatch from a high shelf and strapping it on. "Never any goddam umbrellas back here," he muttered and then stomped down two concrete steps and out through a service door, followed on camera. He was an ordinary-looking man carrying thirty pounds too many, smoothing back brown wisps of hair over his balding crown. A new red pickup waited for him underneath the black oak tree limbs bordering a parking lot where rain came down sideways.

Having no umbrella, Everett had to pull his short windbreaker up over his head and make for the pickup in a flailing knock-kneed trot, keys at the ready.

Goddam strange newscast, thought Phil. Must be Sweeps Week.

His television screen began to fog over. Frigid wind blew into the bedroom from an unseen source and the warm screen clouded with thick condensate. He'd never seen anything like that happen, either, and was about to call Michelle again, when he noticed the writing on the screen.

A fingertip had printed some words on the glass, visible now when fogged, like fingerprints left on a bathroom mirror. They appeared superimposed over the videotape of the mortician gunning his red pickup out onto the street with a hasty squeal of tires, a Saints fleur-de-lis on its bumper.

The words said, all in capital letters, HE'S COMING STRAIGHT ON FOR YOU, PHI

Phil read them and was about to call Michelle a third time, but then he woke up.

HE WOKE INTO a high fever, with a raw throat that felt like he'd been gargling with drain unclogger. Michelle lay asleep beside him and he tried to calm down and breathe easier.

If Savoie's got something to say to me, I wish he'd just *say* it, Phil thought, resting a forearm across his hot forehead. Some of us have to make a living. Some of us have to get enough decent sleep to stay healthy enough to do that. Some of us have been working our asses off all Super Bowl Week in order to keep a whole bunch of kids fed.

A deep and nasty cough began to stir in his chest. When it erupted like a geyser, Phil knew that he was going to have to drag himself out of bed to go take something.

"Whassamatter, honey?" Michelle murmured as he sat up and swung his long sweaty legs out from under the coverlets into the cool dark.

"Just got a little cold," he said between coughs. "I'm okay."

"Are you *okay*?" she asked the question that he had just answered, putting a hand to his back.

"Finally got the kids' virus, I guess," he said, standing, making his way in his pajama bottoms across the carpet to the bathroom without turning on any lights. "Tomorrow's Monday, I can sleep all day, I'll be fine."

"Oh, Philip." She clicked on her bedside lamp. Its sudden light hurt his eyes. "Can I get you anything?"

"No." He rubbed the back of his wet neck. It ached. Every place on his body ached. "I'm just going to go in here and take something and then I'm coming on back to bed. You get some sleep, Shell, you've got Tulane in the morning..."

She nodded finally and allowed her eyes to close, but left the lamp on. "I'm not going back to sleep until you get back in bed."

Phil urinated in a loud stream and then lowered the toilet seat. He opened drawers under the sink and found various medications, including the Benadryl he kept on hand for his occasional hay fever. This is no allergy, he thought, straightening, taking in the reflection of his own bloodshot eyes and damp mashed face in the mirror. I look like shit.

Skip my morning run, for sure. Just sleep late, get fat, whatever.

All those hungover tourists in town, looking worse than me, got planes to catch…Shit, makes me nauseated now to even think about getting on an airplane. Quick, think about something else. Think about fresh air. Think about snow.

He swallowed some NyQuil and then turned out the bathroom light and let himself back into the bedroom where Michelle's small bedside lamp still burned.

I'll probably give her my germs, he realized, going to his side of the bed, starting to climb in beside her. But then she's already been exposed. Nick and Cam have been coughing for weeks.

He realized stupidly, just before getting under the coverlets and lying down, that Michelle was probably already asleep again. Unable to turn her lamp out.

Goddammit! Phil thought, and considered just leaving it on. But the idea bothered him, its expense and waste of electrical energy, and he could see the glow like red flame through his closed eyelids. He thrashed to his feet, thinking, Shit, I'll probably dream about fatal conflagrations if I don't turn it out. Have nightmares about the Chicago Fire or *The Towering Inferno,* or that little Savoie boy with matches…

He wearily rounded the foot of the bed, noticing how cold it was. The chill felt good, actually, to his burning skin.

He stopped in front of the large television that sat atop the antique chest of drawers and saw that its silent gray-green screen was frosted over with water vapor.

A fingertip had printed HE'S COMING STRAIGHT ON FOR YOU, PHI in the fog.

TWENTY-SEVEN

Father Dominic

"SO WHAT DID Michelle have to say about it?"

"I didn't tell her."

Phil's brother Dominic sounded incredulous. "You didn't *tell* her?"

"Nope."

"So— Well, what did you do, you just wiped off the TV screen—?"

"I just wiped it off, yeah." Phil coughed, a soggy rumbling in his chest. "Look, I didn't want to upset her. Like Cam's poem."

"I thought Cam's poem made her happy."

Phil lay inert with the phone against his ear, looking toward the foot of the bed where he could see the large blank television screen in all its inscrutability above his toes. "It's just possible that she wrote it herself, Nonnie. Shit, anybody could imitate his handwriting, he printed everything in caps."

"Why would she do that? And if she wrote it herself, how'd she fog up the screen?"

"Nonnie," said Phil, "Cam could be pulling something."

"Could Cam get you to have the nightmare?" Dominic's nose whistled into the receiver as he breathed and then paused. "Phil, listen. This has all the earmarks of a genuine psychic experience of some kind."

"Yeah, well, what if I'm pretty tired of psychic experiences?" He was unable to tell how much of the heat that was causing him to kick off the blankets now was fever and how much was ire. "It's worrying about all of these psychic experiences that has me flat on my ass now. I haven't lived one single day with anything like peace of mind since November, Nonnie, it's always *Tales From the Crypt* around here, and I'm sick of the whole damned thing. Literally sick."

"You had the opportunity to obtain fingerprints," his brother sounded agitated at the idea, "and you wiped them off."

"You bet."

"And what if they were provably genuine? What if they were really his?"

"Just what the hell kind of priest are you anyway, Nonnie? What kind of voodoo seminary did you go to?"

"Seminary taught me to both hope for and believe in eternal life," Dominic answered. "I was taught to watch for miracles but to demand proof. Jesuits are big on free will, perhaps even that of disembodied spirits. And we're real big on proof."

"Proof."

"Notice, too, that the topic of our conversation here also touches upon eternal life."

"Aww bullshit, I've done some reading…" Phil rubbed his greasy face with the palm of his free hand. "I've read up on how disturbed adolescents can generate poltergeist activity. Cam Savoie is enough to generate a whole horror movie festival."

"Phil, what you've got over there is much more than a poltergeist and you know it."

He had a great comeback all ready but a coughing fit robbed him of it. He had to sit up and reach for the carafe of water on the night table that Michelle had left for him. He washed down more medication while he was at it.

"Think this through, Phil. What if you're being warned about something dire? Your own death?"

"Oh yeah, like Savoie's going to warn me."

"Well, for Michelle's sake he might want to. For his children's sake, since they're becoming attached to you."

Phil coughed again. "According to that psychic we visited, the danger comes from Savoie. It originates with him. So why would he warn me? That makes no sense."

"Didn't the TV thing scare you at all?"

"I'm terrified!" Phil shouted into the phone. "Some overweight undertaker is after me, I'm fucking *terrified,* Nonnie, what do you want me to say?"

"'Adding to his own substance'... maybe it's an inadvertent sort of harm, like a parasite killing its host. Perhaps it's something that Savoie can't help."

"No, I think he enjoys keeping all of us fixated on him, just like in life, it's this power thing. Keeping Michelle and the kids and me fixated. Because it's always been all about him. That marriage to Shelly was all about him. He jerks our chains, we dance."

"Dance how?"

"Well, we fixate! Thinking about him! Talking to him, like he can see me! I can't help it, I do it automatically, Nonnie. Like talking to myself, only I'm talking to him instead, sometimes. Maybe he gets off on it someway, how the hell should I know?"

"But is *fixation* the correct terminology here? Addressing him in your mind..." Dominic took a long breath. "What if the term we should be using here is more like—God help me—*prayer?*"

Phil had an urge to just fastball the cordless phone at the TV screen. "Don't even think it, Nonnie. This guy was no kind of saint, lemme tell ya. Take my word for it."

"Who are you to be speaking for God?" The priest's voice was mild. "In the eyes of the church you're still married to Regan. In the eyes of the church, Phil, you're an adulterer. So who speaks for God? Just what is it that you want from me?"

"Shit, I don't know."

"Why did you call?"

"Guess I just wanted to see what you'd think," said Phil. "About the TV and stuff."

"Look—off the record," said Dominic, "metaphysics may not be what dogma would have us believe. So I'm not talking saints and demons, I'm talking disembodied intelligence, something living and acting in, like, four dimensions—or six, or ten—when we're stuck here in the body in only three, Filbert. It may be difficult for such an intelligence to focus its concentration upon us and our limited time frame, to narrow itself down enough. Like trying to follow only one single conversation among all the diners in your restaurant from the kitchen."

"So where does that leave us?"

"Phil," he sighed, "you need to identify exactly what specific resentments you harbor about Michelle's past relationship with this man. And then you need to go talk everything over with your own parish priest—to whom you're not related, and for whom you presumably have more respect than you have for me."

"I respect you a lot."

"No, you manifestly do not. You've been presented with a great mystery here, a great puzzle. And I keep trying to get you to look upward for the solution. To look heavenward, or at least to look inward. But you approach everything like it was all spilled grease and stomped cabbage."

"Some of us are realists."

Dominic's voice lost several degrees of its professional mildness. "You call me up, you ask for advice, well, this is *it,* baby! If an intelligence is involved here at all, maybe it'll eventually recognize just how futile this is, since you display no intelligence of your own."

"Blow it out your ear, Nonnie."

"Even if it's trying to warn you, you moron. Perhaps it'll just give up and go away when it understands what a 360-degree-round asshole you are."

"Aww listen: 'He's coming straight on for you, Phi'—there's

more taunt in there than warning," Phil parried. "Even sounds clichéd... I think it's a line from some rock song."

"Man's a musician—"

"No, listen! It's like, 'This big bad undertaker's going to bag up your poor doomed ass and there ain't a thing you can do about it.' A modern-day Grim Reaper driving a red pickup."

"Is this an argument you want to win, Filbert?" Dominic asked. "Do you sincerely want my input here, or would you rather be right all the time?"

Phil watched his own hand twisting off the lid of the cough syrup bottle. It was a strong hand, its nails short and clean. He was suddenly conscious of the blood beneath its skin, the matrix of tendons and muscles and the skeletal structure that made it function.

Its very complexity struck him, the vulnerability of its raised veins, its snappable bones. It would not move always. Surrender to some mortician, sooner or later, was inevitable.

I'm familiar with the idea that my body will eventually stop, I'm an organ donor, he thought. The realization doesn't keep me awake at night.

So it's not that. We all live with that.

"What happens to your soul, Nonnie," he spoke, "if you die disturbed and befouled by hell, or by what you imagine hell to be?"

"That needn't happen. That's where the church comes in."

"And what happens to you if you *live*? Disturbed and befouled?"

"Phil—"

"Because I know I'm out of my depth here, and I admit it," he paused to swallow another mouthful of cough medicine, realizing that he would not sleep well tonight no matter how much syrup he downed. "I don't seem to do well with the unknown. Maybe I shouldn't've wiped off the TV screen, maybe you're right. Shit."

Dominic made no comment, breathing audibly into the phone.

The sound was like a scythe rushing through the air: HE'S COMING STRAIGHT ON FOR YOU, PHI

Phil set the bottle back down onto the night table where it stuck, glued to its own sticky pink rings. "I need your help, Nonnie."

"That's exactly what I've been trying to give you."

"Your help as an ordained priest."

"That's what I've been trying to give you, Phil."

"Not as a counselor, as a *priest*."

"That's—"

"Please, Dominic!" He didn't choke on the plea, not with the sound of the scythe so close. His aching head was like a melon, something that would cleave readily in two with no resistance to the blade. Phil lay it back down into the wet pillows sandbagging the headboard and spoke one more word to his brother.

The word he spoke was *Father.*

TWENTY-EIGHT

Hold Your Breath

EARLY THE NEXT MORNING, just before her alarm clock was set to go off, Michelle was awakened by peculiar deep wheezes coming from Philip's side of the bed.

"Philip?"

He was shaking his head from side to side, trying to cough, but couldn't suck in enough breath to do it. He suddenly rolled onto his side away from her and kicked out with both feet at the snare of the sheets and blankets.

"Honey?" She jumped and groped, turning on a lamp.

His back heaved with effort. Strangled sounds came out as her hand cupped his burning shoulder and she leaned over him to see both forearms clamped against his chest in a spasm. His knuckles and the protrusions of wrists were white.

Lurching out of bed, shouting for Cam and Nicole, she called an ambulance and looked for her shoes. The alarm clock sounded but she wouldn't take the time to shut it off, its battery would just have to give out. She located Philip's wallet, his Ochsner HMO information, the phone numbers of his brothers.

Please, Adrien, she thought. *No!*

It's *me* you've got a beef with, remember? Not this man here.

Send me a coronary, send me cancer! Do your worst, I deserve it, she addressed him mentally, racing around the house to collect her purse and a long coat she could throw on over her nightgown.

The mattress dented under her weight as she sat to cradle her husband's head and smooth back the wet hair while he took speechless breaths, hugging his own chest as if it would break. She kissed the side of his face, his cheek, his ear, murmuring encouragement while they waited for the ambulance but thinking through chattering teeth *Please please please* leave Philip alone, Adrien, he's innocent and he's better to me and the kids than we deserve. I'll do anything you want. *Anything.*

Cam and Nicole stood in the open doorway, centered in her field of vision when she looked up.

Her fear was like a brick in her heart.

"MOM, IS PHIL GOING to die?" Nicole's eyes were solemn.

"No, sweetheart, thank God."

"But you were real scared this morning."

"Well, sure, yes, I was a little scared, because I thought he might be having a heart attack." Michelle led her daughter by the hand to the end of the serving line in the hospital cafeteria, hefting plastic trays onto the chromed rails. "Men Philip's age are susceptible to heart attacks. But this isn't anything like that, thank goodness. Okay?"

"So Phil's going to be okay," Nicole affirmed in her most adult voice, her just-getting-it-straight voice, nodding to herself like a miniature dowager.

"Absolutely." Michelle regarded a generous selection of food she had no appetite for. "Well, he is pretty sick, no kidding. But his prognosis is real good."

"For real?" Cam pursued, worried. "'Cause he does look kinda bad, Mom, with those tubes in his nose and everything."

Stress made her short-tempered. She had to literally count to three and take deep breaths before she answered. "I've never lied to you two. I refuse to start now. Just pick out something and let's eat fast, because we've got a lot to do."

Nicole studied the cafeteria foods laid out before her. "What if I'm not hungry?"

"You can have cake."

"What kind of cake is that?" her sticky little fingers pointed.

"Carrot."

"Yuck."

"Cam?" Michelle wheeled upon her tall son. "Tell me what you want to eat and then go save us a table."

"How do I know what I want? Without looking at all of it?"

The pressure of her own blood pounded in her ears. "Pizza? Look, they have pizza. Fries. Coke. Junk out the wazoo. Go get us a table and I'll bring it."

"Well, if it's all the same to you, Mom, um...could I just have a salad? Spinach salad, if they've got it."

"Salad."

"Yeah, with, like, ranch dressing." He grinned.

"Okay," she nodded, wishing that Adrien were alive in the flesh to hear his son ask for spinach salad.

"I want french fries," Nicole spoke up, "please, Mom. What's that stuff over there? Is that pudding?"

"It's bread pudding, yes."

"I hate bread pudding. What's that stuff way back there?" She rose on her tiptoes. "The choc—"

"Cam?" Michelle called him back as he was halfway to the seating section. "Please take Nicole with you."

He shot her a questioning look and she mimed ripping her short hair out. His expression didn't change but he returned, shuffling in unlaced sneakers. He snatched up the small hand of his sister as if he had caught a fly.

Michelle selected foods like a robot, pointing to salads and pie slices and fries and drinks on automatic pilot. She didn't know what she had chosen for herself until she had carried the loaded tray to the table and saw what was on it. Red beans and rice, oh yeah.

"So what's the deal?" Cam unloaded the tray and served the ladies.

"Somebody's got to go run Tasso," said Michelle. "I've canceled my class."

He chewed and reflected for a moment and then almost smiled. "Cool."

"Yeah, I've already spoken to Frank Favrot—Philip's second-in-command—and to the hostess. The kitchen staff can handle the cooking part all right for a few days, even if they're shorthanded. But payroll and bookkeeping, and ordering the meats and ingredients and even the napkins or whatever, paying the linen service, buying the seafood, writing the checks—Philip does all of that. And none of that can stop. Nobody else has the authority to do it."

"Then what does the hostess do?"

Michelle shrugged, biting at a piece of sausage she'd unearthed in her red beans.

"Couldn't a hostess be more like a manager? I mean, what does Phil even need a hostess for, if he does all the rest of that himself?"

Michelle watched Nicole dunk fries into ketchup. "I have no idea. She's probably the cashier, I guess, I don't know." She almost said, *Your father is a control freak, you know that,* but then heard her own thoughts and realized her error.

"Do you know anything about running a restaurant, Mom?" Cam squinted.

"No. But I can balance a checkbook and sign my name on a line, son, and I'm Mrs. Philip Randazzo—I think my signature'll be legal. I can see that all of the employees' hours are kept track of and that they get paid. If I don't do things the way that Philip would do 'em, then tough. But I want him to conserve every ounce of his energy and use it in getting himself well now, not lying there stewing over his pride and joy crashing and burning without him."

"What can *I* do?" Cam asked. "Because you know, Mom, Phil's showed me a few things. I can cook…"

"Then ask Frank and Vanessa when we get there, son, I don't even know what to tell you."

"When do we go?" Nicole asked.

"This afternoon. As soon as we finish up here."

"Cool! I can draw pictures of everybody. And show the little kids how to draw, if anybody brings any little kids, 'cause I'm real good with little kids." She kicked her short legs.

"Well, y'all finish eating and then we'll go back upstairs. And you two can tell Philip good-bye, and tell him not to worry." She pushed away her plate. "I think he'll probably believe you guys more than me."

"Why wouldn't he believe you, Mom?" Cam looked at her.

She shook her head. Pushed herself away from the table. "Figure of speech."

"Please don't screw this up, Mom, this marriage to Phil."

"Believe me," she finally answered, wanting to shout something retaliatory at her son yet understanding why she must not, "that's the last thing I want to do."

SHE KISSED PHIL good-bye up in his hospital room. His dry lips were parted and tasted like ash. There was that oxygen tube in his nose. The perfunctory pat on the back he gave her was just that.

He looked smaller, nowhere near his usual sturdy self, the topography of his body draped with a white sheet. She was used to seeing him against white, he wore white to work. But this was different. It even smelled different. The healthy stink of fried grease and garlic, the exuberant splashes of sauces and roux were missing, replaced by antiseptics that spoke of weakness.

What exactly does Adrien take from us in order to add to his own substance? she wondered, the brick of fear still in her chest.

She took Philip's hand. "I love you."

"Shelly…," he began with no energy, and then said nothing more.

She straightened and hugged herself under her sheepskin coat while Nicole and Cam approached the bed. "We're going to go run Tasso for you, Phil," Cam said as Nicole climbed upon the other side of the mattress, "so we don't want you to worry about anything at all, okay? You just get better, okay?"

Philip found smiling words to say to them.

Michelle stepped outside the heavy blond wood door and onto beige tiles, immediately blundering into a thickset figure in black. She got a glimpse of the Roman collar.

"Oops," he said. "Sorry."

"My fault, Father, I'm sorry," she said. "Not looking where I was going, was I?" The cleft chin got her then, the eyes behind the black rims of eyeglasses. "Oh, you're Dominic! —Father Dominic, I mean, please excuse me. It's been a while."

"Michelle." He kissed her on the cheek. "How're you doing, dawlin'?"

"I've been better…"

A thick thumb jerked at the closed door. "How is he?"

"Pretty much like I told Joey over the phone this morning. The pneumonia brought on the panic attack, is all they can figure."

"Phil's not used to being flat on his back. Or not in charge."

"No, he isn't," she agreed, and then realized that she hadn't known Philip Randazzo long enough to discover this on her own. The thought left her empty.

"May I buy you a cup of coffee, dawlin'?" The voice was Philip-ish with similar intonations, yet somehow more studied: the vocal tool of a professional.

"Well, I've got to get to Tasso…," she waved a hand at the hospital room door, "and my kids're in there with him. I need to get them out so we can go."

But Father Dominic stuck his round gray head through the

door and spoke a few cheerful sentences to everybody inside while Michelle waited. He retracted it and then came to take her by an elbow. "Very well, I'll not take up too much of your time, so we'll limit ourselves to the soft drink machine down the hall here, shall we? I told the kids we'd bring them one."

She had nothing to say. She let him lead her down the corridor to a vending machine.

"What's your pleasure?" He waited, broad face clean and smiling.

"Uh…iced tea, I guess. Thanks."

Quarters dropped into the slot and a cold aluminum can rolled out. The priest popped open its top and offered it to her. "Michelle, I know all about your paranormal happenings. Phil's kept me informed."

The tea tasted metallic. She didn't know why it surprised her that Philip would confide in someone. His older brother. A clergyman. "Father—"

"My name is Dominic, you're family." Additional coins were fed into the machine. It coughed up an orange soda. "I realize it's none of my business, and you're free to tell me to go jump off a bridge. But meddling in the affairs of other people is sort of in my job description, when you get right down to it. And Phil's my brother and I love him."

The simplicity of his words carried no offense. She took another sip of her tea and considered her words. "Well, as you say, we're family now. So I guess it's as much your business as it is anybody's, outside the four of us living in the house with it."

"The five of you," he corrected, buying Cokes for Cam and Nicole.

"Well." She mulled that over. "Yes."

"So your children are being helped by these phenomena?"

"Yes. Very much, so far."

"How about you?"

She had been raised a Protestant and the transactions of the confessional meant little to her. But something in Dominic Randazzo's plump, clean face discouraged lying. "I am helped."

He gathered up the children's Cokes against his black chest with one hand and held his opened orange soda with the other. "And Phil?"

"I imagine he's told you some things that he hasn't even told me, so you probably know a lot more about his state of mind than I do. I don't think we're as close as we should be now, he and I." She swallowed resignation along with iced tea. "I don't know what to do."

He initiated a slow return to the hospital room. "But if you could make the choice between the solace of these paranormal events and a return to normalcy with him, which would you choose?"

"I have no say-so in the matter, Dominic, I hope you know that. My...Adrien comes to us when he likes, and goes when he likes. And does what he pleases." This whole conversation had begun to feel dreamlike. Her mind seemed to drift inches above her head as if she'd taken too much flu medicine. "We don't know what he's up to, why he's here. And I'm frightened...not of him, he was a sweetheart. I mean, I'm not frightened at all of what he was. But I don't know what he is now. And as for his possible intentions in regard to Philip...yes, I'm very uneasy."

"But what if you *could* choose? What if I could give you the means to make that choice?"

She licked her upper lip. "What're we talking about here?"

"Some species of exorcism, I suppose."

"Ah," she stifled an inappropriate laugh. Unreality settled on her, white as fog, like the one she'd experienced that terrible December night when an emergency room doctor had taken her by both hands.

She pushed open a door in a different hospital now, thinking: This certainly has all gone far enough. I've had enough. I didn't hear that word I just heard. People don't seriously speak that word in the USA because they don't need to speak it.

Let me just get on back to my anthropology and my academic distance from cultures that routinely utter words like *exorcism,* and I'll be fine. Let me get my cranky husband well and let me take him home, and the Casper stuff'll just fade away if we all stop believing in it.

Please, just *stop.*

TWENTY-NINE

Faith

"I'LL HAVE TO GIVE IT a lot of thought, you know, so don't expect an immediate answer," she reminded Dominic one more time as she opened and shut desk drawers in Philip's restaurant office at random, adjusting the height of his swivel chair to her own build, wondering which task she should tackle first. "I have a lot to consider here. And I've already got a lot on my plate, you can see that."

"Naturally. Take your time."

"I mean," she kept her tone neutral as she moved the telephone within easy reach, "it's like killing Adrien all over again, isn't it."

He took down several heavy ledgers from the top of a gray steel filing cabinet. "Well, no, it's not like that, really. That's not exactly the case."

She looked at the small framed photograph of herself on the desktop, displayed near a group snapshot of Kerri, Hunter, and Brendan. Her frozen emotions registered but did not stir at the absence of photos of her own children. "It might be. To me."

"He'll be as alive as he is now. Just as much in the hands of his God, maybe even more so." The priest waited. "It's mostly just playacting, Michelle, really, for Phil's mental health, more than anything else. This wouldn't technically qualify as an exorcism, what I propose. Since nobody is possessed. I'm not casting a demon out of a possessed person—something that I'm not up for, few priests are these days. Something that'd scare me to death to even try. Unless there was no other recourse."

She squelched an observation about her own mental health. "I find it difficult to come up with a vocabulary to even address this."

"Me, too, actually."

"Why do we need to do this, again?"

"So that Phil gets some peace of mind. So that no genuine, full-blown possession has a chance to develop. Even if only in his imagination."

"Just who does he think is at risk of becoming *possessed*?"

The priest said nothing. His eyes spoke.

"Maybe you ought to just give me some space now, please, Dom...Sorry—is it okay if I call you 'Dom'?"

"Oh, fine, I've been 'Dom' now and then...actually, I'm 'Nonnie' in our family..." He leafed through a ledger. "Phil couldn't say 'Dominic' when he was little."

She sighed. "I guess what I need is some time to sort everything out before I decide. Because I've had a lot of stuff thrown at me all at once here today, you know."

He handed her a large, fat black business checkbook. She had no idea what to do with it. "That's why I'm here. Just to help out." He waited. "So where shall we start?"

"I have no earthly idea."

He was patient, still standing, while she looked around herself at the surface of another planet.

"When are your seafood deliveries? Whom do you buy from?"

He might as well have asked her the chemical composition of jet fuel. "I don't know. He doesn't have a computer. Why the hell doesn't he have all of this on computer?"

An unfamiliar terrain of collected invoices and Rolodexed telephone numbers, receipts and canceled checks and employee hours, handwritten notes in Philip's jagged slant, spread out before her like an obstacle course in neat little stacks.

"Get up, dawlin'," Dominic suddenly ordered, plopping the ledgers onto the desktop in front of her, seizing the office chair by its back and trying to dump her out of it. "Just stand up, Michelle, and let me take over here."

"That's not necessary, hon, but thanks." She stood anyway, in the fog again.

"Hey, I grew up in a restaurant, remember. Now get out of the way…"

"But you hated it."

"Well, maybe so. Yes. It's eating someone else's cooking I enjoy—you can tell how much just by looking at me. But I'll suppress any vestigial distaste for the restaurant business long enough to get us going here… Just trust me, it'll all come back to me."

"I hope so."

"It will," he insisted pleasantly. "We still get 'erstas' from water and eggs from chickens, I suppose. Nothing new."

She smiled. Oysters.

He examined the contents of the Rolodex and then found what he was looking for. Taking up the telephone receiver, he gave Michelle a glance. "When I need you to sign some checks here, hey, I'll come find you. So why don't you take a break and go look in on your kids now. I know it's been a tough day for them, too. See if they need anything."

He did seem to know what he was doing. Michelle was able to stand up straighter, feeling lighter, recognizing his competence. "Thank you, Nonnie. Thank you so much, bless your heart."

"But we do need to talk later," he eyed her through his bifocals and wouldn't let it drop—here it came again. "You need to hear some positive input. About my proposal."

"And I'm also going to need a lot of time to think about it, whatever that input," she warned him again, but with respect.

THE DINING ROOM was silent and pristine when she looked in on it now, chairs taken off the tables where they had still been resting upside down not thirty minutes ago. The potted palms were healthy and almost too green to be real. Linen napkins lay on the tablecloths in complex folds. Each table displayed several fresh-cut flowers in crystal vases next to unlit votive candles in white glass.

Lord, Michelle thought, heading for the kitchen, I don't have a clue about which florist those come from. I don't know who cleans these floors, or how much he's paid. Or even who has keys to this place.

The kitchen itself was orderly bustle, water running, pans clanging, and voices conversing. Two cooks worked at their stations, clad alike in white tunics and large shapeless black-and-white checked pants. (*Why do your pants have to be so baggy?* Michelle recalled asking Philip soon after she had met him. His answer had been *If hot stuff spills on you,* accompanied with the plucking of fingers and thumbs at the fabric covering his thighs, pulling imaginary boiling custard out and well away from his skin.) She immediately saw Nicole, in a chair near the freezer where she couldn't be in anybody's way, Xeroxed menus in her lap, pencil in her fingers.

"This girl can some *draw,*" a slim young brown woman came from the sink and took Michelle by an elbow—Vanessa Augustine—after wiping her hands on a towel. "This girl is some artist for real, I don't believe how good she is, you know that? She drew me, I'm going to take it home and have it framed. Might be worth a lot of money someday."

Cam squeezed past carrying a tall stack of white dinner plates from the dishwasher, scurrying carefully but rapidly, sneakers giving him adequate traction on mats not yet splattered with the night's cooking oils. His long bangs were darkened and wet, wilting over a blue bandana tied around his forehead like a sweatband.

He grinned and waved two free fingers at Michelle.

"Don't wave," she cautioned him.

He stooped with a grown man's strength and laid down the white breakables at a cook's instructions, and then rested with his hands on his hips, waiting for further orders. "—kitchen grease'll rot your tennis," the young man was warning him as Michelle approached. "Got to get you some kitchen clogs, man. Store at Uptown Square'll give you a work discount, just ax for a lady named Nancy…"

"Hey, Mom," he said, greeting her as if he belonged here, as if she were a visiting tourist come to the kitchen to compliment the staff. "This is Da'Shaun Wooten."

Michelle took the offered warm hand of the cook. "Pleasure to meet you, Mr. Wooten."

"How's Chef feeling?"

"Not too good right now, but I think he'll be okay, thank you."

"Tell him we thinkin' about him. Tell him we ain't just screwing around here while he's out."

"And this is Tyrone Dennis." Cam still waited, hands at his sides, as Tyrone stepped up behind him to slip a clean white apron over his head and then tie it around his waist. "What's next, y'all?"

"Know how to separate eggs?" Vanessa asked him.

"Child's play."

Is this where my son's heart really lies? she wondered. In a restaurant kitchen?

Am I going to have to get used to that?

Well, is there anything wrong with that? If he doesn't go to Yale? Other than what my own mother might think? Since when have I ever listened to her?

The alcove that hid the bar was deserted, she saw as she exited the kitchen. At the thought of her mother, on impulse, she stepped behind the bar herself, secure in her right to be there and yet feeling furtive. The premium bourbons were tempting but she chose a midpriced brand.

"You know, here's my little Cameron, son of the only Cajun ever born who couldn't cook worth doody," she remarked to Dominic as she retreated back to the office with her drink, "in the kitchen of a nouvelle-Louisiana French restaurant owned by his

Italian stepfather, just happily egg-beating his little heart out under the tutelage of a Creole lady. Wow, I love this town."

"Ah." Dominic regarded her glass, visibly perking up. "You bring me one of those?"

"No."

"Naughty girl."

"See?" she crowed. "Clergy who imbibe! Hey, if all those fussy ol' Baptists and Methodists back in Texas had openly enjoyed the fruit of the vine, I might've just stayed in church."

"You're Baptist?"

She shook her head. "Episcopalian. Underwent Catholic instruction and converted so I could remarry my first husband in church, something that meant more to him than to me. Respectfully agnostic, now. I don't mean to offend…"

"No offense taken."

"Good." She realized that she liked him. "That's good."

He put down his pen and rubbed both hands up under his glasses, over his eyes, and then down over his mouth. "So are you ready to get heavily metaphysical but undogmatic with me yet?"

"I don't think so."

"Too bad, because the time has come." He stood, rubbing one red hand against the other like a housefly. "You owe it to me, you know you do. Since I'm Superman, I've saved the day here. So just sit right down over there in that sofa and get comfortable while I make myself a drink and bring you another."

"THE FATHER OF my children was not an evil man," Michelle began, minutes later, fortified with bourbon and Dominic's good humor. She watched the way he loosened the knees of his black trousers with fingers and thumbs before he sat. "Deeply flawed, yes, I'll admit that. But he had such a sweet soul, you just don't know."

"Okay."

She sipped her second drink. "I have had some—what's the

term?—*impure* dreams about him lately. But that's my own psyche generating them. Not Adrien."

"Why those dreams, why now?" He set his glass down onto the desk blotter, pushing the paperwork aside. "If conjugal relations are satisfactory in your marriage to Phil."

"They are," she affirmed. But then had no answer to his question.

Dominic leaned back in the swivel chair and took up his drink. "Phil say anything to you about the television set?"

"Television? Our TV set?"

"Just something he saw on television, nothing important." He took a long and slow mouthful. "Something to do with the spirit world, few days ago. Minor thing. Forget I asked."

"No, but look, no spirit can hang around us like this forever, I'm pretty sure," she said. "Adrien can appear only two more times, and then that's that, he told us through a psychic. Maybe he's here just to comfort the kids. He's certainly doing that."

"But you're frightened for Phil, aren't you? You said."

"Well, yes. All this just seems to be a bigger drain on him than on the rest of us. I know he's a workaholic, but *double pneumonia...*"

"So here we are."

"But nobody'll ever be able to get me to believe that Adrien is demonic, Nonnie."

"You don't have to believe that." His voice was mild. "If I actually believed it myself, I'd never propose meddling with him, not by myself, not without the help of an experienced exorcist. A real demon would chew me up and spit me out, from what I've read. Nothing to be trifled with."

"But you're willing to trifle with him because he's trivial, huh? Or at least relatively benign, compared to your real demons, I take it."

Dominic shrugged. "I'm willing because Phil has asked me to."

"But three of us knew Adrien: me and Cam and Nicole! We know what a sweet soul he had, what a good heart! Lord, was he a good-hearted person, his entire life. Looked after that mob of family he had. Always slipping some down-and-out musician money he couldn't spare. Do anything for you. Put up with *me*, forgave the unforgivable in *me*, ultimately." She fell silent.

Dominic finished his drink and did not speak.

"He found it in himself to forgive such a big failing in me, Nonnie, such a rotten betrayal of him, you cannot imagine." Her hands and arms began to shake in a private earthquake, not just tremble. She set down her glass. "Damn damn *damn!* Why do I feel like we're both on trial here, him and me?"

"Shelly, dawlin', listen. I don't believe he's evil, either," the priest's voice slid out quiet and easy. "It just doesn't fly. This isn't the classic pattern, at all, of any kind of diabolical activity."

"Then why on earth—"

"Because *Phil* is beginning to believe it. And I'm afraid that the notion itself has begun to affect him. I mean, pneumonia? A panic attack?"

Michelle pondered this. "I see."

Dominic pushed his glasses higher up on his nose. "This is where real danger could lie, in his own negative attitudes. That danger your psychic mentioned. What if it's self-fulfilling, in some sense? Psychosomatic?"

"This is the last conversation I would've ever predicted myself having, this time last year," she said dully.

"I also fear that he's beginning to hallucinate certain…ah… events. Like that TV show he says he saw. So what, exactly, are we saying when we acknowledge that Phil is 'sick'?"

She shrugged and shook her head again, wishing she could travel back in time to those first few lovely uncomplicated months right after she met Philip Randazzo. Or go even further back in time and not meet him at all. "But this can't be a nervous breakdown, that's ridiculous, he's just not the nervous-breakdown type."

"My point exactly."

Her arms crossed beneath her breasts in a self-hug.

"Would you be a dear and fetch us another one of these?" He held out his empty glass to her.

"I guess so," she grunted finally and got to her feet. "Because I'm going to have to be dead stinking drunk before I allow the Catholic Church to cast Adrien Savoie into hell. Not that y'all need my permission, because I don't guess you do."

"BUT THAT'S NOT what would happen to Adrien Savoie," the priest told her when she returned from the bar with her cheeks still hot from what she had just said.

She handed him his refilled glass. "How come?"

He put down the drink. "Look: The old ritual, very rarely used anymore—and never performed by any priest of my own acquaintance, I had to get hold of a copy of it through the Loyola library—it applies only to demons, dawlin'. *Unclean spirits. Incursions of the Adversary. Phantoms, legions, in the name of our Lord Jesus Christ* are instructed to remove themselves. That's literally what it says, Shelly, line by line, translated from the Latin. And I honestly do not believe that A. P. Savoie falls into any of those categories."

But one word stood out. "'Phantoms'? It's a ritual to cast out phantoms, isn't it?"

"Out of people, mostly. Possessed people."

"People, houses, cigarette lighters, what's the difference? He's a phantom."

"Shelly, this term couldn't possibly apply to him. I can't exorcise a benign spirit."

But *exorcism,* the very word, the idea that an educated cleric actually thought that some homemade type of one was called for here, finally caught up with her, compliments of this whole day of nothing but frightfulness, this alcoholic haze. She put down her drink, careful not to spill it, feeling something slip. And suddenly pounded her knees with both fists, surprised and then seized by sobs of frustration and fury and fear.

Dominic swiveled the chair and jumped up. "Oh sweetheart, I'm sorry!"

"Get away from me." She stood and fled.

But he caught and embraced her, his capturing black bulk smelling of soap and aftershave. "Shelly, I'm so sorry, what a fool I am...I'm making this so hard for you, when all I want to do is set everything right."

"But what if you're wrong?" She grabbed his clerical suit by its shoulder seams, shaking him. "What if this ritual turns out to be more than just 'playacting'? What if there *is* a real hell? What if you're wrong, and you unintentionally send him there?"

"Hells begin on earth, Shelly," he said, steadfast, not letting her rock him. "And A. P. Savoie might have inhabited his own hell here at one time, from what I understand. But I do believe he escaped it before he died."

She couldn't speak for a moment, she could only sniffle and shake him by his shoulder seams like a dusty throw rug. "God damn everybody," she said, "I wish everybody would just leave us alone! You want to know how he got into hell? My parents and I sent him. Got him evicted from a houseboat full of matchbooks."

His hand stroked the back of her head.

She held on to his fat biceps and then finally gave up, pressing her nose into his black chest, fury all spent. "Shit. I don't understand why you need my permission. You'll do whatever you want, in the end."

"I'd never try anything like this if you were against it, Shelly, honestly. I'd never in a million years go behind your back."

"Bullshit. You just need me to get into my house. You need me to give you the burglar alarm code, if Philip's too sick to remember it."

"Dawlin', look. I'm not saying that I believe it, because I don't believe it. But if it's just barely possible that some dark spirit," Dominic was saying, rubbing her back, "some adversarial spirit, is appearing in the guise of your first husband to create mischief and grief, wouldn't you want to examine that remote possibility and have it checked out? If it were so, wouldn't you want it to be cast out, removed from any proximity to your children? To Phil, who's so susceptible?"

"I don't even believe in dark spirits. I remember not believing in ghosts."

"Oh, c'mon!" It was his turn to shake her, but gently. "You've lived in the so-called third world, you've studied shamanism! I know you've witnessed inexplicable events, don't give me that. You might not 'believe' in them, officially, but you had to have witnessed some."

She sighed. "So what happens if you whip out your crucifix in my house and this big nasty demon pops up?"

"I'll run like hell and approach the archbishop the way I'm supposed to be doing here in the first place, and let him call in somebody who has some experience."

"Why aren't you going by the book right off?"

"Because your Adrien can't pass an archdiocesan evaluation, sweetheart, he's just not demonic enough. And no one here is actually possessed. Yet."

"So what you're saying is, if he's innocent, no kind of exorcism can hurt him. But if he's a big scary devil…"

"You know anything about the Navajo?" He stepped back.

"Well, Mesoamerica is my field, but I suppose you're referring to the *chindi* in Navajo belief systems. Ghost Sickness. Like in Tony Hillerman."

"Yes," he nodded. "I taught for some years at a school in New Mexico just after my ordination, long time ago. And became familiar with a few folkways in spite of myself, which I guess it was more my job to try to eradicate, but that's neither here nor there. Anyhow, when you die, says Navajo tradition, your soul goes on—"

"—to an unspecified afterlife," she finished for him. "And what gets left behind, the less wholesome fragments of the personality, linger on as a largely unconscious, unintentionally malevolent presence called the *chindi.* Capable of causing Ghost Sickness in the living, who weaken and die. Unless the proper Sing is performed by a shaman. Is that about it?"

"Well?" He waited. "Notice any similarities?"

She sat down, spent, sinking into the vinyl cushions of the sofa again like a stone into Jell-o. "You believe that? Shall we call a medicine man?"

"Not officially, I don't believe it." He sat beside her. His weight created a hillside. "But it does make you think. It's funny—I saw Jesus in clouds sometimes when I was a young boy. I'd see the Virgin in angel-hair pasta. I think I craved the numinous, that's why I went to seminary. And here at long last are the visions I wanted, here's that contact. But it's Phil who's having it, not me."

"And you don't know what he's contacted."

"Do you?"

She searched her boozy mind for alternatives but kept seeing the hospital room at Ochsner, the depleted figure on the bed, the alarming way the twin-branched oxygen tube bisected his face. She felt the cold of it again, the unreality. The fog.

Chindi, she thought. Causing Ghost Sickness, or something like it? Something like whatever Ghost Sickness really is, is that why Philip is ill?

"Tell me what to do, Shelly," said Dominic.

Are we haunted by something like the *chindi,* after the real Adrien has gone on to somewhere else? To wherever it is that we all go. And mere fragments of his personality, the baser aspects of it, linger behind like prions now, like protein fragments, toxic and harmful? Capable of killing, no intentions needed or required?

Dominic drained the last of his drink and then he spoke. "Absolutely no way around it, dawlin'. It's your call. You're going to have to choose."

Bedside Visions

FAINT DRUMBEATS from St. Charles Avenue disturbed the Chestnut Street house's silence, where sunlight came spilling from the multiple windows above the indoor patio and dust motes hung suspended in the air.

Weatherwise the day was a ten, just cool enough for sweatshirts or sweaters, Phil had been informed. Not damp enough for jackets, the overarching hard blue sky unsoftened by clouds.

Great parade weather, he had been told repeatedly. And he well knew, as he rested alone in the stillness of the house, what it would be like out there right now on the parade route. Sequins giving back the sun, gold leaf on the rocking floats, toddlers belted in above the heads of the crowd on stepladder seats. Masked float riders tossing beads into forests of outstretched hands.

There would be old ladies in beach chairs and young guys with ice chests. Out-of-state college kids doing Carnival for the first time, getting drunk and sunburned too fast, wearing too many leis of plastic beads to be comfortable, moving in loud swarms. Armies of middle school students following their school bands on the sidewalks on parallel marches that would take them all the way to Canal Street. Men riding horseback in faceless masks and plumes, Prince Valiant wigs and velvet, jeweled capes spread over their mounts' rumps in fanciful throwback to a royal France that had never looked even remotely like a Mardi Gras court.

Phil lay on the bedspread and knew what it was like to be out there and he didn't miss it. One parade was much like another: seen one, seen 'em all. If he missed anything it was the camaraderie, the excitement of his kids, cold beer in a plastic cup, the thunder of the bass drum passing just two scant feet away from him like a crashing concussion in his chest....

Or maybe that's because I'm just getting over pneumonia, he thought as he sipped water and stretched out his socked feet, warm in clean sweatpants and a maroon Loyola sweatshirt.

The illness had passed but had taken all of his stamina with it. He was amazed to feel this weakened, astounded at the effort it took to stand up and then shuffle into the bathroom to urinate.

"You going to be all right here, honey?" Michelle had asked him before rounding up Cam and Nicole and heading off to the parades.

He understood that it probably wasn't really there, the implication that he wasn't expected to answer her with a no. The implication that she would go anyway.

"Cell phone's in my backpack," she told him, searching out her sunglasses and pulling on a Mexican sweater, "just call me if you need anything..."

"You won't hear the phone out there, Shell."

"Yes I will."

Regan and Lyle and his own three kids would be out there with Cam and Nicole and Michelle now, having crossed the lake for Mardi Gras Saturday. Scheduled to spend the night here as well so that they could do tomorrow, too, the parades of Thoth and Bacchus, unless something like emergency heart surgery changed Lyle's plans.

Divorced people aren't supposed to be this chummy with each other's families—I guess this is what I get for marrying a woman with a house just three blocks off the parade route, Phil told himself,

trying to make his head comfortable. He'd lain in bed so much
lately that his ears were sore.

Are you sure you're going to be all right here by yourself, Philip?

Sure. Y'all go on. Have fun out there.

Are you sure, honey?

I'm too tired to piss. It hurts my sore ears to talk on the phone
with Frank and Vanessa, shit, do whatever y'all want to over there
at Tasso, you and Nonnie. Burn it down. I'm too fatigued to give a
rat's ass. Forget about me.

If I've got to live like this, a stranger in my own haunted house,
with Lyle Gaspard out there catching beads for my kids and my
first and second wives hitting it off so well while I lie here like a
beached whale, I'd just as soon be asleep.

HE WOKE WITH drums still going, the white rectangles of sunlight
higher on the bedroom walls. The house was quiet. He was thirsty
again, a craving that couldn't be wished away, but there was no
more water in his bedside carafe.

Aw fuck, he thought, swinging limp legs over the side of the
bed.

He stood and balanced, turned, and then saw what was on the
floor.

A man lay on the carpet near the foot of the bed, on his right
side with his head raised slightly, looking at a fixed point just to
Phil's left with one eye. The other was gummed shut by gore and
torn tissue.

"*Holy God!*" Phil jumped back, stumbling in his weakness,
settling onto the mattress with thighs and bent elbows.

The man's head fell back onto the carpet. Blood and saliva
dripped through cut lips into its white tufts. He looked up again
but not at Phil, his flannel shirt and jeans rucked up and red. He
lay barefoot in a posture that suggested he could achieve no other,
scalp lacerated, blood soaking his dark hair and dyeing its graying
places.

Phil recognized the left hand with its missing fingers and couldn't make any kind of sound except the wheeze of inhalation, blasted so deep into shock that he had emerged on its other side. He held himself rigid at the bed's edge and heard his own breathing coming out in shakes and hisses.

The single eye was all dilated pupil. The fine long nose was broken.

"Savoie?" Phil spoke with not enough air.

This was real. This body was casting a shadow on the floor.

Phil heard no words meant for him and didn't expect to because the pulped lips never moved. Yet words were growing audible inside his skull and they were not for him: ... *Mère de Dieu, priez pour nous pauvres maintenant et à l'heure de notre mort, amen* ...

The psychic was right, Phil marveled irrelevantly, about thoughts in French. About thoughts. About about about—

In spite of all reason he was compelled to crouch down, to attempt to help. He extended a half-furled, badly shaking right hand. "Savoie?"

Savoie suddenly flinched at something that Phil couldn't see, wrapping an arm around his head as if he expected a blow, trying to curl into a fetal position to protect genitals and belly with his other hand. One leg would not curl.

"Hey, it's okay!" Phil reached out instinctively.

It took him a millisecond to realize that his fingertips were making contact with warm and wet flannel. When he did realize it, with a sucking intake of breath like he'd touched a hot stove, the apparition vanished.

There was no blood on the carpet. There was no blood on his fingertips.

HE LACED UP HIS running shoes with hands so numb they felt like someone else's and sprinted right out of the house without even locking it, jogging two short blocks before his debilitated condition caught up with him.

Then his jog dwindled to a walk but it was a rapid walk and he maintained it. His breath came short and his pulse would not slow, because those fingertips of his kept remembering their impossible contact. Phil wiped them against his sweatpants over and over as if they were soiled. He repeated the motion so often that they began to redden and become raw.

Fucking freaked out, man, his own brain diagnosed him as he stepped off the corner at Chestnut and Josephine, winded by the pace yet unable to drop back. Fucking freaked out here, mind blown, yes indeed. A mind can pop just like a circuit breaker, for real.

Just need to walk around for a little bit, I'll be all right...Just need a major change of scene here for a while...Get my breakers reset...

A white minivan drove past. He followed it across the street, not knowing where he was bound, intent only upon putting as much distance as he could between himself and Michelle's house. Heading away from the river on Josephine he turned right on Prytania, shaky with incomplete convalescence and a terror so pure that he experienced it as intoxication.

The parades were just a block away and the shouts of the crowds and the drums of the marching bands echoed from buildings in irregular acoustical patterns as he passed. Each footstep jarred him like a drumbeat, a heartbeat. Houses unreeled past him like cinema footage, distinct and very alive, pale pink or gray-lavender or Victorian white, iron fences spiked and lacy. Greenery waved branches out to him as he passed, large and torn banana leaves, thorny holly, crepe myrtle twigs reaching like skeletal hands from sculpted trunks.

He looked up to see the Norwegian Seaman's Church with its replica lighthouse and finally paused in front of it on Prytania while he tried to put it all together, perspiring. Tried to decide what he should do next. What he wanted to do.

He didn't want to do anything in particular except stay away from the house.

He didn't know what specifically to fear. He resumed walking.

Reaching the bridge approach ramp after making it through many blocks of shabbier buildings and less tidy front yards, he ran out of both breath and strength. Then he stopped and bent over, palms on knees, listening to drums and his own blood for countless minutes while lactic acid flooded muscles unused for too long. Pigeons roosting high overhead among the steel supports of the overpass spattered his right shoulder with falling dung. There wasn't enough air in his lungs for a cussword.

The sidewalk was studded with broken beer bottles and urban parking lot dirt, windblown brown paper sacks, a single blue knit glove in the gutter. Unsuccessful and lonely weeds stood in cracks of the pavement, not quite living and not quite dead.

Christ, he thought, rubbing a hand over his own forehead and eyes. Holy God.

Wild music from the marching bands echoed in the steely trap of the overpass. He became aware of eighteen-wheelers rumbling high over his head and then had a sudden premonition of some sleep-deprived long-haul trucker losing control up there, speeding into the guardrail like a runaway army tank. Smashing his way right over the side and dropping his rig like a fiery mountain to crush Phil where he stood. He suddenly perceived his own thoughts as actual *things,* actual forces, powers that might cause an accident to happen by calling out to it and shaping it.

He wiped his sore fingertips against the knitted cotton of his sweatpants and trudged out of the shadow of the overpass into sunlight, half expecting the stupefying wreck behind him that never came. His pulse refused to slow. After a couple of blocks he passed a pay phone and then doubled back and stopped, placing a credit card call to his brother Dominic because he had no money on him and had run out of ideas.

"If you can come get me, Nonnie, I'd like to maybe crash on your sofa for the rest of today and maybe tonight, if that's okay…" He propped himself upright with both elbows upon the gray steel of the telephone's shelter, wondering if the Jesuits had prohibitions against laity sleeping over.

"But what's happened?" Dominic kept asking.

And Phil kept trying to tell him, to hear him and be heard over the Carnival din. "You remember that business about adding to Savoie's substance? Well, we've added to his substance pretty damned good, all right, for real."

"Give me your location again. Let me get a pencil or something."

"He's substantial enough now to be touched. Listen, do you hear me?"

The line rustled. Dominic's voice barked: "Okay, here's a pen. Where on Prytania?"

"Nonnie, do you hear me?" Phil repeated, knowing that he was shouting now only by the pressure at his neck. "I just now literally *touched* him."

"Who?"

"Savoie!"

"Touched…?"

"That's what I said." He rubbed his face again, slimy with sweat, with madness. "I touched him, he's substantial. Please come get me."

THIRTY-ONE

Emptiness

"IT WAS JUST AFTER we'd conceived Nicole, like maybe the next morning after, in December of '89 when it happened…" Michelle kept trying to make sense of things for Phil the next afternoon. He listened to her with one ear, comparatively glad to be back home in his own sickbed, too fatigued from his insomniac night on Nonnie's ancient sofa to remain very freaked out now.

He had realized along about eleven o'clock this morning at Nonnie's that the skipping of two doses of the antibiotics left behind at Chestnut Street might possibly land him right back in Ochsner again. He hadn't thought of that at all yesterday when he ran out the door, obsessing about the ghost when bacteria should've remained his top priority. Just sentencing myself to more hospital food, he thought. Savoie must be laughing his head off.

She watched him place his palm against his sternum now. "Are you all right?"

He couldn't tell if he was wheezing. He didn't know if he felt feverish. "I'm okay, go on. Who beat him up?"

"My boyfriend."

This was just going to be more Shelly shit, wasn't it? Phil closed his eyes, sorry that he had ever brought up the subject. The ghost could wait now, the ghost had dematerialized. Pneumonia might be what was rematerializing right now, deep in his lungs, while she confessed him to death.

"But see, I'd been trying to break off a relationship that wasn't working out with this really jealous and really abusive person who'd been slapping me around for months—a younger man, somebody I never should've gotten involved with in the first place, Philip."

"I know the feeling."

"Who had a terrible temper. Suspected me of infidelity and just went totally insane on me that morning."

"What a goddam rocket scientist—you still leaking Savoie's fresh DNA from at least two orifices." Stress and discomfort were steadily transforming yesterday's fear into fury without losing a single degree of intensity.

All this morning over there at Nonnie's while he'd waited for him to finish saying Mass and doing whatever a Jesuit educator did on a Sunday and finally get around to dropping him off home, Phil had worried on the lumpy sofa bed, knowing he'd been due for medication again at eight. Wondering what he should say to Regan and Lyle and his kids, how he should explain his sudden overnight absence.

Now, after barely an hour of being back in the Chestnut Street house and belatedly taking his medication, he was finding that he didn't give a rat's ass what anybody thought.

Michelle was patient. Her very patience was maddening. "We were breaking up, Philip, I've already said that, this abusive man and I. Because I was afraid of him, honey—he'd blackened my eyes a couple of times before this. So on this particular morning he begins to knock me around like a crazy man, calling me all kinds of obscene names in front of Cam, punching me and everything... Adrien just happened to witness some of it and he intervened."

"'Adrien intervened.' Anything sound the least bit familiar here?"

"He got the shit beat out of him, Philip, it wasn't something he particularly wanted to do!" Her voice rose in this brief privacy, the

absence of Regan and Lyle and all five kids who had left early to
stake out a good spot for the Bacchus parade. "Cam and I were
there, okay? That's probably another reason Cam's such a traumatized mess. Neither of us could get it stopped before the cops came.
But Cam did see his father stand up for his mother. Maybe he
learned something valuable, I don't know."

"Sometimes, you know…" Phil had to shake his head. "I wonder why anybody goes to the trouble to stand up for you, Shelly, I
mean, Jesus! How much shit have you caused?"

She held back whatever knee-jerk response she wanted to de-
liver. But her cheeks, nose, and forehead flushed pink. "We'd been
separated, me and Adrien, for almost five whole years. We were
going on with our separate lives until Cam just suddenly ups and
wants to go visit him. Cam was barely eight years old at the time,
so I didn't want him flying all the way down here from New York
all by himself. Adrien was just this lost soul from my past by then,
a nonentity bar band musician, drinking himself to death. Apparently unsalvageable. I mean, not *everything* is my fault, Philip, okay?"

"You're too easy," he countered. "Cheap date."

"Look, when he came to my rescue that next morning with
nothing but sheer heart, attacking this huge young gym rat who was
threatening to kill me, slapping me around, who stood on two good
legs and was a whole head taller—!"

"Goddam, didn't the two of you ever show some kind of learning curve?" Phil sat up in bed. "All you ever brought to this poor
bastard in his entire life were hospital beds."

She didn't take the bait. "Well, I was ready to take him as he
was, after that. I remarried him as soon as he was able to kneel in
church. Married him in the sight of God and the Catholic Church,
plus the state and federal governments and our families and whatever else kind of officialdom I could think of to tie us together for
the rest of our lives."

"Yeah—Missus Devotion Savoie. I notice you never took his
surname."

"That's not about me loving him less," her tone became tighter. "That's about him loving me more."

He half-accidentally swept away with an elbow the aspirin and the prescription medication standing at attention on his night table. But thrashed on, getting to his feet, striding into the kitchen for a real drink, convalescence be damned. "Sleeping with two guys at the same time—there's a name for that and it ain't *love,* baby doll."

"But let me tell you," she began to shout, following him like his shadow, "about ghosts! About *ghosts,* Philip, goddammit—listen to me!"

Suction made the freezer door hard to open and he jerked at its handle, seeking ice. Found it, threw four ice cubes into a water glass, and then dumped in some bourbon while she stood in his peripheral vision and watched him.

"Oh for God's sake, like that's a smart thing to do," she said. "Mix alcohol with medication, just what the doctor ordered."

He swallowed half of it right off, turning his head to regard her over the rim. "So you don't even know for sure that Nicole's even his, do you?"

She ate air for a moment, astounded. "*Look at her,* Philip, for God's sake!"

His drink was balm soothing him into indifference. Ten feet away his wife's breath began to come in noisy heaves. He watched her, unmoved, feeling no emotion except satisfaction at being able to put two and two together. "Poor bastard, you jerked him around and fucked him over so many goddam times, no wonder he haunts us, no wonder he bleeds on our carpet."

"*God!*" she suddenly screamed at him like a wildcat with a raving face, clawing at her own head, ripping at her hair with frenzied fingers. "*What do you want of me?*"

"I don't know." He finished his drink. "But I sure as hell ain't been gettin' it."

"It was *his brother,* you asshole, you emotionally stunted…!" Her invective gave out and so did her legs. She folded herself onto collapsing knees, blindly easing herself down onto the floor in the doorway, hair in tortured spikes. *"He saw his brother!"*

Phil's initial interpretation of this was something so kinky that he could only stare at her.

"Oh Christ! I don't mean his brother beat him up or that my abusive boyfriend was his *brother,* for God's sake!" She was shaking her head with such rage that tears flew off her chin. "I mean his *little brother,* the one who burned to death in the fire! *Adrien saw his little brother,* you evil-minded asshole! That's what I keep trying to tell you!"

"What I keep hearing is something about some nympho."

She threw her clogs down the kitchen's steps and out onto the bricked patio. They were all she had to throw. "You don't understand one goddam thing. You don't want to understand. You're not emotionally advanced enough for it, is my guess."

"Yeah, well, we're all certainly beneficiaries of your own emotional maturity, Professor Wickham. Your son is a nutcase. Your daughter wets the bed." He put down his emptied glass, bolstered by his observations.

Michelle sat there in the doorway and waited thirty seconds before she spoke. The palms of her hands lay against the floor at the sides of her thighs. "Nicole is his daughter, Philip. I know it and he knew it. She's the spitting image of Delphine, her grandmother. But if you want her to undergo some fucking DNA test…"

"C'mon, I'd never put a child through that."

"Look what you're willing to put me through."

"Well—"

"He wanted to remarry me. In church. It was his idea, he knew I was pregnant. So I guess even if Nick had been born with, like, red hair and blue eyes—"

"I very much doubt that, baby doll. No man alive thinks like that."

"Listen to yourself." She leaned her head back against the doorjamb, looking at nothing, looking tired and defeated. Looking her age. "What you just said. Your own true take on stepfatherhood. I guess it's time I found that out."

He deposited his used glass into the stainless steel sink with a ringing of crystal. "I'm going back to bed. Tell Regan and the kids good night for me."

She remained there, making him have to step over her knees and feet. "So I don't suppose it makes any difference to you that Adrien saw his little brother, does it? Right before the cops got there, right after he'd been kicked in the head about twenty times."

"I don't know if it does or not…" Phil visualized that battered apparition again—kicked in the head about twenty times seemed like a reasonable description.

"He saw his dead little brother standing right there in the room with us, smiling and healthy and jumping around…Saying that he was really happy where he was and that he totally forgave Adrien for leaving all those matches in the houseboat…"

Phil stepped over her.

"He *forgave* him," she repeated loudly to his back. "It changed our lives, Philip—don't you care about what I'm saying?"

"Did you see the child? You or Cam? Your boyfriend?"

He heard the sigh and rustle of her clothing as she finally stood. "No."

"A hallucination, then, not a ghost." His anger was spent. "Just something like a near-death experience, another head injury. Wasn't real."

"It was real enough to Adrien." She padded along barefoot several paces behind him as he stepped down to the patio and then went up the two steps to their bedroom. "What's the difference? If all his dysfunctional shit just stopped immediately after that, I'm telling you—the drinking, the drugs, the women—just stopped on a dime? And I was ready to take him as he was. And he was ready to take mean, shallow me as I was."

He knew where she was going with this and he didn't want to give her the satisfaction of getting there. Flinging back the coverlets, he flopped onto the bed in his sweatpants and let a grunt come out of him, all that she was going to get from him right now.

"Philip?"

Lying on his side, resolutely facing away from her, he heard her opening and shutting closets. She left the bedroom and went upstairs and then returned.

Large zippers zipped.

The glide of her handbag sounded across the marble top of the dresser. Keys jangled. She jostled the bed as she reached under it for shoes that were not clogs. "Philip, I'm going to walk up to St. Charles to get my kids and then go to a hotel for the night. I'm taking my Saturn. Don't try to call me on my cell phone because I won't answer."

He didn't speak. He didn't move.

"I'm not going to go into any details with Regan and Lyle, so you're free to tell them anything you want. You can tell them what a slut I am, anything you want to."

He heard her feet move away across the carpet and then down onto the brick and out through the front room with a clicking of hard soles. He heard the door open and slam.

Yesterday's distilled terror was gone, as vulnerable to medication and bourbon and anger as any fear less pure. Recalling it did not reproduce it now. Phil didn't think he had the strength to reproduce it. He couldn't pull himself together enough to make it happen. Rage had sucked him dry, leaving nothing behind except anxiety and a tight chest.

I touched him, whatever he is, he remembered, looking again at his fingertips, still slightly reddened. I touched him and that means something dire, but I'm too beat to give a good goddam right now, God bless bourbon.

No wonder Savoie drank.

So Phil lay on the bed and thought about nothing, trying to relax, mind boozily blanked. His fingers located the remote control for the TV and he clicked it on, a pastime that wouldn't involve much reflection, not if he kept clicking through the channels fast enough.

He clicked.

REGAN AND LYLE spoke to him in quiet and detached voices upon returning from Bacchus, pretending that they hadn't noticed how tightly wound Michelle had to have been when she'd appeared on the parade route to fetch Cam and Nicole.

They didn't ask him where she was now or much of anything else as he lay across the bed and channel surfed. Everyone moved through the house like wraiths, searching out personal belongings and getting packed up for the trek back home to Mandeville.

"Bye, Dad," each of his kids came wanly to him in turn to hug him, to lie about what a good time they'd all enjoyed. He could tell from their unease, from what they weren't saying, how disturbed they were at Michelle's decampment following on the heels of his own. "Come see us, Dad," one of them said. Then: "Hope you feel better soon, Dad." "I love you, Dad."

"I love y'all, too. Be good. Take care of yourselves."

"You going to be okay for supper, Phil?" Regan herself finally stood at his bedroom threshold in her own afterthought, overnight bag in one hand, staring from her perspective at the soles of Phil's socks. "Can we get you anything before we go?"

"I'm fine," he shrugged lying down. "Y'all be careful. Drive safe."

"Was it," she hesitated, "anything we did?"

He raised his head and looked at her from between his feet. "No. Nothing like that. Nothing to do with y'all."

Savoie saw his little dead brother, he was thinking, detached, as he studied Regan studying him. A. P. Savoie saw his little brother, and now we're seeing Savoie. He's touchable now. My wife has run off. And all I can do is watch television.

"I'm sorry, though, Phil," she said. "Kerri's really confused. She and Cam were having such a good time…"

He suddenly jacked himself up off the sheets and then stood, and Regan stepped back from the doorway one step, tinted auburn hair very bright. Phil hustled past her, down the steps to the bricks and then up to the foot of the staircase. "Wait a minute," he told her. "I've got to go get something. Where are the kids?"

"Out front with Lyle. In the car."

"Wait here a sec. I'll be right back—" He mounted the steep steps to Cam's room and shouted back down, "I'm coming right back!"

The room was rank, disordered, but did not smell of tobacco. Phil waded in among soda cans and video games, kicking obstacles out of his path as he homed in on Cam's dresser. Its top was heaped with Mardi Gras detritus, beads and doubloons and plastic souvenir cups printed with the names and themes of parades, but Phil furiously rummaged underneath it all, fumbling for the small and cold metal object he suspected might be lying hidden somewhere beneath the mess.

Oho.

He pulled it out, a silvery rectangle with the inscription SAVOIR FAIRE stamped unevenly in block letters into its surface by some unknown Saigon artisan.

"Regan?" he called.

"Yes?"

He trudged back down the stairs to her level, the lighter clutched tightly in his hand like something that might try to get away and escape. He took her by an elbow and steered her to the front of the house.

"Don't go out there without shoes!" she told him when his intention to accompany her out to the Lexus registered with her. "You'll catch your death out there, Phil! What's going on?"

"I've already caught my death," he passed through the front door. "I'm trying to keep it from catching me."

"Hey, sure had a swell time, Phil," Lyle told him through the driver's side window, his grin insincere on his mustachioed face. "Thanks again for having us. Sorry if we caused you any trouble."

"'S'okay, no problem..." Phil stooped and searched the darkness behind the car's tinted windows. "Kerri?"

"Over here, Dad," she said from the street side of the back.

He stepped upon sticks and acorns with his tender socked feet, off the curb and onto the asphalt, and then thumped two knuckles against the dark glass. The window slid smoothly down.

He reached in with his fist. "Here. Keep this for Cam."

She examined the object as if she'd never seen it before.

"You know what that is, right?"

She nodded, closing freckled fingers around it, green eyes making contact with his. Her lips were slack, exposing braces.

"Just keep it a while, okay?" he instructed. "Keep it somewhere safe until Cam can come get it himself. Okay, sweetheart?"

"But are you sure he'd want me to—?"

"Kerri, there's nobody on God's green earth he'd rather have as a guardian for this right now."

Her delicate brows went up in pleasure and she pressed her lips together. "Okay..."

"Because I don't know how long his mother is going to stay mad at me, so I don't know when he's going to get to come back home," Phil went on, telling some truth, making up the rest. "So you keep it safe, okay?"

"Okay, Dad."

Phil circled the car into the glare of the headlights, briefly seizing Lyle's hand and shaking it. He had nothing to say.

Then they were gone, nothing now but retreating red lights, and Phil climbed the steps back up to the porch with knees that didn't hurt him. The enforced bed rest dictated by his pneumonia had weakened and fatigued him but had also allowed his jogged-out joints to heal some. He had not gained weight during his convalescence only because his appetite was depressed. He could feel his abdominal muscles sag and noticed the slackness of his hamstrings and thought: I've got to get up off my ass and get back into shape and back to work. God alone knows what they've done to

Tasso, Michelle and Nonnie and Frank, God knows who they've hired to take up the slack. We might be a burger joint by now, a pizza parlor, a greasy spoon. We're probably called *Da'Shaun's*.

He let himself back in through the front door with a sigh and closed it behind him. The house was chilly. He went to the thermostat and dialed it higher and heard the rattle of ductwork as the heat kicked in.

The phone lay among unpaid bills on the breakfast bar. He considered calling Michelle and apologizing despite her warning about not answering, but decided not to try.

Just fuck her, he thought. I don't remember why the hell I married her now. I don't even recall what made that seem like a good idea in the first place. I don't know what love is—romantic love, sexual love—if it's so conditional that it doesn't seem remotely related to what you feel for your kids.

Romantic love, there should be another name for it. For these unspoken rules: I'll leave your ass if you get too fat and begin to turn me off; you'll leave me if I become inattentive or lose my job or lose my hair; I'll leave you if I run across somebody younger and sexier who makes me feel virile; you'll leave me if I seem wooden and unresponsive. Shit. Can't count on it, nothing here to count on. Just empty air and broken promises.

Empty house, empty air.

He threw himself down onto the wide bed where the sheets were twisted into ropes, secure, at least, in the house's very emptiness. Because it had been deserted now in every way possible by every entity except himself. He could sense its desertion and its loneliness like the distant but expectant humming of a telephone left off the hook.

I've done it, he realized.

Hey, I think I might've just *done it,* was it always this simple?

Savoir faire—means mostly, like, social skills and ability, doesn't it? Adaptability. Tact. What a suave little bastard he must've thought he was, getting that lighter engraved like that, punning on

his name. You can just see him lighting smokes for francophone
Saigon b-girls with it like some bayou Maurice Chevalier. But what
it literally means in French, I believe, is, "knowing what to do."

Knowing what to do—you can sure interpret that in a lot of
ways.

Does he still know what to do? Did he foresee that I'd finally
take some action, perform this one simple little act?

Can this be what he's wanted all along?

But the house was as dead now as an old tomb, Phil realized.
Still whole, but unoccupied and lifeless.

Well, tough shit, he thought, solitary, too drained to feel anything like triumph. A faraway thunderstorm began to rumble.

The joists of the house popped in response but they popped in
emptiness, not in the fullness of some occupying personality. The
sound was subtly different. It held no resonance.

No, Phil sensed, all personality had vacated this building for
the moment. All four members of the former Savoie nuclear family, even the memory of their cat, had been sent off in all directions
tonight. The ingredients needed to cook up a ghost were thoroughly dispersed for a while, Cam and lighter and house, separated
like yolks from shells and egg whites.

And Phil searched inwardly for the peace he knew he should
be feeling, as a result.

But was not.

Just fuck her, he thought again.

TWO BLOCKS AWAY, on Prytania Street, amid the litter of crushed
cups and windblown multicolored trash dropped by Bacchus
parade-goers, a speeding red pickup with a Saints bumper sticker
drove past Seventh Street and on into the heart of the lightning-lit
night.

THIRTY-TWO

Warren

THERE JUST WEREN'T any vacant hotel rooms on Mardi Gras weekend.

Which is something I should've thought about before leaving home in a snit, Michelle realized now, parked at the Circle K convenience store on Magazine Street after having been politely turned away by the Park View Guest House. She dialed yet another hotel desk on her cell phone while Nicole slept in the backseat and Cam listened to rap music over his headset.

The western sky flared. Thunder muttered.

"Sorry, ma'am," came the familiar feedback, this time from a Holiday Inn all the way out in Kenner near the airport. "We're all full up. I can try Mississippi for you..."

"No," she said, "that's okay. Let me think about it."

Yeah, there might be some vacancies in Mississippi, she considered, kind of close by. No reason why I can't just drive to Mississippi, since neither Cam nor Nicole have classes again until Wednesday, and neither do I. We could stay in, like, Bay St. Louis or even as far away as Biloxi, if that's as close as I can find a room...

Wait, you're forgetting something.

Tasso is open tomorrow, even though it's a Monday, *dammit!* We're opening for Lundi Gras since we'll be closed on Mardi Gras day, and I told Nonnie I'd fill in for him. And Frank's counting on Cam to be there and help out because we're going to be insanely busy, all booked up already, not a single reservation left.

So do I want to drive all the way back in from Biloxi tomorrow morning? In all the tourist traffic, vans full of drunks on the I-10, if the weather's as bad as it looks like it might get?

Let me think this through some more.

Fuckhead Philip, she silently seethed, restoring the cell phone to its resting place between the front seats. I wouldn't be out here right now like this if it weren't for that judgmental asshole. I'm seeing a whole new side of him since he got sick, and I don't know if I like what I'm seeing. At all. Maybe I ought to hit the Louisiana state line and just keep on going, what the hell.

The night was oppressive and muggy. There was no wind.

A slender young woman with bobbed brown hair stood fifteen feet away in conversation at a pay phone while two little girls waited for her in a white minivan, sipping Icees. Cars circulated in and out of the lot, hauling revelers in shining carnival beads.

Lightning from nowhere suddenly ripped down like a vertical train wreck at some hapless oak in Audubon Park, setting off two nearby car alarms. Nicole leaped to life: *"Mom?"*

"Be cool, we're okay!" Michelle reached around and patted her daughter's ankle. "Everything's okay, sweetheart. We'll get us something to eat, an Icee or something, in just a minute…"

I sure don't want to have to risk driving with my kids to Mississippi in a bad storm, she told herself, making up her mind about it.

She had parked the Saturn underneath bright lights near the pay phones and she sat there for a moment with both of her hands on the steering wheel, trying to figure out a plan of action. The woman who had been using one of the phones hung up now and fished around in her shoulder bag for something.

Cam pulled off his earphones. "Mom, I wish you and Phil would just get over whatever this is, and let's go back home. This really sucks. I mean, we've even missed *X-Files!*"

"They'll repeat all the episodes," she said, watching the woman at the pay phone come up empty, "in the summertime. Chill out."

The woman noticed Michelle noticing her. She approached the Saturn in expensive sneakers, a raincoat partially covering her short tennis dress. Her palms were spread, eloquently empty. Michelle lowered the glass as she came up to the window on the driver's side and stooped slightly. "Ma'am, would you happen to have a quarter on you?"

"You have car trouble?" Michelle took several quarters from her parking-meter stash. "You can use my cell phone..."

She waved a dollar bill. "I'm not going to put anybody else out, you're so nice! Here."

Michelle took the dollar because the stranger wanted her to. The wind was picking up. Cellophane sandwich wrappers blew across the street with rattly brown oak tree leaves. "Everything okay?"

"Accidentally locked myself out of my house, how stupid is that? I'm just right over there on Calhoun. My girls could care less, they got to see all of Bacchus...Thank you so much, ma'am. Y'all have a nice night."

"Can I do anything for you?"

"Locksmith's already on his way. Thanks anyhow. I'm going to leave one more message on my husband's voice mail and then head on over."

"Y'all be careful." Michelle looked past her at the two little faces.

The young woman smiled and straightened. "You're a mom, I see—you know what it's like to be on the road all the time. We just about live in this minivan, we'll be fine."

Yeah, my own car certainly looks like the day-care center from hell, Michelle laughed in empathy, nodding. She waved and then pressed the button to raise her window, stowing away her Guatemalan handbag near her thigh. The other woman signaled her gratitude through the closed glass with an answering wave and nod, raincoat blowing against tanned wiry legs.

The Saturn's driver's-side window exploded outwards in an earsplitting crash of white light like the end of the world.

Struck by lightning! was Michelle's first thought, astonished that she could still think, that she had not been killed and that she still had brain cells to think with. She whipped her head around to check on her children, Nicole openmouthed on the backseat, Cam similarly intact but dumbstruck next to her.

Drops of rain the size of grapes began to plop through the missing window. Michelle glimpsed the young woman madly sprinting to her daughters and heard her calling to them, dark raincoat flapping like wings.

"Mom?" Cam put out a hand and touched her. "Are you okay? Are you cut?"

She looked out of the hole in the car door where a window should have been. Gleaming tiny squares of broken glass, pounded by rain, littered the parking lot from here to the phones like miniature ice cubes. "I'm not cut, the glass exploded *outwards*! It's all out there on the pavement!"

"That lady didn't get hurt, did she?"

She shook her head, watching the woman's taillights circle away. "I don't know, I don't think so—she was too far away—she's getting her girls to safety now. Yes, she's okay, look—she's waving."

"Mom!" Nicole leaned forward against the tension of her seat belt. "Rain's coming in on me!"

Michelle turned the key in the ignition. "Cam? Help Nick get buckled in on the other side of the backseat, please."

He complied. Rain was falling in sheets now, the wind driving it sideways. Her headlights swept a wide arc of falling water as she reversed and then came about.

"Where're we going?" Cam asked her, facing around in his own seat, refastening his seat belt.

"Getting away from the park and all these trees and these big electrical transformers, that's for sure."

"To where?"

"Tasso," she instantly decided. "Just a couple of miles down-town on this same street."

"Exactly what just happened here, Mom?"

"I'm not really sure," she said and told the truth, blinking her eyes against the rain. Not as much was blowing through the open window and onto her now as she had expected, but driving all the way to Mississippi was no longer any kind of option. "Sudden drop in atmospheric pressure outside the car, that's probably the answer, son."

"Let's just go home, Mom!" Nicole called from the back. "It's scary out here!"

"No, we're going to Tasso! I've got keys, even if there's nobody there." She drove down Magazine trying to see, windshield wipers running at their maximum. "It's not too far away, Nickyboo—it's closer than home is—and I know the alarm code to get us in if everybody's gone."

"It's just a little past eleven," said Cam, "kitchen's just closing."

She realized that she had no idea what time it was. The reces-sion of adrenaline had left her shaky and retroactively terrorized. She kept replaying the exploding window in her mind, the crash of light, the indescribable sound.

"Okay, we'll help 'em with cleanup," she told her son, "and then just bed down in Philip's office for the night, me and my old bones on the sofa, you and Nick camping out on the carpet. We'll be fine. An adventure."

"But what was it, Mom?" he asked again. "Something to do with lightning?"

"Something to do with barometric pressure," she spoke with professorial authority as if she knew. "Bad storms—like the ones containing funnel clouds—are very low-pressure areas. This car's just three years old with rubber gaskets still sealing all the doors and windows pretty tightly…" At least its age was the truth, she knew without doing the math, because she had bought this Saturn only about a week before Adrien died. "So if our inside air pressure remains greater than a sudden steep drop-off of pressure outside— *boom*. It happens. It's happened to a lot of people. I felt both of my ears click just before it happened, as a matter of fact. Don't you guys remember your ears clicking just now, like in an airplane?"

"Yes," said Nicole, anxious to please.

"No," said Cam.

"Well," Michelle lied, "mine certainly did."

"So we've been near a tornado?" Cam's face was white in the corner of her eye.

"Possibly. Maybe."

The rain kept up. "Cool," he nodded, but lowered his head to see as much of the city-lit clouds through the windshield as he was able, on the lookout for funnels.

Michelle drove, blobs of colored light running down her field of vision between wiper strokes, biting her lips.

"We'll try to hear the news, tonight or tomorrow, and see how close it was. Whether a tornado ever touched down anywhere or not," she told them, gratefully pulling up at the Tasso loading dock near the kitchen door in the rear of the building. "Well, we're here. Let's see if Da'Shaun or Tyrone can give us some garbage bags to tape up the window so that more rain won't come in and ruin the upholstery. Nickyboo? You awake?"

"Uh-huh."

"Go on inside with Cam, sweetheart. I'll get our stuff out of the trunk."

The kids splashed through puddles to the door while Michelle followed more slowly with their overnight luggage. The rain was slacking off. She slammed shut the door on the driver's side. Big chunks of greenish glass broken into gridded squares fell out of the doorframe and into the front seat.

She thought about Philip, remembered what he had said to her and how he had said it, and started to cry. She wiped her eyes with the heel of one hand, deciding to blame her wet face on the rain if anybody noticed.

SHE MADE TWO telephone calls from Philip's office while Nicole fell asleep on the sofa and Cam helped the staff load the dishwasher, clean the range, and mop the kitchen floor with chlorine bleach.

The first of her two calls was to Warren Pailet, the psychic, and she apologized extravagantly for disturbing him at so late an hour. She recalled his rules and broke none of them, remembering not to identify herself beyond mention of the Tulane Psych Department, but she pleaded that he consider this an emergency call. "...And I'll reimburse you in any way you want," she told him, knowing that he was probably able to identify her, at least superficially, as someone he had already read for, by her Texan drawl. "You did read for me once, and you warned me that you can't maintain accuracy if you read for any one person too much, but somebody's marriage and maybe even their sanity might depend—"

"No, don't tell me anything, ma'am, or there's no hope at all for any kind of authenticity." The mild voice sounded resigned to this intrusion but nevertheless reassuring. He probably got follow-up calls like this all the time, despite all his warnings that they wouldn't be fruitful. "So just take it easy and try to relax, okay?"

"All right." She felt guilty. Like just another loopy New Ager with too much time on her hands, needing to commune with her dead koi fish. "But this is sort of an emergency, Warren, I wouldn't dare bother you if it wasn't—"

"Ma'am, I'll do what I can, don't feel you have to pass any kind of qualifier. But I'll probably turn out to be way off target, if I've read for you already."

"I'll risk it. I'm so grateful to even get you on the phone, I'm hyperventilating."

"Don't do that. Just let me get a pencil...," he paused and she could visualize him pushing his glasses up higher on his nose, reaching for something to write with. And at last, beginning to doodle. "All right, all set. Ah…yeah. Do you know a letter *A*?"

"Yes."

"Man's name, passed."

"Yes." She closed her eyes against the sight of the sleeping Nicole curled into the Naugahyde of the sofa like a kitten.

"Oh man, this is coming through as clear as a bell! 'I love you,' he's telling you."

A hot rill of water instantly blurred her vision and spilled down her cheek. "I love you too, pal," she whispered to the air.

"—Because I get this encouragement vibration, like he's encouraging you."

"Yes."

"Some decision you need to make."

"Well, I don't…"

"He's showing me, like—wow, this is clearer than a bell—a man with a cleft chin, wearing a white…white lab coat or jacket…first initial is *B* or *P*…"

"Yes."

"*A* is pointing to this man's wedding ring and he's saying, 'Yes, yes.'"

"Yes how?"

"Like, yes, he's affirming that this man, his marriage is a good thing. Yes. I'm getting a name here—'Bill'?"

"Oh Lord. Close enough."

"'I've been trying to get Bill out of the way,' he says—but maybe that's the wrong tense, actually. Maybe it's: 'I'm trying to get Bill out of the way.' Or an instruction to you, like, '*Try* to get Bill out of the way.' You making anything at all out of this, ma'am?"

What she was making out of it wasn't helping her, it was frightening her. "I can't answer yes to this, Warren, I don't know what it means."

"Okay…" There came hisses while the psychic breathed deeply through his nostrils. "Then let's try this—here's something else:

'Save Bill,' I'm getting… Okay, he's saying it over and over now, this is *A* speaking: 'Save Bill. Save Bill. Save Bill.'"

Michelle closed her raw eyes. "Yes."

"You get that?"

"Yes."

"'I've made errors,' he's saying. 'Bill will die. Death is coming straight for Bill.'"

Shocked, she pictured Philip saying the vile things he had said to her, how he had looked, how he had sounded. She spoke desperately to the air, to Adrien, "Please don't hold his behavior against him! I'll get over it, I know! He's a good man and I love him. The kids are beginning to love him, too, baby. Please don't take him from us. *Please* don't."

Warren's voice came out slow like something extracted from him with tweezers. "'I don't want to harm him,' he's saying. 'Save him. I make errors. Timing is off. I try to speak. Glass breaks.'"

She felt her eyes roll and then open at the ceiling. Cam had not been carrying the Zippo in the car tonight, she was almost sure of it. "Oh *wow.* Oh Lord."

"'I can't control—' *something.* He's saying, 'I can't always control—' the…um…manner of his contacts with you, I think is what he's saying…"

"Yes. Oh Lord."

"Here it comes again, ma'am—sorry to be repetitious—but it just keeps coming, over and over: 'Save Bill. Save Bill. Timing is off. Save Bill.'"

"How?" she threw her hands up at the ceiling. "Tell me how!"

"Do you know an initial *D*—man's name, not passed?"

"I—"

"Oh man, this is a strong reaction!" said Warren. "I see him pointing to, like, a little girl asleep on a couch and an older boy—this can't be right—putting shoes into a dishwasher…?"

"It's okay." She saw Nicole stir on the sofa, kicking out one leg but not waking. "Go on, Warren. Please."

He sounded frantic. "Um…it rhymes with 'Donnie' but isn't 'Donnie'—how can it begin with a *D* and not be 'Donnie'?"

She knew. *Nonnie.* Her fingers hurt where she gripped the receiver. "I know who it is. Oh Lord. Keep going."

"'Save Bill,' *A* says again. —Oh wait, he's showing me the kids again…No, it's not them, it's *Bill* who needs help, he's saying— No, wait—it's Bill *and* several kids, and a woman wearing Mickey Mouse ears— Oh man, he's really agitated…I'm getting a migraine, ma'am, I'm sorry…"

"What happens to him if I call Nonnie?" She felt like she was having a heart attack herself. Her chest constricted. "What happens, Warren?"

"To Bill?"

"To *A*! What will happen to *A*?"

There was a long pause. Michelle wondered if the phone line had somehow gone out. She felt her eyes beginning to roll again and finally understood how horses felt in thunderstorms. Then: "He doesn't know."

"Doesn't know what?" She had no breath. "Who doesn't know what?"

"*A*. He doesn't know what'll happen to him."

The dam broke again and tears eroded her vision. "Oh goddammit."

"'Save Bill,' is all he keeps insisting on, ma'am… '*Touts les enfants,*' he says—'all the children.' Like it's important to them. 'Save Bill,' he's saying. Just: 'Save Bill. Save Bill.' Like a mantra."

"Yes."

"'It doesn't matter what happens to me—I'm dead,' he says. 'Bill's alive.'"

She had nothing left in her. She struck herself three times in the head with the phone receiver but that didn't make any difference, didn't make her any smarter or more reconciled.

"I've lost it, ma'am…" The psychic sounded a million miles away. "I can't—I'm done—it's gone. I'm sorry."

"Yes," she answered him automatically.

"Okay, ma'am?"

All of her insides felt as if they had been removed through her esophagus. "Okay."

"Please don't contact me anymore, ma'am."

"Yes. Of course. I mean, no. Whatever you like."

"You're a nice person," Warren enunciated carefully as if he were on the verge of passing out. "But this has been... Ma'am, this was the single most intense..."

"I know," she agreed.

"I can't take any more," he said simply.

"I think that makes two of us."

"Well, good night then, ma'am."

There weren't many Hebrew terms in her accumulated social and anthropological vocabularies but she knew this one: "*Shalom*, Warren."

He echoed this sign-off with exhausted cordiality. "You, too, ma'am. *Shalom*."

She put down the receiver and lay her head on Philip's desk.

Tears became torrents. Torrents became mudslides. Poor little sleeping Nicole, wrung out by the Bacchus parade and everything else since, never woke.

Michelle suddenly became afraid that she would not be able to stop weeping. Inner continents were shifting, Atlantis was going down. She darted quickly into the adjoining bathroom so that she could shut the door. If Cam were to come in, she certainly didn't want him to see her like this. She didn't want to have to explain or tell lies.

Get a grip here! she coached herself, running water in the sink until it got cold. Think of the kids, you nitwit.

Because there was no reason that either of the kids should ever have to learn more about all the weirdnesses that had been going on during these last four months, she lectured herself, pooling water in her hands and then lowering her face into them. Regardless of whether she and Philip found a way to stay together or split up, live or die, kill each other or go nuts, knowledge about their father's apparitions could do neither Cam nor Nick any good and might actually harm them in some way.

Michelle pressed a paper towel against her cheeks and studied her puffy eyelids in the mirror. Nick's dream and Cam's video game had provided just the correct amount of solace, she thought. But anything more would certainly cause anxiety, would upset, would frighten. Especially if Adrien were not in full control—

She looked into her own blue eyes and suddenly foresaw a very particular and terribly possible danger to her children.

The risk that they might witness the fourth and final apparition to come.

Oh no, she thought, transfixed by the idea. Oh no.

It would not bring them solace. Nor would it be anything like a mere shattered car window, just a mysterious happening attributable to nature. No amount of after-the-fact explanations would ever be able to transform Cam's and Nick's certain horror into anything less.

She instantly understood what it would do to them. What kind of subjects Nicole might paint forever afterward on into womanhood, with pigments the color of arterial blood and the dirty white of exposed bone.

And Cam, she saw quite clearly now, would literally lose his mind.

Good Lord, you're right, pal! she told Adrien mentally, unable to dash back to the desk now and dial Dominic Randazzo's phone number fast enough.

THIRTY-THREE

Afternoon Exorcism

"I STILL CAN'T BELIEVE she's letting you do this," Phil greeted his brother as Dominic came toiling up the steps to the green front porch at Chestnut Street that next day, leaving his Camry parked at the curb. It was a messy car, almost as unkempt as Michelle's Saturn, Phil again noted from where he stood, with folders and papers and notebooks cascading all over vacant seats, front and back. Burger wrappers lay crumpled in the floor. "Jesus, fast food can't be good for your heart, as out of shape as you are, Nonnie."

"Associate with teenagers, eat like a teenager..." Dominic wore a gray tweed sports jacket over his Roman collared black shirt and he was indeed breathing hard. One red hand held a small black train case. The other carried a zippered garment bag.

"Coffee?" Phil helped him with the garment bag, walking him into the front room and then closing the door behind them. The day came in shrouded through the white sheer curtains. Dominic's polished black shoes echoed on the hard wood of the floors.

He lay his paraphernalia down on the sofa cushions. "A beer, if you have it."

"Beer?"

"Why not?" He straightened, removed his eyeglasses, and then wiped their lenses clean with a tissue. "Soothe my nerves."

Phil opened the black refrigerator and stooped. "Your nerves need soothing?"

"I don't do this every day, Filbert." Dominic took the cold wet bottle from Phil's hand and wrung off the stopper. "Thanks. Sometimes these kinds of things go rather badly, I hear."

"I still can't believe she's letting you." Phil got a beer for himself.

"Oh, she's more than letting me, she's cheering me on," Dominic grunted, allowing his bulk to sink into the soft cushions. Opening his train case, he took out a slim book, battered and yellowed. "'*Rituale Romanum Pauli V Pontificis*—'" he read from the title page and interrupted himself to take a swig of beer. "You were an altar boy, or was that Martin?"

"Both of us."

"Get your reading glasses, then. There are responses I'll need recited in Latin."

Something minor made Phil choke, just a droplet of beer, but it caused him to cough and coughing worried him. Dominic watched him through his black frames like an owl. "You okay?"

"Beer went down the wrong way, I'm fine."

Dominic unzipped the garment bag to expose a long black cassock, white surplice, and a traditional purple stole. "Well, then…"

"Shouldn't we finish our beers first? I can't see us going through the house, casting out demons, with, like—I don't know— a crucifix in one hand and a Corona in the other…"

"We'll finish first, certainly." Dominic was fidgeting, uneasy. "This is a ritual and has to be performed in a prescribed manner. I'm taking it very seriously. So should you."

"So this is the real deal?"

"I'm an ordained priest, Phil. One of our original job descriptions includes the definition 'Exorcist of Demons in the Name of Our Blessed Lord, amen.'" He crossed himself without irony and then finished off his beer, setting the empty bottle on the coffee table. "I promise you I'll perform this as correctly as its irregularities permit. I do not take it lightly. I'll probably be keelhauled if word ever gets out. And if we do encounter something demonic and nasty…"

"That could be bad?"

"That could be real bad, yes."

"Nonnie, wait, I still don't get any of this. Shelly just called you up out of the blue and just asked you to come over here and exorcise Savoie?"

Soft light flashed from his brother's lenses. "Well, I introduced the subject, back while you were still in Ochsner. But her phone call to me last night, that was her own idea. Yes."

"Why now?"

"I don't know, you tell me." Red fingers clutched black knees. "She just said that you two had been at odds and told me that y'all couldn't go on this way. And she's frightened, finally. Of the phenomena."

Phil reached up and scratched an itchy place just behind his right ear. "Well, I don't know if we need to go to all this trouble now, not if it's actually dangerous to—"

"I don't believe this!" Dominic slapped both of his thighs. "What game are you playing? You're getting what you want, what you've been bellyaching and lobbying for three whole months now to get, and suddenly you decide it's not necessary?"

"Well, yeah…" His scalp stopped itching. "Yeah."

"You've married a lady of great character, Filbert, I have no idea how you managed to pull that off," Dominic leaned back into the cushions and stuck out crossed ankles before him. One black sock was creeping down to expose a band of white flesh where the trouser cuff rode high. "She's running your restaurant even as we speak, she and her children, getting ready for tonight's business, no complaints about how hard or boring it is. Michelle possesses such great charm and intelligence of a very high order, and manifests a mature love for you that I sometimes wonder if you deserve."

"None of us deserves love," Phil muttered. "Isn't that what grace is all about?"

"Touché." He tugged up his sagging sock. "So why must you make her think she's got to deserve it from you?"

Phil, too, finished off his beer. "These have been real trying circumstances, Nonnie, these last few months. It's like I'm possessed by all the petty weak elements in my own personality. I used to be a better man than this."

Dominic reached into his train case to take out a handwritten list on a small memo pad. "Since we're not entirely sure of what, exactly, we're supposed to be casting A. P. Savoie out *of,* she's given me a list of things. Objects, besides the house."

"Yeah." He counted on his fingers. "Keys, Saint Jude medal, wallet, watch, and Zippo."

"Yes. There were also three dimes and a penny in his pockets, apparently, but she doesn't remember what happened to those. Plus some crushed junk the hospital people gave her, which there was no point in keeping. But for the rest of it, she said to tell you to look on the top shelf of Nicole's closet in a Nine West shoebox. Everything else is in there except the lighter. The lighter's in Cam's room."

No, it's not, thought Phil with satisfaction.

Then he thought of something else. "Nonnie, there's one other thing I've never heard her mention and I'm suddenly curious about it. Savoie walked with a cane. Looked kind of Edwardian, like an antique worth saving. He was on his way to a school function that night, lots of socializing with other parents and teachers, lots of standing up, so you know he would've certainly brought it along. Had it with him in the car."

Dominic looked up again. "'Crushed junk,' like she's mentioned? She'd throw it out if it were ruined and no longer of use to anyone, wouldn't she?"

"I guess it doesn't matter, since a cane wouldn't actually be *on* him, not in the sense of all this other stuff. It was probably in the passenger seat, like where I throw my umbrella."

His brother's profile blocked out a portion of the daylight from the windows behind him. "He certainly would've taken it with him. He knew he had to cross several streets on foot, remember."

"Cross streets?"

"To get to the school. Country Day."

"He never got a chance to get out of the car, though," said Phil.

"Whatever makes you think that?"

"He was broadsided by a drunk running a red light," Phil insisted, "somewhere on St. Charles. Wasn't he?"

Dominic just frowned at him.

Phil stared at his brother from across the expanse of coffee table and wondered if his own face was displaying as odd an expression as Dominic's. "*Wasn't* he?" he asked again, feeling strange and detached.

"Where are you getting all this from, Phil?"

"I recall hearing something about it, like, Regan calling me when it happened. It was a traffic fatality of some kind, I'm sure I got that much straight." But Phil was remembering now the details of that vivid dream he had had back in the autumn, the streetcar, the darkness, the rain. "He was driving—?"

"I don't know where you'd get the idea that somebody would be on St. Charles Avenue if he's headed out to Metairie."

"Well, now that you mention it—"

"No, look, what happened, the lack of parking space for these kinds of events at Country Day is notorious and he didn't arrive soon enough to get to park very close to the school, according to the *Times-Picayune*." Dominic folded his hands across his girth. His sock was down again. "He'd had to park several blocks away and then get out and walk. It was right before Christmas—I'd just been transferred back here and the whole thing made a very vivid impression on me because the driver was a student at the high school

I'd just been made principal of. Terrible thing. Seems he and several passengers were late for a party. They'd already had too much
to drink and were lost on all of those winding residential streets,
looking for an address, you know how kids are. He was speeding
and ran a stop sign. He struck Savoie before he saw him."

Phil couldn't make it compute. It wouldn't match up with any
of the puzzle pieces in his picture of past things. "Jesus."

Dominic rubbed his upper lip in reflection. "There were witnesses. Their account of it had the vehicle doing at least thirty-five
when it hit him. He saw it coming, its headlights from behind trees
and shrubbery out of that long curve, but it didn't stop at the stop
sign and he wasn't able to run."

"Holy God."

"Terrible thing. Terrible. The young idiot who was driving
never meant to hurt anybody, he's the one who called 911 on his car
phone," Dominic went on. "Savoie, as I understand it, was dressed
in a dark suit, very dark clothing. The kid said he never even saw
him, and I'm sure he didn't."

"It was raining, wasn't it?"

Dominic shook his head. "I'm not under that impression."

Phil couldn't speak now.

"The human body is a poor match for two tons of metal. Look
at all the lives changed or ruined, Phil. Not just Michelle's and
those of her children, but the young driver's as well, and his parents' lives, and the lives of his passengers. He'll have to live with
this for the rest of his days."

"Unless Savoie shows up to forgive him…" Phil flopped back
in his armchair and rubbed his face from top to bottom.

"You want to go get those personal effects for me now?" Dominic became brisk. "Just forget about the cane. I think we can be
fairly certain that it was broken upon impact, being right at bumper
level."

So were Savoie's crippled legs, Phil realized, feeling blood
draining down into the hands he let dangle over the chair arms.

The priest glanced at him. "Phil?"

"We don't need to do this, Nonnie," he answered. Gravity pressed him into the upholstery. "I've pretty much already done it."

Dominic stopped in midfumble with the contents of his train case. Phil saw the crossed bars of a crucifix. "What're you talking about?"

"It was the Zippo. It's always been the Zippo, mostly, combined with Cam's energy. So I put it into Kerri's hands last night. For safekeeping."

"Filbert, I did *not* go to all this trouble to leave school and drive all the way over here just to drink beer and entertain the notion that you could be right about a cigarette lighter!" said Dominic with asperity. "And I refuse to face your wife and tell her we just decided to wuss out and skip it. So please go fetch me these objects, or I'll climb up into Nicole's closet and get 'em myself."

Phil got to his feet, forcing his healing knees up the steep stairs to the shoebox's hiding place. When he came back downstairs and lay the everyday objects out on the coffee table, the inexpensive watch—no Rolex—and a brown leather wallet that had seen better days, a small gold Saint Jude medal and a set of house and car keys, he wondered if his own existence would someday be boiled down into such temporal insignificance.

There were pictures in the plastic windows of the wallet, a much younger Cam, baby Nicole, Michelle with long hair. Along with a driver's license and a single Visa card in its torn slot were two one-dollar bills.

If A. P. Savoie eventually learned how to make decent money in his life, Phil thought, fingering this humble legacy, it's clear that he never learned how to spend any of it.

I have no business handling these things, goddam, I feel like a sneak thief. My wreck dream was bogus. None of us are clairvoyant, we're just a bunch of dumbasses with a wild hair up our butts.

"Please call Michelle for me as soon as we're done here," he instructed Dominic in a quiet voice, "and tell her I'm an idiot. Ask her to please come back home. With her kids. Tonight."

"I'll dial the number, Filbert, but she'll want to hear that directly from you, baby."

"She'll probably hang up on me…"

But Dominic was already getting to his feet, taking off his jacket. He held up the long cassock by its hanger. "We'll deal with that later. Time I got into uniform here."

Phil watched his brother array himself. "Important to look the part, huh?"

The white surplice went on over the cassock. Dominic arranged the purple stole over his shoulders after touching its fabric to his lips. "I'm not to appear incognito. Even the blindest demon shall notice me."

"How long will this take?"

"Oh, I guess about twenty minutes. To read the prayers. *If* nothing happens." Dominic reseated his glasses onto his strong nose and took up the old book.

"So how soon will we know?" Phil's pulse rate increased. This was really going to happen. He still held Savoie's wallet. "If we're up against something evil?"

"Just as soon as I flash a crucifix, I imagine. Well, what about it? You ready?"

Holy Church is riding to my rescue here like the U.S. cavalry, thought Phil. About to trample whatever's in the way.

Whatever is injured and can't run.

"I guess so," he answered, closing the wallet and spreading all of the items out onto the glass top of the coffee table. He located his reading glasses and looked at the priest. "God forgive me."

"God forgive us all," said Dominic.

IT TOOK TWENTY-FIVE minutes to read through the ritual because Phil's Latin was rusty. In the stillness of the pauses he could hear his watch's tiny clicks as the sweep hand made its circuit. He heard occasional street noises from outside. But increasingly all he could feel was numb peace.

Dominic raised his crucifix, lowered it, raised his voice in the sonorous old prayers, lowered it. He cast glittering droplets of holy water into the stripes of sun that came through the edges of the sheers at the windows.

Absolutely nothing happened.

THIRTY-FOUR

Homecoming

"I'M SORRY, HONEY," was the first thing Michelle said to Phil as she ascended the brick steps of the front porch very late that same night—after midnight, so it was technically tomorrow now, he saw by his watch—dragging overnight bags and a white plastic grocery sack of dirty laundry.

Cam came behind her, leading a groggy Nicole by the hand, stinking of garlic and fried grease as he passed through the door and came into the bright lights of reflector bulbs high up in the ceiling.

Phil noticed the Saturn's taped-up window. He indicated the car with his chin as Cam sprawled onto the hardwood floor, removing his sauce-splattered sneakers. "What's happened? Y'all okay?"

"We're fine. We had an awesome night at Tasso, Phil, even during the Orpheus parade—umpteen billion people, big spenders, big tippers!" Cam's straight white teeth shone up at him. "Frank says I have a natural talent for roux."

"'S' good..." He took the luggage from Michelle and settled it against the breakfast bar, trying to act normal around her, assessing her mood. "What happened to the car, Shell? Somebody break in?"

"We were in a tornado," Nicole spoke up with no particular emotion, dropping to the floor near Cam and settling herself against the luggage, "and we're incredibly tired."

"Tornado?"

"That big thunderstorm after Bacchus." Michelle looked drained. Her hair was unwashed and dull, her face doughy. "Sudden drop in barometric pressure outside the car, all the windows were up. Insurance'll cover it. I'll take care of it sometime on Wednesday." She flopped down into the nearest armchair. "So how are you feeling?"

"More rested." He poured twin bourbons at the kitchen counter, still within her sight lines over the breakfast bar. "Going back in to work on Wednesday, I imagine."

"They all miss you. Da'Shaun told me to be sure to give you his best."

Phil nodded. He carried Michelle's drink around the end of the bar.

"Don't step on Nicole," she said.

Nick was nodding off with her upper body against the bar, short legs sticking out onto the hardwood of the floor. Cam lay on his back on the Oriental carpet with his hands folded over his rib cage. "Looks like a hurricane relief center in here," said Phil, making his way to his wife around the luggage and soiled laundry.

"Restaurant work," she said, accepting the glass. "Thanks, honey."

"Some of us love it," mumbled Cam's voice out of his shut-eyed face.

"Well, you know, if you keep your grades up," said Phil, "and do your homework, maybe we can work out a schedule for you at Tasso this summer, like start you out on Saturdays—"

Cam reached out and tried to hug Phil's ankle.

"What I want you two kids to do right now," said Michelle, sipping, "is to go upstairs and get into bed, guys, if you want to catch Rex tomorrow morning, it rolls at ten."

Nicole scrambled up and Cam followed slowly, his long limbs showing more grace and less of their customary ungainliness. "Can we skip our baths, Mom?"

"No skipping baths. Even Nick's hair smells like grease. Mine does, too, probably."

"But it's Mardi Gras!" Cam protested, heading for the stairs with his sister right behind him. "Let the good times roll, and whatever!"

"The good times will roll tomorrow," said Michelle. "They're out of gas tonight, son."

"Cam?" Phil called out, remembering something, and saw his stepson's legs freeze a quarter of the way up the steep flight.

Cam bent to make eye contact, long oily bangs in his eyes. "Sir?"

"If you notice your lighter is missing, I've asked Kerri to look after it for you for a while. Is that okay?"

His face didn't change expression. He smoothed back his hair with one hand. "But I wasn't carrying it with me anywhere anymore, y'all said not to accidentally risk taking it to school…"

Phil was aware of his wife's eyes on him. "I realize that, son, and I'm sorry for not trusting you more. Just look at it as my mistake— I haven't been myself since I got sick, I've been an idiot about a lot of things. Think of it as an excuse to get to see Kerri again real soon. Okay?"

He didn't move. Nicole stepped under the arm that he held to the banister and climbed on up past him. "It's Kerri who has it? Not Doctor Lyle or Miss Regan—?"

"*Kerri.* I put it into her hands myself."

Cam moved now, one foot to the next step. "Well, that's okay."

"I'm sorry. But you know you'll get it back over Easter if not before. The kids'll be spending Easter here with me this year."

"Okay," his voice came drifting back as his socked feet climbed out of Phil's sight.

Phil didn't need to turn his head to know that Michelle had never taken her eyes off him. He gulped his drink and then set the glass down upon the coffee table.

"We drink too much," she said. "How're you going to get your strength back?"

"Not everybody is an alcoholic, Shelly. I'm gonna be dragging my ass for several months no matter what I do. Might as well enjoy myself."

"Just don't go overboard."

"Well," he responded, meaning nothing. Meaning everything.

"We kept Nicole busy by letting her think she's designing a new menu for you," she went on dully, wiping her hair back. "She drew red crawfish all over the margins of a spare that Vanessa gave her, and some ducks. Looks fairly attractive, actually, in sort of a primitive and funky way. I mean, she's a *'tite Acadienne,* after all. Who better to embellish something with crawfish?"

"Hm."

"Your brother Dominic kind of likes it. Says it loosens up the place's image. He thinks you ought to buy her some real paints and let her do murals in the dining rooms."

"Hah."

"I'm running off at the mouth." Her face was puffy.

"Well," he said again, "I don't know how comfortable I'd be with letting Tasso get loosened up. I'm just more of a white-on-white kind of guy, I guess. That's just me, I'm sorry."

"Philip," he had given her an opening and she was taking it, "I'm sorry, too. I'm so sorry, honey. For everything. What I said, what I did…"

"Me, too, hon. I was a world-class jerk. You were right, calling me an asshole."

"Oh, I call everybody an asshole sooner or later…" Her face was drained of complete emotion. What she showed was incomplete, lacking. "When Dominic phoned me, after the exorcism, and then when I spoke with you—"

"Why're you sitting way over there?"

"I don't know." She looked around herself and then put a hesitant hand to an arm of the chair to get to her feet.

He patted the sofa cushion beside his thigh. She settled into it, not quite pressed against him but not wholly separated from him.

He let his arm drape across the sofa's back behind her head, not quite touching her.

He glanced at the watch on her wrist. "Happy Mardi Gras."

"You going to feel like coming out to the parades with us in the morning?" She held the rim of her glass, cold, to her forehead. "I'm really too beat to be up for it, but the kids'll both bust a gut if I don't let 'em go. And I don't think Cam's responsible enough yet to look out for Nicole out there all by himself."

"I might walk up there with y'all for a little bit," he said, "yeah."

"Because it's hard for Cam and me to keep her sheltered from the crowds, and he likes to catch beads and stuff when he should be watching out for her, you know how it is. She's so little, she can't see over everybody's heads, so he holds her up on his shoulders once in a while. But only after she's had to nag him to death."

"I can probably lift her up," said Phil, "myself."

They sipped at their bourbons in tandem.

"I guess I need to go wash the kitchen grease off me," she said. "Get my own bath."

"We could get in the Jacuzzi," Phil understood that he had to make the offer even if he wasn't sure that he had the energy. Or the desire.

"Honey, I'll be too tired to make anything happen for us in the Jacuzzi, most likely," she warned, not making eye contact with him. "Will you read something into that?"

"No," he said, but privately thinking that he probably would. He tried to remember the last time they had had sex, him and her. How long ago that had been. "That's okay. I'm not much in the mood myself."

"But he's gone, Philip. I can feel it."

"Me, too," he said, knowing it, intuiting what an empty house they were in now. It was as if the house itself had died like a whelk and they were living in its shell. "I feel it, too."

"I mean, he is *outta here*," she spoke with unexpected bitterness, lips pressed together.

Phil was thrown off track. His latent anger at her was suddenly goosed.

But she went on, oblivious, possessed by bourbon and fatigue. "I was always able to tell. Whenever he left me, in our bad old New York days. Even if I was asleep and hadn't heard the door open. Or close. He could move very silently for a man with a cane. Sneaking out, after one of our big arguments, for more liquor or dope or some piece of raw twat, just stay gone for weeks—I never knew where. Damn his guts. He hurt me so bad, leaving."

Phil triangulated one ankle over the other knee and then breathed from the top of his chest.

"I could always tell," her voice faded.

"Well, I can't tell a goddam thing about anything." He moved his arm high up on the back of the sofa, away from the greasy hair he was desperate for her to shampoo. "I don't know a thing about a thing."

She reacted to his tone. "I'm sorry, honey. I never know when to shut up."

"I'm wooden. I don't know when to talk."

"We're both getting old," she said after a long pause, but with no rancor, making an observation. "Inelastic. That's not the same as being wooden."

"Only one way to avoid that. Call the mortuary."

Her head nodded.

He thought about it and then let his arm fall onto her shoulders. She reached up and held his fingertips. They sat in silence broken only by the rushing sounds of water running through plumbing as the kids bathed upstairs. Orange street light came through the sheer curtains of the windows at their backs. No cars passed outside.

"I don't know what else to say, Philip," she pressed his hand after those many minutes. Her face, reflected in the distant mirrored wall of the dining room, was leaden.

"What scares me, Shell, is how just about the time people get to where they're finally able to let go of the past," he said, "seems like they're so goddam old, they don't have any future."

SHE WOKE EARLY, with low morning sunlight filtering through the open window, to the nearby boom of drums and amplified second-line music: probably the Jefferson City Buzzards or a similar marching club, passing by on Prytania just two blocks away in its own private and meandering parade.

Oh shit, Mardi Gras, she remembered, wearily consulting the clock on the nightstand. Only 7:42. Lord.

Philip lay motionless as she stirred, facing away from her. But at least he was still there.

No, it's Adrien who's gone, she reminded herself, still oddly angry at his decampment. Upset at his compliant exorcisability as if he'd just decided to take the easy way out again, away from her and her roiling emotions, and just go. Just sneak out the door, without apology or explanation, like so many times before.

And now we'll never know why the asshole was even here in the first place, she thought, depressed and disgruntled. How unreasonable I am. How conflicted and hard to please.

She rested a forearm over her eyes and wondered how long she could get away with faking sleep on Mardi Gras before Nicole and Cam woke up and became excitedly active. It was like Christmas morning—Christmas morning in any normal household, anyway—kids up at the crack of dawn and rarin' to go, grown-ups dead on their feet and seeking coffee.

Yeah, and I've promised Nick that she can do some face painting on all of us, I don't know how that's going to go down with Philip, she thought now, hauling herself to the edge of the mattress and then sliding off with as much don't-shake-the-bed care as she could.

That's when she heard the first juvenile footfalls overhead. She moved very quickly now, rushing to intercept any bushy-tailed youngster before he or she could come stomping down the stairs and wake Philip. She located her robe and fled.

The morning seemed pleasantly warm and was certainly bright as she mounted the stairs in her bare feet and came up to the kids' high sanctuary. The sky was blindingly blue.

It was Nicole who was up, mouth in a happy hyper O. "Mom! I hear the parade!"

"*Shhh*— It's not Rex yet, sweetheart, don't wake up your brother." Michelle came into her daughter's room to sit on the small rumpled bed. "It's just one of those walking clubs like Pete Fountain's—you know, the guys with paper flowers on sticks, and you have to kiss one of 'em to get one."

"Oh yeah." Nicole rocked back on her heels and swung her arms, and then couldn't help jumping in place. Twice.

"Sweetheart, please don't do that! You'll wake up Philip!"

"Oh yeah. Sorry."

"Let's let the menfolks sleep just a little while longer, you and me," said Michelle, going to Nicole's small television set and turning it on, "while we investigate the weather reports, why don't we? So we'll know whether or not we'll need to bring jackets with us."

"We won't need jackets, Mom," Nicole announced, raising her window four more inches and putting her small hand excitedly against the screen. "It's incredibly beautiful outside."

So it was, Michelle saw again.

"Can I wear my long princess costume, Mom? From Halloween?"

"I don't know if you'll still fit into your princess costume, you've been growing so much," Michelle bent down and hugged her daughter from behind and inhaled the sweet smell of her neck, "my *big* girl! Gimme a smooch."

Nicole giggled and turned her head to give her mother a smacking kiss of the lips.

It was self-evidently a gorgeous morning, which was good,

Michelle thought, because she couldn't find weather reports on any of the local TV channels. One newscaster was going on about the revealed identity of this year's King Rex when she punched the off button and took Nicole downstairs to get the coffee started.

This is the first real day of my total and complete commitment to Philip Randazzo and to Philip Randazzo alone, she realized, blue.

I'll probably screw it up.

THIRTY-FIVE

Mardi Gras

WHAT PHIL WAS NOTICING for the first time was just how bizarre Mardi Gras actually was, because he was witnessing it this year through new eyes—the eyes of the formerly haunted—while both Cam and Nicole hustled to capture throws and Michelle worked to keep track of both of them.

The weather was perfect, true Mardi Gras weather, temperature in the high sixties, sun bright enough to burn Caucasian faces. Yet the sunlight couldn't dispel this new uneasiness Phil felt toward the blank and featureless masks of the captains, masks he had seen all his life and had grown up seeing. But he had never before been aware of their strange anonymity, of how much their smooth golden surfaces—with ovals cut out for eyes, for nostrils, for a mouth—resembled gilded human skulls.

Rex the King of Carnival rolled past, waving his scepter, unmasked as was customary, wearing the traditional blond Prince Valiant-bobbed wig, false goatee, and natty mustache. His cheeks were rouged but he looked genuinely regal, not campy—and how hard would that be for an ordinary guy to pull off, Phil wondered, dressed in tights like this and a golden fairy-tale tunic? Two child page boys attended him on his throne float, likewise rouged and bewigged, white ostrich plumes sticking straight up from glittery skullcaps held in place by elastic straps passing beneath their small chins.

"Look, Phil!" Nicole held up a doubloon for his inspection, a souvenir coin with Rex's profile on it, thrown to her by one of the pages but actually caught by Cam who had rescued it from the intervening hands of would-be interceptors.

"Yeah! Great!" he shouted back, more mouthing than shouting, it was that noisy. She had painted his face before leaving the house this morning, blue and black spiders on webs of silver glitter across his nose, cheeks, and forehead. The glitter was working its way into the crow's-feet around his eyes now and causing some minor irritation. It's tough to be beautiful, guys, Phil waved cheerily to the royals as they rolled down the avenue underneath their own makeup.

Here came the traditional *Boeuf Gras* float in the wake of assorted dukes and chattels—the proverbial Fatted Calf, a giant white steer with a garland of flowers around his sleek neck, mounted upon a platform large enough to hold a number of masked men, his symbolic butchers-to-be, all sporting chefs' toques. *Eat, Drink, and Be Merry,* Phil recalled the old motto, *For Tomorrow We May Die.*

"You feeling okay?" Michelle pulled at his arm, masked by her own sunglasses and red glitter crawfish painted on both cheeks.

He nodded, feeling pretty good on the whole.

But just what, exactly, is this really all about? is what he was pondering, watching the familiar spectacle unfold through the new filter of his recent uncanny experiences. Because this is fucking strange, even slightly sinister when you get right down to it, he thought, our annual civic celebration here. What the hell are we celebrating?

Unmasked faces, black and white, brown and pink, lining both sides of the avenue in ranks ten deep, began to appear equally malevolent. It occurred to Phil that many of the thousands out here would statistically be actual criminals, wife beaters and child molesters, purse snatchers, armed robbers, rapists, sadistic murderers.

Whom we walk amongst every day, holy God! he thought, hug-

ging himself. How fragile and illusory what we call "normal" life is.
How blessed we are to wear blinders.

HE MOVED CLOSER to Michelle who stepped down off the sturdy
plastic cooler she'd been standing on. He bumped her with his hip,
accidentally, but she deliberately bumped back and that made him
feel better about everything. He watched as she stooped to raise
the cooler's lid, noticing how her jeans flattered her nice ass. Maybe
the kids'll fall asleep early tonight, he thought, and then we can see
about the Jacuzzi and whatever else we need to see about.

She took out two beers from a fjord of melting ice.

"Thanks, doll!" he shouted to her over the din.

A string of metallic-blue plastic beads hit her right on the collarbone, a rattling missile. Reflexively she slapped a hand against
them, laughing, and then draped the necklace around her neck
with the many others that were already there.

"Great!" he nodded. "Good catch!" Although it had been nothing of the kind. Riders frequently slow-pitched to attractive women.

He saw himself reflected in twin images in the dark ovals of her
sunglasses. With all of that glittery red face paint on her cheeks she
looked more like a college girl than a boomer. With her layers of
beads and her beer, her pale hair in a messy halo. With one hand
held in the air now to beckon for more throws.

She was yelling at the maskers up there on the floats, waving,
gyrating, and beads rained down like Niagara. Phil put an arm
around her to establish ownership and felt proud. Women could
earn even longer and more spectacular strands of beads by raising
their shirts to flash their breasts, mainly inebriated female tourists
farther downtown, and it was mostly male tourists beneath French
Quarter balconies who egged them on. But Carnival in the neighborhoods was a family event, and that was just fine with Phil.

He spotted Cam balancing Nicole on his shoulders, twenty
feet away. The purple netting of her princess costume billowed
over her big brother's back like the train of some Endymion parade

headdress. Didn't women call that net fabric tulle, or something like that? Phil wondered if it would make a good food strainer—like cheesecloth, only with uniform holes.

The Rex parade was nearing its end just as he was beginning to really get into the mood and enjoy it. Yet few onlookers left the parade route now at the passage of the last float because the immense truck parade, the Elks' Krewe of Orleanians, was coming up right behind in Rex's wake.

"Here come the trucks," said Michelle, unnecessarily. "You want to stay for the trucks?"

Phil shrugged, pointing at the two kids. Kids really dug the trucks. Because the truck parade riders always threw copiously, heedlessly, generously, like drunken sailors.

But he winced at the raw honking of the chrome air horns mounted on the cabs of these one-hundred-plus decorated floats constructed aboard the flatbed trailers of eighteen-wheelers, as their drivers signaled milling pedestrians to again clear the route.

There were no bands in the truck parade, just one homemade truck float after another, built and decorated and manned by ordinary citizens, extended families, whole neighborhoods. These were not society people like those in Rex. Phil thoroughly endorsed the democracy of their presentation, finding many of their floats and coordinating riders' costumes astonishing in their eye appeal and high degree of professionalism. But an air horn was an air horn.

Time for another beer, he concluded, consulting Michelle's cooler.

He enjoyed the novelty of a beer buzz in bright noontime sunshine and studied the endless line of trucks yet to come as they crawled toward him through lacy tunnels of oak branches and power lines. Showers of glittery trinkets arced into the air from both sides of each vehicle like spewing fountains, landing tangled in the trees or clutched in the outstretched fingers of onlookers. Voices crescendoed in a roar as each truck passed.

The nearest air horn let loose a blast. He covered his ears, one hand fisted around his beer can.

A shot went off, to his right and across the street, from the wide neutral ground among the ranks of stepladders holding toddlers above dormant streetcar tracks.

TIME STOPPED. Heads were flash-frozen in their turning.

The day went dark.

Michelle seized Phil's arm. "Was that a—?"

"He got a gun!" shouted a panicked young woman pounding up on his left, herding three small brown-skinned children with her out-stretched arms, pushing them up the sidewalk for the shelter of parked cars on Seventh Street. *"He got a gun!"*

Phil looked back to witness the immediate scattering of other people in an ever-widening circle from the point across the street that was ground zero—ripples from a rock heaved into a puddle—black and white faces on the run, babies snatched up, ladders and ice chests abandoned, girls shrieking.

At its center was a sudden police car, blue light bar ablaze. Where had it come from? Phil wondered. How had it gotten here so fast?

"Philip!" Michelle was yelling, pulling him away, tugging him along on the tide, steering Nicole ahead of her.

Two more officers, mounted on horseback and helmeted, con-verged upon the action in a drumbeat of rubber horseshoes. Six or seven blue uniform shirts had already materialized around that first car. Another cruiser approached from downtown, siren shrill.

Wow, they haul some ass, Phil marveled, buffeted by the el-bows of strangers. My tax dollars at work.

Backed-up float trucks honked in protest, immobilized by flee-ing pedestrians, unable to move more than a few feet at a time. Most of them, stranded well away from the incident, probably had no idea of the nature of the delay.

"Philip!" He became aware of Michelle screaming over the air horns, right into his ear, stopped in her tracks. "Where's Nicole?"

"She's okay, honey—calm down—it wasn't no shooting," he answered, looking back, loud enough so that his wife could hear him, gesturing at the stationary blue shirts of the police presence behind them. "No ambulance, nobody seems to be hurt or nothing…"

"I don't see Nicole." She became still, unhearing. Aggressive in her passivity.

Cam was near them now, pointing back at the avenue. "Some moron set off a cherry bomb or something, y'all believe that?"

But the true crisis of the situation had begun to get through to Phil's buzzed brain. "Cam," he took the boy's finger down out of the air, "where's your sister?"

Cam glanced all around himself as refugee parade-goers who had been running past him first slowed to a walk and then a full stop, forming in bemused groups upon the asphalt. "She's right here."

"No, she's not." His mother spoke through vocal cords as tight as piano wire.

The crowd had begun to reassemble itself in clots braying softly with sheepish laughter, relief turning into collective self-consciousness. But Phil's vision scanned the forest of stilled legs for a glimpse of purple tulle.

He didn't see it.

"Shelly, you know she's all right, she's too smart to go off with a stranger…," he reassured his wife but his eyes still searched. "False alarm, nobody got shot, thank God. She's okay, I'll find her. Just stay here with Cam for a minute."

Her voice, monotonous with tension, ratcheted up a notch. "Oh for God's sake. Oh for God's sake."

"Look, she's a smart kid, she knows what to do, I'll find her," he said again, positioning Michelle's spine right up against the one-way sign at Seventh Street. "You just stay here with Cam, right here at this corner, so that she and I can find the two of you when we get back."

"You stay, *I'll* go!"

"Shelly, I'm a runner, honey," he told her. "She's probably headed for home—wouldn't she do that? If we all got separated and she couldn't find us?"

"I don't know."

"I'll just catch up with her and scoop her up," said Phil, "and be right back here before y'all even miss me. Okay?"

Michelle said nothing but she remained with Cam at the tall street sign, arms hanging limp. Phil wondered, as he turned away from her and headed into the crowds, just how long it would take her to miss her beer cooler. Dammit, Nick! he thought, losing Michelle and Cam to the barrier of faceless bodies and featureless mouths that called out to friends and cursed.

But would Nicole actually go home? Without a key to get inside the house?

Phil knew his long legs could take him five times faster down Seventh Street toward home than Nicole's short ones would be carrying her, so he used this luxury of speed to first about-face and then backtrack the route to the beer cooler, just in case she had seen fit to return to it. Kids got lost at Mardi Gras all the time.

One of those goddam maddening truck horns began to blast again, the fucking dickhead, urging people to clear the street. Phil noticed that the army of cops had dispersed, taking with them in handcuffs that transcendent genius who'd supposed a Mardi Gras crowd the ideal setting for a firecracker explosion.

Under two giant black tires of the nearest idling truck float, amid the litter of flattened soft drink cans and fast-food wrappers and broken parade throws, Phil, not looking for it there, spotted a lengthy rag of purple tulle, dirtied and torn.

His heart stopped.

Crouching, he saw clouds of tulle in the darkness beneath the float's fringe, near the place where the cab joined its trailer. Its horn blared again and it hissed like a monster as its driver put it into gear.

When he came back to himself a second later he was already screaming, hammering with both fists against the driver's-side door, taking his voice up to the loudest volume it had ever reached, "STOP! STOP! STOP! STOP!" until the top of his head seemed to lift off.

Gears changed again. A man's head appeared up there at the open window above his own. "Yeah? Whassamatter, what's the problem?"

"My stepdaughter." He still had some voice left. "Under your truck. Six years old. Way up under there."

The engine immediately died. Shining painted metal began to part as the door opened, but Phil didn't wait. On hands and knees he scuttled underneath the decorated vehicle into inked shadow where fringe curtained three sides of it.

Its costumed riders, sequined headdresses reflecting light that he could no longer see, began to inquire above him and then to gradually wail: "What?" "What happened?" "A little girl—" "Somebody's child—" *"Oh my God!"*

But he could also hear Nicole now, still softly alive. Sobbing, unheard in the uproar on the street, "Mom! Cam! Help me! Come get me…!" Silhouetted against the fringed stripe of glare, scrabbling to move and unable to do so.

His insides twisted. Dread fell upon him like a smothering black blanket. "Nick?" his own voice was swallowed up by the cave, by what he was about to see. "Nick, sweetheart?"

Oh please dear Saint Joseph and the infant Jesus, he prayed. Oh please, blessed Saint Anthony of Padua, Saint Rosalia—

"It's Phil!" he called again, creeping on his elbows.

The purple bundle turned a few degrees. Dim light fell onto the small face, striped with tears and smeared glittery paint and misery.

His shaking hands reached her. Touched her.

Miniature fingertips curled into the fabric of his sleeve, raw and bleeding. Her body pivoted in a bizarre manner, horribly un-

solid as he handled her, and despair like a heart attack seized him
in instant and literal nausea.

—Until he realized that she felt that way because she was partially suspended a few inches over the asphalt, hanging from a pro-
trusion. The long layers of her skirt were caught in the vehicle's
undercarriage.

Anxious voices, the heads and shoulders of bystanders and police officers, began to surround them. Phil experienced their presence as dim and distant as he tore bare-handed at the purple fabric.
Flashlight beams illuminated his furious fingers.

"Phil!" Nicole was crying. "Phil! Phil!"

When he realized that he might be hurting her, it was too late.
His strong cook's hands had already ripped into strips the netting
that held her. Her body, at its waist and hips, dropped two inches
in sudden freedom.

She wrapped both arms around his neck like a drowning swimmer. The delicate bones of her back were warm and intact beneath
his palm, and he choked up. The two of them, sprawled out on the
asphalt, were cheek to cheek, face paint mingling.

An EMS rescuer appeared from out of the light at the opposite side, red ponytail dangling over one shoulder, as Phil tore the
entire skirt from Nicole's leotard, releasing her.

"Holy God, sweetheart," he wiped his face with purple tulle,
"Jesus Jumpin' Christ—"

"I'm sorry, Phil, but there were these real pretty long beads on
the ground... I went to get 'em only for just one tiny little second,
I promise you—while everybody was running—but somebody big
knocked me down and then the truck ran over my princess dress..."
She was still crying but calmer, going into excuse mode, as he turned
her over in the low space and got one arm underneath her legs, the
other under her shoulders.

Both of her knees were badly abraded, he saw. Both elbows, the
palms and fingertips of both hands. She'd been dragged. Already
dragged some yards, with nobody knowing or having any way of

finding out. And there would have been three more miles of dragging yet to go.

"Sir?" The EMS woman began to crawl in toward them.

"Yeah?"

"You her father?"

"More or less."

"What is her—?"

"Name's Nicole," he answered, if that indeed was going to be
the question, "and she's okay." He began to inch out backward on
his knees and elbows, coming feetfirst into daylight. "Just skinned
up. And shook up."

Paramedics met him as he emerged, bystanders and float riders breaking into loud cheers and applause, shrill keen whistles.
Someone took the child from him before he could even rise to a
kneeling position.

"Me, too," he muttered in an afterthought, getting unsteadily to
his feet, "as a matter of fact."

"You what, sir?" The redhead was helping another paramedic
settle the unwilling Nicole onto a gurney, gently but firmly strapping her down. The street had become full of white bedding and
aluminum frames, blue official shirts, flashing ambulance lights.

Goddam, Savoie's really *dead,* Phil finally felt the truth of it.
He's completely dead for real, no kind of alive at all anymore. He
wanted to save his kids, here was a prime opportunity to rescue one
of 'em. A big reason to want to become substantial.

Two policemen were instructing the driver of the eighteen-
wheeler to pull it out of line so that the rest of the parade could
pass by unobstructed while they questioned him for their report.
Because the rest of the parade had to go by, Phil knew. Everybody
knew. The day's celebration must resume.

Several onlookers at the edge of the crowd were suddenly
jostled by a tall blond boy pushing them out of the way so that his
mother Michelle could fight her way through, face strained and

wild and relieved. Her sunglasses were gone, long arms and legs jerking in all directions at once, and she was trying to run to both Phil and Nicole at the same time but could manage only Nicole.

"I'm shook, too," Phil finally answered the paramedic, running a hand through his sweaty gray hair, knowing that nobody heard him.

THIRTY-SIX

Another Anniversary

MICHELLE GLANCED UP at the sound of two sharp taps on the glass panel of her opened office door, expecting to see yet another student.

But it was Philip standing there, dressed in the clean jeans and golf shirt of his prework early afternoons, brown eyes widened in some sort of unreadable expectancy.

Her reading glasses slid further down her nose and she reached up to remove them, slightly alarmed. Alarm came so easily to her these days. "What's wrong, honey?"

"Something has to be wrong for me to be here?" He took one tentative step over the threshold.

"No," she said, but remembered that he almost never just showed up at her Tulane office this way, unplanned, unannounced.

"Does anything have to be wrong for me to give you this?" A single red and perfect rose appeared from behind his back. Its fresh perfume beckoned.

The muscles of her face relaxed but her mouth remained open as he approached her desk to offer it to her. Pushing herself back in her swivel chair, she reached at the heaped bookshelves behind her for a coffee mug or something to put it in. "Oh, Philip, honey, it's lovely...! What don't I know about?"

"You free for lunch?"

The terra-cotta Mexican vase she came up with was cracked. That empty plastic cola bottle over there would have to do. "Right now?"

"It's lunchtime, more or less."

"What don't I know?" she asked him again from over her shoulder, stepping past him and out into the corridor to fill the makeshift vase with water from the cooler.

"March eighth," he said. "First anniversary of our first date."

She stuck the rose into the bottle and then brought it back to set it on her desk. "Philip, our first date had to've been a bit later, honey. During spring break, I remember."

"You remember the exact date?"

"No, but I do know it was during spring break, because I had no classes to—"

"Can't we just *say* it was March eighth, for Chrissake?"

She looked closely at his face but detected no anger there, only frustration and some emotion that she could not read. Philip, far from wooden lately, was a fountainhead of new and changeable feelings this spring. Too bad he didn't seem to know what any of them were. "Yes," she answered, "I don't see why not. Close enough."

"I didn't get to celebrate Valentine's with you the way we should've," he began to backtrack and apologize, "what with it being a Friday, and Tasso and all. Cam ate all your candy…"

"Honey," she closed and locked all of her desk drawers, "I keep telling you that having my daughter alive with me on Valentine's was celebration enough, I swear to God."

"Grab your stuff and let's get going." He held the door open for her. "It's real nice outside and we're wasting it."

"Saving Nicole takes care of every Valentine's Day for the rest of our lives, Philip, as far as I'm concerned. We're more than even, honey. You can drop Christmas, too."

He made no comment. He just seemed in a hurry to get out of the building.

She was still mystified, but he had been correct about the beauty of the day. Damp sunlight filtered through a white haze over the green tops of the oaks as he drove toward the zoo, not in the direction of either Tasso or home. "Where're we going?" she quizzed him. "Am I allowed to ask that much, if you're abducting me?"

Now he seemed amused, getting his way. "Trust me."

"Little warning bells always go off in my head whenever anybody says 'Trust me,'" she said. "People always say that when they know they're just about to screw up."

He took the road that led behind the zoo to the river-view park up on the levee, becoming obviously more comfortable with himself and what was happening with every revolution of the tires.

She climbed out of the Acura when he parked, cool river breezes lifting her hair, the sun warm on her skin. The wind smelled of sweet olive. Shrugging off her cardigan sweater, she waited on the sidewalk while Philip opened the trunk to take out a picnic basket and a silver cooler of champagne.

"Honey," she said, watching, "you're definitely not screwing up, I take it all back."

Now his amusement became a broad grin and Philip had such a great grin, firm cleft chin, high color. He slid one arm around her and guided her onto the green lawn near the water's edge where he opened the basket to remove a tablecloth.

It billowed in the wind like a flame as he shook it out and then spread it on the grass, sunlight blinding on both the cooler and his silver head. He settled her onto the fabric where she sank down into a deep cushion of fragrant grass and fresh linen.

A large rusty freighter glided past on its way downriver. She heard the waves of its wake begin to lap at the levee below. She felt solar heat on the shoulders of her embroidered cotton blouse like two soothing hands.

The tight knit of Philip's short sleeves expanded over his biceps as he removed the cork from the champagne bottle with a snowy towel and a soft professional pop. "What on earth brought this on?" she asked him.

He shrugged, filling two crystal flutes with fizz. "No real reason, except I know that we met each other just about a year ago. I think we need to agree if that's a good thing."

She accepted her flute and held it. "Seems like a real good thing right now."

"Salute!" he clinked his glass against hers, and then muttered, "Maybe it's time you learned some Italian to go with all that Spanish and Mayan and whatnot..."

They linked elbows, something they had never done before but did smoothly now with no forethought, and drank to each other. Michelle wondered what all the young joggers and passing dog walkers might be thinking, these two pathetic middle-agers out here like this, nose to nose like college lovers. But I really don't give a damn about anybody else's opinions right now, especially not the young, she thought. They have no idea yet of what a tightrope we all walk with no safety net, and how more and more of a person's contemporaries run out of luck, misstep, and plunge off it every single day.

"Teach me some more," she said when they disengaged.

"Some more what? Italian?"

"Yes."

"That's about all I know," he said. "I need to learn it myself."

She watched him unpack the picnic basket. He wore that glazed preoccupied expression he got sometimes when he worked with food, as if he were trying to remember the exact taste of oregano.

"Well," he handed her a linen napkin and then unwrapped twin *croques-monsieurs* on white china plates, "Shelly..."

Oh Lord, a suddenly terrified little corner of her own brain began to anticipate him, he's going to leave me. My friend Jan's husband took her on a second honeymoon to tell her that he wanted a divorce.

"Shell, I've been doing some heavy thinking since Mardi Gras."

She nodded, outwardly calm, prepared for anything. "So have I."

"I mean, you know, we're luckier than a lot of people, when you think about it. We've got our health, some money in the bank. Everything necessary to enjoy ourselves." He garnished the sandwiches with some kind of fancy little green that Michelle did not know the name of but it wasn't parsley. "So why aren't we?"

Because you're a fucking workaholic, is what she didn't say. "I don't know."

"Well, why don't we talk about starting?"

Her eyes closed with brief relief and then opened again. "This is a start, right here," she said as he served her. "I've never picnicked with a five-star chef before." She bit into fragrant savory layers and coped with their strings of melted cheese.

"Shelly, baby doll," he watched her, "there are still a few things I'd like to do in life, I'm finding out. I don't want to just get old, just dwindle down and lose interest in everything the way my father did, there at the last. Even before his cancer. You know?"

She thought of her own purposeless mother and tried to stop anticipating him. "I'm a hundred percent with you on that."

"'It takes life to love life,'" he unexpectedly quoted poetry, this college graduate who usually affected a macho blue-collar disdain for most things academic. "Edgar Lee Masters. *Spoon River Anthology.* What one of his characters says from her grave, lying underneath her tombstone. A soliloquy from the dead."

She sipped cold champagne, aware of her own sudden love for each passing second. In love with the splendid and subtle flavors of her lunch, the sunlight, the river. She had no idea why a line from Edgar Lee Masters in the mouth of Philip Randazzo should affect her so much, but it did. Her eyes filled.

"I've been thinking about it." He drained his champagne and then poured more for both of them without looking up. "Seems to me, on somebody's deathbed, he probably isn't gloating over stuff like, 'I was the richest guy in the world,' or 'I had washboard abs,' or 'Hey, I won the James Beard Best New Chef Award.' You know?"

She raised her head and looked at the steely Mississippi.

"Maybe the right thing for me to do is adopt your children, Shell, I don't know…"

"Philip, Nicole is already yours, you must know that. She'd walk through fire for you. You're the coolest thing on her personal planet, especially since Mardi Gras."

"But Cam?"

"I think he'd be relieved if you adopted him, yes. In his own way, honey, Cam does love you. It's obvious how much he wants to emulate you. But I doubt he'd let us change his surname." She braced herself for an observation about her own failure to change her name.

It was like he hadn't heard her. "Shelly—what I've also been thinking—I'm beginning to think that I might really want to go cook in, like, Tuscany for a year or six months."

"Tuscany?" Her paranoia raised its head again. "You mean, like, Europe?"

"Tasso could use some infusion—I'm tired of the same old faux-Cajun shit—I mean, how many goddam species of fish are there left for restaurants to blacken anyway?"

"But—"

"Or maybe we'd just open a second place, Italian—I don't know. 'Tasso' isn't much of a name for an Italian restaurant."

"I thought you were Sicilian, not Tuscan."

"This isn't about me." But he seemed almost stereotypically Italian now, struggling with language, trying to grab something out of the air with his free hand. "It's about moving on, not stagnating. Not just fading out. Jesus, I don't want to just fade out as I age, sit around the house like when I was down with pneumonia, watching daytime TV."

"Well..."

"How hard would it be for you to get a sabbatical? —That's what y'all call it, right?"

There was no point anymore in even wanting to anticipate him because he was going too fast for her. "Well, I'll be due for one in about two more years, I think."

"So tell me how we could do this."

This was too strange: Philip Randazzo, proposing a leave of absence from Tasso, no matter how temporary, no matter how far in the future. Michelle wasn't prepared for it. "Honey, my field is Mesoamerica. I just don't know how I could justify central Italy to the department, Philip."

He threw a small stick at the river. "Cam will have graduated high school, he can get a leg up by cooking in Europe, it's a great apprenticeship. Nick'll be old enough to get something out of all the art museums by then. We could maybe travel a little bit. Take 'em to France."

But this whole scenario was spiraling out of control. "Philip, a sabbatical is not a vacation, honey. I don't see how I can do this."

"Fine, fine." He was motionless for a moment. And then took a deep breath, and kept taking it in. And was still drawing it in when it exploded into, "Then *fuck,* Shelly, let's go cook and live in fucking Yucatán, shit. Or fucking Guatemala, if that's what it takes."

"Honey, what's wrong?"

Another dead twig sailed from his hand out over the levee's edge, this one spinning like a boomerang. "Shelly, we've got to let go of everything, and we're not doing that. Everything that holds us back and keeps the two of us apart. Or else we owe it to ourselves—and the kids—to just call it quits and get divorced before all of us become even more involved with one another. If that's where we're headed, then let's do it right now, because it's not going to get any easier on them, the longer we wait."

"We're not apart!" she objected, but knew it wasn't the truth.

Knew that she had just finished fearing that he was leaving her for Italy.

"Let go, Shell."

"What about Regan? You've still got some unresolved feelings for Regan, I know."

Another slung object flew toward the river and oblivion now. This time it was the cork from the champagne bottle. She almost reflexively squawked a protest about environmental pollution but realized in time that cork was a natural product. "You're such a smart woman, Shelly. Such an intelligent woman. And you're so full of shit sometimes, you absolutely amaze me."

The bright day ate into her stomach like acid. "Maybe I'd better get on back to work—I've had about as good a time here as one person can reasonably stand."

"Look, I'm willing to put the entire Atlantic Ocean between me and my own three kids for you, Michelle. Mickey. Whoever the hell you are."

She glanced at her watch and tried not to think about the deadly afternoon that waited for her back at the Anthopology Department.

"We'd be close to Spain, there in Italy," he tried again, but mumbling, defeated. "Couldn't you at least make a case to the department for studying some connections between Spanish culture and Mesoamerica? In Spain? You've lived there. Hey, I can even cook in Spain if that's what it takes to get us onto another track. *Arroz con pollo, tapas,* whatever it takes, I'm willing."

She intertwined fingers with his. "You don't understand."

"What's that term all about, 'visiting professors'? Couldn't you be a visiting professor somewhere?"

"Honey, I don't know. It's getting late. I've got to get back."

"We could serve *tapas,* rechristen Tasso. Call it 'Tosca.'" Here was the old Philip, the irreverent Yat she had begun to fall in love with just about a year ago.

She couldn't help smiling. "I think you mean 'Carmen,' honey—but that is cute, yeah."

"Please, let's do this, baby doll. Let's go find ourselves. Let's go have our own long honeymoon, kids and all. We need something to look forward to, all four of us. We need to get out of Chestnut Street. We need that, Shelly."

"I *can't!*" She felt like tearing her hair out, or his, because she couldn't make him understand what academia was all about.

"Or you could take some kind of academic leave of absence, couldn't you?" He absolutely would not drop it, and she was ready to scream. "Didn't Savoie leave y'all enough money for you to take some kind of leave? I guess if I sold Tasso—"

She pressed both palms to the sides of her head and squeezed. "This is not about money, Philip!"

"Then what is it about?"

"I don't know."

His eyes were like autumn pools of brown leaves she could fall into. *I'm scared to love him,* she realized. *I'm terrified to fall all the way in. Because as soon as I do, I'll lose him. It's silly to think that, but that's what I really think. That's what I know. I don't have the guts.*

He suddenly stood and began to gather the remains of their picnic into a hasty wad, jerking at the white tablecloth while she still sat on it.

"Philip?"

He said nothing. Just jerked and packed up.

"I'm sorry," she spoke carefully, unable to identify her transgression. As if she were a drunk coming off a binge and trying to sober up, obligated to apologize for something that she couldn't recall doing.

"You amaze me," was all he said.

THIRTY-SEVEN

The Red Pickup

CAM STARTED BUGGING HIM about using the food processor that Easter Saturday morning, even before breakfast could be properly finished, because three important guests were expected. One, at least in Cam's eyes, might be more important than the other two, Phil understood.

"Well, I guess so. Go ahead, just don't leave me a big mess to clean up," he gave in, trying to linger over coffee with Michelle and get the paper read while he still had the chance. "We've still got breakfast to clear away, remember. Okay?"

No answer.

"I'll give you a hand in a minute, son, just let me finish this article. Big wreck here on the High Rise, two little girls and a lady killed... Okay?"

Cam whacked and clanged utensils in the kitchen, out of Phil's sight lines. "Okay. Thanks." But it sounded like a garbage Dumpster operating in there.

Phil lowered his paper with a maximum of irritated crackling. "Don't make me a mess, please," he warned again. "Please!"

"I just want to get this into the oven before Kerri and Hunter and Brendan get here—it's a surprise, like!" Cam shouted back and then appeared at the top of the steps. "But I'll get everything all cleaned up, I promise. No problem."

"This your Killer Walnut Brownies again?" Phil asked and then sneezed, his spring hay fever acting up.

Cam was outgrowing this particular pair of baggy jeans. The biceps on his smooth arms were becoming better defined. "Well, I've changed the recipe. Trying to improve on it."

"Wish I'd known that haute cuisine impresses girls when I was your age."

Michelle blotted her lips and then smiled at him from across the table. He smiled back because it was something that had to be worked on together, this effort to create an environment of smiles and harmony. They worked on it day and night. They did not discuss Tuscany.

But it wasn't so bad to be pushed back from the table like this, over coffee and the *Times-Picayune,* spending his free hours before Tasso like this in domestic peace. Or in relative domestic peace, since Nicole had had a sleepover for two other little girls last night and one of them, named Connie, was still upstairs rampaging with Nicole and a herd of pastel plastic ponies. Saturday morning cartoon shows could be heard as accompaniment to their chirrupings.

"Looks like it's going to really pour," Michelle observed, turning her head to examine the darkening sky through the windows. "I hope Regan and the kids'll be all right on the Causeway."

"They'll be fine."

She drained her coffee. "Connie's mom can't pick her up until after two, she's got her nine-year-old's swim meet at Newman…"

"Swim in the streets, if we get some flooding."

She put her chin onto the heel of her hand and rested her elbow on the Mexican place mat. "It'd be nice if I could get out of here for a little while to do some emergency shopping. I know Cam has to've outgrown his good suit by now, and Nick doesn't have a thing that'll serve as an Easter dress."

He interpreted her words. "So you're letting 'em go with me to the Cathedral tomorrow."

"Well," she yawned, "if your own kids are going, I can't let mine feel left out."

"I don't guess you'd care to tag along."

"Don't keep making me out to be *anti*-religion, Philip. I'm just not pro-."

"You could just sit in a pew like I do without participating in the Mass. Lotta people do that, especially on a big holiday like Easter. Tourists, who aren't even Christian."

She didn't move or speak.

The whir and grating of the food processor chopping nuts sounded like a helicopter landing in the kitchen. Phil looked at his watch. "I guess I could stay here until Connie's mother gets here, if she can make it by three."

"I'll have to stop for gas," Michelle stretched and yawned again. "I've left myself an empty tank."

"Take the Acura, leave me the Saturn. I'll fill it up on the way to Tasso."

She stood. "Maybe if I go take a shower real fast, I can be out at Lakeside and back before Connie's mother gets here. And you won't have to drive my nasty car."

He sighed, finishing his coffee if not his reading, as she retreated to the bedroom and its bath. He finally carried the empty mugs to the kitchen where Cam had made a staggering mess and was pouring out rich brown batter with the consistency of lava.

"You know, if this turns out any good," Cam spoke when he noticed Phil's proximity, "I'm going to post the recipe on the Internet."

"No, save it," he surrendered to the inevitable, beginning to rinse off the dishes piled in the sink. "We might do a Tasso cookbook someday, so don't just give it away."

———

KERRI HAD BROUGHT chocolate Easter eggs for Nicole, but she hastily divided them when she was introduced to the visiting Connie. She also carried a big chocolate bunny for Cam, a duplicate bunny for Phil, and a fragrant live Easter lily in a beribboned flowerpot for Michelle.

Her two brothers came barreling into the house, grappling with sneakers squeaking on the hardwood floors and shoving, making the house shake. "Hey hey hey!" shouted Phil, and all remnants of domestic peace dissipated. "Y'all settle down!"

"Sorry, Dad," panted Hunter. "Here's something where I don't have to jump. It's called the Razor's Edge."

"What is?"

"This wrestling move. Bend down, Brendan, so I can show him."

"No!" ordered Phil. "No wrestling indoors."

"But you don't have an outdoors," complained Brendan, hands on hips.

Kerri had no idea where to set the potted lily. Her brown hair spilled over her shoulders as she turned her head. "Where's Michelle?"

"She had to be somewhere, she waited for you guys as long as she could."

"Yeah, sorry to be so late getting here. The rain slowed down everything on the Causeway." She stood near the breakfast bar between Cam and Phil. But it was Cam she looked to. "Can I just put the lily right down here? On the bar here?"

"Sure." He uncovered without drama the brownies he had arranged on a large platter. Phil's nose was too stuffy to appreciate their aroma, but their presentation, he saw, was excellent. Dark fudge swirled atop each in perfect semicircular whorls. Light dustings of confectioners' sugar traced their tops like frost. Marbled strata of lighter-colored batter and nuts showed at their precisely cut edges. "Here." Cam handed Kerri a small chocolaty square. "Taste this and tell me what you think. Sorry it's not still warm."

"That's not your fault, we were late." She sank her braces into the fudge with alacrity and then chewed. "Oh, delicious! Oh Cam, they're wonderful! Totally!"

"You're just saying that," he tossed the hair out of his face, pleased and abashed.

"No, *really!*" But she suddenly held the bitten square away from her, considering it carefully, then looked up at her father. "Uh-oh," she said.

Cam's eyes dodged between them. "What?"

Phil snatched out of her hand what little remained of her brownie and bit into it himself. *Loaded,* he realized in a brain fog. With delicious peanut butter swirls underneath all that fudge, peanut chunks, *loaded.*

"What?" Cam stood transfixed.

"I'm becoming allergic to peanuts," she told him, her face beginning to show white bumps and red blotches, "I'm sorry."

All the pleased pink in Cam's complexion turned into white. "How allergic?"

"The subject just never came up before—," her hands flew about in the air, "I can't believe we never got around to telling you, we're such *dorks!*" She moved carefully to the armchair and sat down.

"*Real* allergic, looks like!" Phil shouted, already halfway into the master bath for the Benadryl in his toiletries drawer. He raced back to the kitchen with two pink lozenges, thrusting them at Cam while he searched for the cordless phone.

"Cam, here—run her some water and give her both of these while I call 911," he said. "Where's the goddam phone? I can't find the goddam phone—"

He collided with Brendan as he galloped down to the washing machine because the phone usually turned up on its top beneath dirty clothes for some reason. Please let it be here, God! he urged, and yep, here it was....

He made the call while Cam held Kerri's hand, apologizing

over and over to her. Her brothers sat relatively still on the sofa, white-faced and moving their feet around.

The Benadryl might help some, Phil thought as he crouched beside his daughter now and waited for the ambulance. She was bright red, breathing hard. Frightened, too, tears squeezing out of the corners of her eyes. "My throat is closing up, Dad," she squeaked and gripped his fingers.

Can a tracheotomy help? he quizzed himself on what little he knew about severe food allergies. Shit, I don't know. Do I have the guts to try it if she stops breathing? You bet. "You'll be fine," he tried to reassure her. "The EMS guys'll give you a shot of epineph-rine or something like that, open you right up."

Cam stood next to her, vibrating like a guitar string. "Cam," Phil hid both his fear and his anger, "this isn't your fault, son, you understand me? Nobody ever thought to tell you, son. No way it's your fault."

He barely nodded.

"She's going to be all right," Phil went on in what he hoped was a calm tone, "ambulance'll be here any minute. Give her a shot and take her on to the emergency room just as a precaution. Nothing to it."

Cam nodded again, not vibrating quite as much now.

"But I'm going to need you to do a few things for me when they get here, okay?"

"Yes sir?"

The front room was in deep shadow from the black clouds gath-ering outside. Thunder boomed. Brendan reached to turn on a lamp beside his elbow. Phil looked away from his sons and straightened. "This is your house, Cam, so I'm leaving you in charge here. That little girl upstairs, her mom is coming for her sometime after two. Don't leave her and Nicole here by themselves for any reason. Got that?"

Cam seemed calmer. Nodded.

Phil crossed to the kitchen space and located his smallest,

sharpest boning knife in its block, just in case. "Try to get your mother on her cell phone and tell her what's happened, and tell her I'll call her from the emergency room. Let her make the call to Miss Regan, okay? Once we know that everything's under control, okay?"

"Okay."

Kerri's breathing was noisy but still successful. He came back to take her by both shoulders. "How're we doin', sweetheart? Hang in there, they're almost here."

Her red chin went up and down.

Thunder sounded again. Phil found his sneakers near the refrigerator and stuck his bare feet into them. A loud siren approached from the direction of Prytania. He almost collapsed with secret relief.

"I'm going to have to follow the ambulance to the hospital," he checked his jeans for ID and money, scooping up Michelle's car keys and his own cell phone from the bar top, "so that I can do the insurance thing and then drive Kerri back home. Cam, you're in charge, handle anything that comes up in any way you see fit. If I've forgotten anything important here, do whatever your judgment dictates. I'll call y'all as soon as I'm able."

"Ambulance is here, Dad," said Brendan unnecessarily from the window.

"You two," Phil pointed at his sons, "behave! I'm counting on y'all, cooperate with Cam and watch out for the girls upstairs! No wrestling, no horseplay, no jumping around!"

But both boys were making faces and Phil was ready to knock their heads together until he realized that they were looking at Kerri and not at him. Kerri, brilliantly red-faced, was sticking out her tongue and trying to stare down at it to see if it were red, too. He felt better about everything. "—Oh, Cam? One other thing: Please call Tasso and tell 'em I'll be late. You know all the staff there."

"Yes sir."

Phil undid the thumb latch and jerked open the front door to admit the paramedics who came running for the porch through the rain.

HE PULLED AWAY from the curb and swung in behind the ambulance, on its way to Mercy Baptist. The hospital was where all three of his kids had been born and it was close by, and it had been the first place Phil could think of when the paramedics had Kerri's condition stabilized enough to ask him about where to go. There wasn't enough gas in the Saturn for anywhere else, Phil remembered, unless he stopped and got some.

Regan is absolutely going to kill my ass, he realized, turning onto Eighth Street. He didn't try to keep up with the ambulance because he couldn't, but he could still see its flashing lights up ahead in the rain as it crossed the intersection with Prytania, intermittently whooping. Phil took comfort from the less-than-constant siren. If Kerri were in real danger, he knew, they'd never turn it off. But Regan is still going to ream me out royally, he thought, and I deserve it. How come I never thought to say a word about Kerri and peanuts? Michelle knows about it, I told Michelle, but who the hell thinks to tell a fifteen-year-old boy? Who cooks? How many other fifteen-year-old boys cook?

The flashing red lights could still be seen receding when Phil made his left-hand turn onto St. Charles. The rain came down in sheets now and blotched them into tiny sparks. He could no longer hear the siren at all.

And goddammit, I've got us going to Baptist Hospital now—fucking lowest ground in town, water over Michelle's hood here if it comes a street flood.... He turned on the radio before he ground his teeth to powder, finding his favorite classic-rock station, making himself take deep calming breaths and hold them and then slowly let them out.

The red traffic light was taking a thousand years to turn green way up there at Louisiana Avenue. The radio was playing one of his favorites but it wasn't soothing—Jim Morrison and the Doors— *riders, storm*... Always gets played on rainy days like this, every dee-jay in the country thinks he's being original and clever, Phil thought, knowing the lyrics and mouthing them.

Lightning briefly painted the distance mauve but everything nearby was greenish black except the headlights of oncoming cars stopped up ahead at the intersection. The purple luminescence of the K & B drugstore up there across Louisiana was a beacon. Long thin parallel puddles on the neutral ground refracted streetlights into the bull's-eye patterns of raindrops.

C'mon, c'mon, c'mon! he flexed his jaws and began his acceleration at midblock in anticipation of the traffic light, seeing Kerri in his mind's eye being wheeled into bright fluorescence among strangers, swiveling her head from side to side on the gurney, she's looking for him, anxious...

C'mon, *c'mon,* goddammit!

The light turns green. He floors the accelerator.

Headlights splash over a pedestrian.

Instantly stomping the brake, Phil feels the Saturn wanting to wildly fishtail but its antilock system holds it to its course. It slides toward certain impact as he nevertheless tries to frantically steer around, thinking, I can't—shit—I can't—shit—I'm going to hit him, shit! in the queer slow motion of disaster.

He has a millisecond's impression of outspread fingers before the revolting jolt of steel into flesh punctuates the end of his skid. Tiny squares of glass left over from Michelle's broken window come flying out from underneath the driver's seat along with music tapes and toys, smacking against his heels. Objects leave the back-seat and strike like missiles at the headrests as the body comes smashing into his windshield, only to be flung off again in the brakes' sudden bite.

Something else immense has blazed past through the intersection at the very same instant, left to right, missing Phil's front bumper by mere inches.

He feels its wake still rocking the car.

His vision turns black and then brighter. He resumes breathing, not really wanting to, not wanting to get out of the automobile and deal with what he's going to have to deal with. Oh Christ, he thinks, shaking so hard that he can hear his teeth chatter in the crazy and surreal calm of too much adrenaline, oh holy God. I've killed somebody.

A streetcar full of witnesses, running on a parallel track, indifferently crosses Louisiana Avenue with a snapping of circuit breakers and the chug of its engine. Phil flips on his four-way flashers, grabs his cell phone, and scrambles out of the Saturn and into the storm, the rain pounding into his nerveless face like bullets, in so much dread that his hair shakes.

He finds no dead body in the street, not even far up ahead. Nobody lies near his car, or on his car, or beneath it.

Drivers lining up behind him lean on their horns and shout as he walks dazedly in the storm all the way around his car where it sits catercornered and flashing. He holds up an arm to motion them around, once he is sure that they won't be running over someone lying on the asphalt if they pass him. Maybe the body's on the neutral ground. He knows where he is, recognizing K & B in front of him to the right, Bultman Funeral Home across the oncoming lanes over there to his left. He recognizes Michelle's gold Saturn, knows how to get to Blockbuster and Tasso and Mercy Baptist Hospital and home from here. He looks down at his own arms and hands. He remembers his name.

Maybe I didn't hit him that hard—a small seed of hope begins to sprout inside Phil's skull. Maybe just some drunk, some whiskied-up relaxed bum, didn't even feel it, just got up and walked away somewhere....

Rivers cascade onto his head and buffet his shoulders but he is compelled nonetheless to keep scanning the sidewalks and neutral ground and flooded gutters, searching for a sodden lump of something human, a broken heap of somebody. Because he very well knows how hard he hit him. What the impact was like. Its sound still echoes in his ears.

Vehicles squish slowly past, drivers regarding him through closed windows and making no comment, on their way to places that don't concern a lunatic walking around a car in a storm. In the pulsing strobe of his own flashers Phil suddenly recovers a memory of the man in his headlights. A man in dark clothing. A bearded man with a walking cane.

Oh Christ—and eye contact, yes, there is eye contact. Phil sees again past the defensive spread fingers of a hand like a ragged starfish and looks into black and bottomless eyes.

He begins to walk in small circles and make wordless voicings.

A police car approaches and slows. The cruiser's headlights and blinding blue overhead light bar reflect from the Saturn's circular spiderweb of broken windshield glass. Phil touches it for reality's sake, feeling its inward bulge. His own head has not created that.

His left headlight is blind, broken, gone. Fender and hood damaged.

"You okay, sir?" the young officer asks him from a rolled-down window. "Anybody here need an ambulance?"

Phil hears his own voice. "I was following an ambulance."

"What's happened here, sir?"

"I don't know. I thought I hit a pedestrian, ran over somebody—can't find anybody—" High winds whip at the black limbs of the live oaks, driving stinging water droplets into his face like needles.

"You got some damage there," the cop says. "Tree limb blow into you, sir? Display sign or something?" He is getting out of his own car now, pulling on a yellow rain slicker in the downpour. His blue lights, so bright they hurt, flash a counterpoint to Phil's amber four-ways and turn the falling rain into strobed streaks.

"I thought I hit a person," Phil speaks to the badge and the patient dark face above it. "Maybe it was just some reflection I saw. From somebody's headlights. Off of blowing trash or whatnot. There was another vehicle kind of involved..."

"Nobody here, sir." Pale-palmed hands are spread. "We need to clear this intersection. Will your vehicle move?"

"A pickup ran a red light," Phil suddenly hears himself explaining, going into mild shock, remembering. Gesturing with the cell phone in his hand. "Coming from the river here on Louisiana, going real fast. Speeding. Coming within inches of plowing right into my—"

"We need to get you out of the intersection, sir, and get your vehicle moved."

But Phil sees again those far-off-the-ground headlights coming right for the place where his own car door should have been. Would have been. He feels again the left-to-right rocking of that oblivious speed, the whoosh of the scythe.

He understands now that if he'd paid more attention to his newspaper this morning, he might've been able to put some of it together—that wreck on the I-10 High Rise killing an Uptown woman and two kids in their white minivan. A woman who now lies dead and naked on a stainless steel table, abandoned by—

"A red pickup," he tells the policeman in somebody else's voice, viewing in memory the chubby profile of the young mortician at the wheel. Understanding now everything. It renders him weightless and hollow. "With a Saints sticker. Coming straight for me."

HE'S COMING STRAIGHT ON FOR YOU, PHI

Understanding everything. Understanding nothing. "He's in a big hurry," he mumbles. "His first child's being born."

"Sir?"

"The wreck would've probably killed him, too." And the unknown cosmos that knows for sure, that *knows,* is covered and muffled now by dark gray clouds and it goes on forever, right above Phil's head. He looks up.

"I believe you might need some medical attention here, sir, just get back in your vehicle and take it easy for a little bit…"

Phil obeys the suggestion in a dream, opening his car door and climbing back behind the wheel in his soaked clothes. Items crunch underfoot. As the officer returns to his cruiser to speak into its radio, Phil reaches a hand down to clear these newly emerged small plastic toys and rap tapes and broken glass from the floorboards. He fails to recognize one object, one so strange-looking that it earns detached attention from him. Black and gleaming, it has sharp points.

He lifts it up into the light.

Two inches of splintered ebony are still threaded into its flattened cylindrical base. Tarnished, abraded, and flattened, the object reveals itself as the sterling silver handgrip of a gentleman's cane.

Phil feels the unknown weight of that infinitude of stars suspended right above him, the unspeakable mystery of black holes and galaxies and supernovae Dopplering mightily away from him on unchartable courses.

He brings the handgrip to his lips like a holy relic. Kisses it. Then immediately throws it out onto the street where it belongs.

He hears no splash or clang over the sounds of rainy traffic. He doesn't know where it landed. All of that weight is beginning to crush big abject sobs from out of his chest. Helpless, he can do nothing but put both hands up over his face.

I can tell them, he thinks in fragments, I can tell the cops who he was and how he looked when he saw those headlights coming out of that wooded curve near Country Day School three years ago. I can even tell them why.

Changing my nightmare, my fate. Saving my ass. I can tell them. Nobody'll believe me.

Only one person in the whole world would ever believe me, he finally realizes as he wipes his face with a palm and then gropes for his cell phone. And it's her voice I need to hear most right now, no matter where she is, no matter how pissed off at me she'll be. No matter if she's an atheist or has had a past. No matter if she doesn't know how to love me any better than I know how to love her.

None of it matters. What's the number? Punch in her number. Wait for her human, human voice.

My Michelle.

Acknowledgments

THIS BOOK HAS a past.

Some of its characters were inspired by imaginary people my sister Donna Thompson helped me dream up in our shared childhood, so I hope she is pleased at how their adult counterparts finally turned out. I'm more than grateful for all her helpful comments and suggestions. She was my very first reader, so all of my books are always for her. She's wonderful.

Two other dear friends, Sallie Lowenstein and Mike Thompson, read in its entirety what was once a hugely bloated manuscript and made their own very useful observations. I owe them my deepest gratitude. A third, Tom Rayer, Jr., read it more than once—I actually lost count—and provided invaluable insights each time. I owe him both the book's dedication and my sincerest thanks, because I'm not sure there would even be a book here if not for him.

I also want to thank my nephews, William Harper Sherrod and Keith Mills Sherrod, who couldn't get enough of my ghost stories when they were little boys and used to tell me, "Auntie, you need to write a ghost story!"

Judy Long of Hill Street Press, queen of editors, has done a fantastic job of "liposuctioning" the bloat and fine-tuning the narrative. I also owe Tom Payton thanks, plus the amazing team at Har-court: Jen Charat, David Hough, and copyeditor Dan Janeck.

Thanks go also to Elizabeth Wisznia for feeding me, Nancy and Joe Ory for unfailing encouragement, Robert Wait for getting me back home to New Orleans in the first place, and to Paul and Marilyn Kullman for a thousand kindnesses, above and beyond.

I've listened to real-life ghost stories at cocktail parties over the years and have twisted their details to suit my purposes. I also took the liberty of reimagining some of the geography of southern Louisiana as well, plus certain other environments like restaurants and academia.

All errors are my own.